ANGEL MAKER

A DI JAMIE JOHANSSON NOVEL

MORGAN GREENE

ALSO BY MORGAN GREENE

The DS Johansson Prequel Trilogy:
Bare Skin (Book 1)
Fresh Meat (Book 2)
Idle Hands (Book 3)

The DS Johansson Prequel Trilogy Boxset

———

The DI Jamie Johansson Series
Angel Maker (Book 1)
Rising Tide (Book 2)
Old Blood (Book 3)

For my father. My teacher. My friend.

ANGEL MAKER

1

HER BODY WAS STILL warm when he carried her into the woods.

His feet crunched in the fresh snow, the cold night air frosting his laboured breath. It caught the moonlight, glowing silver in the shafts that splintered through the trees.

He slowed. She was growing heavy, limp in his arms. Her lips were already turning blue, her skin taking on that deathly shade of pale.

This wasn't going to be easy.

Nothing about this was easy.

But it had to be done. It *had* to be.

He set her on the ground carefully, the snow soaking through the knees of his trousers, numbing him. He paused, looking down into her eyes.

For a moment, they stayed like that. And then he reached to his belt and pulled free the freshly sharpened hatchet tucked there with trembling fingers.

The numbers on his watch glowed in the dark. A little after midnight.

Dawn was still a long way off, but there was lots of work to do.

And time was running out.

2

DI JAMIE JOHANSSON knew that getting a call at 3 a.m. only meant one thing.

Her phone lit up on the nightstand, vibrating, dancing across the wood.

She may have been startled if she was asleep. But she didn't do much of that these days.

Jamie stepped away from the window, the waves of Machir Bay breaking themselves against the rocks below, and crossed the room quickly.

She didn't recognise the number, but knew the extension. Sweden.

'Hello?' she said quietly, not a hint of sleep in her voice. Jamie headed for the door, not wanting to disturb Graeme, and stepped into the corridor.

The air was colder here, outside the embrace of the bedroom.

'Detective Inspector Jamie Johansson?' a voice asked, the accent driving her back to her childhood. 'Of the London Metropolitan Police?'

Not for six months, Jamie felt like saying. 'Yes,' she answered tentatively. 'Who is this?' She pulled the door behind her, hand lingering on the cool brass, waiting for the answer.

'This is Kriminalinspektör Anders Wiik with the SPA, Stockholm.'

Swedish Police Authority.

'Vick?' Jamie confirmed, leaving the hallway and walking into Graeme's kitchen. The frigid flagstones stung her bare feet.

'Anders *Wiik*.'

Jamie swallowed, staring out of the window over the counter. A lighthouse twisted in the distance. 'How can I help?'

'I apologise for the lateness of the call,' he said formally. 'But I need your help.'

'With what?' Jamie asked, turning and leaning against the Rayburn cooker, warmth still clinging to its iron body. She ran her hand through her ash-blonde hair, pushing it off her face, and then folded her arms.

'It's your father,' he said.

Jamie stiffened. 'My father has been dead for nineteen years.'

A hand-carved cuckoo clock ticked loudly on the wall opposite.

'Yes,' Wiik said. 'I know.'

Jamie detected a hint of frustration in his voice.

'It appears, however,' he said, 'that the Angel Maker is not.'

The plane sidled down through the thick layer of cloud, and the snow-covered earth blurred into view.

She sighed and rubbed her eyes.

Sleep had come fitfully. Barely at all, really.

Jesus, what was she doing back here? She knew, but struggled to wrap her mind around it. The Angel Maker. It was one of her father's biggest cases. She remembered it well. How could she not? It was the final case he worked before her mother had left him and taken her to England. It was the final nail in the coffin that was their marriage.

And now the SPA needed access to her father's old case files. And she had to be there to grant it. She *had* to be. She couldn't let someone else go rifling through his belongings. Or what was left of them, at least.

It wasn't fear that kept her away all these years. She didn't know what it was. Guilt? Dread? What would she find? She didn't think she would have ever wanted to visit the long-cold wreckage of her father's life.

And yet it had found her now, taking the choice from her.

Jamie was going back to the place she had once called home.

She hadn't decided how she felt about that yet.

Or perhaps she just didn't want to.

Jamie watched as the city swelled below her, the afternoon defeating the sun behind, the night approaching in front. It came quickly here.

The plane landed in a crosswind, the pilot wrestling it down, and Jamie unlocked her phone, turning off aeroplane mode. A message appeared on-screen. It was from Graeme. It said, *be safe.*

He was a man of few words, and Jamie appreciated that.

What they had was simple.

He fished, he came back, he went to fish again. Gone for days, weeks at a time.

They ate, often in silence.

They made love. Also in silence. Each trusted the other to say something if they needed to. It was rare that either did. It was good. As good as she'd ever known.

She didn't know if that was the saddest thing of all.

Jamie had been on administrative leave since May. It was now January. She'd been living at his cottage since October. And yet, despite leaving her little oasis just hours before, it all seemed very distant. Like her life over the last eight months hadn't happened. Like it was all some fever dream. A temporary escape. A breath between the relentless waves.

And as she stared out at the silhouette of Stockholm, England seemed like another world. Like another 'her' had lived it.

The Met. Her career. Would she ever have gone back to it? She didn't have the answer.

What was it going to be like to be back again? Back among the dead. Back among the darkness. Hers, her father's… She was only going to grant them access, but just being in proximity to it all again…

Jamie clenched her hands in her lap to stop them from shaking.

Her job had always been a way to keep him close. Following his footsteps. Doing what he did.

And yet it had taken everything from her. Inside and out.

Jamie felt her chest heavy and drew in a deep breath, forcing her ribs to expand. Her last case had earned her a promotion and a commendation. But she didn't think that shooting a person was worth that. They had cleared her for active duty again, told her she could return whenever she was ready. She scoffed to herself a little, listening to the engines wind down, the plane rolling to a stop. Ready? There was no such thing in this job. Bad shit happened, and then the rest was down to you. Whether you were looking for it or not, the darkness would always find its way. Drawn to you, moth to flame.

And here she was again.

Jamie unfastened her belt and let the tension drain out of her.

She took one last look at the Stockholm skyline.

It was too late to turn back now.

Jamie always went carry-on, and breezed through security, her red passport helping the process along.

'Välkommen hem,' the customs officer said, smiling broadly as he handed it back. Welcome home.

Jamie nodded to him, failed to return his expression, pocketed her passport, and headed for the exit, her mind falling back into Swedish as though she'd never left.

Utgång.

Exit.

It was only the second time she'd set foot in Sweden in nineteen years. The first was for her father's funeral. Nineteen years ago. She thought about it as she walked. She'd been with her mother. Neither had said a word to each other the whole journey.

This time, Jamie hadn't even told her mother she was coming back. She hadn't told anyone. There was no one to tell, really.

The silver doors slid open in front of her, the quiet din of the road outside echoing through the airport.

A clean-shaven man in his late-forties was standing at the kerb, a new Volvo saloon sitting behind him. He was leaning against the front fender, watching Jamie carefully as she exited.

He pushed off and crossed the damp concrete slabs,

meeting her halfway. He nodded courteously, wasting no time. 'Kriminalinspektör Anders Wiik,' he said, hands firmly in the pocket of his black coat. 'Thank you for coming.'

'My pleasure,' Jamie said, hoping it didn't sound too disingenuous. It wasn't a pleasure, in fact. It wasn't even close.

'Would you prefer we spoke in English?' he asked, measuring Jamie.

She detected a hint of patronisation in his voice, though she didn't know why. '*Svenska går bra,*' she answered flatly. Swedish is fine.

Wiik gave a quick, polite smile and then carried on in his native tongue. 'I apologise that I could not share more information over the phone. The nature of this case, as you can imagine, is sensitive.'

Jamie stretched her back, her duffle bag hanging at her side, already keen to get this over with.

Her boots squeaked a little as she shifted her weight. Lightweight trail boots. Trusty, sturdy. Ready for anything.

Just like she used to be.

Jamie sighed, feeling much older than her thirty-seven years. Aeroplane seats always seemed to have a way of doing that. 'I understand. You said that this case was to do with my father's personal files. I don't understand what would possibly be in them that wasn't in the case files, though.'

Wiik inhaled, glancing left and right. He seemed uneasy. 'Please,' he said, gesturing to the car. 'We have a lot of ground to cover. I'll explain on the way.'

He pulled away from the kerb and accelerated smoothly, the electric motor whining softly as they left the airport behind.

It was dark now, and the air was cold, the wind biting. Snow was piled up at the sides of the roads. Jamie watched the city swim into view out of the window, the lights burning on top of the tall, modern office buildings. This had been her home for fourteen years.

The first fourteen years of her life.

There was a part of her that always wished she stayed.

'The Angel Maker,' Jamie said quietly, remembering as much as thinking aloud. She turned her head and measured Anders Wiik. The skin on his face was smooth, completely clean. Shaved meticulously. His dark hair was pushed back over his head. Not a single strand was out of place. He had a strong, sharp jaw, a square nose. Intelligent eyes.

'Yes,' Wiik confirmed. 'Do you remember the case?'

'I was thirteen,' Jamie said. 'It was the last case my father worked before my mother and I moved to England. Seven teenage girls were murdered. Raped. Suffocated. Their bodies left in the forest.'

There was a time when Jamie would have found it difficult to say that, to confront those memories. But she didn't seem to feel things like she used to. The words just seemed to come easily, not even catching in her throat anymore.

'Yes,' Wiik said. 'Did he discuss the case with you in detail?'

'Enough to anger my mother, but probably not enough to help you,' Jamie answered. 'What exactly is going on?'

Wiik sighed. 'The man your father caught, Hans Sjöberg – the man who was convicted of killing those girls – died in prison four days ago.'

Jamie set her jaw and looked at the road ahead. The red haze of headlights swam in the distance.

'Yesterday morning,' Wiik went on, 'a body was found,

the circumstances of the kill striking a remarkable resemblance to those of the Angel Maker.'

'A copycat?' Jamie asked, turning to look at him.

He shook his head. 'The particulars of his kills were never released to the public, the details too…'

Gruesome. Shocking. Disturbing. Jamie had seen the photos. You could take your pick.

'Someone could have read the case files,' Jamie said. 'Leaked the information?'

'That's one theory. But we suspect the reality of the situation is much worse.'

'How so?' Jamie asked, studying the side of Wiik's face. He wasn't an expressive man.

'They're missing.'

It clicked. 'That's why I'm here,' she said. 'You're hoping my father has some copies stashed somewhere.'

'It would certainly help,' Wiik said reservedly.

Jamie noted the way his fists tightened around the wheel and flexed as he spoke. It didn't seem like the case was off to a flying start. The fact that his best lead was flying Jamie in from another country confirmed that. 'Who could have taken them?'

'Someone with the knowledge of how our security systems worked. Someone who knew how to disable the security cameras and get through the security gates.'

'A police officer.'

'A detective.' Wiik glanced at her now. 'Robert Nyström. Your father's partner.'

Jamie suppressed her surprise. 'He must be in his sixties now.' Jamie recalled the man. Tall, thin. The darkest, thickest eyebrows she'd ever seen. And a good friend to her father. A good man, too. She'd liked him. 'Did you question him?'

'We would, if we could find him.'

'Do you suspect him of taking them?'

'We cannot say for certain. But his key card was used to access the archives – we know that much. And it appears his apartment was broken into the night that the files were stolen. There's no DNA or trace evidence to suggest anyone else had been there, but we're not ruling anything out.'

'Signs of a struggle?'

'No, Nyström was not at home at the time, as far as we can tell. His car was clocked at a toll gate a hundred kilometres north of the city three days before that – the night before Sjöberg died. It never passed back through. We sent out a notice countrywide and alerted border crossings to the north. If the car moves, we should pick it up. But so far there's been nothing.'

'Was anything else taken?'

Wiik shook his head. 'No. Nyström was retired, but was kept on as a consultant. Still retained his credentials. Whoever broke in, it seemed, knew that Nyström would have access, that he would not be home, and exactly what they were looking for.'

'Why him? Why not any of the hundreds of other people who had access?'

Wiik clicked the indicator up, sailed across the lanes, and pulled off at an exit.

Jamie glanced up at the sign, felt her body tense a little as they dropped down onto a roundabout and headed for the suburb she used to call home.

'Sjöberg maintained his innocence right up until they handed down the verdict,' Wiik said. 'Always claimed that your father and Nyström had it wrong.'

'The evidence was overwhelming,' Jamie said, remembering how the case had ended. 'And he confessed, didn't he?'

Wiik nodded. 'Yes – but Sjöberg was not the only suspect.'

'You think they convicted the wrong man?' Jamie searched Wiik's face for any hint of what he thought. The passing streetlights burned his skin orange in time with her heart.

The thought was terrifying. The Angel Maker had stalked the city for nearly a year. Parents had stopped their children from going out. People were afraid to walk alone at night. Not a day went by that Jamie's father – and the entire city – didn't dread finding the next victim.

And now, if he was back… the nightmare would begin all over again.

'I cannot say,' Wiik said. 'But Sjöberg is dead, the case files stolen, the surviving detective who worked the case missing, and now a teenage girl has been found in the woods, her body posed. Just like the others.'

Jamie pictured it, clamping her jaw shut. They drove through a town Jamie had once known well, not slowing down. 'Where are we going?' she asked, watching as the building that contained the solicitors who had handled the sale of Jamie's childhood home passed them on the right.

'Your house,' Wiik said.

Jamie narrowed her eyes. 'My father's belongings are in storage, the key left with the executors. I assumed you needed me to open…' Jamie trailed off as Wiik pulled left into Jamie's old street.

'In storage?' Wiik asked. 'No, your father's things are still at the house.'

It came up on the right, tired and dirty. The once beautiful wood panelling had rotted and fallen in places, the tiles slipped from the roof. The front garden was wild and knotted with long grass, the tops curled down with snow. The windows were shuttered and dark.

He eased the car to a stop outside and Jamie looked up at it. 'My mother sold the house after he died,' Jamie said, not understanding, her voice distant in her ears.

'No,' Wiik said, killing the motor. 'She didn't.'

3

WIIK EXITED the car and crossed the street towards a man Jamie recognised.

Jamie watched through the window as they shook hands.

His name escaped her. Osland, or Oberland or something. He was the solicitor who had handled her parents' estate. The supposed sale of it.

In the four years between Jamie's mother moving her to England and her father's death, her mother had said that her father had squandered their savings and fallen into debt. Gambling, women, drugs.

All his vices. All believable.

She had said that when he died, he'd left nothing to them. That he had *had* nothing left to leave to them. That she had been forced to sell the house to pay what he owed.

Jamie got out, steeling herself with a cold breath of Swedish air, and rounded the bonnet to address Osland.

'Ms Johansson,' he said, smiling brightly. He was over-weight, his tie perching on his stomach, the buttons of his shirt straining a little under it. His face was kind, though, his chin covered in a black-and-white beard, his thin eyes hidden behind thinner spectacles. 'It is good to see you again.'

'I'm sorry,' Jamie said, shaking his hand briefly. 'I don't understand what's going on. What are we doing here? My mother told me that the house had been sold.'

Wiik clasped his hands behind his back while Osland spoke.

'Your father left the house and his estate in its entirety to both you and your mother.'

'No,' Jamie said. 'There was nothing to leave.'

He pushed his glasses into his face with a chubby finger and glanced at Wiik before looking back at Jamie. 'Monetarily, perhaps not. A small amount in savings which went to your mother. His pension was forfeited due to the nature of his death.'

That he'd killed himself, Osland meant. 'Okay,' Jamie said, willing him to hurry up.

'But the house was mortgage free – it belongs to both you and your mother in joint ownership. She would not be able to legally sell it without your written consent. Had you been under eighteen years of age at the time of his death, she would have had full ownership, as they never legally separated. But as you were eighteen at the time…'

Yeah. I was. It was my birthday. He killed himself on my eighteenth birthday.

Jamie's head whirled. She could feel blood rushing in her fingers – they were stiff, aching – and a weight, like someone's boot, crushing her chest.

Her mother hadn't sold the house? Couldn't. But she said she had. Why? She had hated Jamie's father. Deeply. But to do… But…

Her mind couldn't comprehend.

Osland's mouth was moving then, his cheeks pushed out

into reddened balls by a wide smile. He lifted his hand towards Jamie.

She couldn't hear anything over the roar of her own blood in her ears.

Osland dropped a key into her hand, nodded to both her and Wiik – they exchanged a few muted words – and then he went back to his car, leaving the two of them standing in front of her father's house.

Her house.

Jamie's fingers curled over the cool brass and she drew a rattling breath, staring up at the ruin of her childhood, unsure what to do next.

'Are you coming?' Wiik asked, already on the path.

He looked back at Jamie as she willed her feet to move, a well of anger bubbling inside her.

'I…' she started, clearing her throat. 'Wait… just wait a second.'

Wiik looked tense.

'Can we just…' She glanced back at the car, trying to process everything. The last years of her life here were all coming back. Like she'd been thrown from a great height, the earth of her memories rushing up to meet her.

She couldn't. She couldn't do it. Couldn't face it. She didn't have it in her. Not yet. Not like this.

She thought, hard. Looking for an out, for any path that led away from here.

'Take me there,' she said finally.

'What? Where?' Wiik narrowed his eyes.

'The scene. Of the murder.' The words tumbled from her mouth.

He took a step back towards her. 'I am not able to do that.'

'You can,' Jamie said, wrestling with her voice, her fist

now tightly balled around the key. 'This is what I do.' She needed this. She needed to focus her anger on something. To keep her mind straight. It was too much to take in all at once, just standing here. 'I'm a good detective. You can use me.'

'We have this firmly under control—' Wiik answered back.

'What are you expecting to find in there?' Jamie asked, nodding towards the house. 'My father wasn't the note-making type. Not exactly organised.'

'Anything will be of use in this case,' Wiik said.

'Anything?' Jamie stepped forward. 'It sounds like you have no leads, no files, and no information to go on. And if the scene was rife with evidence, I wouldn't be here.' She met his eye. 'And if there's nothing in there, then *all* you have is me.'

Wiik measured her, pushing his hands into the pockets of his thick coat.

'I was there,' Jamie said. 'I remember the case. I remember what my father told me about it. You can use me. You *should* use me.'

'You are a civilian.'

'I'm a detective inspector with the London Metropolitan Police. And if you got my personal number, then you got it from my DCI, Henley Smith. Because if my mother hid this place from me all these years, then she sure as hell didn't give it to you knowing I'd come back here.' She read the lines on his still face. 'You called her first, didn't you? Asked her to come and grant you access here.'

Wiik looked down.

'And she told you where to stick it, didn't she?'

'With more profanity, yes.'

'And if you're working this case – the Angel Maker? Then you must be pretty good at what you do, too.'

Wiik didn't say anything.

'So I'm guessing you checked me out. Even just cursorily. Even if you just asked Smith what I was like. Professional curiosity – it's a bitch.'

His lip twitched almost imperceptibly, his face a mess of shadows and orange in the glow of the streetlights.

'You know I'm a good detective,' Jamie said plainly, one step short of begging. 'And I'm the only one in the world who knows this case. So whether you think this is someone else carrying on his work, or my father caught the wrong man all those years ago, you're going to need my help.'

By the look on his face, Wiik knew she was right. 'It will be difficult to arrange.'

Jamie huffed a little, turning towards the car. 'You seem capable. I'm sure you'll manage.'

'This case will be trying,' he added.

Jamie's hand froze at the handle.

'Are you sure you're ready for it?' Wiik didn't move, his hands still in the pockets of his coat. 'Chief Inspector Smith told me of your situation. Of the circumstances of your leave. What happened last May.'

Jamie ground her teeth and pulled the door open, casting Wiik a cold, hard glance. 'Just get in the fucking car.'

4

THEY SWEPT out of the city at pace. The scene was a few kilo-metres north, just off the side of a well-worn path through the forest that was perfect for runners and walkers. Popular, too. The trail wound endlessly through the zebra-striped birch trees.

The Angel Maker's kills had never been hidden away. They were always meant to be found.

Jamie looked over the initial assessment of the scene as Wiik drove, putting distance between them and the house. With every streetlight that washed past, her tension eased. The file on her lap showed an aerial shot of the area. A few hundred metres to the east of the scene, a road ran away from the city. What looked like a lay-by had been circled as a possible site that the killer had parked in.

Jamie leafed through the other papers – copies of the witness statements from the couple who had found the girl while out for a morning run in the snow.

They had seen no one. Heard nothing. Just glimpsed the girl through the trees and stopped. Gone closer. Then had realised what they were looking at.

Officers arrived fifteen minutes later, and the scene had been locked down since.

The body was still in situ, the whole area cordoned off. No one was going in or out on Wiik's orders. He wanted the scene as untouched as possible until they had Jamie's father's notes, the original case files. And Robert Nyström in an interview room.

Jamie had to hand it to him, Wiik was a focused man. She appreciated that.

'Do we have an ID on the victim yet?' she asked, reaching the back page. There was nothing in the file about the victim.

Wiik shook his head. 'Nothing yet. No missing persons matching her age and description so far.'

Jamie stared out of the window. Droplets of moisture had beaded on the glass and streaked backwards as they drove. 'Teenage girls don't just disappear without anyone missing them,' Jamie said.

Wiik met her with silence, seemingly not having an answer, and drove on.

They were waved in at the side of the road, a two-lane that connected Stockholm with a small outlying town called Vallentuna, and pulled to a halt in front of a police officer. He had a baton and was directing traffic to keep moving. To not slow down and gawp at the procession of police vehicles that had carved deep, muddy welts into the verge with their tyres.

Wiik clicked the engine off and rubbed his eyes in the driver's seat. Jamie wondered how many times he'd been to this scene in the last two days.

It was nearly thirty-six hours since the body had been discovered.

Usually, they would have cleared it long before, but the cold air was keeping everything preserved.

Jamie remembered walking through her father's study at fourteen, stepping lightly not to wake him as he lay asleep on the sofa, clutching an empty whisky bottle. Snoring. He always snored so loudly.

She had looked at each of the photos on his wall in turn. All seven girls, all posed.

She swallowed, remembering how frightened she had been.

They were all around her age. Maybe a little older. But girls. Like her.

'Ready?' Wiik asked.

Jamie nodded, not trusting her voice, and climbed out the car and her memories.

The cold grabbed at her cheeks and she screwed her eyes up, staring into the darkened sky, the swollen underbelly of the clouds hanging still above them. On her right, the birch trees swayed in the wind, a snowy bank letting down into their shadow. On her left, the road stretched away, wet and shimmering in the flashing blue lights coming off a patrol car in the middle of the pack.

Jamie pulled her peacoat tighter around her shoulders and waited for Wiik to walk around the bonnet and head down into the forest.

He judged the slope with careful confidence, made little steps, and then lurched forward so as not to slip.

Jamie followed, crunching through the snow at the side of the muddy bank. She was tired and didn't trust her footing.

The sound of the road died behind them as they reached the interior of the woods, their breath close in their ears. Wiik strode quickly, following the thin and twisted line of blue-and-white police tape. It bounced from trunk to trunk, guiding them deeper, until the flashing blues were eaten by the trees.

Jamie swallowed, keeping her fists balled in her pockets and her eyes on Wiik's broad shoulders. The only sound was their footsteps cracking through the frost underfoot and squelching into the mud beneath.

She was surprised he hadn't put up more of a fight before bringing her here. Maybe her DCI had told him what she was like when she got the scent of a case. Maybe Wiik really didn't expect to find much in her father's house. Or maybe he just read that look on her face and knew that forcing her to go inside would have set the investigation back.

He seemed the pragmatic type.

Either way, Jamie was glad she was here and not there.

As terrible as that was.

Wiik slowed ahead, and Jamie drew up at his shoulder, squinting at the sudden onslaught of light.

In front of them, plastic sheeting had been stapled to trees. It spanned the gaps roughly, bunching on the snow, creating a shield all around to protect the scene from onlookers.

Inside, Jamie could see floodlights burning, the translucent sheets glowing against the inky backdrop of the forest.

'Ready?' Wiik asked. A vertical slit cut in the sheet in front of him billowed softly.

The thickness of the forest had culled the wind here, but the tops still swayed high above, groaning gently in the winter silence.

Jamie nodded, pushing her hands deeper into her pockets, and stepped through.

The victim was about thirteen.

Jamie clamped her teeth together, her eyes moving across the girl's pale blue skin.

A thin layer of snow had settled on her shoulders, her hair, her outstretched fingers.

They were held in front of her face, palms flat together, wrists bound with rope to hold them in place.

She was on her knees, doubled over so that her back curved slightly.

The soles of her naked feet pointed upwards, the tips of her toes blackened by the cold.

A thin white confirmation dress hung from her exposed shoulders. It was soaked red in the front where sharpened limbs of birch branches pushed through the fabric, burying themselves in the earth, propping her up in position.

Her elbows rested on two of them, allowing her hands to remain aloft in front of her closed eyes.

Jamie began to circle, taking it all in, using the path in the snow that Wiik and everyone else who had attended the scene had walked.

She breathed slowly, steadying her heart as best she could.

Wiik stayed back.

The boughs – six in total – had been driven through the girl's back.

The cuts in her dress were fine. The cuts in her skin, fine. Done with precision and care.

Each of the boughs was the same thickness – an inch. Maybe a touch thicker. Just small enough to be pushed between the ribs without causing them to break.

The branches stretched upwards, curving, splitting into thinner and thinner limbs. They drooped under their own weight, the tangle of them supporting a dusting of fresh snow.

Three each side of her spine had been positioned such that they looked like wings, arcing away from her back.

She was ready to take flight.

An angel.

Jamie stopped, realising she had done a full circle of the scene now, had drowned in its grim radiance.

Her eyes ached.

'Well?' Wiik said, barely above a whisper.

The photographs in her father's study lined themselves up in front of her eyes. 'Mm,' she replied, her throat tight.

'Is it him?' Wiik asked.

He couldn't seriously expect her to know.

'I don't know,' Jamie replied, voice thin and quiet. 'But it's good.'

'Good?'

She looked up, seeing his raised eyebrows, his enquiring eyes. 'A good imitation, if it's not him,' Jamie said. 'My father always thought that Sjöberg had killed before. Was convinced of it. You can't kill a girl for the first time and then create this.' She didn't have to gesture for Wiik to know what she was talking about.

His silence was enough invitation to explain.

'If this is a copycat,' Jamie said. 'Then we're probably looking at the same thing. Someone who idolises Sjöberg, someone who wanted to emulate him. But someone who has killed before. Someone who knows what it's like to take a blade to flesh. To work on a human being like they're a thing, not a person.'

Jamie sighed, glancing down at the pool of blood around the girl. It had melted the snow, forming a circle of flatness around her, the undergrowth visible around her body.

'Have SOCOs been through?' Jamie asked.

'Hmm?'

'Shit, sorry, uh,' she said, racking her brain. 'CSTs.' Crime scene technicians.

'Yes,' Wiik said plainly. 'Though they are not confident.

A single set of footprints led from the road to the scene' – he turned, pointing with two fingers the way that they'd come – 'and back. The killer stepped in his own prints heading in the reverse direction, which has destroyed any hope of identifying any sizing or shoe tread patterns.'

The killer knew what they were doing.

'The branches were dusted for prints, but they weren't able to pull anything from them here. They suspect the killer wore gloves. But they'll test for trace residue of polymers and particulates once the body is removed to the lab.' He drew a deep breath. 'The girl herself,' Wiik went on, 'was dead before she was mounted like this, but not for long. She was washed and dressed carefully before being carried here. Her body shows no signs of bruising or trauma.'

'Apart from the wooden stakes driven through her back,' Jamie muttered, taking another circle. She noticed more with every step. Saw more. Felt more.

Anger churned in her chest.

Wiik kept talking. 'The rope used is a standard unbleached linen or cotton – natural fibres. Of that much they're sure, but we're still waiting for confirmation. We'll check security footage from all nearby shops that sell potential matches. But I doubt the killer would be so sloppy.'

'Mm,' Jamie said, taking the kill in. She paused as she moved behind the girl, staring at Wiik through the wings. *Her body shows no signs of trauma.* That's what Wiik said.

'Was she raped?' Jamie asked plainly. There wasn't any other way to approach it.

'We don't know,' he said, meeting Jamie's eyes over the girl's head. Her brown hair fell in clean strands around her serene face, framing it.

'That was one of the hallmarks of the Angel Maker,'

Jamie went on, again. 'He raped his victims before he killed them.'

Wiik pressed his mouth into a crumpled line. 'It is impossible to say until she is examined by the pathologist. That the girls historically chosen have all been of pubescent age suggests that there is a sexual element at work – that the angelic element is linked to purity. Virginity. There's a sorrowfulness to his kills,' Wiik said. 'An attempt at the restoration of innocence.'

Jamie drew a slow breath. She didn't want to conjecture anymore. 'What about the dress? The original dresses were taken from the church that Sjöberg and his wife attended. They held a Bible group there every Sunday.'

Jamie was surprised at how much she was dredging from her memories. She had suppressed them for so long. She considered what else would rise from the recesses of her mind.

And then decided that whatever did, it was worth it to catch this bastard.

Judging by Wiik's expressionless face, Jamie suspected that the insight about the girl's attire wasn't new information. No doubt they'd already questioned all of the officers and detectives at the SPA who were working at the time, had cobbled together as much information in lieu of the missing files as they could.

'We have taken photographs. We will make enquiries,' Wiik said. 'That church is now closed. A ruin. It was burnt down after Sjöberg was convicted. It won't have been from there.'

Jamie didn't think it had been.

'We need those files,' she said. 'The originals.'

Wiik nodded. 'We do. Your father's notes, too.'

Jamie didn't know if that was a shot at her.

She exhaled, hard. The faint taste of blood lingered in the frozen air. 'When is the pathology lab going to take possession of the body?' She needed to know what this girl had gone through.

'When I say so,' Wiik replied curtly. 'I will want to examine the scene again in daylight. Once I have read your father's notes.'

Jamie approached him slowly, her boots crunching in the snow. 'Okay,' she said, not needing to do more than whisper to be heard in the quiet of the forest. 'Take me home.'

5

THEY PULLED up outside Jamie's childhood home for the second time that day and Jamie exited the car.

The air was biting. The hour dwindling into evening, the temperature going with it.

Jamie exhaled, a long stream of steam expelling itself from between her lips. God, she'd missed the cold. The crisp, sharpness of the air that cut at the inside of the nose and made the chest ache.

London never came close, even on its coldest days.

Jamie looked up at her father's house. She corrected herself. *Her* house. And felt the key in her pocket, digging into her palm.

'Ready?' asked Wiik, standing beside her.

She nodded. She was. Now that she had a reason to go. A train with a track to follow. Something to move her through the place. Before, this was just a case in a far away country that rubbed up against the raw edges of her childhood. Now it was real. There was a girl – an innocent girl – brutalised and mounted in the woods like a trophy – and a killer who thought they were smart enough to get away with it. Well, they weren't. Not now that Jamie was here.

Jamie leaned forward, trusting the sensation of tipping over to jump-start her feet. She couldn't lift them herself.

The houses around were quiet now, the driveways busy with cars. People had come home from work and gone inside out of the cold. All that surrounded them were dim squares of light. Windows glowing in the darkness.

The key seemed to guide itself into the lock. It slid in rustily, and she began to twist. It resisted at first, and then gave. Jamie listened to the tumblers turn and then the creak of the hinges.

Stale air hit her and then she was inside, being shuffled forward by Wiik. He was wasting no more time.

She stood there in the hallway, the stairs stretching up in front of her, the house all but pitch dark.

On the left, an archway led into the kitchen, their old family table sitting in the middle of it. On the right, another archway opened into the living room.

She looked both ways, remembering the last time she was standing in that spot.

Jamie had been fourteen. Her mum had been in the car, screaming, crying. Her mum's voice had been shrill, echoing through the open door behind her. 'Don't you go up those stairs!' she had shrieked. 'Get in the car! Now, Jamie. I'll leave, I'll do it. I'm counting to three! Don't think I won't do it.'

She wished she had.

Jamie was calling her father's name. Asking him to come downstairs. To say goodbye.

'Dad?' Jamie had called. 'Please – come downstairs. Tell her. Tell her you're sorry. Tell her it was the last time. Tell me it will be okay. At least, say goodbye.'

But he hadn't.

And her mum had got to three and then laid on the horn.

And Jamie had backed out of the door, keeping her eyes on her parents' closed bedroom door for as long as she could.

Her mother had spun the front wheels, hit the rev-limiter, her mascara running down her cheeks in thick black lines. The car juddered forward and then crunched horribly as she rammed it into second and sped away.

'Inspector Johansson?'

Jamie pulled her eyes from the door at the top of the stairs, wiping her cheeks roughly with the back of her hand. 'Yeah, sorry, what is it?'

Wiik was standing next to her, flicking the light switch. Nothing was happening. 'No electricity,' he said. 'Where's the fuse box?'

'The house has been empty for nineteen years,' Jamie said, her voice quiet. 'It won't do any good.'

He made a dissatisfied noise. 'Do you know where your father kept his notes?' he asked.

Jamie peered past him into the gloom of the living room, seeing letters and paperwork spread out on their coffee table, perched on the TV, the bookcase.

The kitchen, too, was full of junk – the table had what looked like a half-rebuilt lawnmower engine on top of it.

'No,' she lied. 'They could be anywhere.'

Wiik let out a long breath. 'We'll have to come back tomorrow,' he decided. His anxious face portraying an awareness that every minute delayed was a minute burnt. Another minute closer to the Angel Maker's next victim.

Jamie knew it too, but it wasn't the reason her throat was tight.

'Which hotel are you staying at? I can give you a lift,' Wiik said. It came across as more of an insistence than an offer. Jamie had no doubt that he didn't want to disturb the house until they could see what they were doing. Didn't want to miss anything.

'It's fine,' Jamie said. 'I'll get a taxi.'

'I don't mind,' Wiik repeated. His tired expression failed to match the politeness of his offer.

'Honestly,' Jamie said. 'I'm going to take a look around anyway. If I find anything, I'll let you know.'

He clicked his teeth together behind closed lips. Looking like he was deciding if he wanted to stay and help her.

'Look,' Jamie went on, wishing he'd just piss off. 'I know the house. I know my father. But there's no use us both blundering around here in the dark. We can cover more ground if we split up. Let me go through my father's notes, you dig into Sjöberg. Find out everything you can about him, what he died of, who visited him, his doctors. Check out the original trial, get the transcripts – they should keep those records at the court archives. The original autopsy reports — they should still be at the pathology lab, in storage, probably. We need to gather all the information we can about the original murders. Compare them, contrast them to this one.

'If this is a copycat, then he had a connection to Sjöberg. We find that, it's a start.' She met his eyes in the darkness. They caught just a glimmer of light from outside, but were otherwise black holes in his shadowed face. 'Someone may have stolen the Polis case files, but there are still breadcrumbs out there to follow.'

Wiik looked back at her, a statue in her front hallway. His mouth widened but didn't curl up. 'Chief Inspector Smith was right.'

Jamie kept her eyes on him but said nothing back. She wasn't sure whether that was a good thing or not.

Wiik turned, pulling a card from his jacket pocket. He

held it out to her and Jamie took it. 'Let me know where you're staying,' he said stepping towards the door. 'I'll pick you up in the morning.'

Jamie watched him through the door. 'Does this mean you're letting me assist on the case?'

He raised a hand over his shoulder to wave goodbye, but didn't turn. 'It doesn't seem like I have a choice.'

He dropped her duffle at the kerb and then gave her a nod before getting in the car and driving off.

Jamie brought it inside and closed the door. Jamie took another look around the dark interior and breathed in the scent of her childhood home. It hadn't changed much. It still stank of stale whisky and cigarettes.

She flicked on the torch on her phone and swallowed, stepping slowly, beginning a lap of the house.

The living room was a mess of old books, magazines and papers. They were everywhere, all over the floor and coffee table, stacked on top of the old TV. Newspapers had been left in piles next to the sofa. Old clothes were draped over the back. Socks had been kicked off and left on the carpet. Jamie counted five empty whisky bottles.

Everything was covered in a layer of dust.

She tried to distance herself from her own memories and tilted her head to read some of the envelopes and letters on the table. Bills, mostly. Electric, gas, water... Past due. Late Payment. Final warning.

Jamie took in a slow breath.

Shit, he'd just given up. Knew he was winding down to the day he'd kill himself.

Jamie leaned in and picked up the envelope on top. It was dated the 17th September 2001. A week before her 18th birthday. It said that the electric would be cut off in four days.

She put it down, replacing it just where it was, thinking about how her father had held out, living in the dark for four days before he took his own life on the day she was old enough not to have her mother sell the house out from under her.

It hadn't stopped her lying about it though.

Jamie circled back through the hall and into the kitchen.

The fridge was still awash with photos of her as a girl, held on by stalwart magnets.

She moved closer, stepping past the rusted engine on the table. The wood around it was stained with oil, the floor littered with screws and bolts. They skittered into the darkness as her boots clipped them.

Her fingers stretched out.

The photos.

Her and her father camping. Her and her father fishing. Her and her father at the finish line of the one-hundred-metre sprint at her school sports day.

She had won.

Her and her father at the beach.

Jamie swallowed, her fingers only a few inches away from them.

Her eyes burned.

She touched one of the photos and the magnet gave out, held on only by the friction of the years.

It hit the ground and bounced, the photo coming away in her hand.

The rest, like dominoes, disturbed after all these years, finally let go, and rained down onto the tiles.

The photos all fell away and spun and flew into the darkness around her.

'Shit,' she muttered, looking around to see where they went.

Jamie sighed, feeling a tear warm on her cheek, her breath still misting in front of her, and looked at the one she had managed to save.

Her father was standing between two larch trees on a rocky outcropping. It was in the foothills under Stäjan, a mountain near the Norwegian border. Jamie was on his shoulders, her hands around his head. She must have been seven or eight. And he still made her look tiny.

Her mother had complained that entire trip. Her feet hurt. It was too far. It was too hot.

Jamie had grown tired, and her mother had insisted they go back to the car instead of pressing on to the top.

Her father had lifted her up like she was nothing and put her on his shoulders. Told her to hold tight.

They had left her mother behind and not returned for hours.

Jamie smiled down at the photo, remembering how funny she thought it was.

When it began to grow dark, they stopped and her father gathered firewood, used the flint and steel he carried on his keys to start a fire. And they'd sat in front of it and looked up through the trees at the stars. He'd told her about constellations.

Jesus, she couldn't believe she remembered all that.

But she must have fallen asleep, because the next thing she knew, they were hammering down a motorway in the car, streetlights flashing past. Her parents were arguing in the front seat.

Hell, her mother must have been waiting for hours before they got back.

Jamie swallowed and tucked the photograph into her back pocket.

She still thought it was kind of funny.

The dining room beckoned. Jamie headed out of the kitchen and into it.

They had rarely eaten in there other than at Christmas. Her mother had always kept the room neat. There was a glass cabinet against the left-hand wall, filled with the 'good china', glass decanters and crystal glassware her parents had received as wedding presents.

Jamie looked over, remembering there being more decanters. Remembering them always being half-full of various shades of amber liquids.

There were just a few left, and they were all empty.

Jamie stared for a moment and then let her eyes drift across to the glass doors at the back of the room. They let out onto the garden.

Thin slits of moonlight bled through the shutters. A slat was missing and Jamie could see the grey of fresh snow covering the lawn.

There was only one room left now. Her father's study.

Her mother had always hated her going in there. And Jamie could see why. As a child it was always exciting – the thrill of seeing these dark, mysterious things her father did, and having the luxury of not understanding them. In her mind, her father was a superhero. A man who wasn't afraid of anything, who'd punch the bad guys in the face. Who carried a knife and a revolver on his belt like a western gunslinger, and who never let the villain get away.

That amazed her back then.

Now she knew him to be a quick-to-violence man with more problems than anyone was prepared to admit. Let alone Jamie.

She had to see a counsellor. Had been forced to confront what she'd done. To one girl. To one mixed-up girl who'd rushed her with a knife. Who'd helped a killer murder four others. Who'd killed a man herself. Who had left her no other choice.

Her father had just been expected to get on with it.

Jamie steadied herself, staring down at her hand halfway to the door. It was going numb in the cold.

She had to move.

Jamie stepped forward, pressed the handle down, and stepped inside.

The air was slightly warmer in here.

Her phone threw a harsh light around the room, and Jamie took it all in.

There was a desk on the right, cluttered with papers, an ancient grey computer. The back wall was a tangle of pinned-up newspaper clippings, photographs from crime scenes and permanent marker drawn right onto the paint.

Jamie cast her eyes over it, picking out the bright yellow of evidence markers in the gloom. The shine of blood in the camera flashes of the CSTs. These were all crime scene photos. Her father's last cases. The crimes varied and brutal.

Jamie set her jaw and came forward.

She could see no angel wings among them.

The carpet underfoot groaned a little as she walked, the fibres gone stiff with time.

Beneath the photos and the papers pinned to the wall was a low, wide bookcase. Jamie remembered it and knelt, running her fingers across the volumes and spines.

There were books on everything crime-related. Criminology, psychology, sociology. Books written by other detectives, by psychologists, some by criminals even. They covered everything from Cesare Lombroso's *Criminal Man* right through to studies and books on 'the warrior gene'. He had been a voracious reader, among other things. Insomniac. Philanderer. Addict. Drinker.

Jamie looked past those and found what she was looking for. A stack of small leather notebooks. His work notebooks.

She hadn't been lying when she'd said her father wasn't one for making a lot of notes. But he'd always carried a notepad. To take down names, thoughts, anything of use he saw or thought of.

Jamie didn't know what she expected to find, but she needed to see.

There were three stacks.

She lifted the one on the top of the left-hand stack, peeled back the cover and saw the dates *1984–1986* written in it.

No, way too early.

The Angel Maker killed the girls from 1995 to 1996.

She moved across to the second stack and checked.

1992. Getting warmer.

The third stack was slightly shorter. She took the top notebook and looked at it. The date inside the front page said *1995*.

Jamie exhaled and flipped through all the pages, letting the near-silent flap of the paper punctuate the room. This was it.

She held it close to her chest and let her eyes drift over the remaining ones.

Her mother had taken her to England in the winter of 1997. Just before Christmas. To make it hurt more. It was her dad's favourite time of the year. On the twenty-third, he would take Jamie north, and they would hunt a goose for Christmas dinner.

She never liked hunting. But her father had always

reminded her that the ones bought in supermarkets or butchers were farmed, brutalised, culled for their meat.

At least they were giving the goose a fighting chance doing it their way.

1997 had been the roughest year for him. For Jamie's mother. For all of them. The Angel Maker had broken her father, and that trip was going to be their first chance to get away. To normalise.

Two days in the frozen north. Two days, just the two of them at the little hunting cabin they always went to. The goose was inconsequential. Jamie couldn't have cared less whether they shot one.

But lying there on an icy ridge was one of her favourite places in the world. Spread out on the ground next to him, the barrel of his old Remington 700 resting on the rolled-up blanket that was always spread across the back seat of his car...

God, how it stunk. He'd shoot on it and then wrap the goose in it. Jamie could smell it now, all grease and gunpowder and feathers. She shook her head, remembering how much her mother complained about it. But how much she'd loved it.

He always kept the rifle in good order, had it hanging above his...

Jamie turned to look at the desk and then tilted her head back.

There it was, on the shelf, like always. Cut out in a dim silhouette, the polished stock catching the residual light from her phone.

Too high for her to reach as a child. But always there.

She couldn't help but smile looking at it. It didn't mean death, or shooting, or even Christmas. It meant her father.

And these notepads – she turned her head back to the

third and final stack – chronicled the last years of his life. The years she had lost him. His final cases, his final thoughts. His final hours.

She let out a long exhale, unable to leave them behind, and grabbed the whole stack, standing up in the darkness of her father's study, and turned. She froze.

Against the back wall, there was a leather sofa. One her father had often sat on to read.

And she had often sat there with him while he did.

Had often sat there, watched him as he typed up his reports on a beaten-up old Imperial 200 typewriter too, falling asleep to the sound of his tapping and clacking.

Tap, tap, tap. Her eyes growing heavy.

She looked at it now, clutching at his notebooks, and then turned away.

Jamie left the sofa where she'd fall asleep a thousand times behind.

Along with the chaotic black stain on the wall above it.

The ancient blood of her father.

From where he'd blown the back of his skull out with his snub-nose .38 Smith & Wesson Special.

6

Jamie,

Not a day goes by I don't think about you.

There was a squirrel in this garden this morning, trying to get at the bird feeder. It reminded me of you that time you tried to climb the pine behind the house. You were too small to reach the lowest branches and spent hours trying to get up the trunk.

You told me if you were a squirrel, life would be easier.

It still makes me smile.

7

WIIK ARRIVED a few minutes after eight the next morning.

Jamie had been there since six and was running on a few snatched hours of sleep, getting up in spates to read her father's notebooks.

Her mind was her own worst enemy in the dark.

But she was used to it now, and numb to all but the worst of it.

Wiik's boots squeaked on the stairs as he came up, approaching the open door to her childhood bedroom.

He slowed, looked left and right, and then stepped inside.

The sun had just risen, the light pale and weak. The room was silent, dust motes floating in the brilliance coming in through the window. The shutters had been opened.

Wiik glanced around, found the room empty, and then turned, jumping a little to find Jamie standing in the doorway.

'I went to your hotel,' he said, straightening the cuffs of his shirt under the sleeves of his grey sweater. His jeans were straight-legged, not quite skinny, his boots polished black with enough tread to hold in the snow. Just. And just as before, his face was impeccably shaved, his hair gelled back over his head.

'I wasn't there,' Jamie said, stepping inside to join Wiik in her old room.

The walls were a dark shade of purple.

She'd chosen it.

Her mother had wanted white.

Her father had let her have it.

'I know,' Wiik said, not trying to keep the tone of frustration from his voice. 'You could have called.'

'You would have been asleep,' Jamie said, stepping around him and going to her bedside table. She picked up a braided bracelet that was draped over her reading lamp. The room was exactly how it had been the day she'd left. Nothing had been touched.

She looked down at the piece of string in her fingers.

He made a disgruntled noise behind her. 'I would have come earlier.'

'Then why didn't you?' Jamie glanced up and met his eye, There was a strange coolness in them that morning.

Wiik folded his arms, his jacket twisting under his biceps, revealing the SIG Sauer P226 semi-automatic pistol hanging from his ribs. He hadn't been wearing it yesterday. 'Where were you just now?' He nodded to the door.

'I heard you coming.'

'And hid?' he raised an eyebrow.

Jamie half shrugged. 'I didn't know it was you.'

'Who else would it be?'

'Whoever kidnapped Nyström.'

'You think someone kidnapped him?'

'Maybe. It seems strange that he'd leave the city and not take his credentials with him. And you yourself said that they knew he wouldn't be home when they broke in.

What better way to ensure that than to make sure of it yourself.'

Wiik took that in. 'And you thought that same person would come here to try to… what? Kidnap you, too?'

'Or kill me.' Jamie looked around the room. 'Maybe the killer got rid of Nyström because he knew he'd be on to him first.'

Wiik processed that too and didn't seem displeased with the extrapolation. He sighed. 'Did you find anything?'

'You walk very loudly, do you know that?' Jamie asked, running her finger over the tops of the books on her bookshelf. Dahls. Tolkeins. Pratchetts. Charting her intellectual maturation.

Wiik spoke through gritted teeth, his fist curling at his side. 'I wasn't trying to sneak.'

Jamie smiled at him now. 'No, clearly.'

A vein throbbed in Wiik's temple.

There. She'd found it. His line. His threshold. He was quick to anger, easy to frustrate. She needed to know what kind of man he was. And now she did.

Now she could work with him.

'Come on,' she said quickly, walking out the door. 'I've got something to show you.'

Jamie used to torture her old partner like that, too. But that was mostly just for the fun of it. She found no pleasure in doing it now. Not when she was placing her life in someone's hands. She needed to know that she could count on Wiik.

She had no idea what had happened to Nyström, but she had a list of things she wanted to check out today, and the security footage from the toll gate his car was clocked at was one of them. Crimes like this weren't done on the spur of the moment. They required meticulous planning. And waiting for Sjöberg to die, stealing the case files, staging the kill, they all required a lot of timing and effort. Precision was the word that came to mind. Nothing could be left to chance. And if it was Jamie, leaving the only remaining investigating officer from the original case hanging around wasn't something she'd be interested in doing.

Nyström would be a hindrance, and taking him out of play would only make things easier. Getting the car tagged at a toll booth meant that it was *supposed* to be seen. Either to push the investigation in the wrong direction, to split resources, or just to show the police that they weren't safe. Not even in their own homes.

Jamie didn't know who they were dealing with. But she did know one thing. And that was that he was smart. And he was a goddamn monster.

Wiik followed Jamie downstairs and into the kitchen. He took one glance at the magnets strewn on the floor. 'What happened here?'

Jamie looked over her shoulder briefly, heading for the dining room. 'How should I know?'

The photographs had been gathered up and were all neatly bound in her duffle at the hotel.

Wiik came into the dining room behind her and pushed back the hems of his coat, putting his hands on his hips, staring down at the table in front of him.

Jamie had spent the morning going through her father's notebook, and had transcribed what he'd written out onto a full-sized pad, then removed the pages and laid them out on the kitchen table in front of her. The information was far from comprehensive. But she did what she could.

'You've been busy,' Wiik remarked sourly.

'I don't sleep much,' Jamie replied, not even looking up.

'Okay, so this notebook' – Jamie held it up – 'chronicles the original Angel Maker case. This first entry, here, dated the nineteenth of November 1995, is the first recording of the case. The first girl.'

Wiik licked his lips.

'I wrote out what my father observed here,' Jamie said, pointing to the top left sheet. There were seven in one row on the table. One for each girl. She read aloud. '"Victim, girl, teens. Posed in white dress, wooden stakes through her back. Angel wings?"' She stared at it for a moment. 'He knew, right from the off what he was looking at. But without the finer details of the scenes – photos, reports from the CSTs – it's hard to make any solid assumptions about likeness. The rest of these are the subsequent scenes.' Jamie cast her hand across them. 'Again, not much in the way of notes. A few comments, a few little illustrations. One drawing of parallel lines that sort of zigzag. I think it's supposed to be the tread marks of a boot. But I can't be certain.'

Wiik held his hand out, signalling that he wanted to see this drawing for himself.

Jamie handed him the book, and he took it from her, turning it over and flipping the pages.

'The pages are marked where—'

'I got it,' Wiik said curtly, the vein in his temple back again.

Jamie went on, regardless. She didn't consider stepping on his toes or making him feel threatened important in comparison to catching this killer.

'The significant bit,' Jamie said, dropping her hand down a row to the middle section, 'is this. These are all the notes my father made on the suspects, the clues, the trails… Everything he picked up on during the investigation.'

Wiik lowered the book and looked down at where Jamie was pointing.

'There are four names here – on one of the pages. Tomas Lindvall. Per Eriksson. Leif Lundgren. And Hans Sjöberg. Sjöberg was convicted of the killings, so I assume these are the names of the other suspects. We need to check them out. Find them, interview them. We work backwards, retrace his steps, from the end' – her hand cut the air – 'right back to the beginning.'

Wiik raised an eyebrow. 'You want me to just come back later? You seem to have this all worked out already.'

Jamie took a breath and turned to him. 'Don't act like a child. I'll be more helpful working *with* you.'

'Than against me?'

'Than not at all,' Jamie said, narrowing her eyes. 'This is your case, but I'm going to do whatever I can to help catch this guy.'

He turned to face her fully now, folding his arms. 'And why is it so important to you?'

Jamie opened her mouth a little to speak, but she didn't have a straight answer for him. To prove her father was a good detective? To connect with him in some way?

To catch a killer before he hurt anyone else?

Because she missed it? Because she missed *this,* detective work*?* As much as she hated to admit it.

She cleared her throat. 'Isn't it important to you?'

He cracked just a hint of a smile. 'Pick this up,' he said, nodding at the papers. 'We have to go.'

'Go where?'

'There's someone who wants to meet you.'

. . .

Wiik drove smoothly, but wasn't interested in making small talk.

When they pulled into the underground car park at Stockholm Polis HQ, Jamie's stomach churned a little. The hours she'd spent here as a kid sitting in front of her father's desk, sitting behind it, exploring the corridors – much to the dismay of everyone else in the building.

Everyone knew Jörgen's little girl. She'd yell at the other officers and detectives in the corridors. 'Slow down!' if they were running, or 'Get back to work!' if they were standing around talking. She thought she was so tough.

'Sorry, Kriminalinspektör Johansson,' they'd say, playing along, and then stride off, grinning at how cute she was. Her white-blonde hair trailing the full length of her back. Her big blue eyes.

'You'll grow up to be just as much of a ball-breaker as your father,' people said, laughing.

They couldn't help but laugh at her. And care for her.

She remembered them bringing cups of hot chocolate and biscuits from the break rooms when her father disappeared. He'd be right back, he'd say. And then leave. Be gone for hours sometimes.

Jamie only found out where he'd been going years later.

The women, the drugs, the drink.

He was a superhero to her.

But even superheroes have their weaknesses.

Wiik killed the motor and got out without saying a word.

Jamie followed silently, and they headed for the elevator.

She glanced at the stairs, but Wiik didn't seem in the mood to discuss anything, let alone the benefits of getting your daily steps in.

She'd walked to her house that morning from the hotel.

3.6 kilometres by her watch. Barely a warm-up by her usual standards.

They got out on the seventh floor and Jamie slowed a little to take it in. The layout was familiar, the sound of people's heels on the tiled floors sending her through a time warp. But otherwise the floor – and probably the building – had been modernised. The stale haze of cigarette smoke and dim desk lamps had given way to a bright interior drowned in light. Large windows and open spaces replaced what used to be narrow corridors between wooden desks. Now they were made of white… plastic. Jamie tapped her short, unpainted nails against the surface of one as she passed, following Wiik towards the glass office at the back.

Some detectives glanced up from their desks as they went by, looking away as they realised it was Wiik, not giving Jamie a second look. The guy carried weight here. Though she wasn't surprised considering he'd just been handed the Angel Maker case.

A woman in her fifties was sitting in the office. She was behind a modern glass desk with steel support struts, leaning forward a little, reading something on her computer screen.

Her features were fine – a thin nose and pointed chin, dark hair cut short, parted in the centre and swept back, the ends flicking out behind her ears.

Wiik stopped at the door, raised his knuckles, and knocked once, lightly.

The woman looked up, went from him to Jamie and back again, and then motioned them in with two fingers, a pen curled into her palm with the others.

Wiik pushed through and Jamie followed.

The woman leaned on her elbows, clasping her hands under her chin. She stared up at Jamie with bright eyes.

'Little Jamie Johansson,' she said, smiling widely. 'I don't know if you remember me, I'm—'

'Kriminalinspektör Ingrid Falk,' Jamie said, nodding. She smiled back. 'I remember you.'

'*Kriminalkommissarie*,' Wiik muttered.

Falk waved him off with her hand and then gestured to a chair in front of her desk. 'Please, sit down,' she said to Jamie.

Jamie obliged.

'We're so glad to have you,' Falk said.

Behind Jamie, Wiik stood, turning to face out of the window, his hands going to his hips again, his jacket pushed back behind his wrists.

'I just wish,' Falk went on, 'that it was under better circumstances.' She looked down at her desk, removed her hands from under her chin. 'This is a dark time for the city.'

'I can imagine,' Jamie said, pressing her lips into a line. 'If there's anything I can do to help...'

'Yes, well,' Falk said, looking up at Wiik's back and then back to Jamie. 'Wiik already informed me that you wished to assist on the case, and while normally we wouldn't accept outside help, the circumstances are... special. The Angel Maker was one of your father's biggest cases, and any light you can shed on it will be invaluable. Is there anything you remember that might help?'

Jamie bit her lip. 'It's difficult. I can't place anything specifically, but it's coming back in pieces.'

Falk nodded silently.

'My father said so much,' Jamie went on, looking down, staring into her memories, 'it's difficult to separate it all. But when I see something, read something...'

'It comes back.' Falk was being more understanding than

Jamie expected. 'Do you need to get back to London by a specific date?' she asked, her voice soft.

Jamie read the lines of her face, analysing the way she'd asked. 'You've spoken to my DCI,' Jamie guessed.

Falk seemed a little amused. 'He said you were sharp.'

'What else did he say?'

'That you were on administrative leave after being forced to shoot a suspect.' She wasn't dancing around it, that was for sure.

'She came at me with a knife.'

'That must have been difficult,' Falk said tactfully. She'd had to deal with this before in her team. That much was clear.

'It was.'

'Why haven't you returned to work?' she asked casually, looking at her screen as though something interesting were on it.

'I've been waiting for the right time,' Jamie replied, trying to keep herself even.

'What is the "right time"?'

'When I was ready.'

She nodded. 'Are you ready now?'

'Yes.'

'But you weren't before.'

Jamie narrowed her eyes. Part of her wanted to wipe the polite smile off Falk's face. She remembered her from the floor when she was a kid. She was always studious, quiet. Great at paperwork. She wasn't a detective like Jamie's father. A different breed. She was the sort that always filed her reports, always had glowing reviews from her superiors. Never put a foot out of line. She was the sort that rose through the ranks and couldn't wait to be shoved behind a desk and out of the firing line.

And here she was.

She'd always disliked Jamie's father, and Jamie couldn't help but wonder if there was a little lingering resentment spilling onto her.

Jamie cleared her throat. 'No, I wasn't. I think I'd forgotten what it was like.'

'What *what* was like?'

'The feeling that if you stand by and do nothing, people will die.'

Falk studied the woman in front of her, a little amused, a little curious, a little derisive. 'You don't think our detectives could handle this case?'

'I don't have any reason to doubt them,' Jamie said. 'But I'm here. I was asked to come here, maybe just to help find my father's notes, but Wiik can attest to their vagueness.'

The man behind her didn't move. Falk didn't even bother to look at him. She kept her eyes fixed on Jamie.

'So it seems more likely that my memories can shed light on the original case. And frankly, if this one turns out to be anything like the first, I don't know why you wouldn't want the extra assistance.'

Falk didn't speak for a second, weighing her words. 'We'd never turn it down. The SPA have always maintained a good working relationship with the London Metropolitan Police, and I'm keen to continue that relationship.'

She was in full diplomacy mode.

'But I have a duty of care,' she went on, 'to both my own officers and those under my purview, to ensure their safety to the best of my abilities. Do you understand what I'm saying?'

'You're asking me if I'm going to be a liability,' Jamie said, not trying very hard to keep the scorn from her voice. 'I've been cleared for active duty.'

'I was informed. But still, I must do my own due diligence. I can't just let anyone go running around in my city

without vetting them first, no matter whose daughter they
are.'

Jamie watched her carefully, looking for cracks in the
wax mask. She couldn't tell if Falk was insinuating that she
didn't think Jamie was capable of working this case, or if she
was trying to ascertain whether she was going to behave like
her father.

Jörgen Johansson had been a decorated detective. But also
a brute, a drunkard and someone who was pulled into an
office like this at least twice weekly for use of unnecessary or
excessive force. Often both.

'I can assure you,' Jamie said, slipping into her own
mask, 'I'll do nothing but be a gleaming representative of
both the Met and the SPA. You have my word on that.'

Falk smiled broadly now. 'I'm glad to hear it. But don't
think about it too much,' she said, going back to her paperwork. 'Wiik will tell you if you're overstepping your bounds.
And then report right back to me. Isn't that right, Wiik?'

The man behind her grunted in semi-confirmation.

'Now then,' Falk said, grinning and clasping her hands
together and laying them on the desk. 'What have you got for
me so far?'

8

'GIVE ME THOSE NAMES AGAIN,' Wiik said as they headed for the old church a few miles north of the city. For the home of Hans Sjöberg's widow.

'Per Eriksson, Leif Lundgren, Tomas Lindvall,' Jamie repeated.

Wiik nodded taking them in. 'Eriksson, Lundgren, Lindvall.'

'That's what it says,' Jamie confirmed, reading her father's old notes back for the hundredth time.

They were the three other suspects that her father had noted down when investigating the original Angel Maker case. Their first three stops. After this one.

Wiik swung a right off a main road and trundled down a narrow two-lane with birch trees growing on the left. Their spindly branches dangled over the asphalt and dropped blobs of snow onto it.

The sky was bleak and grey as they drove, the air still and cold. Winter had closed in on the city like a noose. Same as it did every year.

The lonely spire of a church rose up at the end of the

road, blackened support struts sticking up from its base like a ribcage. The place had fallen to ruin after a fire, its once bright exterior now flaking and charred. The ground around it was overgrown and covered with snow. Brambles arced from the white surface and dived back in at odd angles.

The word *rapist* was still visible, spray-painted on the side of it in huge red letters, despite the years and flames. It looked like someone had come back after the blaze to reiterate their point.

Wiik slowed just short of the locked gate and then pulled up onto the verge.

Nestled on the edge of the church grounds was a house.

Jamie and Wiik looked out at the modest half red brick, half white panelled bungalow, the two steps leading up to the front porch, the rusted access ramp next to them.

Wiik's phone buzzed in the centre console, and he pulled it up in front of him, the corners of his mouth curling down. 'They've removed the body,' he said.

'From the scene?' Jamie asked.

'It's attracting too much attention. The press have got wind.' He reached up, pushing his slicked-back hair against his scalp. 'It's at the lab already.'

He didn't seem happy about that, and it looked like Falk had gone over his head with it. But it was getting on for two days, and there was still no sign of Nyström or the files.

They couldn't have left her there forever.

Wiik shouldered the car door open, stuffing his phone back into his pocket, and headed for the house, not waiting for Jamie or looking back.

He was making it painfully clear who was in charge here.

Wiik swept up the path, climbed up onto the porch and knocked firmly, standing back so that Jamie couldn't get up next to him.

She rolled her eyes and stepped onto the ramp, navigating the slick surface, and then drew level with Wiik.

He didn't look at her.

They waited for a long time before the door opened, a woman in a wheelchair appearing in the doorway. She was in her sixties, her face lined, the skin around her throat baggy. Her long grey hair was pulled back into a loose ponytail, her dark eyes magnified behind thick glasses. Each lens had a different prescription, which made one eye look larger than the other.

She coughed, the sound wet and laboured, and then wheezed, sucking in a deep breath. It sounded difficult for her. 'Yes?' she asked, her voice rasping.

'Kriminalinspektör Anders Wiik, Stockholm Polis,' Wiik said, holding up his badge. 'This is my colleague, Jamie Johansson.' He nodded to Jamie, then smiled at the old woman.

Jamie ignored the fact that he left off her title and gave the woman a smile too.

Wiik went on. 'Eva Sjöberg?'

The old woman looked at the both of them. 'You're here about my husband,' she said, her voice tired. She reached down with thin hands and rolled herself backwards with some difficulty. 'Come in, then,' she said, her face dropping. 'You're letting the heat out.'

Jamie and Wiik sat on a plastic-covered sofa in the living room, Eva across from them. The television was playing daytime gameshows with the volume off. Subtitles flew across the bottom of the screen as two contestants bashed buttons furiously to fill up a giant meter with liquid.

Wiik cleared his throat and Jamie looked back at Eva Sjöberg, the widow of the infamous Angel Maker.

'I'm sorry for your loss,' Wiik said plainly, before driving the stake in. 'Your husband always maintained his innocence in the Angel Maker case, is that correct?'

Eva was staring at Jamie, though. The question didn't even seem to register. 'Have we met before, dear?' she asked, her expression absent, her head shaking just a little.

Jamie was sitting back on the sofa so that she wasn't crowding Eva. Wiik was hanging off the end, elbows on his knees.

'No,' Jamie replied. 'I don't think we have.'

'You seem familiar.'

It's probably because my father put your husband in prison for the murder of seven teenage girls, Jamie resisted the urge to say. 'I'm sorry, I don't think so.'

Eva shrugged a little, her pointed shoulders like the corners of a tent beneath her cardigan.

Jamie didn't know how she could wear one. She was sweating, as was Wiik. It must have been a hundred degrees in the house.

'Mrs Sjöberg,' Wiik tried again. 'Your husband.'

'Hans,' Eva confirmed, inflecting it almost like a question.

'Yes. He always claimed his innocence – that he wasn't the Angel Maker.'

'He is innocent,' Eva replied evenly, focusing now on Wiik.

She caught the tense mismatch. *Is?* Surely she meant *was*. Jamie swallowed, studying the frail old woman.

This wasn't a road Jamie thought they should proceed down – arguing a case that neither of them knew anything about with a woman who wasn't playing with a full deck anymore.

They still hadn't checked the court records – they weren't digitised, and it would be a real job to go through the archives manually to find the originals. And nor had they been to the pathologist yet. They didn't even have an ID on the victim. But the day was young, and they both needed to get as deep into this case, and the original, as they could. As fast as they could. And if Eva Sjöberg could point them in the direction of any of the other suspects, then it would give them a big head start. She couldn't argue with Wiik's logic there. Even if she didn't wholly agree with it.

Wiik cleared his throat. 'I apologise for dragging all of this back up, but we're trying to clarify some of the finer details of the original case. There were other suspects in the investigation,' Wiik went on. 'What was it that tied Hans to the crimes so strongly?'

Eva Sjöberg's eyes drifted to the window, out at the husk of the church. 'We used to run a Sunday school for the children, Hans and I.'

Wiik's fist tightened between his knees.

'We knew those girls. Those poor, poor girls. All of them. All seven of them. They came to the services. With their parents. Sweet girls. Special girls. Innocent girls. What was done to them was just…'

Jamie listened intently. Someone knowing two of the victims outside of the church was coincidence. Three or four would be uncanny. But someone knowing all seven of them? No wonder her father had zeroed in on Sjöberg.

Wiik kept his eyes on her. 'Was there anyone else that might have had a connection to the victims?'

Her eyes seemed to widen at the word. 'Victims…' she parroted. 'Only… I don't know. He was the groundskeeper,

for the church, you know? His name was Erraldsson...
Eriksson?'

Jamie sat up. 'Per Eriksson?'

Wiik shot her a look and she nodded, confirming it was
one of the three names in her father's notebook.

She nodded. 'Yes, yes. He was the groundskeeper, for the
church.'

'You said that,' Wiik said, his frustration growing. 'Did he
know the girls?'

'He may have done. He came to the church regularly.'

'Do you know where he is now?'

Eva seemed to think for a moment, and then shook her
head.

Wiik changed tact. 'Did anyone visit your husband before
his death?'

Eva's eyes widened again, as though she'd forgotten that
fact before he'd reminded her. 'His...' She trailed off, then a
look of knowing came over her face, remembering that she
already knew. 'I – I don't know.' Her voice had grown quiet.
She looked at the chair she was in, a blanket spread over her
lap. 'I didn't get to visit much. It's difficult for me to move
around. In the winter especially. And, you know,' she said, a
sadness coming to her eyes, 'people aren't lining up to push
around the woman they believe is married to a child-killer.'

Jamie swallowed, wondering how this woman's life had
been.

'Do you have children of your own?' Wiik asked.

She shook her head. 'I wasn't... Hans wanted children.
But I couldn't. I had an accident, years ago, that... It
meant...' She trailed off, looking down at her chair again, as
though just seeing it for the first time and realising all the
things that came with it.

Jamie reached forward and touched Wiik on the arm, gave

him *the look* that all detectives know; They wouldn't be able to extract anything else from the poor woman for now. They'd need to check the prison records for visitors and go from there. Whether Wiik had thought she'd plead her husband's innocence and reveal the real Angel Maker, Jamie didn't know. But whatever his reasons were for coming here first, he didn't seem satisfied with the outcome.

All they had otherwise was a nameless girl frozen in the snow, a missing ex-detective and three names scrawled in a twenty-five-year-old notebook.

'Thank you for your time,' Wiik said, getting to his feet. 'We might be back to ask a few more questions.'

Jamie added, 'If that's alright with you.'

Eva beamed at her, widely, brightening suddenly as the sadness fell out of her mind. 'Of course, dear.' She reached out and took Jamie's hand, grasping it tightly with bony fingers. 'If there's anything else I can do to help.'

Jamie let her hand be held for a moment, thinking about the man her father was. Thinking about Eriksson having the means and opportunity. Thinking about Hans Sjöberg. A cold feeling crept up under her shirt and took hold of her spine. 'Mrs Sjöberg, do you mind if I ask, did your husband plead guilty to the crimes?'

'No,' she said, shaking her head, her expression conflicted. 'Not at first. But he had to in the end.'

'Was he going to be convicted on the evidence alone? Do you remember?'

She furrowed her brow, trying to dig the answer out of her fading memories. 'No – not alone. That other man was the prime suspect for a long time, but then Hans…' She seemed to choke on the words. 'They made him confess.'

'*Made* him?' Jamie queried, still holding the woman's hands. 'Your husband's confession was taken under duress?'

The woman's lip began to quiver. 'Yes,' she said, barely above a whisper. 'He beat him. He beat him so badly,' she said, devolving into a sob. 'He beat it out of him, f-forced him to say that he did it.' The woman jerked now, her shoulders rising and falling. Her other hand came up and grabbed Jamie's now, too.

Jamie's mouth had gone dry. 'Who was "he"?' she asked, knowing already that she didn't want to hear the answer. 'Who beat the confession out of your husband?'

Eva Sjöberg looked up then, and a moment of stillness seized the room. She met Jamie's wide blue eyes, her voice dripping with venom. 'The detective,' she spat. 'Johansson. Jörgen Johansson.'

WIIK AND JAMIE drove in silence.

She stared out of the window as they wound back towards the city, watching the trees go by, trying to get the image of her father beating a murder confession out of an innocent man out of her head.

Jamie shook that thought off. *Possibly* innocent. He still had the means, the opportunity, and she was sure that despite the way the confession was obtained, that her father was positive Hans Sjöberg was the guy.

She could only operate under the same assumption.

At least for now.

Wiik reached out and touched the screen in the centre console, dialling for the HQ.

It rang twice and then a woman answered, her voice bright.

Jamie hmphed a little as the woman said, 'Hello, Polisassistent Hallberg.' Hallberg was the equivalent of a constable, and from her disposition it sounded like she hadn't yet had the shine taken off her by the scum of the earth.

Jamie caught herself smirking sardonically. Damn. When did she get so cynical?

She returned to looking at the trees, the high-rises in the distance darkening as they swam out of the cold winter mist.

'Hallberg,' Wiik said.

Just that one word, in that tone, told Jamie that Hallberg was Wiik's workhorse. The one that proofed his paperwork, the one that did the research and the running around, the boring stuff. The one that fetched his coffee and made his phone calls.

The one that would probably be sitting in this seat if Jamie wasn't.

Had she shit all over the biggest case of this poor girl's career? Jamie thought back to the times she was brushed off as a DC. How much she had hated it.

No, it would be a good lesson for her. And plus, this case was already well above her pay grade.

'We're heading back from Eva Sjöberg's house. I need you to do some things. Got a pen?' Wiik asked.

There was scrabbling on the line as Hallberg jammed the phone against her shoulder and grabbed a pad. 'Go.'

'Take these names down. Leif Lundgren, Tomas Lindvall, Per Eriksson. Got that?'

'Uh-huh. Who are they? Suspects?'

'From the original case, we think. Names in Johansson's notebook.'

Jamie perked up, then realised Wiik meant her father. She never wanted to live in her father's shadow. And yet the warmth of the sun had never felt further away.

Wiik went on. 'The last one – Eriksson. He was the prime suspect before Johansson's focus switched to Sjöberg. He was the groundskeeper at the church where the girls were targeted.'

'Oh,' Hallberg said. 'Want me to try and track him down?'

'I want you to track them all down. We need to rebuild the original case from the ground up. Find out where Johansson fucked up.'

Jamie shot Wiik a cold glance, but he either didn't care, or made a point of seeming like it.

'Find me addresses – historical addresses, too. I want to know where they lived at the time of the original murders as well as where they live now, okay?'

'Sure. You have any more info? Dates of birth, or—'

'No, nothing,' Wiik said, then sighed. 'Just the names. But you'll get it done.'

'Might take some time,' Hallberg replied tentatively. 'A lot of records to comb through.'

'Just get it done. And Hallberg?'

'Yes?'

'I'll need copies of the court transcripts for the original trial. And get me a list of all the visitors that Sjöberg had in prison. Security footage if you can, too.'

'In the last twenty years?'

'I don't think it will be a long list.'

There was quiet on the line for a second as she scribbled down the items. 'Anything else?'

'Any word on an ID for the girl, yet?'

Hallberg sighed. 'No, I'm searching missing persons, but no hits yet matching her description. The girl can only have been gone three, four days. Maybe a report hasn't been filed yet.'

'Search wider. Outside the city, too,' Jamie said suddenly, turning her head. 'The girl could be from anywhere. We don't know how she was chosen.'

Hallberg didn't respond for a second. 'Who's that?' she

asked, doing her best to keep what Jamie thought might be jealousy from her voice.

Wiik clenched his jaw, as though already annoyed at the idea of there being any animosity between them. 'The consultant. From the London Met.'

'Oh.'

Jamie sat straighter. 'Detective Inspector Jamie Johansson,' she added formally.

'Johansson?' she asked, surprised. 'As in…'

'Yes,' Wiik said, his voice taking on a cold edge. 'Johansson's daughter.'

'I didn't realise that she— I mean, it's… Never mind,' Hallberg replied, clearing her throat regaining herself. 'I apologise.'

'I don't want your apologies,' Wiik said. 'Just get what I asked done.' He huffed and then hung up on her before she could say anything else.

Jamie eyed him, trying to decode what had just happened.

Wiik put both his hands on the wheel now and tightened his grip, looking ahead.

Being forty-eight hours into a murder case with no possible ID on your victim was a nightmare for any detective. And when your breadcrumbs were this stale – two decades stale – things could only get tougher. But there was something else, too. The whole *consultant* thing? Something was off.

'Where are we going?' Jamie asked as Wiik sailed into the other lane, swooping around a caravan doing forty, before cutting back in. He seemed to have sped up considerably since the call.

'Pathology lab,' Wiik muttered, seemingly unhappy about the fact. 'And whatever you do, don't tell him your name.'

.   .   .

Dr Peter Claesson was the head pathologist at the Swedish National Forensic Centre's Stockholm lab.

Jamie was the same height as him. Wiik was a head taller.

The man wasn't overweight, but his narrow shoulders and slouching posture did nothing for the fit of his shirt and lab coat. His weak chin, narrow mouth, and bald pate all came together to make him look utterly unapproachable. And that's exactly how his demeanour was, too.

'Wiik,' he said, walking out from the sealed lab, pulling bloodied latex gloves from his hands. His white lab coat came down to his knees, his beady eyes bouncing from Jamie to Wiik and back. 'I suppose you have a good reason for inter-rupting my examination?'

The door hissed and clicked shut behind him so that he was crowded into the corridor with them.

If Wiik was in a bad mood before, the thirty minutes he'd been forced to wait in the reception area before being allowed back here had done nothing for him.

The body had been at the lab for a few hours already, and Wiik was like a rabid dog pacing behind a fence. He clearly had a sharp mind, but his judgement was clouding. Jamie wondered if he had it in him to hold back when he needed to the most.

'My good reason,' Wiik snapped, 'is that there's a maniac out there cutting up girls.'

'Oh, I wouldn't say maniac,' Claesson said evenly. 'If anything, the wounds show a great degree of patience, care and focus. Quite the opposite to a maniac, in fact.'

Jamie observed the little man closely, the way he never broke eye contact with Wiik, the way he kept his face completely straight. She saw right through it: Claesson thought he was hilarious. That getting to poke the bear was the highlight of his day. Hell, probably his week. He and Wiik had obviously crossed paths before. And much like Jamie, Claesson had his number from the very first meeting.

She wondered if lots of people did. Whether it irked the shit out of Wiik. It probably did.

Wiik growled. 'Show me,' he demanded.

It was clear that Claesson was in the middle of the examination, and that as much as he liked screwing with Wiik, he was smart enough to read the look of determined rage on his face.

The doctor raised his key card against the pad and pushed through the door into the lab.

Rows of counters ran from left to right in the large room, filled with various glassware, microscopes, centrifuges and everything else that a pathology lab of this calibre would need to conduct tests.

Beyond, in the direction that Claesson was headed with short, quick steps, were the slabs. Four of them lay in a row, gleaming silver under the articulated lamps hanging overhead.

Three were empty.

The furthest away contained the body of a young girl. The same young girl that Jamie had seen in the forest.

The long brown hair that had stretched down to her sternum was now laid neatly under her back.

Her green eyes stared blankly at the light, shining and milky.

Her skin had taken on a deathly pallor, but her fingers and toes had blackened completely.

Otherwise, she was clean. Faultless. Flawless.

Her frame was slight, her body not yet having taken on the curves of puberty. A privacy sheet had been laid across her pubis, but her chest was exposed, the skin around the exit wounds turned out to face the sky. They glimmered like tar.

Claesson circled absently and leaned on the slab over her.

Wiik pulled up a little short, didn't even look down at the girl. It was tough to keep that sort of mean expression when you were faced with horror like this. 'Well?' he said.

'What do you want to know?' Claesson asked, smiling politely. 'I haven't got to the autopsy yet.'

'I can see that,' Wiik said through gritted teeth.

Jamie stepped forward, seeing that there was clearly a path this was headed down, and it didn't seem like an efficient one. 'Would you mind just going over your preliminary findings for us, please? We're trying to ascertain whether this kill holds a significant resemblance to those of the original Angel Maker case.'

Claesson kept his eyes on Wiik but turned his head slowly, letting his gaze fall on Jamie after a second. 'You could learn a thing or two from this one, Wiik,' Claesson said. 'There is such a thing as manners, you know.'

Jamie didn't realise someone could glare at her without even looking, but Wiik was somehow doing it.

Claesson softened then, and looked down at the girl. 'I had hoped I'd never see another body like this.'

'You were here during the original case?' Jamie asked, stepping closer again, so she was ahead of Wiik.

Claesson gave her a brief smile, his small mouth struggling to shape upwards. 'Unfortunately, yes,' he said. 'I was a junior pathologist at the time, but I assisted with the examinations, the autopsies. It is hard to forget something like that.'

Jamie nodded. 'Of course. Well, any insights you can give us on this victim – and the others, would be very helpful.'

He stared at her intently now, as though trying to place her face.

Jamie set her jaw, recognising that look.

Wiik had said not to give her name. And judging by

Claesson's exchanges with Wiik, he was the torturous type. And if he was a stalwart here, he'd no doubt crossed paths with her father. And if there was one thing she knew about her father, it was that he didn't respond well to people intentionally trying to annoy him.

Claesson began speaking slowly, his brain still working to identify Jamie. 'Well then, it's a good thing that I dug the original files out the moment I saw the body.' He pointed to one of the counters, a cardboard box sitting on it. It was dusty, the denotation *CX-231-07-95* written on it.

Jamie looked over. CX-231 was the case reference, 07 the number of victims in the case, she guessed. Seven girls. It made sense. And 95 the year.

She swallowed.

Wiik took the opportunity to leave the conversation and head over to it, lifting the lid without invitation.

'Help yourself,' Claesson said, seemingly unable to help himself.

Jamie cleared her throat. 'Doctor?'

He looked back at her. 'My apologies.' He wasted no more time. 'The girl, like the original victim, appears to have suffocated. I performed a preliminary endoscopy, and identified some light damage to the lungs congruent with smoke inhalation. I have taken blood samples to test, but I would be inclined to believe that this girl died in the same manner as the original victims.'

'Which was?' Jamie asked, watching as Claesson trailed off, looking down at the girl again.

'Carbon monoxide poisoning. Likely caused by the exhaust fumes from a car being fed into an enclosed space.'

Jamie drew a slow breath, the lingering scent of bleach and chlorine in the room burning the inside of her nostrils.

'This was the favoured method of the Angel Maker,'

Claesson concluded. 'And by all accounts, a relatively humane method of killing his victims.'

Wiik scoffed from the box, but didn't look up. He was flipping through the top file. Claesson scowled at him.

'Painless,' Jamie added, pulling Claesson's attention back. 'Were there any marks on the girl's hands?' She held up hers. 'On the outside and heels?' she asked, running a finger from the tip of her pinkie to her wrist. 'Her nails, maybe?'

Claesson shook his head. 'No, there is no bruising or damage to suggest that she tried to break or claw her way out from whatever space she was locked in.' His eyes narrowed slightly at her. 'An astute observation, though.' He looked at Wiik's back. 'Your new partner?' he called.

Wiik grunted in reply.

'She's a smart one,' Claesson added.

Wiik met that with silence.

Jamie was keen to press on. 'The frostbite, was that sustained—'

'Post-mortem, yes,' Claesson confirmed. 'All of the wounds were. Not long after, but yes. She was dead when he displayed her.'

Jamie nodded. 'What can you tell me about the cuts?'

'Done by someone who knew what they were doing, had a working knowledge of anatomy—'

'Or lots of practice,' Wiik said darkly, dropping the file onto the counter and picking another up from the box.

Claesson cleared his throat. 'Six cuts were made in total, using a sharp, smooth blade. A retractable knife or even a small hunting knife, I would think.' He gestured down to the six cuts on the girl's chest, starting just below her collarbones and finishing just above the bottom ribs. Three on each side of her sternum. 'The killer made an incision between ribs two and three on each side of the spine on her back, approximately five centimetres in length. The cuts were deep, but it took just a few incisions to get through the skin and muscle tissues.'

'Confident,' Jamie observed.

Claesson nodded. 'Quite – they don't appear tentative, I know that much.' He sighed, then pointed to the other wounds. 'The killer repeated the cuts between ribs five and six, and eight and nine. And mirrored them on the girl's chest.'

Jamie pulled her lips back into a line, trying not to look the girl in the eyes.

'Once the incisions had been made,' Claesson continued, 'he inserted the boughs of wood. They were sharpened, skil-fully, and then forced through the body' – Claesson held his left hand up flat in the air and mimed pushing something through the space between his thumb and index finger – 'to the corresponding intercostal space here.' He gestured down to the girl's front now. 'Judging by the photographs, I believe he placed her in a kneeling position first, made the incisions all at once going by the blood on her body, and then began the process of...' He trailed off, shook his head.

'Skewering her' seemed like the only way to put it, but it didn't need to be said.

'I understand,' Jamie said, filling the silence, but she didn't. How could anyone?

'The ends of each bough were then pushed into the earth, keeping the girl in place. The first would have been the most difficult. The rest...' Claesson swallowed, showing the first sign of emotion Jamie had seen. Though with a career as long as his, she doubted there was much that rattled him anymore. 'The ligature marks on her wrists here are paler than you would see with perimortem binding. The tissue damage doesn't show evidence of haematoma, just superficial tissue damage, which leads me to conclude that he bound her wrists at the end of this process, after she had bled out.' He cleared his throat again, then reached up and pinched at his neck, as though something was caught in it.

Jamie had to ask the one question she didn't want to. It came out quieter than she intended. 'Was she— Was she raped?'

Claesson seemed to need a moment for this and clamped his teeth together before answering. 'I performed a cursory examination,' he muttered, looking up now, over Jamie's head. 'In order to establish congruency with the original murders—'

Wiik was suddenly at the table. 'Just answer the question,' he said coldly, his knuckles white around the file marked *03*. Three of seven.

Jamie corrected herself.

Three of *eight*.

'Yes,' Claesson said. 'There is evidence to suggest that she was raped. Though it doesn't appear that the killer assaulted and then killed her in quick succession. Some early-stage healing of the damaged tissue had occurred before—'

Wiik silenced him with a hand and returned to the box.

Jamie steeled herself in the face of this new information. 'Thank you, Doctor. I know it's difficult to tell, but do you think…'

He nodded gravely. 'This method of murder, followed by this method of display does lead me to believe that this crime was committed by the same perpetrator.' He looked over at the files on the counter next to Wiik.

Jamie let her eyes rest on him. A file was open in front of him but he was hunched over the counter, arms spread wide into a triangle, his head hung. She couldn't tell if he was reading or steeling himself against the gravity of what Claesson had just said.

She let out a long breath, her jaw quivering.

Her father was wrong.

He'd beat a confession out of the wrong man, and then put him in prison for twenty goddamn years.

Claesson was staring at Jamie now, brow crumpled, lips pursed.

She met his eyes over the slab.

'I'm sorry,' he said, his voice quiet. 'You seem very familiar to me. But I cannot say where we've met before.'

'We haven't,' Jamie choked out.

Wiik picked his head up and looked over his shoulder.

'But, uh,' Jamie began. She wasn't going to hide from who she was. 'I think you knew my father.'

Claesson's face unscrewed itself, his eyes widening in realisation. 'My God,' he said.

'Yeah,' Jamie sighed, extending her hand over the top of the girl's pale corpse. 'Detective Inspector Jamie Johansson, nice to meet you.'

10

'I TOLD you not to tell him who you were,' Wiik grunted, walking fast back through the corridors of the lab.

Jamie was practically jogging to keep up. Wiik's long legs gave him a distinct mechanical advantage. 'I think he took it pretty well,' Jamie said, not seeing what the big deal was.

Wiik scoffed. 'He was in shock.'

Jamie grabbed his arm now, halting him. He glanced down at it, apparently deeply offended to be touched. She uncurled her fingers from the fabric. 'What's the problem? What happened between the two of them?'

Wiik drew a breath, held it, and then exhaled hard, looking left and right. 'Claesson has a way of getting under people's skin.'

'I noticed,' Jamie said.

Wiik scowled at her for a second. 'And your father was easy to get at.'

Jamie said nothing.

'Claesson likes to push his luck…'

'And one day he pushed it too far?'

Wiik looked at her for a moment, as if unsure whether he wanted to tell her. 'About six weeks before he, um…'

'Yeah,' Jamie said, cycling her hand in the air for Wiik to carry on. Why people had such trouble with the words *he killed himself,* she didn't know.

'He was here to see Claesson over a case. Something happened – they argued – the details aren't clear. But what was clear is that your father broke his nose, then put him on one of those lab counters and sent him through about twenty thousand kronas' worth of beakers. Face first.'

Jamie's jaw tightened, her heart beating in her ears as she searched for any hint in Wiik's face of that being a cruel joke. She found none.

'He was in the hospital for two weeks. Needed recon-structive surgery,' Wiik said, pushing his hair back again. 'He was going to have your father drawn and quartered. He was suspended for the incident, prior to…'

'Yeah, yeah,' Jamie said, hurrying him on.

'Claesson was gathering evidence to press charges. And then…'

Jamie stepped back and slumped against the wall, closing her eyes. 'Jesus. Six weeks before he died?' she asked, opening them again.

Wiik nodded. 'Yeah. A bad case. Guess your father wasn't in the joking mood. He had a string of bad ones at the end. One after another. Grizzly shit. It took its toll. This one was maybe… the last straw.' He looked at her, something like compassion in him, then. 'I'm sorry, Johansson.'

Jamie felt a throb in her throat at the use of her second name. 'It's okay,' she said, not wanting to expand on that. Add to the story that he'd killed himself on Jamie's eigh-teenth birthday. That leading up to it he'd called dozens of times. That Jamie hadn't even known. That her mother had told him that she didn't want to speak to him. That he didn't get to speak to her after what he'd done. To her. To them.

He'd called on the morning of her birthday.

She had been asleep.

Her mother hadn't told her.

Three hours later, they received a phone call that police had responded to the sound of a gunshot at the house, and he had been found dead from a self-inflicted gunshot wound.

Jamie's eyes burned there in the corridor as she pictured him wilting away at the house, alone. Drowning himself in booze, in misery.

If only she could have spoken to him.

If only she had known.

'Hey,' Wiik said, his voice soft. 'Come on, let's get some fresh air.' He tilted his head down the corridor and Jamie nodded wordlessly.

As they walked, his left hand quivered a little, as though he was going to reach out, comfort her.

A hand on the shoulder, a squeeze of the arm. Something. Anything.

But he didn't.

He left it as his side as they reached the front door and stepped through.

The cold air of the city hit Jamie liked a wall, punching the air out of her lungs.

Threatening to freeze the tears on her cheeks.

11

Wiik stood with his hands in his pockets, staring out at the trees in front of the lab. They rustled softly, their leaves wet, their trunks hugged by snow.

He looked to be waiting for her to tell him she was ready.

'Where to next?' Jamie asked, regaining herself.

Wiik pulled out his phone. They'd heard nothing from Hallberg. He held the device between the knuckle of his index finger and the pad of his thumb, and drummed it on the palm of his other hand, still watching the trees.

Jamie watched him.

After a moment, he sighed, shaking his head. 'Do you still have the notebook?'

Jamie took it out of her pocket and offered it up to him.

He pulled it open to the page Jamie had dog-eared as the start of the case, and started leafing through, pausing when he got to one that said Sjöberg in large letters. It was circled a few times, a few dots of ink around it where Jamie's father had tapped the nib of his pen on the paper. 'Your father,' Wiik said, 'was so sure.'

'He was wrong,' Jamie replied, surprised at the surety in her own voice. Even more so by the bile.

Wiik inspected the other notes on the page.

A.M.
   Strong.
   Annika Liljedahl.

Wiik looked down at them, written around Sjöberg's name.

Jamie stared down at it too. 'Any ideas what "A.M." means?'

He stuck out his bottom lip. 'I don't know. Who's Annika Liljedahl?'

Jamie shook her head. 'At least "strong" speaks for itself.'

'Mm.'

'Did you meet Sjöberg?' Jamie asked as Wiik let the notepad drop a little. He went back to looking at the trees.

'No,' he replied. 'I saw photographs, though. He was tall, well built.'

'Strong.'

The corner of Wiik's mouth curled into his cheek a little bit, but he said nothing.

A minute passed, the only sound between them the distant roar of rubber on cold asphalt beyond the wall of foliage. And then Wiik's phone rang.

'Wiik,' he said, pulling it to his ear. 'Yeah, one second.' He lowered the phone and put it on speaker. 'Okay, go.'

It was Hallberg. 'I have something.' She took a quick breath. 'We got a lot of results for Per Eriksson and Leif Lundgren in public records. It will take some time to narrow down the search. But I got a hit on Tomas Lindvall. He's got a file all of his own.'

'Oh,' Wiik said, filling the pause Hallberg left. Jamie could tell he'd be happier if she just got on with it.

'He's got a string of prior offences for indecent assault, indecent assault of a minor, possession of indecent images, attempted kidnapping, unlawful imprisonment…'

Wiik's grip tightened on the phone.

'And his file lists him as being a person of interest in the Angel Maker case in 1996.'

Wiik nodded slowly. 'Okay.'

Jamie held her breath.

Hallberg went on. 'No charges were filed against him during the case, but it looks like Johansson pursued him as a lead for a while. The note on his file says he lived close to one of the sites.'

'He still live there?' Wiik asked, glancing at Johansson and motioning for her to follow him.

'No – changed addresses a few times. Seems he's been in and out of a couple of secure units by the looks of things, too.'

'Secure units?' Wiik parroted, eyeing Jamie to gauge her response.

'Psychiatric wards,' Hallberg said, then made a clicking sound with her tongue as though she was searching the information in front of her. 'Looks like he was diagnosed with paranoid schizophrenia in 19… 1999.'

'Jesus,' Wiik muttered, turning the corner and heading down the ramp into the underground car park.

'He received treatment on three separate occasions. Two separate facilities. 1999 to 2000, then again at the same facility from 2005 to 2006. Then a different facility in the city from 2011 to 2012. The last change of address and offence we have him for was in 2016. Looks like he's been quiet for a few years. Maybe he got his shit together.'

Wiik flashed his badge at the parking attendant and
dipped under the gate. 'Or just building up to something more
serious.'

'I'll send the address over now. You want me to meet you
there?'

Wiik glanced back at Jamie, who was firmly in tow.

'No,' he said. 'We've got it.'

'Of course.' The disappointment was apparent in her
voice. 'Guess I'll just stay here, keep digging into Lundgren
and Eriksson, then?'

Wiik stopped at the car and fished Jamie's father's notebook from his pocket. He rested his phone on the roof of the
car and flipped through pages. 'I have another name for you,
too. Annika Liljedahl.'

'You said Liljedahl?'

'Uh-huh.'

'Anything specific?'

'No, just check it out, see what you get. The name was
written in Johansson's notebook, next to Sjöberg's name.
There's a connection there.'

'Got it. And, sir?'

'Yes, Hallberg?'

'Be careful.'

He smirked, then glanced at Jamie. 'I'll be fine. I've got a
Johansson watching my back, remember?'

They rolled quickly through the city, closing in on a cluster of
dank high-rise apartments.

The city slowly grew darker, dirtier around them as they
edged into the worse parts of town. The day was wearing into
the afternoon, and the sun waning at their shoulder.

Wiik pulled in at the kerb on the main stretch, not wanting

to drive into the car parks in front of the towers. Probably because he didn't want to alert anyone to their presence. But also because he likely didn't want to leave the denizens unsupervised around his new Volvo.

She didn't blame him.

Jamie wasn't sure if it was his own car or a plain-clothes police vehicle, but the cream leather interior told her it was expensive either way.

She glanced over at him and saw the shine of a heavy, silver watch peeking out from under the sleeve of his coat. The *fine black wool* sleeve of his coat. His boots, too, were high-quality leather.

Wiik took pride in himself. Liked the nicer things. But wasn't intent on showing them off.

Before Jamie could make any more observations about his attire, the driver's door opened and he was out of the car and striding fast. She had to run to catch up.

Wiik was a man of few words. Jamie had to give him that.

And she didn't mind at all. Maybe it was the Swede in her, or maybe she'd just got sick of hearing people talk. Either way, just like with Graeme, she welcomed the silences between them.

There were three blocks in a line, and Wiik headed for the middle one.

A series of raised lawns studded with trees littered the front of the buildings. The low walls that ran around them, dotted with benches, tried to do something to bring up the general standard of the place. But they failed.

The once bright stone was marred with spray paint and old urine, and the benches designed to allow people to bask in this puddle of greenery were either broken or played host to sleeping homeless.

Jamie glanced down, grimacing as the smell hit her. A

man who could have been in his thirties or sixties, lay strung
out in a thick puffer jacket, drenched in his own piss. He was
sprawled back on the bench, legs splayed, chin on his chest, a
dark patch stretching from his crotch to his ankles, soaking
his navy sweatpants.

Wiik motioned her to speed up. 'Come on. You'll see
plenty more before we're done here.'

Jamie exhaled, locked away the memories of cases gone
by, and pressed forward. They were here for Tomas Lindvall.
And that's who they were going to get.

Tomas Lindvall lived in an apartment on the eleventh floor.
Apartment 1117 to be exact.

The block's ground floor was open as though the whole
building were on stilts. Beneath the concrete body, a car park
had been placed. But there were only a few cars parked there,
one of which was a burnt-out wreck, another abandoned and
spray-painted with massive phalluses and worse swear words.

Teenagers and residents rode in circles on pushbikes,
smoking joints and shoving each other around, laughing like
hyenas.

Wiik headed towards the lifts wordlessly, not looking
twice at the kids. They seemed to clam up, catching his scent
on the breeze, as if they knew, and turned their heads away,
holding in lungfuls of smoke until Wiik had passed.

He did have that look of a cop about him. Maybe as much
as anyone Jamie had ever met. The permanent mask of
expressionlessness. The distrustful eyes. The taut shoulders.

He covered ground quickly, taking long strides, and
pulled a blue latex glove from his pocket, using it as a barrier
between the call button and his skin. It wasn't about contaminating potential evidence. The place was just filthy.

Jamie glanced over at the kids, who were still eyeing them cautiously, then took stock of the surroundings, the fire escape on the far side of the building, the rustling trees on the green, the network of paths there. She visualised the layout, the routes. The exits.

Jamie sighed, her eyes coming to rest on the silver doors in front of them. Another set stood at their right. Damn, the lift was taking forever.

The lit panel above it was caked in dirt, same as everything down here, and the noise of grinding cables didn't do much to dispel Jamie's unease.

The doors finally opened before them and Wiik stepped in, screwing his face up at the stench of old urine.

Why everyone had to piss on everything, she really didn't know.

Jamie took one last breath of fresh air and went in after him.

Wiik, still holding the glove, called for the eleventh floor, and they went up, cables grinding again, the progress painfully slow.

The lift opened onto an open corridor and squares of grey sky appeared on either side as they got out. Wiik looked up at the wall, a tarnished metal sign told them they'd find 1101 to 1120 to the right, 1121 to 1140 to the left.

He went right, heels clicking on the concrete.

This high up, the wind was colder, more brutal. It whipped across the balcony and blasted leaves around the walkway in front of them, scarcely wide enough for them to move side by side. Though Wiik's pace told Jamie he wasn't really that interested in doing that anyway. Or in small talk. Or in anything, really. Whether it was the haze of the case, or he was just an unfriendly bastard in general, Jamie didn't know. But she didn't think she'd like to spend eight hours a day with the guy for the foreseeable. But then again, maybe Hallberg knew her way around him.

Or maybe he was struggling with the weight of this case, the weight of the lives of the girls it had already claimed, it would claim, on his shoulders.

Or maybe it was just Jamie.

Wiik stopped at 1117 and looked back at her for the first time to make sure she was with him. A narrow window ran vertically next to the door, presumably providing some semblance of natural light to the inside of the flat. It was covered by a thick curtain, though, and no sound was coming from within.

Jamie shivered and pulled her peacoat tighter around her shoulders, her heart picking up a little as Wiik raised his knuckles to the composite door. The knock was hard and even. Four loud, distinct raps. The noise was dull, carried away instantly by the wind.

There was shuffling inside and then after a few seconds, the bolts began to slide.

Wiik slid his left foot forwards so that it was near the corner, ready to be jammed into the gap if need be.

The door swung inwards a few inches, a chain spanning the distance to the frame, and a pale face swam into view above it. The man's eyes were wide, his pupils dilated. There were bags under them and his skin was gaunt, his hair tousled and unwashed, somewhere between blonde and brown.

His eyes twitched, going from Jamie to Wiik and back again. The two detectives looked at each other, Wiik no doubt reaching the same conclusion as Jamie.

Tomas Lindvall was high.

'Yeah?' he asked, keeping as much of his scrawny body behind the door as possible.

Jamie looked at his knuckles around the wood, noted the

chewed nails.

Wiik raised his badge. 'Kriminalinspektör Anders Wiik, SPA,' he said flatly.

Lindvall swallowed hard and looked at Jamie again.

'Detective Inspector Jamie Johansson,' she said, reading the strange look of curiosity on his face and holding up the SPA lanyard Falk had given her. The guy was out of his skull.

'Can we come in?' Wiik asked.

Jamie watched him sniff the air, detect the scent of stale sweat and marijuana.

'Or perhaps you'd prefer to step outside so we can talk?' Wiik added.

He shrank behind the door a little. 'What's this about?'

'We'd like to ask you about your whereabouts three nights ago,' Wiik said plainly, not overplaying his hand.

'My whereabou…' Lindvall trailed off halfway through as though a three-syllable word was too much for his addled mind.

Jamie remembered that Hallberg said this guy was a diagnosed schizophrenic. She watched him closely.

'Where were you,' Wiik pressed, moving a little closer, 'three nights ago? You got an alibi?'

'An alibi?' he repeated, narrowing his eyes as though the word was alien to him.

'Stop fucking around,' Wiik said, his voice cold now.

'W-what is this about?' Lindvall asked again.

Jamie could see he wasn't all there. At least not when he was mixing whatever drugs he seemed to have been. There was a delay after each question as his brain did its best to process.

'A case,' Wiik said, his teeth gritting, temple vein bulging. 'A murder investigation.'

'Murder?'

Wiik's hand flew out, slapped against the wood. 'Yeah, you piece of shit.' Spittle flecked onto the surface and crystallised in the sub-zero wind. 'A girl. Young, brown hair, suffocated, raped, murdered, left in the goddamn woods. You know anything about that?'

Jamie set her jaw. Wiik was pushing too hard.

Lindvall's bottom lip began to quiver.

'Open the door, now,' Wiik demanded.

There was fear in Lindvall's eyes for a second, and then it was gone.

Jamie tensed.

He looked from Jamie to Wiik and back, and then nodded, slowly, his nostrils flaring. 'Okay,' he said quietly. 'Just let me...' He stepped back, his thin trunk and round shoulders appearing in the gap for a second before he pushed the door closed, the sound of the chain sliding off audible behind it.

Wiik exhaled hard and plastered his hair against his head with his hand.

Jamie stepped back, feeling the air change.

And then it happened.

The door flew open and Lindvall burst out, shoulder dipped, and drove it into Wiik's chest.

Wiik grunted and stumbled back hitting the balcony guardrail.

The long red strips of wood shuddered and the whole thing rippled under the force.

Wiik's fists curled around the barrier and his body bent back over it, his head swinging out into space as he fought for balance.

Jamie was already out of the way, pressed against the barrier herself. Her hand flew out, grabbing a fistful of Wiik's coat, and dragged him upright.

Lindvall was running, his bony elbows and fists pumping

like train rods at his sides as he headed for the lift they'd come up on.

Wiik got back to his feet and swatted Jamie's arm away, shoving past her after Lindvall. He fired her a hard look, as though she should have grabbed for Lindvall and not him, and then took off after the man.

Jamie watched them go for a second, then looked right, sticking her head through Lindvall's front door.

The smell was stronger inside, the flat no more than a studio.

She could see white powder in a small pile on a dinner tray perched on a coffee table, an ashtray full of smoked joints and cigarettes. A laptop was open, pointed at the wall.

Jamie stepped back, glanced after Wiik, who was halfway to the lifts and not making up ground on Lindvall, and then sighed.

She closed the front door firmly and then turned in the opposite direction, cracking her neck as she walked, picking up speed with every step.

The lift hit the ground floor and Lindvall oozed through the gap, stumbling, his shoelaces untied, and then bolted towards the trees in front of the blocks.

Wiik dragged himself through the gap in the second lift's doors five seconds later and hammered after him, his cheeks bright red, his styled hair now a mad tangle of dark strands around his crown.

He was panting hard, his long, heavy heavy coat and stiff jeans preventing him from picking up any real speed.

Wiik took care of himself, but he wasn't a runner.

Lindvall, on the other hand, was thin, like a whippet, wearing just a pair of sweatpants and a loose T-shirt dotted with ash-holes. He reached the first walkway, streaking past the homeless man in the piss-soaked trousers, and stole a look over his shoulder, grinning with yellow teeth as Wiik began to fall behind, clutching his ribs, at the stitch there.

Lindvall turned his head back, his eyes widening, a shocked squealing sound escaping his lips. He was moving too fast to get out of the way of Jamie, who moved cleanly into his path, sticking her leg out and twisting away from him so that his foot hooked under her calf.

She threw her shoulder into him, letting physics do the rest, and watched Lindvall sail into the air, spinning and landing hard on his side. He bounced, swore, and rolled to a stop, his head snapping up to look at her. Whatever was in his system was dulling his senses. Amphetamines, cocaine. Could be anything.

Jamie came forward, shaking the dull ache from her right leg where Lindvall's shin had connected. *'Stanna nere,'* she commanded, holding out her palm. Stay down.

Wiik was trundling now, fighting with his own breath, still twenty metres away.

Lindvall clocked him, then measured Jamie, figuring he could take her.

In a blur of flailing arms, he was on his feet, charging.

His fist balled and came up behind his head, telegraphing his punch from a mile off.

Jamie watched it, took stock of his feet, and then danced onto her right foot, baiting him, preloading her next move.

Lindvall got in range, unwound his arm.

Jamie sprung backwards onto her left foot, out of his path, his hand flying down in front of her, missing completely.

In the half a second it took for Lindvall's brain to catch up, Jamie's knee had cocked, and then sent the toe of her right boot flying upwards in a steep arc.

Lindvall doubled over the top of her foot, the sharp, well-placed jab from the toe of her boot enough to knock the wind right out of him.

He stumbled, mewled, and then collapsed into a heap, clutching his stomach.

Jamie's heel touched down again and she brushed the loose strands of hair from her eyes, barely having broken a sweat. Her long plait settled between her shoulder blades and hung still.

Lindvall began clawing at the ground to get away, but he was going nowhere fast with no air in his lungs.

Wiik arrived and sank forward, hands on his knees, breathing hard. He eyed Jamie, his face a mix of displeasure and exhaustion. 'How did you' – he hawked, then spat the phlegm caught in his throat onto the ground – 'get down here so fast?'

She shrugged. 'Stairs. Elevator was too slow.'

'Eleven flights?'

'I keep fit.'

He narrowed his eyes, nodding at the prostrate Lindvall. 'And this?'

She drew a slow breath. 'Tae Kwon Do and Kevlar toecaps.' She waggled her boot at him a little.

He didn't look sold and after a second, let out another long sigh, and then knelt down, rolling Lindvall onto his front. He folded Lindvall's hands up behind his back and pulled a cable-tie from his pocket, zipping it tight around the man's wrists before wiping the beads of sweat off his forehead with his sleeve.

'You got any other hidden talents I should know about?' he asked sourly, leaning his knee into the small of Lindvall's back as he fished his phone out of his inside pocket.

'Guess you'll have to wait and see.'

12

THE DOOR to Interview Room 5 opened with a creak, and Wiik and Jamie walked in.

Lindvall had been sitting there for three hours, and whatever was riding high in his system had now begun to wear off. His face was bruised from where Jamie had tripped him, and his nails had been chewed so low that the tips of his fingers were raw.

There were little shards of them on the top of the table.

He shifted in his seat and slid back, the handcuffs clinking gently on the metal surface.

'Comfortable?' Wiik asked, eyeing Lindvall. He sat down on one of the chairs opposite and Jamie joined him.

Lindvall swallowed, looking from one to the other. His pupils had now normalised, and his eyes appeared heavy. He'd refused water and had sat in silence since he'd been thrown in there.

Wiik dropped a file in front of him and pressed his two forefingers down onto it, the others curled into a fist. 'Tomas Lindvall, forty-four years old. Stockholm born and bred,'

Wiik said, a disgusted grin on his face. 'And what a credit to the city you are.'

Lindvall looked away, his hands balling loosely and pulling taut on the chains as he shrank as far as they'd allow.

'We searched your apartment,' Wiik went on. 'Found some interesting things. Amphetamines, cannabis, your stash of child pornography.'

Lindvall straightened and looked at them now. 'It's not—'

'It's more than enough to put you back in a locked box for a very long time. And not one of those padded ones you're used to. One with bars, and no fucking toilet seat. One where they just *love* guys who fuck with children.' Wiik's grin widened. 'What do you say. Does that sound like fun?'

'I've done nothing wrong,' Lindvall said, wincing as though Wiik was about to reach over the table and punch him in the head.

'Bullshit.' Wiik slammed his fist onto the file. 'You've not done *nothing* since you were a fucking child! And with your history, this will be an easy fix. So if you don't want to go away for the rest of your measly life, you better start talking.'

Jamie eyed Wiik cautiously. He had a hair trigger. That was for sure. He'd go from cool and calm to explosive in a heartbeat. And with guys like Lindvall – who were hanging by a thread anyway – he needed to be careful. The guy was a diagnosed paranoid schizophrenic – pushing him too hard would only lose him as a suspect and derail the case further. And chained up or not, you could never anticipate what guys like Lindvall might do.

They'd got a look at his file. A partial case history. But a lot of it was sealed and not immediately accessible. Still, they already had a picture forming. He was delusional – haunted and terrorised by voices, hallucinations – as a child, as a teenager and as an adult. Demons, monsters. The sorts of things that push you to do crazy things. Who tell you to – *force* you to – do the worst things, to yourself, and others. Things like biting through your tongue to drown yourself in your own blood.

It happened. Jamie had seen it. And she definitely didn't want to again.

Lindvall stared back at Wiik. 'I don't…' he began.

'1996,' Wiik said coldly. 'Seven girls. Raped. Suffocated. Left in the woods. Ringing any bells?' He'd narrowed his eyes to slits now.

Lindvall's jaw began to quiver. '1996?'

'The Angel Maker,' Wiik spat. 'A nice name, don't you think? Though I expected someone a little more… imposing.'

'I-I'm not…' Lindvall started.

'And now, you just couldn't resist doing it again, could you? You're sitting up there in your cosy state-provided apartment, getting high and jerking off to pictures of children, and you start thinking that it's not enough. That you could, you know, have a taste of the real thing, huh?'

'What? No!' Lindvall protested.

'And then you read about it, right? In the paper or online, that Sjöberg died. The man who went away for your crimes. And it reminds you of the good old days. You start to think about it, plan it, and then, before you know it…'

'No! I didn't. I wouldn't!' Lindvall was getting worked up now.

'Admit it,' Wiik said, his voice rising, booming. 'You went out looking for a girl, you took her, you threw her in the back of your car, gassed her with exhaust fumes, then took her into the woods, and mounted her like a fucking stag!' Wiik was almost out of the chair now. 'You cut into her like a piece of meat. Some sorry fucking excuse for an apology, was that it? Made her an angel to make up for the fact that you defiled her and—'

'I don't even have a car!' Lindvall exploded, shrieking it, jerking violently. Tears spilt from his eyes.

Jamie set her jaw. Wiik had pushed too hard. Broken him. She hung her head and exhaled.

'Bullshit!' Wiik continued to yell, futile as it was now. 'You borrowed one, stole one. Admit it. You killed them then, and you killed her now!'

Lindvall was shaking, pulling at his restrains, twisting up in his chair, bringing his knees to his chest like a child. He was regressing, spilling back into his past psychoses. Jamie watched as his mind began to detach itself from the reality he'd grounded himself in. She knew enough about psychology to know that Wiik was undoing twenty years of therapy and support in as many minutes.

She reached out, grabbed Wiik's arm.

He looked around at her and she shook her head as subtly as she could.

Wiik's jaw quivered, but Jamie's grip tightened.

She shook her head again, their eyes locked, and then she felt the tension in his arm release.

He exhaled and sank backwards himself, hitting the seat and causing it to slide backwards an inch.

Wiik was about to start again, maybe this time with a little more forethought, when the door behind them opened.

A woman hovering on the young side of thirty with dark hair pulled back into a ponytail and fine, sharp features knocked twice and pushed her head through the gap simultaneously. 'Wiik,' she said, her pale, grey eyes glowing in the harsh interview-room light.

'What is it?' Wiik turned on his chair.

Lindvall was still sobbing.

The woman held a file up. 'You should take a look at this.'

Wiik bit his lip, glanced back at Lindvall and then pushed himself to his feet. 'We'll be back,' Wiik warned him, as though there was any doubt, and then headed for the door.

Jamie rose beside him, letting her eyes rest on the man in handcuffs, trying to weigh him up. Trying to ascertain whether he was capable of this. Running from the police, taking a swing at a detective... Sure that wasn't a good start for his defence, but multiple abduction, murder...? That took planning. A focused mind. Something she didn't think this man had. But then again, if he was under the advisement of one of his voices. If he was ordered to...

Jamie drew a slow breath and then followed Wiik out.

Delusion was powerful. It had power over life and death at times. Lindvall may not have been able to consciously mastermind the crimes. But that wasn't to say his mind wasn't able to. Perhaps just not the part that belonged to him.

Outside in the corridor, Wiik was staring down at the file now in his hands.

The woman now had hers free and wasted no time in offering one to Jamie.

'Polisassistent Hallberg,' she said formally, smiling with perfect teeth.

Jamie took it. 'Detective Inspector Jamie Johansson.'

'Oh, I know,' Hallberg said, grinning. 'It's a pleasure.'

'Is it?' Jamie asked, raising an eyebrow. She didn't know if she was ready to hear anything else about her father's career today. Wiik's revelation at the pathology lab was enough for the whole week.

'I read about your cases,' she said quickly. 'The guy

hunting the musicians, the trafficking ring you took down… the organ harvester…' She shook her head. 'And all as a detective sergeant, too.' She couldn't stop grinning.

It was making Jamie squirm.

Wiik looked up briefly, surveyed Jamie in a way she'd not seen him do before, and then went back to the file.

Hallberg put her hands on her hips. 'It must run in the family—'

Wiik cleared his throat, and Hallberg fell quiet mid-sentence. 'That's enough,' he said, sighing and handing the file off to Jamie. 'Lindvall was telling the truth. He really doesn't have a car. At least not one that's registered.'

Jamie pressed her lips together and scanned the report. 'Wouldn't need one if he stole Nyström's,' Jamie said, not looking up from the file. It contained all the information Hallberg had gathered on Lindvall so far. The sealed case files detailing his treatment and case history. Everything the CSTs had grabbed from his apartment. Jamie and Wiik had only gone in armed with the prelims. But now they had more detail. And it didn't look promising.

Jamie checked her watch.

It hadn't been long since they'd collared Lindvall, and it was late in the afternoon now. Hallberg was efficient. She had to give her that. And the report was impeccably compiled and ferociously detailed considering the timeframe.

'You need to be somewhere, Johansson?' Wiik asked, seeing her glancing at her wrist.

'No,' Jamie replied, going back to the report. 'Looks like the pornography recovered from Lindvall's computer was all legal. Fetish, but legal.'

'Loli,' Hallberg added.

'Hmm?'

'It's short for "Lolita",' she expounded. 'It's a book written by Vladimir Nabokov where—'

'I know what it is,' Jamie said, her tone a little more cutting than intended.

'Of course, I'm sorry.' Hallberg reddened a little.

Jamie felt bad. And worse, that this girl seemed to be putting her on some kind of pedestal. And even worse again that it was because of three cases she wasn't proud of.

She sighed and then started leafing through the other pages.

Hallberg bit her lip, folded her arms and then reached out, flipping for Jamie to a specific page. 'This was the sealed file,' she said quickly, retracting her hands. 'Lindvall's psychiatrist sent it over a few minutes ago.'

Jamie scanned it. 'Jesus, when he was seventeen?'

'What is it?' Wiik asked, taking the file back without asking.

Hallberg interjected. 'The report says Lindvall assaulted his twelve-year-old sister – tried to...'

Wiik nodded, reading it in front of him. 'They arrested him, put him on the register, but no charges were brought,' he muttered, his eyes darting along the words. 'Apparent psychological problems... He was sent to live with grandparents following the attack in 1993, which put him in proximity to one of the Angel Maker sites.' He said it like a statement, but inflected it like a question, glancing at Hallberg for confirmation.

She nodded.

Wiik started reading again. 'The parents put him in for counselling while he was there. He was in and out of therapy for a few years.' Wiik made a clicking noise with his tongue. 'Then after a public outburst in 1999, he was arrested again at twenty-three years old – resisted arrest, clear signs of psychosis, finally diagnosed with paranoid schizophrenia...'

Jamie watched Wiik closely. 'What about the prior offences that Hallberg mentioned, the indecent assault, the assault of a minor, possession of indecent images, attempted kidnapping, unlawful imprisonment...'

Wiik kept reading, was silent for a few seconds, then spoke. 'The indecent assault was the offence that got him arrested and diagnosed – he groped someone on a train, was subdued by staff and pleaded that the woman was his mother...' Wiik shook his head, trying to process that one. 'The assault of a minor, attempted kidnapping, possession of indecent images – they were in 2005, just before he was placed into secure care again. It says here that he took an eleven-year-old girl by the hand and tried to lead her away from her mother, then freaked out when she started screaming, tried to grab the girl. He was convinced it was his sister – who would have been in her twenties by then...' Wiik exhaled hard. 'He was arrested, his phone searched. Looks like the search history was pretty damning.' He ran a finger down the list. 'Nothing too gruesome, but any search beginning with the words *little girl* isn't going to be pretty.' He grimaced now and turned the page. 'Unlawful imprisonment charge was lodged against him by his... girlfriend?' Wiik was surprised. 'In 2013. He moved in with her. Then, it says, he became paranoid that she was going to leave him, was cheating on him, was talking to people about him behind his back. He locked her in the house for three days, and then became agitated, and she shut herself in the bathroom, afraid for her life... Neighbours called the police following screaming and banging on the wall... He was taken into custody. Formal charges were dropped following declaration of non compos mentis, and he was sentenced to outpatient care and community service.' Wiik closed the file, looking drawn.

'We need to speak to her, see if we can't get a better gauge of what this guy is capable of,' Jamie said, filing it all in her mind.

'I think it's pretty clear what he's capable of,' Wiik growled. It seemed he'd already made up his mind about the guy.

'I'll admit that's a hell of a track record,' Jamie said, 'but it's not concrete. Not by a stretch.'

Wiik looked at her intensely, file still open in front of him, and silence fell between them as they sized each other up.

Hallberg shifted from foot to foot. 'So, do you think it's him?'

'Maybe,' Wiik answered, looking at her. 'He's definitely capable of it.' He lifted the file a little to illustrate.

Hallberg looked from one to the other. 'But to go from that to... *this*,' she said, staring into space, visualising the crime scene. 'It's a big leap.'

Jamie could see that Hallberg agreed with her that the file was nothing but indicative that Lindvall had some serious problems. She was dead right in saying that it was a big leap from locking your girlfriend in a house to abducting, suffocating, and then mounting your victim in the woods.

Wiik looked hard at Hallberg, not liking the insubordination. 'We can't make any firm assumptions, you're right. But he was linked to the original case, and if the conversation we just had with him told me anything, it's that it doesn't take much to push him over the edge.'

Jamie watched Wiik now, seeing the angle he was working.

She'd thought he'd been blind to Lindvall's limits, but it was the opposite. He was trying to find his breaking point.

Maybe she was underestimating Wiik after all.

'Right,' Jamie said. 'And he did make a run for it the second we showed up at his door.'

Wiik nodded and folded his arms. 'We need to let him stew for another few hours, calm down, reflect on where he is.' He sighed and handed the file back to Jamie so he could rub his eyes with his fingers.

He looked as tired as Jamie felt.

'Where are we on the court transcripts?' he asked Hallberg.

'They aren't digitised yet,' Hallberg replied. 'But I've got a requisition order in with the court archives. They're going to send us copies when they've got them. I expected them to be here by now, so they shouldn't be long, I don't think.'

'If they're not here by tonight, I'll be sending you to the courthouse myself,' Wiik said, without a hint of humour.

'Hopefully, it won't come to that,' Hallberg replied, just as little in hers.

'When they arrive I want them typed out as quickly as you're able, and then saved securely, okay?'

'All of them?' Hallberg asked, her brow creasing.

Wiik nodded. 'That be a problem?'

She opened her mouth – to say yes, Jamie assumed – and then closed it again and smiled. 'Of course not.'

'What about the information from the prison – Sjöberg's cause of death, visitors?'

'I managed to speak to the doctor at the prison – Sjöberg was undergoing treatment for pancreatic cancer. It was progressing quickly, and after the first round of chemo, he refused further treatment.'

'Why would he do that?' Wiik asked.

Hallberg shook her head. 'I don't know, it can be brutal. Maybe he didn't want to put himself through it. The sickness, the pain. Locked in prison, it would be—'

'I was looking for a solid answer, not conjecture,' Wiik cut in.

'Right, of course,' Hallberg said. 'My apologies.'

Jamie eyed her. Jesus, she was like a kicked dog. She knew Wiik was a hard-ass, but the poor girl couldn't catch a break.

He didn't know how good he had it. Hell, if he had to suffer through just one shoddy report compiled by her old partner...

Wiik went on with his demands. 'And the visitors list?'

'They're combing back through,' Hallberg answered. 'They changed their security system in 2013, so everything before isn't as easily accessible. They should have it to us by the morning.'

Wiik wasn't happy. 'Get back on the phone to them. I'd rather have it in two halves than wait another twelve hours. Get the list from 2013 onwards, and any footage they have of visitors, too.'

'Okay,' Hallberg said, trying to keep her expression positive.

'And what about the victim? Any word on an ID yet?'

'Nothing. I'm still looking, but so far, no missing persons match her description.'

'Jesus,' Wiik muttered, running his hand over his head, smoothing down his hair.

Jamie wondered how many times a day he had to top up on product to keep it so perfect.

'Is there anything we *do* have?'

'Uh,' Hallberg said, rolling through it all in her head.

'Yeah, the stills came in from the toll gate that clocked Nyström's car.'

'What? When?'

'An hour ago?' Hallberg said.

'Why didn't you tell me?' Wiik growled.

Hallberg did her best not to scoff, but gestured to the report in Jamie's hands all the same. 'I was a little busy. And plus, they don't show anything. It was dark out, and you can't make out whoever was driving anyway—'

She stopped talking as Wiik walked away, heading for the main floor again.

Hallberg closed her mouth, stared at the ground for a second, and then looked at Jamie, her pale eyes shining in the halogens in the corridor. 'What can you do, huh?'

Jamie closed the file and smiled, holding it up. She knew that feeling all too well. 'This is great work, really.'

Hallberg returned it. 'Wiik's okay. This is just how he is. You get used to it, you know?'

Jamie watched him disappear around a corner, tail of his coat swinging. She sighed. 'Honestly, I hope I won't be here that long.'

13

WHEN JAMIE GOT THERE, Wiik was already at his desk, his face pressed into the V between his thumb and index finger, concertinaing the skin of his cheeks into folds around his knuckles.

She circled it and looked over his shoulder at the screen.

It displayed a big, grainy image. A beaten-up old Mercedes sat in the middle of the photo, its headlights flaring in the dark. The aged night-vision mode on the camera had turned everything a sub-nautical shade of green. *Detailed* wasn't the word she'd use. Big white lumps littered the image, too – snow. Heavy snow.

The picture was head on to the car, but the driver was no more than a dark smudge. Impossible to make out.

'Piece of shit,' Wiik muttered, shaking his head.

The only thing clear in the photo was the number plate.

Jamie squinted at the photograph of Nyström's car and then gestured to the headlights. 'Looks like he put his full beams on, fog lights too, to blind the camera.'

Wiik slouched backwards. 'It's dark, snowing – everyone

drives with full beams and fog lights. If they value their life at least.'

Jamie stared down at him. He looked exhausted.

The sky had darkened outside and the light inside had changed to a shadowless glare courtesy of the LED strips that hung off the ceiling on thin wires.

'Basically,' he said, throwing his arms out at the screen. 'It's shit. And it's worth shit.'

Jamie was waiting for him to sweep the keyboard and mug full of pens off the desk. The latter had the words *Min pappa är en superhjälte* written on it.

My dad is a superhero.

She didn't know if she could picture Wiik in dad mode. But she didn't have long to try before they were interrupted again.

Hallberg appeared, hanging up her phone. 'Okay,' she said, pushing it into the pocket of her black skinny jeans. 'That was the prison – they're sending over the visitor logs from the new system via email when they can.'

'When will that be?' Wiik asked, staring at his underling.

She dared to shrug. 'I don't know. Soon as he could. But the guy I spoke to, the head liaison officer, said that Sjöberg only had two visitors since he's been working there. Wasn't a popular guy, as you can imagine.'

'I can,' Wiik said. 'Who were they?'

'He couldn't remember off the cuff, but he said one was definitely his wife. She visited once or twice a year.'

Wiik pursed his lips. 'Doesn't seem like a lot for a loving wife who believes her husband's innocent.'

Jamie folded her arms. 'The prison isn't exactly close, and the woman is in a wheelchair,' she argued. 'And she said that people aren't exactly lining up to take her.'

Wiik drew a slow breath and then motioned for Hallberg to continue.

'The other visitor came just once, a week before Sjöberg died.'

Wiik sat up straighter.

'He can't remember the name,' Hallberg said, answering the question before he asked it. 'But they take a scan of every visitor's ID when they arrive and keep it on file.'

Wiik was nearly salivating.

'He'll email it across, too,' Hallberg finished.

Wiik nodded slowly. 'Okay. Let me know the second it arrives.'

Hallberg nodded, did a strange sort of half-bow, and then backed away like a servant before turning and heading to her desk.

Jamie thought it was strange it was so far away, but then again, she doubted she'd be able to concentrate with Wiik breathing down her neck, either.

Wiik was leaning back in his chair now, his hands on his stomach, fingers interlaced, thumbs drumming together.

His coat was draped over the back of his seat, and he was in a white shirt with a grey sweater over it. He stared into space. 'You hungry?' he asked.

Jamie was still standing next to his desk, her coat in her hand. 'Yes,' she said, thinking about her empty stomach. She'd had a sandwich from the vending machine after they'd brought Lindvall in for questioning, but otherwise she was running on fumes. 'What do they have around here?'

'Pizza?' Wiik asked.

Jamie pressed her lips into a line. 'Anything else?'

He raised an eyebrow. 'You don't like pizza?' He cast an eye down the loose knitted jumper that was bunched at Jamie's elbows and covered her butt, and down her muscular legs. His eyes paused for just a moment on the curve of her quads as they narrowed at her knees, the defined, triangular shape of her calves as they dived into her boots. His gaze didn't look salacious though. More like the way a trainer might appraise a new race horse before buying.

Jamie still shifted from foot to foot uncomfortably anyway. Yes, she took care of her body, she felt like saying. Seriously so. So what? The eleven flights at Lindvall's apartment block, the run to cut him off. She was built like a Kudu, and moved like one, too.

Jamie always hated that comparison, but her old partner had told her she wasn't skinny enough to be a gazelle. Then added that it was a compliment.

Wiik then turned his detecting powers to her upper body, as if trying to visualise whether it matched.

It did. But he had no business knowing that.

Jamie set her jaw and pulled her phone out, looking for takeaways nearby.

'You're not one of those health freaks, are you?' Wiik asked dryly. 'A "*vegan*".' He even put air-quotes around it.

Jamie glanced up at him, her thumb stopping on the screen. 'No, I'm not,' she replied, though she thought she'd be offended by his comment if she was.

'Well, that's something,' Wiik said, his face straight.

She honestly couldn't tell if he was joking or not and quickly went back to looking for a decent place to eat.

'Married?' Wiik asked now, still clapping his thumbs on his stomach.

'Nope,' Jamie replied, not even looking up.

'Boyfriend?'

'No. You?' She glanced up from under her brow.

He scowled at her a little. 'Funny.'

Jamie went back to her phone, her mind crawling back to

the little cottage in the Scottish isles she'd just come from. To the bed there. To the warm space next to Graeme. She'd not text him back since she'd landed, and he'd not text again. Hell, she didn't know if he was out on the water or at home. And what were they, anyway? They'd never discussed it… Did she even care?

'Divorced,' Wiik added, gesturing to himself and nodding slowly. 'No surprise there, though.' He sighed.

Jamie kept looking. Discussing their personal lives wasn't something she was keen to do. All she wanted from this trip was to finish what her father started, finally lay his memory to rest, and then move on with her life.

'We have a son.' He seemed hell-bent on filling the silence. 'He's nine now.'

Jamie wanted to talk about Wiik's children even less than she did her own love life.

'The job, you know.'

Jamie sighed and lowered her phone, looking at Wiik, who was staring at her now.

'Why haven't you asked me if I knew your father?' he said.

Jamie shook her head slowly, at a loss. Both for an answer to the question and as to why he'd driven the conversation in this direction. 'I don't know.' She should have just let him order the pizza. 'Did you?'

He nodded. 'I did. Not personally. But I knew who he was. Everyone did.'

'Great.'

'I was young – in my twenties. Just a uniform during his time.'

Jamie felt her fist tighten around the phone, the number for a Thai place on-screen, ready to be dialled.

'He was a good man,' Wiik said.

Jamie felt her shoulders begin to tension, like someone
was ratcheting them into her spine. She pulled in a breath, but
they wouldn't loosen.

'Troubled, though.' He seemed intent on continuing,
despite the resistance from Jamie.

'Oh yeah?' Jamie asked vaguely, her thumb retracting
from the screen.

'It broke him, you know?' Wiik looked up at her wistfully. 'I remember it – there was a distinct change.' He looked
over towards Falk's now dark office. 'Falk warned me to
steer clear of him. He had a short fuse anyway, but after…'

'After what?'

'You left.'

Jamie stiffened a little, pushing her phone into her
pocket now.

'I remember you, as a girl.'

Jamie measured him, sitting there in the chair, spouting
shit about her family.

'You were always so full of energy – of course, you don't
remember me. Why would you?'

She raked in a difficult breath and looked away. 'Is there a
point to all this?'

'Your father changed, when you'd gone. We could all see
the decline in him – we knew it was just a matter of time
until…'

'Until what?' Jamie asked, her voice dripping venom.

'Until something like what happened with Claesson…'

She swallowed hard.

'That was the worst thing of all, that everyone knew.'
Wiik shook his head. 'A ticking time bomb. And everyone
was just waiting for it to go off, praying they weren't the one
to *set* it off.' He huffed a little bit, looked down at his thumbs.
They'd fallen still now.

Jamie's teeth were about to shatter under the force of being clamped together so hard.

'Everyone gave him a wide berth, not wanting to be the one sucked under his wheels, you know? When in reality, it was the opposite that—'

'You know what,' Jamie cut in, 'I'm actually not hungry.' She let her coat fall open in her hand and threw it around her shoulders. 'I'm going back to the hotel,' she said, pulling her long plait out of the collar and already making for the door. 'Let me know if anything—'

'Detective!' Hallberg's voice carried across the room, her footsteps hurried.

Jamie froze in her tracks, her eyes closing. She exhaled and turned slowly to see Hallberg standing at Wiik's desk, a little out of breath.

'You might want to see this,' she said.

Jamie went back over, looking at the piece of paper Wiik had in his hands. It was a black-and-white printout of a photocopy of a driver's licence.

As she approached, Wiik held it up to her, scoffed, and then smirked. 'Sjöberg's mysterious deathbed visitor.'

Jamie took it and stared down at the face on the page.

A guy in his fifties looked up at her, his expression bordering gormless. He was thin, with a narrow jaw and a long neck that ran down into an unbroken white collar.

'Jesus Christ,' Jamie muttered, looking at it. 'He's a priest.'

'Yep,' Wiik said, taking it back and spinning around on his chair to face her. 'Per Eriksson is a goddamn priest.'

14

Jamie,

I wonder how your mother will react. What she will say. I'm afraid of that, probably the most. I don't know how to reach you. And I don't know that I'll be able to.

But maybe you will read this.

Read this and know. Know that I never meant to...

I am sorry.

For everything. For the things I couldn't give you.

There are things I want you to have. That they would take. Things that only you can find. I know you will. One day.

15

JAMIE'S EYES opened slowly and she woke from a dreamless sleep.

She swung her legs off the side of the bed and looked at her phone. It was just after six.

Wiik was picking her up at eight.

She reached for the lamp on the nightstand and flicked it on, picking up the courtesy card next to it. Breakfast at seven. Facilities at eight. Pool. Sauna. Gym. She wondered if they'd make an exception and reached for the phone next to the lamp. She needed to shake off the cobwebs, along with Wiik's words from the last night.

Her father had needed someone. Anyone.

But everyone had been too afraid to.

And Jamie hadn't even known.

Wiik pulled in at the kerb at two minutes before eight, the electric Volvo humming gently.

Jamie climbed in, the thick smell of coffee rich in the interior.

He looked tetchy, his face a silent scowl. 'Here,' he grunted, lifting a cup from the centre console. 'Didn't know how you took it.'

Jamie took a mouthful. 'Black – safe guess.' She held it in her hands, letting the warmth seep into her fingers.

Wiik pulled swiftly away.

'Everything okay?' Jamie asked, reading the tension in him.

'No,' he replied flatly. 'Lindvall threw himself a tantrum in his holding cell at about three o'clock this morning – started screaming, threatening to smash his skull open against the wall if they didn't let him out. Made a real mess – smeared his shit all over the place, pissed himself, threw up everywhere and then passed out, started convulsing.' Wiik grimaced and shook his head.

'Jesus,' Jamie muttered, taking a big gulp of coffee. It sounded like she'd need the caffeine. 'He okay?'

'He was moved to hospital. He regained consciousness on arrival and tried to attack the nurse who was treating him – he's been sedated now. They think it was a psychotic break due to the stress of the questioning.'

'Who does?'

'The state-appointed psychologist tasked with his mental wellbeing,' Wiik practically spat. 'If you ask me, a piece of shit like that should just be left to rot.'

Jamie raised an eyebrow and looked out of the window. She had wondered if pushing Lindvall like he had would yield results like this. Sometimes she hated being right.

'The last thing I need is an investigation into my methods clogging things up.' He sighed heavily. 'I spoke to the attending doctor just before heading over,' he went on. 'Seems like Lindvall has gone into acute withdrawal now as well, and apparently he's dehydrated, not eaten in days. Been on a real bender. System is overloaded with amphetamines. Self-destruct mode.'

Jamie listened, knowing where he was going with this. 'Guilty conscience, you think?'

He shrugged. 'Not like we'll know until he comes out of it. Could be days.'

'Shit,' Jamie breathed. She wasn't inclined to think Lindvall had murdered the girl, but it wasn't out of the question. She sighed, focused on her coffee and let Wiik drive on.

The church grew in the distance until it was a white spire cut out against the grey sky above them.

They parked down the street, a row of single-story houses with red-tiled roofs between them and Per Eriksson's church.

Wiik eyed it carefully through the windshield, massaging his chin.

On the drive over, he'd handed Jamie Hallberg's summary of the kills – both the originals and the new. Including Claesson's autopsy report and the original seven.

All the victims were posed with birch boughs, freshly hacked from nearby trunks with a sharp hatchet. The boughs were then stripped of branches to a length of around a 140 centimetres. The thick ends were then chopped to a point with a single, hard blow, before they were pushed through the victim's backs and into the frozen ground.

If Eriksson was a groundskeeper, he'd have access to and experience with a hatchet. He'd know trees and how to handle wood. And with a priesthood lying in his future, the religious element was hard to ignore. And what better way to throw long-term suspicion from yourself than to enter into the church?

And now, Sjöberg was dead, and the only two people to

see him alive in the last few months were his infirm wife and one of the only other suspects from the original case. The righteous Per Eriksson.

Jamie thought back to the shapeless green blob in Nyström's front seat and wondered if it could have been Eriksson. If Nyström was bound and gagged in the boot.

'Ready?' Wiik asked, glancing at her.

She nodded and they got out, leaving the file on the seat.

Eriksson's church was a modest one, its steeple stretching just a few metres above the pitched roof.

The building was made of stone, painted white, with a wide staircase leading up to it. A cemetery surrounded it on three sides and green algae stretched up the walls from the sodden earth.

The brown wooden door at the top of the steps was open, but there seemed to be no service in session.

Jamie and Wiik ascended to the church and entered, both quiet. The whole place was quiet.

There was no wind. The surrounding trees stood still, as if waiting for something.

Wiik led, not bothering to wipe his feet and shoved the inner door open, letting out as much warmth as he could.

The air inside was close. Jamie counted at least eight electric radiators in the space, all old and ticking away as they blew hot air into the rafters.

A pitched ceiling overhead was clad with wood, and rows of pews stretched towards the pulpit, a stained cross standing behind it, a circular window above like its own halo.

Wiik tsked and approached. 'Per Eriksson?' he called out, his voice echoing in the space.

It sustained for a few seconds and then died.

Wiik inhaled to repeat, but a door opened at the back-left of the room and a man walked out in a pair of jeans and a black shirt, a white dog collar around his throat. He was drying his hands in a tea towel, and then threw it over his shoulder. His hands were red and raw as though he'd just been washing up in boiling water. 'Can I help you?' he said.

Jamie measured Per Eriksson. He was about six foot two, with a full head of white hair that stuck up from his angular face. His eyes were kind, his smile disarming.

Wiik came forward. 'Kriminalinspektör Anders Wiik,' he said curtly, showing his badge. 'This is my colleague, Detective Inspector Jamie Johansson,' he added, gesturing back to Jamie.

She nodded.

He looked at her. 'Johansson?' he said to himself, his eyes resting on her for a moment, a look of familiarity there. He cleared his throat quickly then and turned back to Wiik. 'What can I do for you, Inspector?' he asked innocently.

'We're looking into a case that may be related to Hans Sjöberg,' Wiik said diplomatically. 'A murder.'

Eriksson folded his lips into a line. 'I'm sorry to tell you, Inspector, but Hans Sjöberg is dead.'

'We're aware,' Wiik said quickly. 'But it seems that you were one of the last people to see him alive – and one of only two people to visit him in prison at all in the last few years. And, it's curious to us that, after all this time, you would visit him while he was serving a sentence for the murder of seven girls, and then shortly after, another goes missing and then shows up murdered in the same way. The details of which only Sjöberg and a handful of others knew about.'

Eriksson was a statue before them, his hands clasped in front of him.

Wiik went on, turning out his bottom lip. 'And considering the way they treat men like him in prison, I doubt he would have been keen to share his war stories. He spent most of his sentence in private quarters, locked away from the other inmates for his own safety. Did you know that?'

'No, I did not,' Eriksson replied quietly.

'Do you see where I'm going with this?' Wiik asked.

Eriksson didn't speak.

'You were one of the original suspects in this case, were you not?'

'I was,' Eriksson said carefully.

'So then tell me, why does an acquaintance show up after twenty years to visit a child-killer on his deathbed?'

'An acquaintance?' Eriksson seemed thrown by the word. 'Because he asked me to,' he finished.

'He asked you to?' Wiik pressed.

'Yes. Hans and I were close friends.'

Wiik glanced at her. She was still studying the tall man's features.

Eriksson explained. 'At least, before he was convicted. I was the groundskeeper at the church. We all knew that girls were going missing – Hans and I often talked about it. We thought it must have been someone from the congregation. We heard that they were being murdered, but we never thought that...' He coughed and then carried on. 'When Hans was arrested, I was more shocked than anyone. As I said, we were close friends. He was a kind man, a caring man. But afterwards, I felt betrayed... disgusted by it.' He swallowed, tightened his shaking hands into a knot in front of him. 'I didn't speak to him again, didn't visit him. Not once.' He bowed his head a little.

'Until a few weeks ago,' Wiik corrected him. 'Why?'

'He wrote me a letter,' Eriksson said forthrightly.

'We need to see that letter,' Wiik said, looking at Jamie again.

Second time in a few seconds. Was he looking for confirmation of his instincts? He'd already pushed Lindvall too far. Was he hoping Jamie might temper him this time?

'Of course,' Eriksson said. 'Would you like me to get it? It's in my desk drawer.'

'We'll come with you,' Wiik replied, not wanting to leave the man alone with what could be their first piece of crucial evidence.

Though Jamie didn't think that he'd be this forthcoming if he was guilty. And he didn't strike her as the type. But then again, brutes of this nature rarely did show their monstrous side. Jamie knew that from experience. In fact, they were usually the most charming. The smiliest. The most easygoing. They were invisible to the naked eye. Disguised in plain sight as helpers, as shepherds of humanity. Doctors. Solicitors. Police Officers. Priests.

Jamie nodded to confirm Wiik's intention to trail the man, and all three walked through the door from which he'd exited.

A modest kitchen with units on the left under a window and a tired table on the right greeted them. The draining board had a few plates on it, suds slowly running off them.

Eriksson led them through into a small hallway. Ahead was his bedroom and to their right a bathroom.

He didn't seem bashful or embarrassed as he continued through to the room in which he slept. Jamie often found people got squirrelly as police entered their most private space. But not Eriksson. Was that because he didn't feel nerves? Or was it simply because his room was spartan, as priest-like as one might expect. A single bed with a crucifix hanging above it, neatly made. A bookshelf that contained no less than six different bibles. A bedside table with a glass of water on it. A desk with a lamp and a computer, the screen displaying a website that helped you locate scripture excerpts based on keywords. A notebook was open in front of it, a few quotes written down.

Eriksson wasted no time in reaching for his desk drawer.

Wiik backed up, raising one hand to motion Jamie backwards, the other hovering next to his hip, ready to reach for his pistol.

Eriksson could pull anything from that drawer.

The wood creaked as it opened and Wiik visibly tensed, but then Eriksson was turning, a piece of paper in his hands. 'Here,' he said easily, handing it over.

Wiik took it and began reading.

Eriksson leaned slowly back against the desk, wincing a little as he did. The man wasn't as spry as he used to be, it seemed. He was sitting as though his back hurt. A show for them? To throw them off? How could a clergyman with back problems carry a body into the woods and chop down trees? Surely he couldn't.

'Sjöberg reached out to me,' Eriksson said unprompted, looking at the letter. 'He knew his prognosis was grim and said he wanted to make amends.' Eriksson sighed. 'Apologise for lying to me all those years ago.'

Wiik snorted. 'Rich.'

'I'm sorry?' Eriksson said.

'That he wanted to make amends to you,' he muttered, looking up from the letter. 'Rather than the families of the girls he murdered.'

Eriksson made his mouth into a line again and offered an apologetic look. 'I wrote back, and told him that I'd forgiven him years ago, that after I lost my faith in him, in God, that I found my way back to the church. That I now had my own congregation. And that if he was truly sorry, for lying and for everything else, that I could offer him absolution.'

'What a load of shit,' Wiik said, unable to keep his own views in check.

Eriksson did the Christian thing and smiled politely despite Wiik's unveiled rudeness.

Jamie was thinking on something else. 'How did he find you, Father?'

Eriksson turned his attention to her. 'What do you mean?'

'If you hadn't kept in touch with him, not seen him in twenty years, how did he know how to reach you?'

Wiik's gaze drifted from the page to Jamie and then to Eriksson, at which point it stopped and burnt a hole in the side of his head.

Eriksson shook his head again. 'I don't know – I expect that he either looked me up or—'

'Looked you up?' Wiik interjected. 'We're the police and we had a hard enough time "looking you up". And plus, how would he do that in prison?'

Eriksson looked at Wiik, not a waiver in his face. 'By all accounts he was a model prisoner, and prisoners have access to the internet – supervised, of course. My details are not hidden, my name, date of birth, address, it all appears on the National Lutheran Register as a matter of record, along with the date of my appointment here. And of course, contact details. I expect that simply searching for my name and date of birth online would yield accurate results.'

Jamie peered around Eriksson at his computer and wondered if a browsing-history search would show that he'd confirmed that fact recently.

Wiik didn't look so convinced.

'Or,' Eriksson offered casually, 'he got the information from his wife.'

Jamie tweaked, exchanged a look with Wiik. 'His wife?'

Wiik jumped in. 'Why would his wife have your information?'

'Not my current information,' Eriksson said, looking at each of them, 'but the information of the seminary school I attended. I gave it to Eva before I left, in case she needed anything. They would have happily passed along the details of my appointment.'

Jamie bit her lip. 'We questioned Sjöberg's wife. She barely remembered your name. When were you in touch with her last?'

'I spoke to her just a few days ago.' Eriksson's brow crumpled. 'I called to offer my condolences for Hans's death. They were still married, believed in the sanctity of marriage. I wanted to honour that. And I suspected that few others would be calling to do the same.'

Wiik made a stern humming sound. 'She didn't mention it.'

'I'm not really surprised,' Eriksson replied, exhaling slowly. 'She was rather out of touch when I spoke to her.'

'Out of touch?'

'Detached. Incoherent. Lacking a grip on reality.' His mouth made the line again, cheeks bulging around it. 'Diagnosed or not, I fear the woman suffers from Alzheimer's. Or similar. It's not uncommon at her age. It's just a shame that she has so little support.'

Wiik looked to be seething a little now, though Jamie didn't know exactly what was getting his back up. She took over the questioning all the same.

'I'm sorry, Father, this is all just coming as quite a shock to us. When we spoke to Eva Sjöberg, she made no mention of you. But you're saying you were in contact with both her and her husband recently. That you and her husband were close friends. That what you discussed was of a biblical nature?'

He nodded. 'Yes, we spoke at length about the—'

'Murders?' Wiik said through gritted teeth.

'No,' Eriksson said slowly, glancing at Jamie to make sure Wiik wasn't about to launch himself at the man. 'About the Bible – God. The nature of life, death. Heaven and hell. Absolution.'

Jamie stepped forward a little so that Wiik was behind her. 'Did he tell you why he did it?'

'Why he murdered those poor girls?' Eriksson either was very good at feigning emotion, or was genuinely displaying it. 'No, he didn't. And I didn't ask. What was done was done, the reasons inconsequential so long as he was genuinely repentant.'

'They don't seem inconsequential to me,' Wiik growled.

Jamie cleared her throat, stepping forward a little more. 'And was he? Repentant, I mean.'

Eriksson nodded. 'Yes. I believe he was.'

Wiik scoffed behind her, and Jamie turned, shot him the sort of cold look that said, *Remove yourself before I do it for you.*

He set his jaw, folded the letter in his hand and held it up. 'We're keeping this,' he said to Eriksson.

The priest proffered his own hand. 'Of course,' he said. 'Anything I can do to help.'

Wiik exited the bedroom, then the kitchen, too. Jamie expected she'd find him outside, cooling off with some luck. She felt her shoulders ease a little, but wondered for a moment if he'd just left her alone with a serial killer.

She stepped back a little, shook off that train of thought, and got back to it. 'Apologies for my partner, I don't think he takes a very understanding stance to faith.'

'I'm used to it.'

'I'm sure.'

'Do you?' Eriksson smiled at her.

'Take an understanding stance on faith?' Jamie raised her eyebrows. 'In the same way that I do quantum physics. I don't hope to ever grasp it myself, and know that I won't, but I accept that there are people who do and that doesn't upset me.'

Eriksson chuckled a little, amused by the answer. 'Very well. Do you have any more questions?'

'When exactly did you speak to Eva Sjöberg?'

'It must have been Saturday. Yes, after my service. Around eleven in the morning, I think. Maybe a little after.'

Jamie nodded, felt for her police notebook instinctively and realised that she didn't have it, but felt the bulge of another in her pocket. She withdrew it, looked down at the red cover and swallowed, and then turned it upside down, flipped it over, and opened the back cover. 'Do you,' she started, her voice catching, 'have a pen?'

Eriksson reached behind himself and offered one to her.

'Thanks. And I expect that phone records will show you called her?' Jamie looked at him.

He was watching her intently. 'Yes.'

'What's your number?'

He gave it, eyes never straying from her.

She wrote it down.

'What did you speak about?'

'I offered her consolation, told her where she could find my church if she wanted to come to a service. I offered her transport – we have a church bus with wheelchair access we use to pick up some of our older members.'

'Did she come?'

'Not yet, but I'm hopeful.'

'How did you get her number?'

'Hans gave it to me at our meeting, asked me to call her.'

Jamie nodded, writing it down. 'How many letters did you exchange?'

'He sent the first, I replied in turn. Then he called me to arrange it.'

Jamie didn't ask when. She'd be able to confirm that with the prison. 'Same number that you called Eva from?'

'Yes, the landline here at the church,' he said.

'Good. Thank you.' Jamie's pen hovered and then tapped the pad.

'Was there something else?'

'Do the letters "A.M." mean anything to you?'

'Ante meridiem?'

Jamie shook her head. 'I don't think so.'

'Some context may help.'

'It was written next to Hans Sjöberg's name in an old notebook – the detective's who worked the original murders.'

'Jörgen Johansson,' Eriksson said, looking down at the worn notebook in her hand. 'Your father.'

Jamie froze.

He smiled, amused again. 'You bear a resemblance, share his second name – and I'd never forget that notebook. He'd pull it out and tap his pencil on it, while he spoke.' Eriksson smiled a little. 'Quite like you're doing, actually. Never write a damn thing in it, though.'

'You remember him? And that?' Jamie's voice was quiet suddenly.

'He is a difficult man to forget. And he questioned me several times. Vigorously.'

Jamie didn't know what to say in response.

'How is he? Still working?'

'He's dead,' Jamie said, a lump in her throat.

'I'm sorry to hear that.'

She nodded once, looking at the notebook.

'Was that the notebook? From the case?' Eriksson asked, nodding to it.

'No,' Jamie said, holding it against herself. 'A different one.'

'But one of his?'

She swallowed. 'Can we get back on track?'

'Apologies.'

'A.M. It was written next to a name – Annika Liljedahl. Does that mean anything to you?'

Eriksson thought on it for a moment. 'I know that name.' It seemed to dawn on him then. 'A.M. Army medic?' He held his hand up, finger outstretched with realisation. 'Hans was a medic in the army for several years. I suspect "A.M." refers to that.'

Jamie processed. It made sense that he would have some anatomical knowledge considering the kills – that's what Claesson had said. An army medic would have just that. 'And Annika Liljedahl?'

'That was Hans's first girlfriend, if I remember rightly.'

Jamie waited for him to continue before writing anything down.

'He never went into detail, but I believe there was some sort of altercation – something to do with her parents. It caused Hans some trouble, and he left for the army soon after.'

'What kind of trouble?'

'As I said, he never went into detail, and I'm recalling a thirty-year-old conversation at that.'

Jamie drew a slow breath. 'Right, of course. Thank you. Can you tell me anything else about her?'

He shook his head. 'I can't, I'm afraid. It was a passing

topic in one of our many talks as friends when I was a groundskeeper at the church. I lived next door to Hans and Eva at the time. I spent many evenings there. They were such good people. Warm, friendly—'

'Thank you,' Jamie said, cutting him off. 'I'll be in touch if I need anything further.'

'Of course. You know where to find me.' He stood now, wincing again. His voice turned grave then. 'I hope you find the man you're looking for. If this killer is modelling himself on Hans Sjöberg, then it seems you may have your work cut out for you.'

'Yes,' Jamie said, closing the notebook and pushing it slowly into her pocket. 'It does seem that way.'

'Let me show you out,' Eriksson said.

'I'll find my way,' Jamie replied. 'You've been very helpful.'

He followed her into the kitchen all the same. 'Oh, and, Inspector?

'Yes?' Jamie asked, stopping at the threshold to the church and looking back.

'If you ever need help understanding quantum physics, my door is always open.'

Jamie laughed a little. 'I'll remember that.' And then she pulled it closed behind her.

16

WIIK WAS LEANING against the railing at the bottom of the church steps. He pushed off as Jamie emerged and immediately started speaking. 'I had Hallberg follow up on the story about the seminary school. Apparently, they did pass Eriksson's information on to someone a few weeks ago.'

'That was fast,' Jamie said, surprised. It could only have been about five minutes – no more than ten at most – since Wiik had left the room.

He nodded. 'Yeah, Hallberg is good like that. The forensics reports on the original murders were delivered this morning, too. Hallberg is going to go through them and let us know what she finds.'

'You're lucky to have her.'

He scoffed. 'Yeah, sure. *Sir, sir,*' he parroted emphatically, waving his hands next to his head. 'I hear that a hundred times a day. "*How do I do this? What do you think about this? What would you do in this situation?*"' He snorted derisively.

Jamie gritted her teeth. 'She's eager to learn – don't

punish her for it. She'll make a great detective one day, and she clearly just wants guidance.'

He exhaled, walking fast for the car. He ran his hand over his head and smoothed down his hair. 'I just wish she'd focus on the cases, not so much on her own footing. As if I don't have enough to worry about without mollycoddling her all the time.'

Jamie let it go. She didn't feel like getting into an argument, and saying, *Well, if you cut the kid some slack every once in a while, maybe said thank you, she'd realise she was actually doing a pretty great job,* could only cause one.

Wiik got into the car and sat down hard, closing the door behind him.

He sighed and exhaled hard. 'You want to get some breakfast?' he asked suddenly, staring out of the window.

'I ate already,' Jamie said, looking at him. 'What happened in there?'

'I don't like churches.'

'I kind of got that.'

'My parents used to make me go as a child. I always thought it was ridiculous.'

Jamie bit her lip for a second. 'You still should have been careful in there. Eriksson gave us some good information.' Provided it wasn't all a complete fabrication, she felt like adding. But she didn't think she needed to feed Wiik's distrust any more.

'Yeah? Like what?' Wiik leaned on his hand, his elbow on the sill of the window.

'Information on Sjöberg – the name in my father's notebook, Annika Liljedahl. What A.M. stands for.'

'And who is she, exactly?' Wiik asked, seemingly bored by it all now.

'Sjöberg's first girlfriend, Eriksson said.' Jamie watched

him, but he didn't seem to perk up. 'Apparently they had some sort of disagreement, and then Sjöberg left for the military – he was an army medic for a couple of years.'

'A.M.,' Wiik said quietly, nodding. 'Great. But how does that help us?'

Jamie did her best to keep her cool. 'Any lead right now is a good one. And filling in the blanks from the original case can only help us.'

'Whatever you say.' Wiik brushed her off and started the motor, accelerating away from the church at speed.

'Where are we going?'

'Like I said: breakfast.'

Jamie had already had her fill of cold meats, muesli, fruit and coffee from the breakfast buffet at the hotel. She'd worked up an appetite after her swim. But judging by the way he was stuffing a breakfast sub into his mouth, Wiik had skipped the most important meal of the day altogether. The smell of it filled the cabin of the car, but because of the cold he refused to let Jamie roll the window down.

The screen in the central console lit up, the word *Hallberg* appeared there, and Jamie quickly jabbed the answer button to drown out the sound of Wiik's chewing and slurping.

'Hallberg,' Jamie said brightly.

'Oh, Inspector Johansson,' she replied, a little surprised. 'Is, er, Kriminalinspektör Wiik there?'

'I-ng-here-ngg,' he said, mouth full, spewing crumbs all over the steering wheel. He swallowed – painfully, it looked like – coughed, and then spoke. 'What is it?'

'I was just looking through the original files from the coroner's office, and one of the girls – victim seven – her name was Hanna Lundgren.' She paused after it.

Wiik looked at Jamie, then took another bite of his sandwich. 'Lundgren?' he said, lowering his sandwich a little.

'As in Leif Lundgren?' Jamie interjected, glancing at Wiik. 'The third name in the notebook?'

'I don't know, yet,' Hallberg said. 'But I have her information here. I'll try the next of kin that's listed, but I doubt the number is still in use after all these years. If it's not, I'll check with the hospital, get a copy of the birth certificate, and see if I can get a match. I'll let you know what I find.'

'You do that,' Wiik said, reaching out and hanging up on her. He turned to Jamie and took another bite from his sub. 'See what I mean?'

'Oh yeah,' Jamie said, shaking her head. 'She's fucking heinous.'

Hallberg was back on the line in twenty minutes.

Wiik had finished his meal and his coffee, and the caffeine seemed to be lifting his mood. But the church had struck a nerve of some kind, and Jamie wasn't keen to open that can of worms, especially not right in the middle of a murder investigation.

'Okay,' Hallberg said, taking a deep breath. 'Leif Lundgren. I found Hanna's birth certificate, but Leif isn't listed as her father. It looks like Hanna's mother died when she was four and her father was unable to care for her. Public records show that she was taken into care and was then adopted by Helena and Leif Lundgren in 1987. In 1996, when she was killed, she was only fourteen years old.'

'Why was Lundgren a suspect?' Wiik asked, his voice cutting.

'The forensic report on Hanna showed that epithelial cells

were recovered from under her fingernails – and the DNA was positively matched to Leif Lundgren.'

Wiik stuck out his bottom lip.

'The report says that build-up like that was consistent with defensive scratching.'

'Why was Leif never arrested?'

'Uh,' Hallberg said, hedging. 'I don't know whether he was or not. The case files are missing.' She did her best not to sound patronising, but it was obvious Wiik still took it that way.

'You have a current address for Lundgren.'

'Of course.' She knew not to call a second time without everything in front of her.

'Send it to me. We'll head there now—'

Jamie interjected. 'Actually, I'd like to follow up on the Annika Liljedahl lead.'

Wiik fired her a strange look like she'd just driven a knife into his ribs. 'Why?'

Jamie thought for a second how best to phrase it. 'I'd like to know more about Sjöberg. If my father was wrong about him, I need to know where he went off course. Lindvall, Eriksson and now Lundgren... They're solid suspects. Means. Opportunity. But if they got away with it twenty years ago, then my father did something wrong. And I need to know what that was. If you need backup, take Hallberg.'

Wiik's jaw tightened. 'You're here to help catch a killer, not prove your father's competence.'

Jamie could have torn him apart, wanted to. He was acting like a child. A spoilt one at that. The way he treated Hallberg, the case, now this... She didn't feel great about pushing Hallberg back into the firing line, but as the girl had said herself, you get used to Wiik. She knew her way around him. And obviously Jamie didn't just yet. 'You're more than capable of handling Lundgren, yourself,' Jamie replied finally. 'You didn't even want me on the case to begin with, remember? Let's just divide and conquer. If my father was onto something with Sjöberg, then this helps prove it's a copycat. If he was wrong…'

Wiik huffed. 'Whatever you want. Hallberg – get Johansson an address for Annika Liljedahl. There can't be many people born around the same time as Sjöberg in the same town with that name.'

'I can find it myself,' Jamie protested.

'No,' Wiik said. 'Hallberg is good at this sort of thing, and she doesn't mind.'

Hallberg was silent on the line, but Jamie could picture her fist around the receiver, ready to crush it.

She knew how she felt.

Her own fist was balled at her side. Knuckles white with tension.

But she didn't feel like crushing a phone with it.

She could think of a much better use.

17

JAMIE RENTED A SMALL, economical hatchback and set out for Rättvik, a town on the edge of the Siljan lake three hours outside the city.

The afternoon was closing in, the sun swimming around somewhere near the horizon by the time she arrived.

Hallberg had forwarded her an address along with Annika Liljedahl's details. The woman was fifty-nine years old. A school teacher. No criminal record. And she lived less than a kilometre from the house she grew up in.

Jamie pulled up outside it and sighed. What was she doing here? What would she find? Was she that determined to prove her father was a good detective, or was she terrified to find out that he was the opposite? Either way, it had brought her all the way out here, and there was no point going back empty-handed. Especially not to face Wiik's 'I told you so.'

Jamie got out of the car and crossed the street towards the house, a red-and-white wood-panelled home surrounded by trees. They were dusted by snow, and a layer of it lay on the roof.

She approached the gate and pushed it open, shivering as she did, and paused, looking back.

The road was rural, the houses spaced distantly. There were no other cars, parked or driving. And most of the driveways were empty, the inhabitants still at work.

And yet Jamie couldn't shake the feeling that there were eyes on her.

She scanned the houses in turn, looking in both directions, but nothing moved. She strained her eyes in the twilight.

The day was slowly being bludgeoned into submission, and the air was biting at Jamie's cheeks as she stood.

A light came on in her peripheral and Jamie turned again, seeing an older woman step onto her porch, wrapping her arms around her stomach, flattening a long cardigan against her body.

She squinted out at Jamie, a lone stranger halfway through her front gate. *'Kan jag hjälpa dig?'* she called. Can I help you?

'Ja,' Jamie replied smiling. 'My name is Detective Inspector Jamie Johansson. Are you Annika Liljedahl?'

The woman looked back at her in confusion. 'Yes,' she said warily.

'I was hoping I might ask you some questions?'

'About what?' She wasn't defensive, but she was understandably cautious. 'Can I see some identification?'

Jamie patted her coat pockets and pulled out the lanyard and card that Falk had given her. She walked forward, holding it out.

Annika took it and held it up to the light. She had a narrow face, lined with the years, her hair cut into a bob around the nape of her neck. It was the colour of charcoal. *'Konsult?'* she asked, reading it aloud. Consultant.

Jamie nodded. 'I'm with the London Metropolitan Police. I'm here assisting with a case.'

'A case?'

'A murder,' Jamie said, taking the lanyard back. Shards of ice on the path to the house crunched under her heels. Snow had been shovelled back onto the grass either side, but the walkway was narrow. Jamie guessed she'd done it herself. The woman was slight and shovelling snow was no easy task.

'I don't know how I could be of help,' Annika went on, not grasping the connection yet.

Jamie swallowed, knowing it was easier just to get it out of the way. 'It's concerning your relationship with Hans Sjöberg,' Jamie said.

Realisation dawned on the woman. 'Ah – I haven't seen Hans since 1975,' she replied quickly. 'And as far as I know, he's still in prison for what he did.' She turned the corners of her mouth down a little. 'And if you're about to tell me that he got out and—'

'Hans Sjöberg is dead,' Jamie said.

Annika stopped speaking, holding her mouth open a little while she gathered herself. 'Then I really don't know how I can be of help.'

Jamie's fingers were numbing in the cold. 'Another girl is dead,' she said plainly. 'And I'm looking for the man who killed her. I don't know if you can help, but if we don't catch him, he will kill again.'

Annika let her hands fall, looked down the street, and then settled on Jamie. 'Okay. Come inside. I'll put on some tea,' she said, beckoning Jamie up.

As she stepped onto the porch, Annika eyed her. 'You know, you remind me of someone – but I can't place who.'

'You know what,' Jamie said, laughing a little. Just one quiet, sardonic note. 'I've been getting that a lot lately.'

18

'HANS WAS NINETEEN, and I was fourteen,' Annika said, looking down into her mug of tea. She was perched on her sofa, legs crossed, leaning on the arm. Her shoulders were at odd angles, her expression vacant as she dug into the deepest recesses of her mind. 'That's why there was so much fuss over it.'

Jamie nodded slowly, watching the woman from the chair opposite. There was an elegance to her, a certain restrained beauty that she hadn't noticed before. She wasn't stunning, not head-turning, but she held herself gracefully. Jamie could imagine that she would have matured early. She was slim but shapely, womanly in every sense.

'Rättvik was a small town then – smaller, I mean.' She sipped some of her tea. It was camomile. Jamie didn't really like it, but was glad for the warmth in her hands. Annika went on, 'We lived just a street away from each other, out there' – she nodded towards the window – 'across the lake. There were just a few houses – and we were the only two kids. My parents moved to the house in the early spring of 1974. I was just twelve at the time – Hans was seventeen. Of course, he wanted nothing to do with me.' She shook her head, smiled a little. 'I was in love with him from the moment I saw him, though.'

Jamie looked at her, at the softness of her eyes as she recalled him as a young man. As she recalled a serial killer. A convicted child-killer. Jamie swallowed and looked down into her tea.

'The house my parents bought was falling down – and Hans was good with his hands, a skilled woodworker.'

Jamie thought about the expertly trimmed birch boughs used in the killing but said nothing.

'He came around to ask if they needed help with the garden or with any repairs – that sort of thing – for pocket money. That summer he was there often. But he never looked twice at me.' She chuckled a little. 'But then, by that winter, I turned thirteen, and was beginning to grow up.'

Jamie nodded that she was still following, that she wanted Annika to go on.

'Hans didn't work as much in the winter – the snow, the rain. And you know, thick jackets, scarves to cover yourself up... But then, when the spring came around, he came back, and the coat came off...'

'And he began to notice you.'

'Yes.' Annika shook her head again, unable to help the smile on her face. Jamie found it disconcerting. But she reserved judgement until the story was over. 'He did. He was eighteen, me thirteen. Still just a girl, but beginning to know myself. And my friends, from school – we were all at that age, you know? Where dollies were replaced with boys, where shoes became heels, where face-paint became make-up.'

'A difficult age,' Jamie added quietly, not wanting to derail her.

Annika nodded, swallowed, and a glimmer of something like remorse shone in her eyes. She adjusted herself on the sofa and clutched her tea a little tighter. 'My father was impressed with Hans's skill and wanted him to do some work to our roof – replace some battens and tiles. It was the summer by that point, and we'd exchanged glances, but nothing more. He was a sweet boy – and some of the older girls in my school had talked about him. He was handsome, charming. They all told me I was lucky to have him working around the house.' She let out a long breath. 'That second summer had now worn into autumn and the weather was beginning to turn. I had just turned fourteen – and the house was nearly finished. I feared that I wouldn't see him around anymore, and that I was going to miss my chance.'

Jamie set her jaw, listening intently.

'He was cutting wood in the back garden, finishing the roof of the back porch, and I took some cola out to him. I had it in my hand and held it up in front of me. He came closer and reached out for it. I took his hand before it reached the bottle and held it. He looked down into my eyes – now nineteen years old – and looked at me for the first time. And that was it.' Annika trailed off, inhaling slowly.

'What happened next?' Jamie asked.

'He was cautious, of course – I was just a girl, and he a man by all accounts. He seemed secretive about his feelings – I didn't know why. I thought it was fine – love was love to me. But I agreed to meet with him that night, in the forest between our two streets. There was a path leading through the trees. We said midnight. So after my parents fell asleep, I crept outside, crossed the road, and went into the woods…'

Jamie felt her spine straighten, her shoulders tighten. Imagined that her father had sat opposite this woman two decades ago and had heard this exact same story.

'I did not know what to expect, or what I was doing. But Hans was there, and he knew. He had brought a blanket and laid it down at the side of the path among the birch trees. His breath smelled like beer – I remember thinking how sour it was. And that I should try not to make a face – that it was just something I would grow to love, like the taste of the wine or cigarettes that my parents seemed to enjoy so much.' She laughed a little. 'We laid down there, and spoke for a while, in whispered voices. Hans told me that his parents thought he should join the army – that there was no money in wood-working. But that he didn't want to. I told him he should stay, of course. I wanted that. And then he kissed me – his top lip bristling with hair…' Annika reached up and touched her own lips, staring into space. 'He was gentle – he asked me if it was okay. If I felt alright. If it was hurting. I lied and said no.' She sipped her tea. 'But it was my first time – and he knew that.' She bit her lip now, stopped speaking for a few seconds. Then she swallowed, placed her mug on the table between them. 'When we were finished, we stayed there for a long time, and he held me in his arms.' Her voice had lost the warm quality it had. 'Our eyes had grown accustomed to the dark, our skin used to the chill of the coming autumn. But then, as I looked up at him, I saw his face more clearly, a glint reflecting in his eyes. They were fixed on something over my shoulder – and then he was scared. He rolled away, pushed me off, and got to his feet, pulling on his jeans and boots as quickly as he could. I kept saying his name, "Hans? Hans? Hans?" But he didn't answer.

'I glanced back and saw that the lights in my house were on – my bedroom light lit. My parents were awake and knew I wasn't there. The light in our front hall was burning, my front door open. A beam flashed through the trees, catching the silver peeling skin of the trees around us. A figure was approaching, a torch in hand. And then I heard my name – my father's voice carrying in the darkness. "Annika?" Hans was full of fear, but I didn't know why. How could my parents not understand love? I clutched the blanket against my naked body as my father came closer. And then Hans was running away, my father's torch on his back.

'My mother's voice penetrated the quiet then, and lights came to life around us as other houses woke up to the sound of the shouting.

'My father shouted at Hans to stop, but he didn't. They reached me and fell to their knees. My mother hugged me hard, sobbing. My father was swearing, asking if I was alright, what had he done to me? Who had done it?'

Jamie could feel a lump of hot iron in her throat, but she said nothing.

'They took me back,' Annika went on, nodding, her own voice strained now, 'and sent me to bed. They made a phone call, argued in the kitchen about something. I was afraid then, myself.' She wiped a tear from her cheek. 'A police car arrived an hour later, my father spoke to the officer on the porch, and then he was gone. I watched it from the top of the stairs, peeking around the corner, still not aware then what I had done wrong. What the problem was.'

'And then what happened?'

'I never saw Hans again.'

Jamie processed it. 'I'm sorry.'

She nodded. 'Of course, I was young. Too young – and Hans, at nineteen. He a man, me a child still. It happens – a lot. Then, now. Older boys and teenage girls. But my parents were very conservative. Hans's too. I found out later that his parents and mine spoke while Hans was in custody, arrested on suspicion of…' She cleared her throat, not wanting to use the word. 'It was never that – *never*. But the age difference…

Hans's parents pleaded, offered to send him away if my parents didn't pursue it. They agreed, reluctantly. And so Hans was sent to the army, and life went on.'

Jamie reflected on the story for a moment. 'So my fa—' She cut herself off, seeing Annika looking at her. 'The detective who came to speak to you twenty years ago. You told him all this?'

Annika looked at Jamie, a little amused. 'Your father, yes.'

Jamie cursed herself.

'Your name is Johansson, his name was Johansson. You look alike... And the fact that you're here asking about the same questions he was... You wouldn't have to be a detective yourself to work it out.'

'I wasn't sure if you would remember him that well,' Jamie said, meeting her eye again.

Annika smiled warmly. 'I do. And yes, I did tell him this story.'

'Do you know how he found you?'

'I suspect he looked into Hans, came to Rättvik, found out that he was arrested and what for, and then tracked me down...'

Jamie couldn't help but be impressed by the idea of it. For all his faults, he was a great detective.

'As I told him, I could see his face changing,' Annika said. 'I could see that he was deciding that Hans was guilty.' She sighed. 'He wouldn't tell me what the investigation was about, but we'd heard stories of girls going missing in Stockholm. Aged thirteen, fourteen... When he confirmed how old I was when it happened...'

Jamie nodded. 'The same age.'

'I assume there was a sexual element at work in those crimes?'

Jamie nodded again. 'Yes.'

Annika saw now the train of logic. 'Hans was arrested soon after your father came to see me. I remember reading about it in the paper. "Angel Maker Suspect Finally In Custody." That was the headline.'

Jamie could see the guilt on her face. 'You may have helped put away a serial killer. You did a good thing.'

'May.' She laughed.

Jamie looked at her quizzically.

'You said "may". I *may* have helped put away a serial killer. You're not sure it was him, are you?'

Jamie said nothing.

'This girl who is dead – you think it's the same killer? As before?'

'I don't know.'

'Do you think Hans could have been innocent?' Annika probed. She had a keen mind. Was connecting the dots as she went.

'We're exploring all avenues of enquiry.'

Annika filled her chest and studied Jamie. 'What were you hoping to get out of this? Coming here?'

'I wanted to know what my father knew.'

'And now you do.'

'And now I do.'

Annika smiled softly. 'Has it helped?'

Jamie thought on it for a moment. 'No,' she said with a sigh. 'It hasn't.'

19

JAMIE STEPPED out into the cold afternoon air, the weight of darkness pressing down on her shoulders.

She looked right and left down the streets, saw nothing but a quiet road, and then headed down onto the steps, shrouded in a mist of her own warm breath.

Annika followed her out onto the porch, the deathly silence of Swedish winter hanging in the air. 'I'm sorry I couldn't be of more help,' she said as Jamie paused on the path and turned back.

'No – you were very helpful,' Jamie said, telling the truth. 'I don't know if Hans Sjöberg was guilty, but at least I know why my father thought he was. And that helps – a lot.'

Annika smiled sadly. 'I can't tell you whether Hans murdered those girls or not. But the boy I knew was sweet and gentle.'

'People change,' Jamie said cynically.

'Sometimes,' Annika answered optimistically. 'But not always.'

Jamie bit her lip, wondering which way to turn now. She had her hands in her pockets, rolling her phone over and over in her hand. She should call Wiik. Debrief. Hear what Leif Lundgren had to say. Tell him what Annika had told her. Then go from there. Jesus, she was struggling to keep it all straight in her head.

Annika lingered on the porch. 'Was there something else?' she asked.

'No,' Jamie replied, nodding a goodbye. 'I'll be in touch if anything comes to mind. But I don't think it will. Sorry to bring all this up again.'

'It's no trouble,' Annika answered, waving as Jamie stepped backwards. 'Drive safe.' She shuddered in the cold and then went back into the house, closing the door behind her.

Jamie squinted into the frigid wind that seemed to have picked up while she was inside. It whipped down the deserted street and threw the hem of her peacoat behind her. 'Jesus,' she muttered as it sank its teeth through all four layers she was wearing.

Jamie froze then, right in the middle of the street, no more the five paces from her car.

It was slouched low on its tyres, the alloys pressed flat against the surface of the road.

Something white flapped against the windscreen, pinned under the wiper.

She narrowed her eyes, pricking her ears, her right hand instinctively going to her belt. It grabbed at nothing and then her brain kicked into gear. Shit, she hadn't carried a gun for nearly a year now.

Jamie scanned the night-drenched street – nothing moved – and started forward.

The wind whistled in her ears, the trees rustling all around.

As she got closer, she saw her tyres had been slashed.

The clouds moved quickly overhead, thinning in bursts, creating waves of moonlight that illuminated the sharp edges of sliced wet rubber.

Jamie crouched and ran her fingers over it – a sharp blade. Small. Smooth. Not serrated. She thought about what Claesson had said of the cuts in the girl's back. A retractable knife or small hunting knife.

Jamie swallowed.

The wound was tight, the edges of the exit widened like puckered lips. Someone had stabbed in and then dragged the knife out. With force. Four times. Once on each wheel.

She stood now and looked around again – but there was no sign of anyone.

Jamie still felt eyes on her, though, her hackles firmly up, heart beating quickly against her ribs.

She wasn't cold anymore, her skin prickling with hyperawareness.

Her fingers touched the windscreen and felt their way down as she kept inspecting every shadow and crevasse on the street.

They stopped as the paper hit her knuckles, and stole a glance, pulling the rectangular page free.

It had three smooth edges, one jagged, as though it had been ripped from a book. Jamie's eyes widened as she recognised the shape. It was unmistakable – the same as her father's notebook.

She dragged the one she was carrying from her pocket to confirm and held the paper against it to make sure.

A perfect match.

But that would mean... Jamie felt her body stiffen, her stomach knot. Jesus, they'd been in her house? The thought made her feel sick.

But perhaps the only thing more unsettling than that were the words scrawled across the back.

YOU DON'T UNDERSTAND. STOP.

WIIK WAS ANGRY – which wasn't what Jamie was expecting.

'See,' he said shortly. 'This is why you shouldn't have gone.'

Jamie didn't understand. 'What? You think this is my fault?' she snapped as she watched a tow truck drag the little hatchback up onto its bed from across the street. An orange flashing light spun lazily on its roof.

'Yes,' Wiik said, a tone of clear condescension in his voice. 'If you hadn't gone out there, this wouldn't have happened. We should have both gone to see Lundgren.'

'But if I hadn't come out here, then the killer wouldn't have tried to scare me.'

'Exactly.'

Jamie closed her eyes, shaking her head at Wiik's stubbornness. 'This is a good thing.'

Wiik stayed silent.

'At least now we know we're on the right trail – the killer doesn't want us looking into the original case,' Jamie went on. 'We're close.'

'We've been doing nothing *but* look into the original

case,' Wiik replied. 'And this is the first hint that we've crossed some sort of line.'

'The killer is—'

'We don't know who left that note. It could have been anyone.' Whether Wiik was just trying to punish her for going it alone, she didn't know. But it felt like it.

'Look – someone followed me out here,' Jamie said flatly, checking her watch. It was after seven now and her hands were completely numb. Annika had come out and brought her another cup of tea, but otherwise, she'd been standing at the kerb waiting for the truck. 'And when I was questioning Annika, they slashed my tyres, and put the word "stop" on a piece of paper for me to find. If that doesn't tell you we're on the right track, I don't know what does.'

'I'm under no illusions we're not on the right track, Johansson, but this is serious. There's a killer out there, and it's pretty clear that he's not got any scruples about who he kills. Nyström is missing – and if you're right about the killer taking him off the board, then a badge doesn't scare this guy either.'

Jamie sucked in a hard breath, staring down at the note that was under her wiper.

'It's not that I'm not concerned about what happened – the opposite, in fact,' Wiik went on. 'We're just getting different things from it. You think that this is a path to keep following – to keep pushing this guy until, what? He takes a shot at your life? And I suppose you just expect to see him coming, roundhouse him in the face like you did Lindvall?'

Jamie gritted her teeth.

'Jesus, Johansson, if he did follow you from the city, then that meant you were being tailed for hours and didn't even realise it. Someone followed you all the way out there, waited for you to go into that house, and then slashed your tyres. All while you were sitting, what, twenty metres away sipping a cup of tea?'

Jamie looked up at Annika's house. It was more like fifteen – at the most. She swallowed and said nothing.

'If this guy wants to get at you, he can. This was showing you that. And you've got to think about this – if he's taken Nyström out, if he's threatening you – and you *are* on the right track, turning over the right stones – then what does that mean for Annika Liljedahl?'

Jamie's jaw tightened, her eyes still on the woman's house.

'What's to say the killer isn't still watching the house? Waiting for you to go? What's to say he doesn't go in there tonight and slit her throat while she sleeps?'

Jamie lowered her eyes. 'Okay. Okay.' She sighed. 'I get it.'

'I've spoken to Rättvik Polis – they're on the way over to speak to Annika, advise her to stay with family if she can, do a once-through of the neighbourhood. And they'll increase their presence in the area tonight, too, sweep regularly for anything unusual.'

'Will it be enough?' Jamie asked, as much to herself as Wiik.

'I don't know. But it's all they can do.' He quietened for a moment. 'There's a lot going on – a lot of leads to pursue. And you have to remember – you're not police. Not here. You're a civilian consultant assisting with a case.'

'I know.'

'Do you? I'm glad of your help, really, I am—'

Jamie couldn't tell if he was being sarcastic or not.

'—but I won't risk your life or anyone else's. You're under my supervision, and what you do reflects directly on me. Alright?'

'Yeah,' Jamie said, unable to keep the dejection from her voice. As much as she hated it, she knew he was right.

'Are you coming back to the city tonight?'

Jamie stared at her injured car. It was up on the truck now and the driver was securing the wheels with ratchet straps. 'I don't know – I doubt it. The mechanic said that his garage won't open until the morning. I probably won't be able to get the tyres swapped until then.'

'Okay. Keep that note safe. We'll hand it over to Foren-sics tomorrow and they can run analysis on it. We'll go see Sjöberg's wife to get access to his effects from the prison – get the letter from Eriksson. Get all three in together. Who knows, maybe we'll get a hit on a handwriting match.'

'For Eriksson?' Jamie asked, cocking an eyebrow. 'You don't really think it's him, do you?'

Wiik made an indistinct noise. 'I'm not ruling anyone out just yet.'

The mechanic was beckoning Jamie over now. 'I've got to go,' she said, stepping down off the kerb.

'Sure. Look after yourself, Jamie.'

He hung up, the last word ringing in her ear. It was the first time he'd used her first name.

She approached the truck, pocketing her phone. With her other hand, she reached inside her coat and touched the top of the note tucked in the pocket there. She hadn't told Wiik that it matched her father's notebooks. She'd seen Wiik's – the newer ones were black, square. This was definitely from an older one. And if the killer was trying to scare her, what better way to do it than to use one of her father's own pads?

The killer was taunting her.

The mechanic was talking now, but Jamie couldn't hear him. His voice was just a muted echo somewhere outside her mind.

She needed to get back – to check. As fast as she could.

But right now, she had to think. Who would know about the notebooks? Who would think to use one? Why not any old random slip of paper?

She thought of the writing and what Wiik had said – the priest. Eriksson.

She'd pulled her pad out just that morning in front of him, to take notes. He'd mentioned that her father always had his but never wrote a damn thing in it. Had asked whether it was his?

Jamie exhaled hard. Fucking Eriksson. It had to be. They needed that letter that Hans had received. Needed to run analysis. They needed those phone records. They needed to know where he was on the night that the girl was murdered, the night that Nyström went missing. They needed his computer. They needed everything. And most of all, they needed to get him in an interview room. And fast.

'… is that okay?'

Jamie looked up, realising that the mechanic – a guy in his forties with a scruffy beard – had finished speaking.

'Uh,' Jamie said, shaking her head, having not heard a word of it. 'Sorry, can you say that again?'

He looked confused. 'I said, I'll drop you off in the middle of town – at the taxi rank – then take the car to the shop. You can pick it up in the morning. Is that okay?'

Jamie exhaled, her stomach still not settled. 'Sure,' she said. 'Sounds great.' She shook her head, barely registering, her mind a maelstrom.

He climbed up into the cab and Jamie went around the other side, getting in. The mechanic shoved the truck into gear and then sidled down off the verge and started along the road. Jamie stared out of the window, at the square of yellow cut out in the darkness, Annika Liljedahl's front window, and wondered, frighteningly, whether she was the only one looking at it.

And then it was gone, obscured by trees.

The truck ploughed forward, chugging into the darkness, and Jamie leaned back closing her eyes. It had been a string of long days, and she didn't think they were about to get any shorter.

It was after eleven by the time Jamie rolled to a stop outside her childhood home in Stockholm.

She'd had to bribe the mechanic to re-open his shop and do an after-hours swap on her tyres. It wasn't cheap, but it was worth it.

As Jamie pulled up onto the highway, she'd floored it, pushing the tiny hatchback as hard as the hybrid engine would allow. She sped along in the outside lane, passing car after car. And then, when she was sure no one was tailing her, she crossed all three lanes and left at a random exit for a town a little way outside the city.

She found a quiet street to park in that had clear line of sight in either direction, and waited.

Thirty minutes passed before she was sure that no one was on her tail, and then she set off again.

She wouldn't make the same mistake twice and had no intention of letting a killer track her back to the city. If this was the sick game he wanted to play, then she wasn't about to skip her turn.

Jamie killed the engine, coming back to the present, and stared up at the darkened house in front of her.

She exited the car and pulled her coat tight around her.

The silence in the street was heavy, pressing in on her eardrums.

Jamie moved quickly, approaching the front door, and paused. The path up to it was covered in a thin sheet of crunched-down ice from the foot traffic. Hers and Wiik's.

But there were fresh tracks now, leading off around the side of the house. Through the garden and the snow there. There'd been no fresh snowfall for a few days and the marks were clear. Someone had walked the path and then stepped off.

Jamie leaned out, seeing them disappear around the corner. A low fence separated her house from the one next door. Whoever had walked there wouldn't have been able to stay out of sight.

She tensed her jaw, squinting in the dim light coming off the streetlights, trying to put a timeline on it. When had she been here last? Yesterday morning. And Wiik had picked her up directly from the hotel this morning.

She checked her watch, shivering in the cold night air. 11.19 p.m. As good as forty hours. Shit, that was a big window.

Jamie knew better than to follow the tracks and disturb any potential evidence. She'd get inside, sweep the house, ascertain what was missing, where he'd got in, and then she'd decide what to do. She needed to speak to Wiik – to debrief him on Sjöberg, to find out what happened with Lundgren. But she wasn't going to call him tonight. She didn't feel like explaining why she'd lied. She didn't quite know herself. Up until she'd put two and two together, she had every intention of staying in Rättvik. But now... there wasn't a moment to lose.

Jamie let herself into her house and moved quickly – quietly – through the kitchen, and into the dining room. She slowed, taking a breath, and scanned it. Nothing looked amiss.

Moonlight came in through the broken slat on the shutters in a shaft and fell on the table. She could see her finger marks in the dust from the day previous where she'd laid out the sheets of paper – the transcriptions from her father's notebook.

The notepad that detailed the Angel Maker case was safely back at the hotel in her duffle bag – Wiik – or at least, Hallberg – had the transcribed notes, he didn't need the original. Her father's final notebooks, detailing the years after Jamie left were at the hotel, too, inside a padded envelope, along with the pictures from the fridge, the two medals her father had earned, the braided bracelet from her bedroom he'd made for her as a child, and a few other personal effects of his. His final notebook – the one he'd been using in the weeks before his death – that was in her pocket right now.

But there were still two other stacks of pads still here. Shit. She'd have to take all of them, go through them, see if any were missing, if any had pages torn out.

Jamie gritted her teeth, still staring at the table. No, she couldn't. Wiik was right – this wasn't her case. And she wasn't police. She was here to assist. She'd need to call it in, and as much as she hated the thought, there'd be CSTs crawling all over the place come morning. They'd have to take the notebooks for analysis, take moulds of the boot marks in the snow, pull prints from the...

Jamie's eyes drifted upwards to the missing slat.

The back door.

She walked towards it, heart beating heavily in her chest.

They were old, wooden-framed sliding doors. The shutters outside weren't locked, just shut with a simple latch that fell across the gap and rested on a notch. If someone put a blade between both doors, they could easily push it upwards and free them.

Jamie swallowed and studied the whole set-up.

The lock was a simple tumbler lock – easy enough to pick for those who knew how.

She filled her lungs with a shaky breath and squinted down through the missing slat.

Footprints.

In the snow.

Outside.

Someone had come to this door.

She could see lots of them, like they'd spent time there, moved around in front of it.

A well was worn against the doors, but Jamie couldn't tell if they'd been opened.

The latch was back on the shutters and the door was...

She lifted her hand towards the handle to check if it was locked and froze. Shit – she didn't want to wipe away any prints if there were any.

She couldn't risk contaminating any evidence.

Jamie backed away and turned to the office instead, trying to figure out what she was going to do. She'd call it in the morning – tell Wiik she set off from Rättvik first thing, came here, and saw the prints. Yeah, so long as he didn't check the hotels there, she'd be fine.

Jamie exhaled, looking around her darkened house. It felt different – contaminated. Poisoned, somehow.

She glanced at her feet, wondering whether the killer had stood in this spot. Whether he'd had a smug fucking grin on his face. Inside Jörgen Johansson's house – the detective who *almost* caught him. And now he was screwing with his daughter, too. Raising a big middle finger.

Jamie felt her jaw tighten, her nostrils flare.

Fuck it. If this guy wanted to play this game, then she'd bite.

The joke was on him, though.

Because he had no idea who she was. Or what she was capable of.

Jamie started forward, aiming for her father's office. If the house was about to be full of police and CSTs, then there were a few things she wanted to take care of first.

22

---

*J*AMIE,

Something happened today. Something that I'm not proud of.

I'm sure they'll say I've finally lost it, but if you could have been there – heard what he said.

I'm sorry. For who I am. For the man I couldn't help but be.

I wanted to be different – you need to know that. I just didn't have the strength.

Just... don't believe everything she says about me, okay? She's used you against me since the moment you left. And I'm afraid of going and you living your life thinking that I didn't love you.

I just don't know what else I can do now. Nothing seems to matter anymore.

My only consolation is that I don't feel like I'm leaving you now. I did that a long time ago. But I deserve to feel like this, because I didn't fight hard enough.

Not hard enough for you, at least.

We won't see each other again. I've come to terms with that.

I'm just waiting.

23

It was 7.26 a.m. and darkness was still very much upon the city when Jamie rounded the gates and headed into the *Norra Begravningsplatsen*. The Northern Cemetery.

Her feet pounded the asphalt of the sprawling network of paths, her brow bristling with sweat. It oozed out of her skin and evaporated in a thick mist that streamed behind her.

She was moving fast and had already racked up nearly ten kilometres.

The counsellor she had to see after she was put on administrative leave told her she couldn't outrun her problems.

But she'd never seen Jamie run.

Jamie streaked through the cemetery, somewhere between a jog and a sprint, and let her legs tell her where to go. The hotel had refused to open the pool early two mornings in a row, so she'd been forced to find a twenty-four-hour supermarket and buy a very questionable pair of running shoes.

But they did the job, she was moving, and that was all that mattered.

Jamie was out of her head, thankfully, if only for a few

short seconds at a time. She focused on her heart, her breathing, her feet, and let the road guide her.

And then she realised where she was and slowed to a stop.

Her hands found her hips, her shoulders rising and falling fiercely as she stepped off the path and onto the grass. It was covered with snow, but channels were cut between the headstones.

Her skin prickled, her shoulders slick with sweat, exposed outside the running-vest she was wearing.

Jamie's throat ached as she walked, catching her breath, nearing the place she'd not been aiming for, but that she knew she couldn't have avoided if she tried.

The cemetery was silent around her. The trees bowed a little, holding snow up to the sky in tribute. All quiet, all sombre. All shadows and darkness.

When she got there, she stood back a little, staring down at the stone baseplate, the empty brass vessel that hadn't seen flowers for nineteen years.

The name carved into the headstone: *Jörgen Johansson.*

Jamie stared down in the darkness – there was just enough creeping light in the sky to pick out the letters – and clenched her jaw. The inscription read, *Loving Father, Devoted Husband, Taken From Us Too Soon.*

She wanted to kick the fucking thing down, spit on it.

Not because it was her father's grave, but because of her mother's words written there.

That guilty bitch had bawled her eyes out at the funeral – had been consoled by her father's colleagues. She'd sobbed and sobbed, drowned out the priest who spoke. Made sure it was all about her – that she was seen as the grieving widow pining for a lost love. When it had been her vicious spite that had put that barrel in his mouth.

That was a week after Jamie's eighteenth birthday.

Her father had called on the morning of it. Had asked to speak to Jamie.

Her mother had refused. Had told him Jamie didn't want anything to do with him.

An hour later that gun was in his mouth.

Jamie swallowed hard, her lips trembling with rage. 'Sorry, Dad,' she whispered, the words barely clawing their way up her tightened throat. 'Things should have been different.' Jamie hung her head, felt the sting of the cold on her back, and ran the back of her hand across her face, wiping away what she told herself were beads of sweat.

She picked her head up then and looked around. The cemetery was deserted, but she didn't feel alone. She couldn't help but wonder if those unseen eyes from Rättvik had followed her home.

Jamie checked her watch – just after half past. Why did she have to lie to Wiik? Even if she'd got the mechanic up early, she'd still not make it back to the city before ten at the very earliest. She shook her head, annoyed at herself for being so stupid. She couldn't call him until then about the house or he'd know something was up. She should have just called him the night before. And she definitely shouldn't have gone inside her house. She may have potentially contaminated a crime scene, destroyed evidence. This is what happens when you let your emotions rule you, she thought, anger bubbling in her.

She exhaled, cursing herself, and shifted from foot to foot, staring down at her father's grave. She'd been eighteen the last time she stood here. A strange weight laid itself on her chest and crushed the air from her lungs.

Jamie had to keep moving, or she knew she'd break down.

Her feet were heavy, didn't want to move. But she forced them to. She still had a long way to go and she couldn't crack yet.

She took off, willing warmth back into her muscles, and circled away from the cemetery, taking a wide loop back to the hotel.

Then she would eat, she would rest, she would recharge.

And then she would catch a killer.

It was eleven in the morning when the first of the flashing blue lights rounded the corner of her street and made a beeline for her.

Jamie was standing at the kerb in front of the rented hatchback, staring up at her house.

A patrol car and two CST vans rolled to a halt behind her, and the first of the CSTs disembarked.

A woman approached quickly in white overalls, a hood around her shoulders, a face mask hanging loosely under her chin. 'Inspector Johansson?' she asked, smiling.

'Yes,' Jamie answered.

'I was told you had something for us to put in for examination?' She was holding a clear evidence bag between her fingers and lifted it to illustrate.

Jamie reached inside her coat and pulled out the letter that had been tucked under her windscreen wiper.

The tech pulled on a blue vinyl glove and reached out, taking it from Jamie's fingers and slotting it into the bag.

Jamie was mouthing a thanks when the sound of tyre-roar cut through the din of the engines idling around her.

Wiik's car whistled towards them in the cold morning air, the sky a turbulent grey overhead, and then ploughed to a standstill in the middle of it all.

He was out of the cockpit in seconds, striding across the road towards her. 'What happened?' he asked, wasting no time.

Jamie looked over his shoulder at Hallberg, who seemed to have been promoted to co-driver again in her absence. The woman looked tired. Beaten down by Wiik's insatiable good mood and cheery banter, no doubt.

She turned her attention back to Wiik, her story prepared. 'I was looking at the note again last night,' Jamie lied. 'And I realised that the paper was the same size and shape as my father's old notebook.' She drew a slow breath and effect. 'So I came straight here this morning, and noticed that there were tracks in the snow leading around the side of the house.'

Jamie gestured towards the door, a stream of CSTs in white overalls zipping around her and moving up the path. They all stopped at the threshold and pulled blue shoe-coverings on, and then disappeared into the darkness, hard cases and cameras in hand.

Jamie watched as the final one paused, snapping photos of the tracks. 'I went inside,' she said, and noticed that the tracks came up to the back door. That's when I called it in.'

Wiik set his jaw. 'Did you touch anything?'

'No,' she lied.

He nodded. 'Okay – good. Let them do their work. Do you really think that someone broke in and took one of your father's notebooks?'

Jamie raised her shoulders slowly into a shrug, still watching the tech taking photos of the tracks. Another had joined him now and was tapping things into a tablet he was holding. 'I don't know,' she said. 'But I think if the killer had the foresight to take Nyström out before he made his kill, then the idea of me coming around probably rubbed him up the wrong way. And what better way to send a clear message than to let me know that I'm not safe – not even in my own home?'

She turned to face him and saw that Wiik was staring intensely at her. 'This isn't good,' he said, dropping his voice as Hallberg drew close to them. She stood back a little – not wanting to crowd Wiik and give him any other reason to berate her, probably. 'Falk wants to see you,' Wiik added. 'As soon as possible.'

Jamie sighed. Whether it was her boss or not, getting dragged into the office of a senior officer was never fun. 'Okay,' she replied. 'Did you get anything from Lundgren at least?'

Wiik made a sort of *hungh* noise. 'I'll say. The guy was a pure creep.'

Jamie raised an eyebrow. 'How so?'

Wiik shook his head, put his hands on his hips, looking up at the techs as if disapproving of their methods. A third one had joined them at the tracks now and was mixing what looked like plaster in a plastic cup, ready to pour into the first footmark. 'He didn't want to let us in, first off,' Wiik said, still watching them. 'We had to insist pretty hard – told him we just needed to get some background on the case, cross his name off the list, you know?'

'He didn't like that?'

'I'll say.' Wiik scratched his forehead. 'Hallberg pulled some records on him – he and his wife were registered foster carers until 2012. He worked as a risk consultant for an oil company that operated in Norway – so was back and forth a lot – he tried to tell us he wasn't even in the country when Hanna was killed.'

'Was he?' Jamie asked.

Hallberg stepped in now. 'No, he wasn't,' she said. 'I

checked with the company and their records show that he was flown out to one of the drill sites the day before Hanna died. And after her body was discovered, he was immediately flown back to deal with it.'

Jamie processed. 'So it couldn't have been him, then?'

Wiik tilted his head back and forth. 'Hard to say. Depends how long the body was in the snow for. He could have killed her, posed her, hopped a flight out that day, knowing the body wouldn't be found until the next.'

Hallberg dared to argue. 'Though it's highly unlikely – the original report from the pathology lab said that the body of Hanna Lundgren hadn't been out there for more than about twelve hours at the most – and time of death was shortly before that. His flight departed from Gothenburg at two the previous afternoon.'

Wiik made his mouth into a shape that told Jamie he didn't like Hallberg's information, even though she was dead right. 'He was still a creep.'

Jamie remembered something then. 'What about the skin cells found under her nails?'

Hallberg nodded. 'A positive match to Lundgren – but he said that Hanna used to scratch his back for him – he's a pretty big guy, said he couldn't reach it himself. But she had sharp nails.'

Wiik scoffed. 'Bullshit.'

Jamie bit her lip. 'Doesn't sound like a likely story – but impossible to disprove.'

Hallberg nodded. 'Yeah, I guess we'll never know what happened. But something was definitely off about the whole thing.'

'How so?' Jamie watched her, saw the expression on her face. She looked troubled by the meeting.

Wiik interjected. 'Like I said – the guy was a creep. He was really cagey about the whole thing – and when we asked him about the scar…' Wiik turned his head to the side and sucked air through the corner of his mouth.

'Scar?' Jamie queried.

Hallberg fielded that one. 'He had a scar across his neck' – she illustrated with her finger, from under one corner of her jaw to the other – 'old, faded, but clearly there. Looked like he'd been strangled.'

'Garrotted,' Wiik corrected her, not making any effort to mask the condescension in his voice. 'Strangled is with hands. The guy had been garrotted by the look of it.'

'Jesus,' Jamie said. 'When? By who?'

Wiik let out a long sigh, and Jamie caught the odour of sour coffee on his breath. 'He didn't know – he said he was mugged a few weeks after Hanna's death walking home from the shop in the evening. Someone came up behind him, put the wire over his head, pulled back, dragged him to the ground.'

'Doesn't sound like a mugging to me.' Jamie's brow crumpled.

'I didn't think so either,' Hallberg added.

Wiik fired her a hard look for interrupting, and she shrank apologetically.

He cleared his throat and went on. 'He said he fought the guy off, managed to get away.'

'Did he report it?' Jamie asked.

Wiik shook his head. 'No, and Hallberg double-checked. Nothing on file either. He said that he didn't get a look at the guy – he didn't hear his voice, nothing. His wife took him to the hospital, got it stitched up – but lucky for him it was just superficial.'

Jamie took it all in. 'Jesus – that's…'

'Yeah,' Wiik said, pushing his hand over his hair, slicking it to his head.

'That's too weird to be a coincidence.'

'Maybe,' Wiik said.

Jamie rolled the story over in her head again. 'Two weeks after his daughter dies, he gets attacked? Brutally, too. You don't try to garrotte someone unless you want to kill them. And definitely not just to take their wallet.'

Wiik was eyeing her now, watching her work.

'And you said he said, "on the way home from the shop"?'

Wiik nodded in confirmation.

'The shop,' Jamie echoed.

'Yeah, why?'

'You say "the shop" when it's the one local to your house. Otherwise, you'd be coming home from shopping, or from *a* shop.'

Wiik was expressionless, waiting for her to finish.

'The killer targeted Lundgren – knew where he lived.' She picked her head up, looked back at her house, thinking about the killer in her father's office. Following her to Rättvik. Slashing her tyres. 'Stalked him. Hunted him.'

Wiik set his jaw. 'This is why you should have been there.' The words came from his mouth coldly, and behind him Hallberg visibly shrivelled. If he'd have said another word, she would have been in tears.

Jamie resisted the urge to swing a kick into his testicles and cleared her throat instead. Though she didn't know what to say to that. 'Uh,' she started, unable to look away from Hallberg. She had to throw the girl a lifeline. 'Hallberg.' She looked up at Jamie but didn't risk speaking. 'Can you check out the parents of the other victims in the original case? Dig into them, see what you can find, see if anyone else had any run-ins after the murders.'

Wiik eyed Jamie cautiously. 'You think there'll be a pattern here?'

Jamie thought of the seven dead girls. That made fourteen parents. And they had another girl lying on a slab right now, still without an ID. Though Jamie knew she probably had two parents, too. 'I hope not,' she replied, meeting his eye. 'But I'm right about these things more often than I'd like to be.'

Wiik stared at her, deliberated, and then turned to Hallberg. 'Get on it,' he commanded.

She nodded diligently.

Wiik turned back to Jamie. 'You need anything else from the house? Falk is waiting.'

'No,' Jamie said, shaking her head. 'I'm good. I'll let them work.'

Wiik was already turning on his heel. 'Hallberg,' he called beckoning her like a dog. 'You're with me.'

'Wait,' Jamie said, raising her hand. 'Do you mind if Hallberg rides with me?'

Wiik stopped and looked back, hands in the pockets of his coat. He looked confused. 'Why?'

Jamie thought fast. 'I've got some leg-work I need done on Annika Liljedahl and Hans Sjöberg's families, and you said it yourself – she's good at that sort of thing.' She met Hallberg's eye. The girl didn't look like she could take another punch. 'And she doesn't mind.'

Jamie let just a hint of a smirk slip, and Hallberg understood then.

Wiik sighed and waved them off. 'Fine – just go straight to HQ.' He started walking again. 'Falk's waiting.'

Wiik got into his car, the door closing heavily, and Hallberg came over.

'Do you really need me to look into Liljedahl and Sjöberg?' she asked, a waning hope in her voice.

'No,' Jamie said. 'I just thought you might appreciate some breathing room.'

Hallberg laughed sadly. 'More than you know.'

24

Wiik had arrived at HQ ahead of them, and he and Falk seemed engrossed in a heated discussion by the time Jamie and Hallberg got onto the floor and started towards her office.

Falk caught sight of them, raised a hand to Wiik to silence him, and then beckoned them in.

She was sitting down, but Wiik was standing, arms folded, talking at her. She wondered whether Falk was the sort to crack the whip if needed. She still couldn't really get a gauge on Wiik – he seemed to oscillate between cool-headed and competent, and petulant and impetuous. She was hardly the picture of perfection herself, but Wiik's regular groove seemed to elude her.

Hallberg moved ahead confidently – probably more so than Jamie had seen yet – and looked at Falk. Right in the eyes.

Ah. She was trying to impress her. No doubt gunning for a promotion away from Wiik's leash. Jamie didn't blame her.

The door closed slowly behind them, and they were all inside the office then. Wiik made a point of not moving, so

Hallberg had to speak to Falk over the top of her computer monitor, practically getting on her tiptoes to do so.

Jamie moved behind Wiik, nicking the back of his arm with her elbow. He looked at her and she nodded her head to the side slightly, motioning him over.

He furrowed his brow and then took a few steps towards her, giving Hallberg the space she needed.

'What?' he asked, voice hushed, as though Jamie wanted to whisper something to him.

Jamie feigned ignorance. 'What?'

His brow creased further. 'You just...' He trailed off, reading the look of confusion on her face. 'Never mind.' He turned back to the room now and found Hallberg in his spot.

It probably would have been a little brazen for him to barge her out of the way, so he stood where he was, scowling at Falk.

What had they been talking about before Jamie had come in?

'Right,' Falk said, looking at each of them in turn. Her eyes rested on Jamie. 'From what I gather, things aren't looking good,' she said plainly. 'I just spoke to the head CST at the Johansson house.' The words came out of her mouth with detached ease. 'He said that the tracks lead from the path to the back door but that it's difficult to assess whether entry was gained as the rear door was locked upon inspection. So whoever broke in either locked it after them, or just wanted to peek in the windows.'

He was in there, Jamie felt like saying. But she stayed quiet.

'This,' Falk went on, holding her hands out, tapping them on the table as she spoke to emphasise her words, 'is extra to the fact that Detective Johansson here is being targeted by whom we can only assume is the killer.'

This time Jamie did speak. 'I wouldn't say *targeted...*'

'Then what would you say?' Falk answered curtly. 'Stalked? Hunted?'

Jamie set her jaw. Neither were better alternatives.

Falk drew a slow breath. 'Wiik, where are we on the case?'

'We've interviewed three suspects. Per Eriksson, Tomas Lindvall, and now, Leif Lundgren.'

'Do you have anything to tie them to any of the murders, past or present?'

Wiik rolled his lips into a line but didn't say anything firm. 'We have a letter from Hans Sjöberg addressed to Per Eriksson in for analysis – and we're going to see Eva Sjöberg this afternoon to collect Hans Sjöberg's effects, along with the letter he originally sent to Eriksson.'

Falk didn't look impressed.

'And now that we have the note from Rättvik, we'll compare the two and see what we find.'

Falk looked even less impressed then. 'You're resting this case on what, cryptographic analysis?'

'No,' Wiik said, bordering on sullen. 'Of course not.'

Falk shook her head, turning to Hallberg – much to Wiik's dismay. 'You interviewed Lundgren yesterday. What did you find?'

'Uh,' Hallberg said, surprised to be called upon. Damn, Wiik must really have rubbed Falk up the wrong way. She cleared her throat and gained a little courage. 'We did, yes. Lundgren maintains that he had no involvement with the original murders, but we noticed that he had a scar on his throat, and told us that he was attacked a few weeks after his daughter was killed.'

'Attacked?'

'Garrotted,' Wiik grunted.

Falk kept her eyes on Hallberg. 'By the killer?'

'We don't know,' Hallberg said truthfully. 'He never reported the incident, but we're looking into the family members of the other victims in order to establish a pattern.'

Falk raised an eyebrow now. 'You think the families may have been targeted, too?'

Jamie could see Hallberg was on rocky ground, and this was her theory anyway. 'It's too early to tell,' Jamie said without invitation. 'But if there's another side to the original case that went unnoticed, then we need to investigate it.'

Falk fixed her eyes on Jamie now. 'Yes,' she said. '*My detectives* do need to investigate it.'

That was a shot at her. No doubt about it. Jamie said nothing in response.

'So where do you intend to go from here?' Falk asked Wiik now.

He swallowed, tried on a smile. It fell away after a second. 'We'll wait to see what the CSTs can pull from Johansson's house, run analysis on the letters. Hallberg will stay here and dig into the families of the original victims, and Johansson and I will go to Eva Sjöberg's to see if we can collect her husband's belongings.'

Falk wasn't satisfied yet. 'And what about the current victim? Do we have an ID yet?'

'No.'

'Do you have *any* idea who she is?'

He drew a slow breath. 'No.'

'For God's sake,' Falk muttered, shaking her head. 'Four days, Wiik, and you're telling me you don't have a damn clue who the girl is?'

'We have an alert out for missing persons matching her—'

'I don't care. Find out who she is. And do it now. If this

is anything like the last case, she won't be the last. The original victims were all connected – and it's likely these victims will be, too. So getting a positive ID is our number one priority.'

Wiik nodded in confirmation. 'Of course.'

'I don't suppose you have anything on our missing detective, either?' Falk hazarded to ask.

Wiik just looked down now. 'No. Again, we've got an alert out on his car, but—'

She raised her hand and silenced him once more. 'Jesus, Wiik. You told me you could handle this.'

'I can,' he said firmly, and then glanced at Jamie. 'We can.'

She offered him a questioning look, then glanced at Falk, who was now staring at her.

'Right,' Falk said, taking a moment and brushing a loose strand of hair behind her ear. 'I want up-to-the-minute progress reports.'

Wiik nodded, looked at Hallberg like she'd cocked her leg and pissed on him, and then exited the office.

'Wait a second, Johansson,' Falk said as Jamie began to follow.

The door closed slowly behind Wiik, who looked over his shoulder through the glass, stopping to see why Jamie wasn't following.

Jamie tore her eyes away from Wiik and focused on the woman in front of her.

'Sit,' Falk said.

Jamie did, pulling out one of the leather-and-steel chairs in front of her desk.

'How are you doing?' Falk asked, keeping her voice quiet.

'I'm okay,' Jamie said, a little hesitation in hers.

Falk measured her reaction. 'Good. I wasn't sure if the case would prove too much for you.'

'I'm fine,' Jamie reiterated, a little more sternly now.

Falk gave her something like a warm smile. 'I would understand if you weren't. This case would be trying for any detective. And considering its nature, how close to home it is, and your history…'

'I'm fine,' Jamie said for a third time. 'Honestly.'

'Good. Because if you weren't, I'd have no hesitation in pulling you from this case and shipping you off back to London.'

Jamie didn't respond.

'You're making waves here,' Falk went on, leaning on her elbow. She cast a quick eye at Wiik, who seemed to have found something interesting to inspect on one of the nearby desks outside the office. 'But your input on the case has been invaluable so far,' Falk said. 'Wiik has said as much.'

'Has he?' Jamie asked. 'He doesn't seem like the laudatory type.'

That seemed to amuse Falk. 'Wiik can be… difficult. But he's a good detective.'

'I've noticed,' Jamie said.

'Not beyond reproach though.'

Jamie was the one amused now. 'I've noticed.'

'He's headstrong, needs tempering a lot of the time.'

'He does.'

'He's been struggling since he lost his partner. They worked well together.'

'Are they…' Jamie asked, not sure she wanted to hear the answer.

'Dead?' Falk sat back now. 'No – her and her husband decided to have a child. She went on maternity leave, and Wiik was assigned Hallberg as an interim partner.'

Jamie saw where this was going. 'She never came back?'

'She put in for a transfer to cybercrime. It's not as exciting, but it keeps her behind a desk. Her priorities changed – I can't blame her. They're not all like us, after all.' Falk chuckled a little and met Jamie's eye.

What the hell did that mean? Jamie didn't think they were alike at all.

Falk didn't give her much time to think about it, though. 'Wiik's been sore about it since. Thinks she betrayed him.'

'Partners can be close,' Jamie offered. 'Losing one stings.' She drew a breath, thinking about the confirmatory looks Wiik had been shooting her. 'What was she like – his old partner?'

'Much like you,' Falk said, glancing at the man outside the office again. 'Strong-willed, pragmatic, tough. She kept him in line. They were the best I had.'

Jamie saw it now. 'And he thinks I'll be the one to replace her.'

'I don't know,' Falk said. 'In his mind, maybe. He and Hallberg… They don't really see eye to eye. The first few months they were partnered up, she was in here once, twice a week complaining about him.'

'There's a lot to complain about.'

'He's giving her a hard time intentionally, trying to break her.'

'That's mature.'

Falk shrugged a little. 'Wiik can be fragile, and he doesn't take criticism very well.'

'Who does?'

Falk smiled again. 'Olsen was a good investigator. It was a blow to the department to lose her, but a bigger one to Wiik. This is his first big case since he and Hallberg have been partnered up. I was reluctant to give it to him, and I'm starting to regret it,' Falk said honestly. 'But you seem to have a positive effect on him.'

'Do I?' Jamie was surprised.

Falk nodded. 'You do. But my priority is making sure that you're alright. Wiik is a big boy, he can deal with his own mess. You on the other hand...'

'I'm fine.' Jamie did her best not to grit her teeth. Falk was clearly repeating the question to get a rise out of her.

'Okay then,' Falk said, ending the conversation there.

Jamie pushed up out of the chair.

'One more thing,' Falk said as Jamie was halfway out the door.

'Yeah?'

What are your plans after the case?' Falk asked, her expression neutral. Almost disinterested.

'I hadn't given it much thought,' Jamie answered truthfully, a little thrown by the question.

'Well, make sure Wiik doesn't get the wrong idea if you haven't got any intentions of sticking around.'

Sticking around? Jamie set her jaw.

Falk watched her for a moment, smiled briefly, and then looked at her screen.

Jamie took that as a cue to go, and then left the office without another word.

She hadn't even thought about what came after. Whether it was back to Scotland – back to the Met... Or something else entirely.

Wiik stepped away from the desk he'd been hovering at and into Jamie's path. 'What was that about?' he asked, licking his bottom lip nervously.

Jamie studied the man with the slicked-back hair, the expensive watch, the look that told her that everything had to be *just so* for him. That if his life didn't fit into the nice, neat little boxes he felt comfortable with, that it was like having pins shoved in his eyes.

'Nothing,' she said. 'Just making sure I'm okay to carry on.'

'Are you?' He looked expectant.

'Yeah,' she said, putting a hand on his shoulder and squeezing. 'I'm okay.'

'Good.' He seemed relieved. 'Now come on. Let's get out of here before Hallberg sees us.' He turned on his heel and strode quickly away.

Jamie started after him, looking back at Falk's office.

The woman was sitting back in her chair, massaging her lips with her thumb, watching Jamie through the glass.

Jamie turned away and headed for the lifts, and though she didn't turn around again, she knew that Falk's eyes never left her.

25

WIIK DROVE IN SILENCE, as though afraid to speak.

Jamie stared out of the window, wondering if this is where she wanted to be. If there was *anywhere* she wanted to be.

What was there to go back for, anyway? Back to her job, her… 'life'. It was in tatters. Her old partner had moved on, retired, and their relationship was nothing but ash now. Her doing. But the truth all the same.

She had no home in London, and what few belongings she had were in a long-term storage locker.

All she had to go back to was her job – but could she face that again? Could she throw herself back into the Met? The corruption, the lies… She'd carried secrets away from there, heavy ones. She wasn't proud of what she'd accomplished, of what she'd *had* to do to get the job done. But she didn't expect that her father was proud of his choices either.

There's right, and there's wrong, and the cost is irrelevant. Goddamn him and his right and wrong shit. It was in her bones, her soul, seared into her mind and into her chest. It might as well have been branded on her skin.

Wiik slowed down and swung into the road that lead to Hans and Eva Sjöberg's church. Its shell sat at the end, staring out at them, Sjöberg's house coming up on the right.

Jamie took a breath and shook off the trepidations. She could worry about the shitshow that was her life later. Right now they had a job to do.

She cast a quick glance at Wiik. He looked pensive, but focused, determined.

The afternoon was wearing on now and Jamie was tired. They'd skipped lunch again, anxious to make headway. The case was getting murky, wires were getting crossed, and though neither said it, they both felt like they were tripping over their own feet. That much was apparent from the look in Wiik's eye. Like a caged wolf.

He pulled in on the verge, in what Jamie thought was the exact same spot as before, and turned the key in the ignition.

Wiik turned his head slowly to look at her. 'Okay?' he asked, his question layered.

Jamie nodded. 'Of course.'

'Ready?'

'After you.'

He gave a brief smile – one of the first Jamie had seen – one that revealed a vulnerability in him she'd ignored before. Wiik had struck her as curt, headstrong, perhaps a little full of himself. Definitely vain.

But now she was seeing more. The exterior was nothing more than a shell. And inside, he was troubled, fragile… lonely.

Jamie swallowed, watching her reflection exit the car. They were different on the outside, but more alike than she was prepared to admit to herself.

She got out and went after Wiik, following him up onto Eva Sjöberg's porch. This time, he allowed her enough space to stand behind him. He knocked firmly and pushed his hands into his pockets out of the cold.

Their breath swam around their heads in a thick haze as the door opened in front of them. Eva Sjöberg stared up from her wheelchair.

'Yes?' she asked, looking from one to the other, her head wobbling back and forth a little.

Wiik's brow furrowed as he stared down into her vacant eyes. 'Kriminalinspektör Anders Wiik, Stockholm Polis,' he said tentatively. 'Do you remember us?'

She looked into the distance between them, as though scraping her mind for the memory. 'You're here about my husband,' she said, as though a lightbulb had just gone off. 'I'm afraid he's not in at the moment.'

Wiik opened his mouth to speak, and then stopped, thrown.

Jamie cut in. 'We know, Mrs Sjöberg. We were hoping we might speak to you, instead.'

'I can only tell you the same as I told the other detective,' she said, apologetically. 'I don't know where that poor girl is.'

'Girl?' Wiik asked, moving forward a little.

Jamie touched his arm, quelling him. 'What other detective?' Jamie asked, keeping eye contact with the woman.

'Uh,' she said, delving into her mind again. 'I don't know... Tall man, blonde hair, very serious...'

Jamie understood then. 'Detective Johansson,' she offered.

Eva Sjöberg's eyes lit up. 'Yes, that was him.'

Jamie afforded a sad smile and glanced at Wiik, who seemed to come to an understanding at the same time. The woman thought it was twenty-five years ago.

Wiik exhaled, scratching the back of his head.

They had to press on, hope that Eva would circle back around to lucidity.

Jamie cleared her throat. 'We would just like to ask some follow-up questions if that would be alright – perhaps take a look at some of Hans's belongings. Just to tick some boxes, standard stuff,' she said warmly, pulling her lanyard from her pocket and holding out the ID card so Eva could read it. Wiik did the same on reflex.

Eva Sjöberg leaned forward, squinting at Jamie's. 'Johansson,' she read aloud. 'Are you and that other detective related?' she asked, looking amused by the idea.

Jamie smiled back at her. 'No,' she said. 'Just coincidence.'

Jamie and Wiik were perched on the sofa for the second time, and Eva Sjöberg was staring at them with a smile on her face, completely oblivious as to what was going on.

They exchanged glances and then looked at the woman in front of them. Jamie expected Wiik to start, but when he didn't, Jamie took the lead.

'Mrs Sjöberg,' Jamie said, smiling all the while. She had to tread carefully, try not to distress her too much. 'Do you know where Hans is at the moment?'

She looked thoughtful for a moment. 'No, I, uh, don't really... Um,' she started, at odds with herself. 'But I'm sure he will be...' She turned to look out of the window and then saddened. 'Oh, my. That's right...' she said distantly, and then looked back at the two detectives. She smiled again now, her eyes glistening. They drifted upwards from Jamie and Wiik to the crucifix hanging on the wall behind the sofa. She made a cross on her chest, clutching a tissue in her bony hand as she did. 'I'm sorry – how can I, uh, how can I help you two?' Her voice was barely louder than a whisper.

Jamie breathed a little sigh of relief. Lucid again. 'When Hans passed, the prison would have delivered a box of his effects, along with his ashes.' She watched the woman carefully, trying to be as direct as she could without being blunt. Hans had been cremated two days after his death. The day before the first body had been found.

'Yes,' Eva Sjöberg confirmed, raising her hand. She pointed at a corridor to their right with her knuckles. 'He's in the bedroom – the box, too.'

Wiik tensed next to her, leaning forward. They were both at the edge of the sofa now, elbows on knees.

'Would you mind if we looked through his things?' Jamie asked, keeping her voice soft. 'I'm not sure if you remember us – we came a few days ago, enquiring about the original case that Hans was—'

'I remember,' Eva said, nodding. 'Why do you need to look at his belongings?' Her voice was sharp now. 'He's dead.'

'I know, Mrs Sjöberg—'

'Even now, two decades on, you still won't leave us alone.' She turned her lip out and shook her head in disgust.

'If you'd let me just—'

'That detective put Hans away for nothing! Beat his confession out of him, put the murder on him and—'

Jamie's teeth were clenched now. She exhaled hard, cutting the old woman off. 'I believe your husband was innocent.'

Eva Sjöberg stopped speaking and eyed Jamie cautiously. 'What did you say?'

Jamie met her eyes now. Wiik was a statue next to her. 'New evidence has come to light,' she said, treading very,

very carefully. 'Which throws the original investigation into question.'

Wiik was barely breathing, staring at the side of Jamie's head. She could feel his gaze on her skin, but she didn't stop.

'We're rebuilding that case, and we need access to Hans's effects in order to pursue a lead that may exonerate your husband.' She spoke clearly, making sure every word rang true in the widow's ears. 'Among his effects, we hope to find a letter – and we hope that it might tie one of the original suspects to a new crime.'

Eva Sjöberg looked drawn. 'A *new* crime?' she asked, her eyes drifting to the cross above the sofa again.

Jamie nodded slowly. 'Yes. Another killing – a young girl. Like the others.'

Eva's jaw began to quiver. *'Min Gud,'* she muttered. My God.

'Would you mind if we...'

The woman nodded, swallowed hard, and then pointed to the corridor again. 'Of course – please. In the bedroom – in the wardrobe. There should be a cardboard box.'

Wiik was on his feet before she'd even finished speaking, and Jamie fell into step behind him.

He powered through the hall and into the bedroom, pushing the door open widely.

The room was modest. An old-fashioned narrow double bed sat in the middle, a tarnished brass headboard behind it. A safety rail pivoted down from the wall next to the pillow on the left-hand side – no doubt to help Eva get in and out. Next to that a small dresser stood, a reading lamp on it. At its side was a silver urn. Hans Sjöberg. Or what was left of him. Above the bed, a wooden cross was hanging. The right-hand wall was occupied entirely by sliding mirrored doors.

Jamie and Wiik were both hit by a wall of frozen air and both gasped as they entered. The rest of the house was so hot.

Wiik turned to face the window opposite the wardrobes and made a beeline for it. It was cracked – just an inch or so. But all the heat had flooded out and the cold air had crept in.

He got halfway, about to close it, when Jamie's brain kicked into gear. 'Wait,' she ordered, throwing her hand out.

Wiik froze mid-stride and looked back.

Jamie glanced over her shoulder down the corridor, listening as the sound of daytime television echoed back to her. Eva Sjöberg had resumed her daily viewing.

Jamie pushed the door closed with her heel and then looked around the room.

'What is it?' Wiik asked, turning back to her.

Jamie bit her lip, not wanting to say it out loud in case that made it come true. She stepped cautiously towards the wardrobe and stopped in front of it. 'Have you got gloves?' she asked as Wiik came up on her shoulder.

He pulled a pair of blue nitriles from his pocket and passed them to her wordlessly, watched as she pulled them on and slid the right-hand wardrobe door open.

The smell of dust rose from within, a rail full of old shirts hanging in front of them. Underneath, a unit with square-shaped compartments was filled with men's shoes and socks. They hadn't been touched in years by the looks of things.

Jamie pushed the doors further along and they began to overlap, exposing more of the wardrobe.

The men's clothes became women's clothes as they edged onto Eva's side of the wardrobe. Jamie looked down at the empty space under the rail – saw shoe boxes, old gift bags, black bags full of clothes, and a gap about three feet wide.

Everything was covered in dust, but a clean square was

present in the space. A square where, until very recently, a box had been sitting.

Jamie swallowed and looked up at Wiik. His jaw was clenched, his nostrils flaring as they both came to the same conclusion.

Hans Sjöberg's personal effects were gone.

They both turned to look at the window, and then turned back to the door.

Jamie nosed ahead, pulled it open, and then they were both back in the living room

Eva Sjöberg looked around, startled, and then seemed to remember who they were. 'Did you find what you needed?' she asked.

'Has anyone else come to see you recently?' Jamie asked, not wasting any time. 'Since Hans's belongings were delivered?'

She looked down for a moment, then met Jamie's eyes, shaking her head. 'No, I don't think so?'

Jamie drew a hard breath. 'Has anyone been around the house – have you seen anyone? Through the windows? Heard anything strange? Have you left the house at any point, or—'

'No, no,' the woman said, reading the alarm in Jamie's voice. 'I haven't seen or heard anything – what's wrong? What's happened?' She leaned from the chair, trying to peer around Jamie and Wiik. 'Is Hans alright?' Jamie could hear the fear in her voice now.

Wiik couldn't contain himself any longer. 'Has anyone called you in the last few days?'

The woman stopped, thinking. 'I don't, uh—'

Wiik pushed past Jamie now so that he was assuming the woman's entire field of vision. 'Did Per Eriksson call you?'

Jesus. Eriksson. Jamie saw the train of thought now. When they'd spoken to him – he'd admitted to speaking to

Hans, admitted to sending a letter back, handed over his own letter... But then he'd know. He'd know that they'd come looking for it. Would know to act fast. He knew the layout of the house, too – admitted to having been in there dozens of times back when he and Hans were friends. He'd know where the bedroom was, would know where the window was... And that to make any sort of meaningful text comparison between the note on Jamie's car and Eriksson's own hand, they'd need his letter to Hans Sjöberg.

She and Wiik both looked at each other and he pulled his phone from his pocket, dialling a number and going for the door.

Jamie went after him, pausing for a moment. 'Thank you, Mrs Sjöberg. There'll be some officers along shortly to conduct an inspection – will that be alright?'

Eva Sjöberg didn't seem to be following.

'Don't go into the bedroom, okay?' Jamie said. 'Just wait for the officers to arrive.'

She nodded slowly, a note of fear and confusion in her voice. 'I don't understand what I've done...'

Jamie smiled at her and took a step closer, reaching out and resting a hand on the woman's arm. 'It's okay,' she said warmly. 'You haven't done anything wrong. They just need to take a look around – it will help to prove Hans was innocent.'

'It will?' She began to tear up then, laying her other hand over Jamie's. 'Bless you,' she said, finding a weak smile. 'God bless you.'

26

BY THE TIME Jamie got outside, Wiik was already barking orders at Hallberg down the phone in the middle of the street. 'I want CSTs out here immediately to search this place top to bottom.' He didn't pause for breath. 'And I need an arrest warrant in place for Per Eriksson an hour ago... On what charges? How about breaking and entering, removing evidence from a crime scene, abduction, gross abuse of a corpse, rape, murder – take your fucking pick!'

He clocked Jamie coming and snapped his fingers at her, beckoning her over.

She didn't appreciate the gesture but she let it slide considering the circumstances.

Wiik kept going. 'Send it over the second you have it, and dispatch uniforms to the church to take him into custody, along with a pair of techs to collect his belongings... I want his phone, his laptop, everything. Then get CSTs over there too... I don't care... The same ones, different ones, just fucking do it! I want Eriksson in an interview room within the hour and his life picked down to the fucking bones. We missed this son of a bitch once, we're not going to again.'

Jamie looked at him again, letting it slide. That wasn't a shot at her father. Even though a few days ago she would have taken it as such.

Wiik hung up abruptly, let out a long breath of thick steam, and then slicked his hair against his head, finally looking up at Jamie.

He didn't say anything, and neither did she. But they both knew they'd missed a step – and it may have just cost them the investigation.

Eriksson was smart. Smarter than they gave him credit for.

He was charming, he was cunning and he'd got inside their heads. He'd manipulated them both – pushed Wiik's buttons until Jamie removed him, and then wrapped Jamie around his little finger with stories of her father. He'd played them both like fiddles. And she was half expecting to receive a call in the next few minutes saying that Eriksson wasn't at the church. That they didn't know where he was.

That he'd slipped through their fingers.

A tight knot built itself in her stomach, and judging by the look on Wiik's face, he was feeling the exact same way.

He groaned, cracked his neck and then licked his bottom lip. 'I need to call Falk.'

Jamie nodded, her own phone vibrating in her pocket. 'Probably a good idea,' Jamie said, pulling it out. She glanced down, reading the text on-screen.

'Everything okay?' Wiik asked.

'Yeah,' she said. 'Just a personal thing, give me a sec?'

He proffered her the open road in front of them and then stepped away, dialling Falk's number.

The message was from a number she didn't have saved, and read:

It's Hallberg – need to talk. No Wiik.

Jamie obliged, and called the number back once she was out of earshot. She could hear Wiik bringing Falk up to speed in the distance.

The phone at her ear rang once and then Hallberg answered. 'Detective Johansson,' she said quickly.

'What's up?' Jamie asked, turning to keep an eye on Wiik. She didn't really want to get caught speaking to his partner behind his back, but she knew she needed to give the girl a chance. She wouldn't get in touch without a reason.

'You with Wiik?' she asked quickly.

'Yeah,' Jamie said. 'But he can't hear us. What's this about?'

'He cut me off before I had a chance to say anything, and I didn't want to call him back, so I thought if—'

'Just spit it out,' Jamie urged her, not wanting Wiik to finish his call before her. He was nodding vigorously as Falk spoke in his ear.

'It's the parents.'

'Parents?'

'Of the original victims.'

Jamie held her breath, sinking her teeth into her bottom lip.

'For five of the seven victims, one parent is missing or dead.'

The words rang in Jamie's ears and it took her a few seconds to process what Hallberg was saying. 'You're sure?'

Hallberg sighed. 'Yeah – I'm sure. I've double- and tripled-checked. The first victim – Christina Bergner – her father was killed in a car accident three months after her death. He was run off the road and into a lake. The other driver was never found. The second, Britta Engdahl, her mother disappeared just two weeks after her death. The father was questioned, but the case was never taken forward – the conclusion was that she simply left because of Britta's death. The third, Hilda Nordell – her father was found a little under a month later. He'd hanged himself in their garage. The fourth, Agnes Floden – her father went missing about six weeks after she died. The mother believed he was having an affair and ran off. But no trace was ever found, and he never got in touch again. The fifth, Elin Wickstrom – her father was stabbed during a mugging. Killer never found. Sound familiar?'

Jamie swallowed painfully. Her mouth had gone dry all of a sudden. But her mind was whirling. 'What was the, uh,' she started, the words more like croaks. 'What was the delay between the murders of the fifth and sixth victims?'

'Around three months,' Hallberg said, all the information right there in front of her. 'Elin Wickstrom was killed in March 1996, and Tilde Gunnarson was killed in early June of the same year.'

'And Elin Wickstrom's father – when was he attacked?'

'In May.'

Jamie closed her eyes, mapping a timeline. 'Were all of the parents' deaths and disappearances before the next girl was killed?'

'Uh,' Hallberg hedged. 'Looks like. Yes.'

Jamie exhaled hard, her hand shaking a little at her ear. 'Hanna Lundgren was the seventh victim, right? And we know her father was attacked. But what about the sixth victim? Tilde Gunnarson?'

Hallberg took a few seconds to look over her notes. 'It doesn't look like anything was reported, but I can look into it a little more. See what I can find?'

'Do that,' Jamie ordered.

'There was a much shorter delay between the last two victims, though.'

'What do you mean?' Jamie eyed Wiik now. His call seemed to be winding down now and he was glancing over, keen to know who Jamie was talking to and what about, no doubt.

'Tilde Gunnarson and Hanna Lundgren were murdered just ten days apart.'

'Jesus,' Jamie muttered, thinking about it. Did the killer know the net was closing in? Did they know her father was getting close? Upped their timeline? She swallowed hard. 'What dates?'

'Tilde Gunnarson was sixth of June – and then... Hanna Lundgren was found on the sixteenth.'

Jamie set her jaw. 'And when was Sjöberg arrested?'

'I pulled the records from the solicitor's firm that represented him. The information was privileged, but they confirmed that they began representing him on the sixth of July 1996. So maybe a day or two before that?'

'Jesus. We have to assume this isn't coincidence. It can't be.' Jamie shook her head, laying it out quickly. 'So the killer takes Tilde Gunnarson, lines up her father, or mother or whoever, but then gets nervous? Knows the net is closing, so he acts fast. Takes Hanna Lundgren first. But why?'

Hallberg was quiet, unsure if it was rhetorical or not.

'Can you look into Tilde Gunnarson's parents? They must have been questioned – but it was all in the case files.' Jamie was thinking out loud now. 'See if you can find any contact details. I want to talk to them.'

'Right. Okay.'

Wiik was coming over now.

'I have to go,' Jamie said. 'Keep me posted on what you find – and don't worry,' she said, reading Hallberg's silence.

'I'll deal with Wiik for you.' She dropped the phone from her ear and hung up.

Wiik narrowed his eyes, maybe catching his name before Jamie ended the call. 'Who was that?' he asked.

'Hallberg,' she said truthfully. 'She wanted to run something by me.'

'What?' Wiik probed.

'A potential link between the original case and some unexplained disappearances.'

'Why didn't she call me?' he asked sharply, offended by it.

'She wanted my opinion before she bothered you with it.'

He didn't know how to take that. 'And?'

Jamie drew a slow breath and looked out into the cold, grey sky. It was early afternoon now and the cloud cover was thick today, bathing everything in a flat, dingy light. 'And I think we're in trouble,' Jamie said.

Wiik waited for her to expound.

'One parent of five of the seven victims either died, was murdered, or disappeared without a trace.'

Wiik's jaw flexed. 'She should have called me with it.'

'She knew you needed to speak to Falk – wanted me to confirm it was worth thinking about. Didn't want to waste your time if not.' She met Wiik's eye, remembering what Falk said about him being quick to conclusions and prone to emotional reactions. About him needing someone to keep him in line. 'The girl did everything right, Wiik. And she uncovered another potential lead in this case. A big one. Don't chide her for it.'

The muscles on his clean-shaven chin all bunched and twitched.

'Now,' Jamie went on, dragging him back to the tracks and setting him straight. 'Hallberg's pulling together some more information for us, but meanwhile, we could be looking at an oversight in the original case – twelve victims, not seven.'

Wiik blinked slowly, taking it in, and then seemed to relax, knowing this outranked any sourness he had over Hallberg calling Jamie first. 'Okay. So what do we do?'

Jamie looked down, thinking for a moment. 'A parent of each of the first five victims was targeted – we need to figure out why. Lundgren was attacked but got away with it. The parents of the sixth victim were left alone. But I think maybe Sjöberg was arrested before any attempt was made.'

Wiik was right there with her. 'But why would that matter if it wasn't Sjöberg? Eriksson could have dealt with them anyway.'

'And risk alerting my father to Sjöberg's innocence?' Jamie shook her head. 'He's too smart for that – no, he got away with it. And he just left them be.'

'So why has he started again now?' Wiik was doing his job – he was testing Jamie's theory. Her line of reasoning.

She measured the focus in his face, could see that he was a good detective. And despite herself, she was beginning to warm to him. He had about as much charm as a cactus, but she respected his mind and his will to get the job done, even if she didn't always agree with his methods. 'I think Sjöberg reached out to him – awakened a part of him that he buried, or let go... He went and spoke to Sjöberg, didn't he? And he said they didn't talk about the murders. He said he never asked and Hans didn't tell.'

Wiik nodded. 'And why would he ask if he knew Sjöberg didn't do it?'

'Exactly. He wouldn't.'

Wiik bared his teeth. 'Son of a bitch,' he growled.

'Eriksson, sitting there, listening to Sjöberg talk about

how he was wrongfully convicted for those killings, how he was innocent – telling Sjöberg he could repent, get into heaven, that all was forgiven – hell, it probably got his juices flowing again. Sitting there, face to face with the man who went to prison for his own crimes – he starts thinking maybe he can pull it off again. Get away with it a second time.'

'Shit,' Wiik said, putting his hands on his hips. 'I wish we could get a copy of that conversation.'

'If it was a visitor's conversation we'd have a chance. But a deathbed confession with a priest? No way. No one would think to, let alone enforce that.'

Wiik agreed sullenly. 'So Eriksson takes the girls, kills them, works the religious angle to frame Sjöberg, and—'

'Maybe not just to frame him. He worked at a church as the groundskeeper, then went to a seminary. He must be interested in it – maybe just the iconography or the history or—'

'The way religion is used to indoctrinate and control people?'

Jamie was surprised, but noted the look of semi-disgust in Wiik's face. He really did hate the whole idea of it all. 'It chimes with the classic psychopath profile. They are drawn to professions that allow them to control people. And if he was interested in theism, a priesthood would give him the opportunity to not only embrace that obsession, but also satiate that need to control.'

Wiik looked over Jamie's head, thinking now. 'So he comes back from visiting Sjöberg and starts scheming? He lines up Nyström, knows he needs to get rid of him to clear the field.'

'Kidnaps him, gets him to talk him through stealing the case files,' Jamie added.

'Then he finds himself a victim and goes to work.'

'You don't understand,' Jamie said, bunching her mouth under her nose.

Wiik's brow furrowed. 'What don't I understand?'

'No, not *you* – the note. On my car. It said, "You don't understand. Stop."'

'Okay. So what don't we understand?' Wiik asked.

Jamie shook her head. 'I don't know – but we need to get back. If Hallberg's lead is right and Eriksson is targeting the parents as well, then we need to ID our victim fast – or we could have another kill on our hands.'

Wiik agreed, letting his own hands go to his sides. He raised one then and ran it over his head, slicking his hair to his scalp. 'If Eriksson is following the same method he did before, then we can circulate the photo of the girl – put out a statement to the press. They're beginning to frenzy as it is. They don't deal well with radio silence, and we need to make headway. Throw them a bone before they crucify us, and see what comes back. I don't like doing it, but we're out of options here.'

'Yeah, we are.'

Jamie and Wiik looked at each other for a second, and then Wiik went for the car. 'Come on,' he said, walking fast. 'Let's get going before anything else happens.'

Jamie caught up with him. 'Don't say that.'

'Why not?'

She circled to the other side of the car and looked at him across the roof. 'Because every time someone does, something else happens.'

Wiik cracked a smile. 'You didn't strike me as the superstitious type, Johansson.'

'I'm not,' Jamie said, getting into the car. 'I've just been doing this long enough to know not to tempt fate.'

27

JAMIE AND WIIK got about five hundred yards before his phone started ringing.

It flashed up on the centre console and filled the cabin. He reached out and pressed the button. 'Anders Wiik,' he said, glancing across at Jamie.

'Kriminalinspektör Wiik?' came a breathless voice. Female.

'Yes – who is this?' he asked.

'My name is Sanna Eliasson – I'm a nurse at Söder-sjukhuset Hospital,' she said speaking quickly. 'There's a note on the file here to inform you of any developments concerning Tomas Lindvall.'

'Is he awake?' Wiik asked, leaning forward a little in anticipation.

'I don't know how to... He has—' She cut herself off, coughed away from the phone, and then came back to the receiver. 'He has escaped.'

Wiik stood on the brake so violently that Jamie nearly headbutted the dashboard. Her neck clicked nastily, and she swore under her breath as Wiik wrestled the Volvo onto the hard shoulder at the side of the road, sending it snaking to a stop on the icy tarmac. 'What did you just say?'

'Tomas Lindvall regained consciousness, and while he was being assessed, he assaulted a nurse, took her hostage, and then escaped.'

Wiik slammed his open palm into the steering wheel so hard it made the whole car shake. 'Goddamnit! When was this?'

'About forty minutes ago?'

'Forty minutes?' He nearly yelled it. 'Why didn't somebody call me?'

Sanna Eliasson scoffed. 'Lindvall assaulted a nurse! He threatened her life, terrified half the patients here. We've had our hands full.'

Wiik hung his head between his taut shoulders and muttered something under his breath. 'Did you manage to get anything from him before he escaped?'

'I don't understand the question,' the nurse said plainly.

'Information – did he say anything? Did he mention anyone? Friends, family, where he might have been going?'

'No, inspector,' Eliasson said, her voice taking on a cold air of scorn. 'We concern ourselves with the welfare of our patients – not their interrogations.' And with that, she hung up.

Wiik's nostrils were flaring wildly, his anger bubbling over.

Jamie rubbed her neck. 'We'll find him. If he's got a history of mental illness, then his information will all be on file. Next of kin, family contacts, previous addresses. All of it.'

Wiik said nothing, but slowly picked his head up and looked out of the windscreen. Cars streaked past and made the car rock slightly in their wake. The city swam in front of them, hazy in the cold air. Jamie remembered this weather well. There was an eerie stillness at work now, the clouds sagging low over the buildings. They'd burgeon as night closed in, descend to street level in a freezing fog, and then beckon a frozen drizzle in their wake. By morning, the ground would be covered in fresh snow.

Wiik spoke suddenly. 'Does Lindvall fit into this?' His voice was quiet.

'Into the case?' Jamie confirmed, resting her head back. 'I don't know – he ran when we cornered him. He's got the history for it. He was in proximity to one of the murders – but does he have the guts, the skills, the intelligence to pull off something of this magnitude? I don't know.'

'"You don't understand,"' Wiik repeated. 'What don't we understand?'

That question was like a rasp being run along Jamie's teeth. It made her uneasy to think about it. 'I don't know.'

'I bet there's a lot a paranoid schizophrenic would think we wouldn't understand.'

'Maybe. Though he was unconscious when I drove out to Rättvik and had the note put on my car,' Jamie offered diplomatically. 'But whether he's involved in this or not, we need to find him.'

Wiik nodded slowly. 'I'll get Hallberg to go through his records, and then we'll dispatch officers to see his family, see whether he turns up. But for now, I think we need to keep our attention on Eriksson. Lindvall is just…' He looked pained to say it. 'Collateral damage. This is on me.' He looked at Jamie now, boxing up the guilt and responsibility he felt and stuffing down inside him. 'But we can't let it cloud the investigation. We stay on Eriksson, and we get him talking.'

Jamie nodded to confirm that she thought that was the

best course of action, and then Wiik pushed the car into drive and pulled swiftly onto the road, the electric motor hurling them back towards the city at speed.

An hour later, they were back in Ingrid Falk's office, polishing the statement they were going to make to the press. A press liaison had already been briefed and had lined up a spot on the evening news with the three local channels and sent a photograph of the victim to the local newspapers.

To circulate the photo like this was a last resort. To alert parents to the death of their daughter by way of showing her picture on the evening news? It was the sort of thing that could blow up in the department's face and put them under a microscope for misconduct.

But it was all they had. No one had come forward to report her missing. There were no DNA matches on the database. There was nothing. Total radio silence.

But the killer knew who she was. And more frighteningly, knew her parents as well if history was anything to go by.

They needed to find out who she was, and fast.

Falk was reading over the latest draft of the statement – a matter-of-fact delivery of information that did its best to sound apologetic, consolatory, humble, concise, honest about the potential danger faced by the victim's family, and yet not alarming. Which was proving to be difficult.

Jamie and Wiik sat in silence, watching Falk go through the page, the words reflecting in the lenses of her reading glasses, a pen flicking back and forth between her raised fingers.

A light knock on the door behind Wiik and Jamie made them turn.

Hallberg was hanging through the gap and Falk looked up. 'Officers are on scene at the church with CSTs now,' Hallberg said.

'And?' Wiik asked, trying to read her tone.

Hallberg bit her lip and averted her eyes, looking at Falk instead. 'No sign of Eriksson. And the church minibus is gone.'

Wiik hung his head, massaging his temples with his thumb and middle finger of his right hand, his face buried in his palm. 'He's running.'

Jamie cursed silently, but tried to focus on what they did have. 'Pull his records – see if he has any other properties, another house, an apartment, or—'

'Already did,' Hallberg cut in. 'And he doesn't. A tactical team can be on site at the church in fifteen if you want me to put the request in?' She was still looking at Falk.

'Do it,' she said sternly. 'I want that place pulled apart. Leave *nothing.*'

Hallberg nodded.

'Find him, Hallberg,' Falk commanded. 'If he's driving a sign-written church minibus, he won't be able to go far.'

'Do you want me to set up checkpoints? Put out a notice?'

Falk thought on that for a second and Wiik looked up, waiting for her to answer.

'No,' Falk said measuredly. 'No, it's too soon for that.'

'Falk,' Wiik said, his voice wringing with insubordination. 'You can't be serious?'

She looked at him now, about as sternly as her fine features could manage. 'He's a suspect, Wiik, and we have no evidence to—'

'No evidence?' Wiik scoffed.

'Yes, *no* evidence,' Falk finished. 'We have three words

written on a piece of paper tucked under Johansson's windscreen, and a letter from Hans Sjöberg that quite frankly proves nothing at all.'

'The letter is *key,*' Wiik said, leaning forward and putting his hand flat on Falk's desk.

Falk looked at it and waited for him to remove it before she continued, refusing to rise to his volume or match his tone. 'The letter is a plea to an old friend to come and see a dying man – it mentions nothing of the original case, it mentions nothing of either Sjöberg's or Eriksson's involvement, and it will have absolutely no bearing whatsoever in court.'

Wiik was seething. But Jamie knew Falk was right. She'd read the letter. All Sjöberg apologised for was for not being a better friend: *I'm sorry about what happened – I still don't quite understand how it all worked out the way it did. I'm sorry for not reaching out sooner. I hope you're doing well. I've elected to stop treatment. It would mean a lot if I could see you before the end. I hope you can find it in yourself to hear me out. Blah, blah, blah.*

In legal terms it was jack shit. And whether Wiik knew how to origami it into the shape of a pistol or not, it was never going to be the smoking gun he needed.

Falk carried on, sitting back in a relaxed pose, defusing Wiik by the second. 'We cannot get ahead of ourselves here, Wiik. You know that, don't you?'

He sulked.

'Eriksson could be doing a thousand things right now – and only one of them is fleeing because he's the Angel Maker. We're already going out on a limb here by releasing a photograph of an unidentified victim – and a minor at that – to the public. Which puts us in a *very* vulnerable position, as I'm sure you know. I'm not going to exacerbate the situation by putting up roadblocks and sending every officer we have scouring the city for a borderline-geriatric priest who may or may not even be involved with this crime.'

Wiik's fists had balled on the arms of the chair.

Hallberg was still hovering by the door, but knew not to get in the middle of it.

'And,' Falk went on, beating Wiik fully into submission, 'that's not even taking into account the paranoid schizophrenic you interrogated into a manic state, and then set loose upon the city.' She lowered her head to catch his eye. 'The last thing I want is for the press to catch wind of that, too. I can see the headlines now: "Suspect in original case now prime suspect in new killings – Stockholm Polis bungled original Angel Maker investigation… Paranoid schizophrenic pushed to breaking point by Stockholm Polis, attacks nurse and escapes custody…. Kriminalinspektör without patience causes widespread panic in the city by acting rashly."' She paused for effect. 'Dealer's choice.'

Wiik had clammed up totally and judging by the way he was pouting, he got the message.

Falk drew a breath and looked up at Hallberg. 'Have CSTs go over the church with a fine-tooth comb. Bag and tag everything. Same goes for Eva Sjöberg's house.'

'They're already there and working on it,' Hallberg added.

Falk continued to smile politely, but Jamie could tell by the twitch at the corner of her eye that the woman didn't like to be interrupted. 'Good. You can put out a notice for the church minibus – any officers who see it are to report it, but not to approach – follow at a safe distance. Same goes for the tolls. I don't want him arrested in public. Not yet. But I want to know the second we have eyes on him.'

Hallberg dared to glance at Wiik, but then quickly came back to Falk. 'Got it.'

'Was there something else?' Falk asked.

'Yes,' Hallberg said, looking at Jamie now. 'I've got that information you wanted on Tilde Gunnarson's parents.'

Jamie sat more upright now. 'The sixth victim.'

Hallberg nodded. 'Looks like Tilde's parents are both prominent business people – both still working. Her mother, Åsa Gunnarson, is a solicitor – works in international tax law for a big firm in the city. Her father, Mikael, owns a company that works in renewable energies – he's one of the founding partners in Grön Framtida Industria – they specialise in wind and solar.'

'Green Future Industries,' Jamie repeated, committing it to memory. 'And they're both alive?'

Hallberg nodded. 'Alive and well by the looks of things – Tilde was an only child, and they moved after her death. But both are still working in the city and are still together.'

Wiik was eyeing Jamie, as was Falk.

'Okay, good,' Jamie said. 'Can you send across their details, I'd like to talk to them.'

Wiik spoke up now. 'What for?'

'I want to know.'

'Want to know what?' He hauled himself more upright in the chair.

'I want to know why they're still alive when all the other parents aren't. If there's something we don't understand – then I'm betting we're going to find out what it is with the Gunnarsons.'

Falk clasped her hands under her chin. She seemed pleased with that answer. Or perhaps she was just taking the chance to get Wiik out of her office. 'Go,' she commanded. 'Speak to them – see what you can find.'

Wiik didn't seem enthralled with the idea. 'We need to stay on Eriksson,' he said. 'We need to be here if they find him, to question him, to—'

'Fine,' Falk said. 'Hallberg, you go with Johansson. It'll be good for you.'

Wiik's mouth opened, but he knew he'd just backed himself into a corner.

Hallberg looked down at Jamie, trying to restrain a grin.

She understood what Hallberg was feeling, but couldn't reciprocate it. There was a killer out there, and Jamie was starting to get the feeling that he was toying with them.

And that frightened her.

Too much to smile.

Too much to do anything except keep working the case. And not take her eye off the ball for a second.

Jamie pushed herself out of the chair wordlessly and pulled her coat off the back.

Wiik had found something interesting to look at on his phone and didn't bother to wish them goodbye. That didn't surprise Jamie. Things hadn't gone his way and this was the result. Miserable silence.

Better than the alternative, she supposed.

Though Jamie didn't know how she felt about Hallberg watching her back instead. Then again, if the girl was anything like she was at that age, then things could have been worse.

At the very least, she felt better than she would have going alone.

And Falk knew that, too. Jamie's instincts had taken her to Rättvik, and it had rattled someone's cage.

Maybe Falk was hoping that sending her to see the Gunnarsons would do the same, draw Eriksson, or whoever else was behind this, out of the shadows.

Jamie didn't know if that made her bait or not, but as she walked next to Hallberg, the girl with a spritely bounce in her step, Jamie's fists had clenched at her sides. Not out of anger though, or even determination. Simply, to stop them from trembling.

28

JAMIE WATCHED with a sort of amused curiosity as Hallberg dialled the number for Gunnarsons and put on the most formal phone voice she'd ever heard.

'Hello,' she said when they answered. 'Is this Mikael Gunnarson? My name is Julia Hallberg, I'm a *polisassistent* with the Stockholm Polis.'

They were sitting in Hallberg's car, a compact Mercedes hatchback with a punchy little petrol engine. It wasn't as luxurious as Wiik's Volvo, but it was nice. Jamie had never been fussed on luxury. She preferred function over form, and judging by the smell – Jamie sniffed the air in the cabin and detected the faint whiff of new-used-car-smell – so had Hallberg until recently. Jamie glanced over her shoulder and spotted paper mats in the footwells of the back seats. She ran her finger along the dashboard and felt the greasy texture of faux-leather blackener. Yeah, she hadn't had this long.

Jamie glanced over at her now, tuning out her words as she explained to the Gunnarsons that they'd like to come and meet them, talk to them about the murder of their daughter.

Hallberg was slim – narrow-waisted, narrow-shouldered.

Her features were pointed, her hair dark and pulled into a low-maintenance ponytail, but well looked after. Her clothing was professional yet informal. She had on a pair of black skinny jeans and flat Chelsea-style boots with a slightly pointed toe and a fashionable buckle. Jamie didn't think they'd be much good at a run. Especially not in the middle of a Swedish winter. On top, Hallberg was wearing a grey blazer and a white shirt open at the top button. Jamie didn't know if she'd ever seen such a police-looking outfit.

She lifted her eyes from Hallberg's midsection and saw that the girl was smiling at her. Then she corrected herself. Jamie had to stop calling her a girl, even in her head. She had less than ten years on Hallberg – probably more like seven – and yet they seemed lifetimes apart. Hallberg was energetic, positive, optimistic… youthful, even. Jamie was… tired. Cynical. And broken. If she thought about it, her elbow ached from where it had been cracked by a drug dealer's baseball bat. Her shoulder had a dull throb from where she'd been stabbed. And her back-left molars were still sensitive and just a little loose from where she'd had the shit kicked out of her courtesy of a scumbag she'd been chasing.

She still couldn't drink cold things without wincing.

'Okay?' Hallberg asked.

Jamie snapped out of it, realising how strung out she felt. 'Sorry, yeah. Just sort of zoned out then for a second.' She looked down and found she was rubbing her sore elbow and then quickly dropped her hands to her lap. 'We good?'

'Yeah, Mikael is going to be home in around half an hour, and Åsa is already in the house. He said we can come now.'

'How far is it?'

'A little way outside the city – should take a little under an hour.'

'Okay.' Jamie sighed and rubbed her eyes. 'Want to grab some coffee for the road?'

'Sure,' Hallberg said brightly. 'I know a great little place.'

'Of course you do.' Jamie hated how sick Hallberg's positivity made her.

They pulled out of the car park under the HQ and into the final minutes of sunlight. The fog was descending, just as Jamie thought it would, and soon it would be dark.

She swallowed and looked out of the window, conserving what little energy she had left.

With any luck, Hallberg wouldn't be the talkative type. Though as she stole a look over at the young and determined polisassistent, drumming happily on the steering wheel with her thumb, humming along to a tune only she could hear until she worked up the nerve to ask whatever burning question was on the tip of her tongue, Jamie knew she was.

And what was worse – much worse, in fact – was that she was actually starting to miss Wiik.

And they'd not even got to the coffee place yet.

Hallberg's headlights burnt holes through the fog as they wound along a narrow road a hundred kilometres outside the city.

The fog had thickened to a soup and the temperature readout on Hallberg's centre console was flashing a balmy minus six degrees.

The last of the warmth had gone from the cup in Jamie's hands, but she still held on to it, willing the triple shot of espresso to seep its way into her body and throw some fire on her mind.

Trees flashed by in vertical white strips – silver birch forest as far as the eye could see – catching the headlights.

The Gunnarsons had done well for themselves and lived in a large property set on a hillside overlooking a narrow valley and a small lake. This road served only their house and ended at their gate. Another had branched off about a kilometre back, no doubt to another mansion, but now there was nothing else.

Jamie exhaled, feeling nauseated by the constant pendulum swing of the road.

Hallberg drove smoothly with both hands on the wheel, and had mercifully fallen silent.

Yet that hadn't made Jamie feel better.

The Gunnarsons held the key – the answer to the question, what don't we understand? But she didn't feel right. Something didn't feel right.

An imposing black gate swam out of the gloom, two large stone pillars sitting on either side of it. From them, stone walls ran off into the forest in either direction – they were ten feet high and topped with pointed rocks. There must have been millions of them. And it probably cost that much to put them there.

The gate looked heavy and immovable. Though Jamie expected that security was important when you were thirty minutes' drive from the nearest village – and any potential rescue.

Hallberg slowed and wound down her window, leaning out to speak into an intercom that stuck out of the ground twenty feet short of the gate.

Jamie looked ahead – seeing a slit of yellow light between the join of the two gates. She sat taller and tried to see over it, catching just a glimpse of the flat roof of the Gunnarsons' mansion.

They'd come up on the side of a slope – the ground to their right fell away towards the valley floor, and on the left climbed up to the top of the hill some few hundred feet above. Jamie wondered how much of it they owned.

The house itself seemed to perch on the hillside, and from here Jamie could see that trees hemmed it in at the back, but at the front it was open. She expected a manicured lawn rolled away at the front of the house down to the boundary, giving an unobstructed view of the valley. She pictured it, even from behind the impenetrable gates able to visualise the glass front. If it was her, the whole side of the house would be glass. Plenty of natural light, space, and not a neighbour around for miles. What could be better?

A wash of cold air hit Jamie and she looked around at Hallberg. 'What's up?' she asked.

Hallberg leaned back in and turned to Jamie. 'No answer.'

'Try it again,' Jamie said, keeping her breathing even.

Hallberg leaned out and pressed the call button for the second, and then third time.

The temperature in the car had plunged now and their breath was misting in front of their faces, the blowers on the dash fighting to keep the fog from the inside of the windscreen.

Hallberg withdrew her hand and looked over at Jamie. 'They know we're coming.'

Jamie shrugged. 'Rich people,' she said, brushing it off. And yet, something didn't feel right.

How long could they sit there and wait?

'Should I try calling them?' Hallberg asked.

Jamie leaned her head back, tapping her fingers on the cup between her knees, spying the thin shred of light between the gates. Her skin had begun to goose pimple, and it wasn't because of the cold. 'Yeah,' she said after a second. 'Call them.'

Hallberg wound the window up and pulled her phone from the centre console, getting the number up on-screen.

Jamie checked her watch. It was nearly six thirty now. The cloud cover had blotted out all of the moonlight, and the forest around them was drenched in a black stillness.

Fog swirled in front of the headlights.

Hallberg placed the call and the tinny sound of the dial echoed around them.

A dull bang rang out somewhere in the distance, and Jamie sat bolt upright. A cluster of birds flapped out of the trees in a spray of snow and careened into the air, cawing madly at the disturbance.

Hallberg was sitting up like a meerkat, her head turning on her shoulders. 'What the hell was that?'

Jamie swallowed hard, her heart racing. She knew that sound well – even muted by the glass in the windows, even dulled by the forest and the fog and the distance. 'That was a gunshot,' she said.

To be more precise, it was a report from a hunting rifle. It had a distinct sound. One she'd come to know intrinsically from the trips with her father. Medium calibre. A 6.5mm round. Something designed to hunt bigger prey than geese. That much she was certain of.

Hallberg's voice was strained now, her eyes wide. 'Where did it come from? Was it close? Inspector Johansson?' She was looking around wildly, but by the time she got to her name, Jamie was already out of the car.

The gate was closed before them and from inside the car, Jamie couldn't see over. Hallberg was nearly yelling as Jamie climbed onto her bonnet, stepping up onto her roof to get a better look at the house.

It was as she thought – sprawling, glass-fronted. Open to

the elements, the wilds, and anyone with a long enough rifle and the balls to set up across the valley.

It wasn't far, maybe two, three hundred metres at most. You wouldn't have to be a match shooter to line up a shot from that distance.

Jamie's head turned back to the house now, scanning it for any signs of anything amiss. A small part of her was hoping that their neighbours were just hunting enthusiasts.

But then she saw it.

One of the full-length windows facing the valley was shattered. The top quarter still clung to the frame, but a spider web of cracks ran across the glass, the lower portion lying in shards on the polished oak floor of the Gunnarsons' house.

Her heart sank, her blood running cold.

Hallberg was out of the car now, calling up at her, but she couldn't hear words. All Jamie had in her ears was rushing blood.

Another shot rang out and Jamie flinched, ducking reflexively.

She was shielded by the trees from the shooter, but the house wasn't.

A second window exploded in a shower of glass. It fell to the floor and skittered everywhere, raining down onto the snow-covered lawn below.

Jamie was frozen, staring up at the house.

'Inspector!'

Jamie couldn't move.

'Jamie!' Hallberg was grabbing at her leg now, trying to pull her down – no doubt fearful that she was about to get her head blown off.

Jamie's foot slipped on the frozen droplets stuck to Hallberg's roof and her legs splayed. She landed on her hip and slid down the windscreen and onto the bonnet.

The moisture stung her skin, cold and painful, and the lump of the windscreen washer jet dug into her thigh.

Jamie grunted, rolling down to the ground and onto her feet.

She was moving then, going on instinct and nothing else.

Hallberg was still yelling behind her, but Jamie wasn't listening – the Gunnarsons were in trouble, if not dead already. Was Eriksson across the valley right now? Finishing what he started twenty-five years ago? Would Leif Lundgren be next? Would the parents of his latest victim?

Jamie charged at the gate and leapt up, the Kevlar toecaps of her boots hitting the slick steel, her hands finding the top.

She scrambled up, the tread on her boots raking wet lines down the black paint, her shoulders creaking and straining as she hauled herself upwards and swung her leg over the top.

She stole a glance back, her breath already ragged, and caught a glimpse of Hallberg, rooted in place behind the open door of her car, her mouth open in shock, eyes wide with fear.

And then she was gone.

Jamie's heels hit the tarmac of the Gunnarsons' drive and she was on the other side, already moving fast up the sweeping driveway.

The freezing fog stung her cheeks and made her lungs ache. Her throat tightened and tried to make her cough. Jamie suppressed it and sped forward, the sound of the idling Mercedes already drowned by the fog behind her.

The trees had fallen away on her right now and had been replaced by a sloping lawn. It dropped forty feet or so over twice that distance and ended in the same high stone wall that kept the trees at bay.

Jamie couldn't see anything beyond it but a blockade of grey mist, but she knew somewhere out there a shooter had line of sight to the house over the highest branches.

She looked up at it now – a square building with a flat roof that pushed back into the hillside.

Jamie's legs were burning as she reached the top of the drive, keeping low as she moved, her knees tight to her chest. The asphalt widened in front of a huge double garage next to the front door, and Jamie ducked between the two cars parked there – a top-end BMW coupe and an inordinately expensive Porsche saloon with exhausts big enough for Jamie to put her fist in – four of them.

She caught her breath quickly, fingers tingling, heart hammering, and peeked through the driver's window. Nothing moved in the ocean of fog.

Jamie cursed, glancing back down at the gate. There was still no sign of Hallberg and no sound was coming from within.

Something flashed in the corner of Jamie's eye – a blazing rose in the darkness. It strobed for an instant and then died, and the boom reached her a second later. The glass over her head exploded and the bullet ripped into the bonnet of the BMW behind her, gouging a big silver trough in the gleaming black paint. Sparks danced as the bullet ricocheted up into the trees behind the house, the BMW wobbling from the impact. Its lights began to flash, the alarm blaring in shock.

Jamie slumped to the ground against the door of the Porsche and protected her head, ears ringing, and felt shards of glass raining down on her head and shoulders. She swore to herself, barely able to hear her own voice.

She didn't know how far out the shooter was, but he was no slouch and wasn't afraid to put a bullet in her.

He wasn't here for Jamie, though – he'd put rounds into the house. After the Gunnarsons. They were the target. Jamie was just a witness.

She snatched a breath and rolled over, bear-crawling to

the front bumper, lining up the front door. It was hidden behind a stonework wall – one that was no doubt designed to block out the frigid wind sweeping up off the lake. But now Jamie hoped it would provide her with cover. Hoped.

She had to move, and fast – get inside, find Mikael and Åsa Gunnarson. Get them somewhere safe – then wait for backup to arrive.

Jamie was in the open for just a moment.

She saw another flash, then dived forward, her elbows slamming against the composite front door with a loud crash.

The stones on the corner of the protective wall plumed into dust and crumbled to the ground, leaving a hole the size of an orange. She didn't know what rifle the shooter was using, but they weren't hunting bullets – not jacketed or open-tipped. Jamie glanced at the hole in the wall, the wide gouge in the bonnet of the still-wailing BMW – they were serious. Ballistic tips, she guessed. Bullets that had a plastic nose cone that disintegrated on impact, allowing the flat head of the bullet to bloom and expand into its target. For maximum damage. For maximum stopping power. The kind of bullet that would turn a glancing shot into a kill shot. Jacketed bullets would pierce, could nick, could pass straight through a victim and miss everything important. A ballistic tip as good as exploded when it struck, guaranteeing serious damage.

Jamie stared at the hole in the BMW, wondering what it would be like to get hit by one.

She didn't want to think about it.

There were two people inside that were on the shooter's kill list. Two people who could be the answer to their questions. Who could be the linchpin in this investigation. Who could be the difference between the end of this case or a trail of victims stretching away from them.

Jamie clamped her jaw shut to stop it quivering, raked in as deep a breath as she could, and then turned to the door, pushing down on the handle and plunging inside.

The interior was bright, the floors a dark and rich wood. Walnut or cherry. There was no time to consider which.

On Jamie's left, a door came up. Garage, had to be. She opened it and stuck her head in, was met with a dark interior. A four-by-four sat quietly on the far side, an open roof box on top of it, skis sticking out the front. The Gunarassons had just come back from, or were planning, a trip.

'Hello?' she called.

There was no reply.

Jamie cursed. She didn't think it was going to be that easy.

She left the door open and stepped back into the corridor, advancing. Ahead, the space opened up into a large open-plan kitchen and living room.

Another door lay open on Jamie's left, leading to a small bathroom. Empty again. Shit.

Jamie came up on the corner of the kitchen and slowed, pressing herself to the wall.

The smell of food was thick in the air – Italian maybe, or Mediterranean. Something rich – but there was another scent. A metallic tang.

Jamie looked at the wall she was pressed against. White.

The one opposite, white.

All the walls were white.

She let her eyes drift across the back wall – running from the open bathroom door into the open living room.

She got a third of the way along and stopped, her stomach twisting itself into a sickening knot. On the back wall – between a photograph of the Gunnarsons sitting, arms around one another, on a boat, bathed in golden sunshine, and an old

black-and-white photograph of a young girl Jamie assumed
was Tilde Gunnarson – was a spray of scarlet.

She edged towards the corner and looked out, casting
her eyes over the long room – the gleaming white coun-
tertop of the kitchen island, the white leather sofas, the
brushed-steel freestanding fireplace, the reclaimed-wood
dining table beset with candles and plates of half-eaten
food... and a woman slumped down on top of her dinner,
back to the shattered window, cheek against the surface,
eyes wide and vacant, a blood-red hole between her
shoulders.

Åsa Gunnarson's arms were splayed on the wood, her
wine glass knocked over outside the knuckles of her right
hand, her left still clutching the knife she'd been eating with.

Her auburn hair lay around her head in a tangled mess and
a thin stream of blood ran from her open mouth.

Through the gaps in the wooden slats of the table, her
blood was dripping, pooling beneath her. Her white, body-con
dress was soaked, her feet at odd angles, ankles rolled over on
her heels as she had tried to move, the last dregs of life
draining from her.

Judging by the spray across the table and the wall, the
first round had hit her square in the back – blown the front of
her chest out, and doused the house in her blood.

Jamie ducked back in, forcing herself to breathe. She
couldn't get the stench out of her nose now. Blood. So much
blood. The human body holds around five litres of it. And
Åsa Gunnarson's was soaking into her expensive walnut
flooring.

Jamie swallowed the rising bile in her throat and forced
herself to focus. Åsa was dead. But the table held two plates –
Åsa's and the one opposite. It sat on the table, the wide rim of
the bowl speckled with blood. Jamie could see a knife and

fork on the floor next to the chair that had been pushed back from the table at an odd angle.

Jamie narrowed her eyes, blocking out the dead woman and tried to call out. 'Mik—' Her voice was a croak. She cleared her throat willed herself to volume. 'Mikael Gunnarson?' she shouted across the living room, searching for any sign of the missing husband, her eyes decoding the scene.

How many shots had she heard from the car? Two, three?

One was in Åsa – the bullet in pieces inside her chest cavity. The second had blown out another window.

Jamie leaned out and looked at the windows. Eight of them in a row. The third had been broken by the first shot, right behind Åsa. The fifth and sixth were broken, too. Two more shots.

She went back to the blood-splattered wall and searched past the photo of Tilde Gunnarson.

A corridor led into the back of the house, to the bedrooms, Jamie guessed, and next to it a welt in the wall that showed the concrete beneath the paint. That was the second.

She kept moving, seeing another welt, higher this time – the third shot – and below it, on the floor, another photograph lying in pieces, blown apart, its glass spread around in sharp fragments.

At the far end of the living room, Jamie could see another dividing wall that separated the lounge area with the sofas and the fireplace from a corridor that dog-legged left and out of sight. Bedrooms, laundry room? She didn't know, but the bullets had chased Mikael Gunnarson that way, and that's where she had to go, too.

Shit.

It was thirty feet with no cover.

And a shooter with no intentions of letting anyone walk away from this house alive.

Suicide.

That was the word that came to mind.

Jamie glanced down at her watch, thought about the drive up. The twenty-minute-at-best delay time before the flashing blues arrived.

The shooter would know that, and wouldn't want to let the Gunnarsons slip through his fingers. If he hadn't already, he'd be advancing on the property, perhaps moving to a new vantage point. Jamie had to go quickly, get Mikael and then either hold out until support arrived, or get somewhere safe until the shooter came for them.

She didn't have time to think about who it could have been.

She just needed to move.

Jamie backed up towards the front door to get a running start, pressed her heels into it for grip, and then balled her fists, ready to spring forward and charge across the gap.

She counted to three in her head and then went on two before she lost her nerve.

Jamie sprinted into the open, the wash of freezing wind from the blown-out windows hitting her like a wall and punching the air out of her lungs.

She gasped and kept going, her boots crunching on broken glass as she made for the cover of the opposite wall.

Another flash lit up in her peripherals and the wall in front of her erupted in a shower of concrete and paint.

The bang echoed through the house, deafening her as she threw her hands up to protect her face, grains of concrete smashing into her arms as she broke through the cloud.

Jamie screwed her eyes shut against the dust, feeling it hitting her bared teeth as she moved, and barely caught sight of the dividing wall as it lunged out at her.

She tried to readjust, but she was moving too fast. Her

shoulder clipped it and she spun to the ground, landing hard and sliding into the narrow corridor.

Jamie was panting, flat on her back, and looked out into the living room, a thick cloud of white paint and plaster still lingering in the blood-heavy air.

The shooter had led her across the space, pulled the trigger a fraction too soon, misjudged the travel time of the shot, misjudged her speed. But any closer and the bullet would have ripped through her arms, maybe her whole body.

Jamie wanted to roll over and vomit.

But she wasn't done yet.

Still breathing hard, she pushed herself to her feet and reached out, steadying herself on the corner of the wall.

A hallway stretched towards the back of the house – two doors were on the left, and then at the far end, there was a door on the right leading outside. Jamie edged forwards, tweaking her ears for any sounds of movement. She couldn't hear anything and prayed that Mikael Gunnarson hadn't been stupid enough to try to make a break for it through the back door.

Jamie slowed at a window on her right and glanced out. It faced down the valley – there was no way the shooter could have line of sight from where he was. She saw a flagstone path running away from the house, moving towards a gate at the treeline about fifty feet down the garden.

Was the shooter heading for that right now?

She set her jaw and pushed on. There was no time to waste.

The first door on her left was open. She glanced inside – saw a sprawling bathroom with a walk-in shower. But no Mikael.

She exhaled, trying to calm herself, but her heart wouldn't quit. It was still hammering against her ribs.

'Mikael?' She tried again. 'Mikael Gunnarson? It's the police,' Jamie offered. 'If you're okay, let me know.'

But there was nothing but silence.

Just one door left.

Jamie moved towards it with conviction now and found that it was closed.

She paused for a second, laid her hand on the wood, taking an extra breath, and then she pushed down on the handle and stepped inside.

The door creaked open and her boots sank into a plush carpet. The interior was dark and she could just make out the outline of a bed from the ambient light coming in through the large window on the right-hand side of the room.

'Mikael?' she said into the darkness.

Whether it was the rustle of the carpet, the creak of a tensioned tendon, or just the primitive part of Jamie's brain alerting her to danger, she didn't know. But the instant before it happened, she twisted instinctively to the left and locked her muscles.

Something hard hit her in the guts and she was thrown off her feet, driven sideways, deeper into the room, and slammed against the wall next to the window.

All the wind left her body, along with a sharp yelping sound, and stars danced in front of her eyes.

In the light coming in through the door now, she saw the figure of a man rear back, pulling his shoulder from her chest, winding up a punch. His elbow raised in the darkness, silhouetted against the hallway lighting, and hung there before propelling his closed fist back towards Jamie's face.

She pulled her hands up into a tight guard and rolled to the right, feeling the fist bounce across her forearms and hit the wall next to her left ear.

The attacker grunted and swore, pulling his hand back in

shock, giving Jamie enough space to react. Her training kicked in, the muscle memory doing the work, and she stepped inside the man's reach, leaned into her left foot and threw her right knee upwards as hard as she could, bringing it around in a sharp arc.

The point impacted him in the lower midriff, just above the pubis, and he let out a low groan, clutching at his front and doubling over.

Jamie wasted no time and danced onto her right foot, sent a low kick with her left into the back of his calf.

Her foot sang, the vibration reaching all the way to her hip.

But the man went down to a knee, his eyes wide with fear in the darkness as he stared up at Jamie. *'Nnälla, döda mig inte,'* he whispered, squeezing it out between ragged breaths. Please, don't kill me.

Jamie lowered her balled fist, the one meant for the man's jaw, and glanced at the door, massaging her sternum with her off hand. 'Mikael Gunnarson?' she asked, still not lowering her guard fully.

He nodded, fearfully, raising his hands next to his shoulders. *'Snälla, jag betalar vad du vill,'* he said, looking up at Jamie. Please, I'll pay whatever you want.

She swallowed and let her hands fall now. 'My name is Detective Inspector Jamie Johansson,' Jamie said, proffering the man a hand. 'I'm with the SPA – Stockholm Polis.'

'You're not here to kill me?' he mumbled, not taking it.

'No,' Jamie said, wincing at the pain in her chest and turning her attention to the open door instead. 'I'm here to save your life.'

29

JAMIE WAS SITTING in the back of an ambulance having a torch shone in her eyes when Wiik pulled into the driveway and skidded to a halt on the slick tarmac.

The Gunnarsons' front lawn was a sea of flashing lights. Two ambulances were at the scene, as well as four squad cars, two canine units, Hallberg, and now Wiik.

He kicked his door open and swept from his car, throwing the tail of his long coat from around his arms as he stormed towards Jamie.

She sighed, brushed the penlight away from her face and thanked the paramedic checking her over. He glanced at Wiik, realised that sticking around was probably a bad idea, and then evaporated into the blue haze.

'Hey,' Jamie said, sighing and rubbing her forearm. Mikael Gunnarson wasn't a fighter by any means, but his knuckles had caught her, and it was still aching horribly.

'Hey?' Wiik asked incredulously, standing over her and putting his hands on his hips. 'What were you thinking?'

Jamie narrowed her eyes at him. 'I'm fine, thanks for asking,' she said.

Wiik's nostrils flared, and then he exhaled hard, smoothing down his hair. 'You could have been killed.'

'So could have Mikael.' Jamie set her jaw. 'Åsa was.' She turned and nodded towards the house. Two paramedics were walking out, pulling off their gloves. Mikael had been unharmed, but Åsa hadn't made it. Jamie only had to take one look at the holes in the walls to know there was no coming back from a direct hit like that.

The gunman had shot to kill, and he'd succeeded.

Wiik stood stoically now and looked out into the darkness, the fog still thick around the house.

Torch beams moved intermittently through the trees in the distance as the canine units combed the forest for the shooter. Jamie knew he was long gone by now. But just finding his nest, maybe a few shell casings, anything, would be a start. She wasn't so sure of the shooter's identity, but she knew Wiik had already made up his mind, was hoping the canine units would corner Eriksson out there.

'You shouldn't have rushed in like that,' Wiik muttered, his anger riling against something else. Concern?

Jamie cast an eye past him at Hallberg, who was hovering near the front of her car. She was on her phone, but kept glancing over. How much had she told Wiik, exactly?

'And what else was I supposed to do?' Jamie asked, genuinely not knowing the answer.

'Wait, call for backup,' he answered plainly.

'It would have taken twenty minutes for the nearest officers to arrive – and you know as well as I do,' Jamie said, trying to keep the coldness out of her voice, 'that they'd be some inexperienced bumbling country-born uniforms who'd be about as much help as... as...' Jamie trailed off, shaking her head. She couldn't think of anything that wasn't a joke, and she didn't much feel like laughing.

'I don't care,' Wiik said.

'If I hadn't gone in, then Mikael could have been killed.'

'Åsa was anyway, and did you have any way to know that Mikael wasn't either before you almost got your head blown off? Hallberg told me you were dodging bullets all the way to the front door, and the shooter had no intention of letting you get to him.'

Jamie leaned around Wiik and scowled at Hallberg. She looked away sheepishly. Wiik's reasoning was as sound as she'd heard. 'Look,' she said tiredly. 'I'm fine. Mikael Gunnarson is fine.' Jamie dipped her head to one of the squad cars, where they could just make out the silhouette of the would-be second victim in the darkness of the back seat, hunched over, head hung. 'The shooter didn't get him – and he didn't get me. I went in there, because the case probably rests on Gunnarson now, and I wasn't about to let our best lead catch a bullet.'

Wiik's mouth had become an expressionless line.

'The shooter knew this property, and he knew the targets. This was planned, it was executed to precision. It was just dumb luck that we showed up when we did. And me going into that house might have been the only thing that stopped the shooter from advancing on it and finishing the job. I have no doubt that if we weren't here, there'd be two dead bodies in there, and we'd be no closer to figuring out just what the fuck is going on here.'

Wiik refused to look at her now. He was staring up at their house. 'It doesn't fit,' he said after a few seconds.

'What doesn't?' Jamie asked, shaking her head. She didn't think she had the energy for riddles.

'This,' Wiik said, not looking away from the house. 'The killer – going after Mikael and Åsa Gunnarson.'

'I don't think I'm following,' Jamie said, watching Wiik closely.

'In each case – the other five victims,' Wiik said, looking back at her now and holding out his five fingers. 'Christina Bergner – her father was run off the road and killed.' He pulled one of his fingers down. 'Britta Engdahl, mother disappears without a trace.' Another finger. 'Hilda Nordell – father hanged himself. Agnes Floden's father, missing. Elin Wickstrom's father, stabbed.' He lowered a finger with each one. 'There's a pattern here.'

'It's not gender-driven,' Jamie said, trying not to let on how impressed she was he remembered all that. He'd barely seemed interested in what Hallberg had to say, and definitely not enough to come out here after the Gunnarsons. And yet he had taken that information and memorised it from the off. Jamie was impressed. But she didn't let on. 'We know that,' she went on. 'Britta Engdahl's mother was targeted, as, now, Åsa Gunnarson was, too. The rest are fathers.'

'But why?'

'I don't know,' Jamie answered truthfully.

'Why would the killer go after the girls? Specifically *girls*. Aged thirteen or fourteen. Same church group. All linked. All alike. Young, Christian – ready for their confirmation. All killed in the same way, too. Abducted, suffocated, displayed. But then the parents... The kills were opportunistic, tailored to the victim, not the killer.' Wiik folded his lips into a line again. 'They were careful, too. Hidden. Plausible. Seemingly accidental. A hit-and-run – disappearances, supposed suicide. They were able to slip through the net, unnoticed.'

Jamie sighed, agreeing with him then. 'Taking shots at two high-profile business people with a hunting rifle isn't exactly covert. It doesn't fit,' she said tiredly.

'No, it doesn't.' Wiik looked out at the forest again. 'So what changed between then and now? What made him come at the Gunnarsons like this? Why both of them?'

'If the killer was twenty-five years younger then,' Jamie mused, 'he was probably young enough, strong enough to take them like that. Confident enough to get close. Now, if he's older… a gun is a safer bet. Maybe he didn't want both of them. Maybe he just wanted to take them both so the other couldn't call for help.'

Wiik didn't look sold on the theory. But then again, Jamie was just spewing words at this point. Her head was spinning. She was exhausted, the adrenaline having worn off. She could barely think. 'I don't know,' she said for what felt like the hundredth time. 'But we will.' She looked over towards Gunnarson again. 'The killer has gone after the girls, and then their parents. We need to question the surviving parents, and we need to question Gunnarson. If anyone knows why they're being targeted, it's him.'

'And if he doesn't?' Wiik was watching Jamie now.

Jamie closed her eyes and rubbed them with the heels of her hands. 'Then we're no closer to solving this case.'

30

IT WAS late by the time Jamie got back to the hotel. One of the uniformed officers had driven her. Wiik and Hallberg had both offered, the former practically insisting, but Jamie had told them she wanted to get back, and they both needed to lock down the scene and wait for CSTs.

She reached her room and looked around. The hotel was clean, but basic. After all, no one was covering her expenses here. Jamie was purely there by choice. Allowed to assist on the case by the goodwill of the SPA. She wasn't being paid. It wasn't her duty.

And yet she'd gone charging into a house. Into the jaws of death. And for what? To solve a twenty-five-year-old case that she had no doubt would have been well handled by the dour Anders Wiik and the plucky Julia Hallberg.

Jamie sat on the bed and rested her elbows on her knees, hanging her head between them. Her duffle bag sat on the chair in the corner of the room, open, the two changes of clothes she'd now brought already dirty. She in her second pair of jeans, and now they needed a wash, too. How long did she intend to be here? And when she was done –

whatever 'done' meant – where did she intend to go? Back to the Met? Back to Scotland and to Graeme? She checked her phone then. He still hadn't texted or called. But then again, she hadn't even thought about him. What that said about her, she didn't know.

She could have died tonight, and the person who seemed to care the most was a man she'd known all of three days. And one she didn't even particularly like.

Jamie sat up now and then flopped backwards onto the bed, reaching into the pocket of her coat.

Her fingers closed around the thin red notebook and she pulled it out, flipping past the notes to the final few filled-in pages.

When she hit the blank space that marked her father's death, she stopped and backtracked to the entries addressed to her.

The last things her father ever wrote, in the last notebook he ever wrote in.

Jamie clenched her jaw to stop it from quivering, turned the pages until she got to the next entry, and then read.

31

JAMIE,

I received a letter today that said that the man I hit was going to be filing charges against me.

I suppose this news should make me feel something, but it doesn't.

I don't feel anything anymore.

Last night, I thought I heard you coming home.

I woke up, rushed to the top of the stairs, and fell.

I lay at the bottom, not sure if I was hurt or not, not knowing if anyone would come. And I thought – I realised – then, that you were never coming back.

The only thing that keeps me going is making sure that I leave you with more than memories of what a terrible father I was.

And an even worse man.

I don't expect you to ever forgive me, Jamie.

And I don't think I deserve it.

32

JAMIE STEPPED out of the hotel, the pre-dawn crisp and clear now, the sky that bloody shade of red it turns just before dawn starts to break. A thick blanket of snow had fallen in the night and the cleaners and ploughs had already been out to sweep it into the gutters. It lay there, grey and thick, melting slowly into the sewers under its own weight.

Wiik had texted that he wanted to get an early start on questioning Mikael Gunnarson, and so did Jamie. The man had demanded his attorney be present for any conversations and had been stewing all night at HQ until he arrived. Both Jamie and Wiik wanted to get some answers out of him as quickly as possible, but if he wasn't talking without representation, wasting their breath at three in the morning would have accomplished nothing.

And so she was out before the commuters. Before the sun, even.

The city was still drenched in darkness, but the street-lights were still burning, casting a dim glow over the shining tarmac.

Jamie shifted from foot to foot, willing blood into her

fingers, the salt on the pavement crunching under heels. And then she paused and looked up across the street.

She narrowed her eyes at a narrow walkway between two buildings opposite, and tried to focus. Were her eyes playing tricks on her, or could she see a figure standing there?

Her jaw flexed and she stepped to her right, lining the mouth of the walkway up directly with her line of sight.

The streetlight died at the corner, shrouding the alley in darkness. Jamie cursed silently, forcing herself to breathe.

Her breath misted around her head, obscuring her vision. But then, it didn't matter.

The person hiding in the shadows stepped into the streetlight.

Jamie couldn't make out their features – they were wearing a thick parka, a black hoodie pulled up over their head, their hands in their pockets.

The figure was just standing there, not moving – they wanted to be seen. Wanted Jamie to see them.

She swallowed hard and felt her fists ball at her sides, her mind racing. The shooter? The note writer? Nyström's kidnapper? Eriksson? Damn it. Lindvall? She was afraid to move, afraid to spook them. They had a hell of a head start on her.

But what did they want?

Jamie picked her head up, glanced left and right, seeing the street empty, and then raised her hands to show she meant no harm.

The figure turned a quarter-on, as though ready to bolt.

Jamie exhaled and then took a step forward.

The figure hovered.

What were they there for? To scare her? To let her know that they knew where she was staying? Or something else... to make contact? To reach out?

You don't understand.

'What don't I understand?' Jamie felt like yelling. But she held back, took another slow step.

The figure seemed like they couldn't decide whether to run or face Jamie down.

She was at the edge of the kerb now and glanced down, checking her footing.

The figure squared up a little and came towards the road.

Jamie's heart was racing in her chest.

She took another step, lifting her foot up over the mound of slush piled in front of her, and then dropped her heel onto the road.

The instant it touched, something flashed in her peripheral and she wheeled around, watching Wiik's Volvo skidding to a halt.

Jamie lurched backwards, catching her heel on the mound of snow, and slipped, one foot now either side of the mound. She regained her balance, her hands slamming into the bonnet of his car.

She met Wiik's eyes through the windscreen, a look of shock on his face. He threw the door open and stepped out. 'What the hell are you doing?'

But Jamie wasn't listening. She was already halfway across the road.

He watched as she stepped up onto the kerb and into the mouth of the walkway. But the figure was gone.

'Shit,' Jamie muttered, backing up and going back to the street. 'Did you see them?' she asked.

Wiik was standing behind his door, shaking his head. 'See who? The crazy woman stepping into the street without looking? I almost ran you over.'

Jamie grumbled and threw a hand towards his Volvo. 'It's your damn electric car. Couldn't hear the thing coming.' She glanced over her shoulder towards the alleyway again, but there was no sign of them.

'You're supposed to *look* both ways, not listen,' Wiik said flatly. 'Now get in.'

Jamie sighed, rubbed her eyes, and then circled around the car and got in.

Wiik proffered Jamie a cup of coffee from the centre console.

She took it and sipped.

'Skimmed milk, right?' Wiik asked, knowing the answer. He didn't look round before he pulled off.

'That's right,' Jamie said, eyeing him cautiously.

'Hallberg told me you stopped for coffee,' he added, indicating and pulling down a side street. 'I had her look into Eriksson, see if there was anything that would line him up as our shooter. He doesn't own any guns, doesn't have a hunting licence. By all accounts, the man is as clean as a—'

'Priest?' Jamie offered, arching an eyebrow and taking another sip of coffee. She wondered briefly if Hallberg had been forthcoming with the information on the coffee or if Wiik had probed for it.

'As a priest *ought* to be,' Wiik said. 'But that doesn't mean anything. We still don't have him – not a trace. It's like he just upped and disappeared into thin air. Apparently, he's never missed a service before, has been a model custodian of the church and just all around amazing fucking human being.' The scorn in his voice was unmistakable.

Jamie leaned her head back. 'Eriksson was good friends with Sjöberg, who had a military background. Maybe he taught him to shoot? We'll have to check with Eva Sjöberg, see if they went hunting. In fact, we should check if Hans Sjöberg owned a rifle. Maybe the letter wasn't the only thing that Eriksson took from Sjöberg's house.'

Wiik seemed to like that. He nodded slowly. 'Good call.'

Coffee and a compliment? He was in a good mood this morning. Though you couldn't tell from the scowl on his face. Maybe her brush with death had put his feelings on Jamie into perspective. Or maybe that was just wishful thinking.

'Where are we on the ID for our victim?' Jamie asked. 'Any hits yet?'

'Nothing so far,' Wiik said. 'But it'll circulate on the news again this morning. With some luck we'll get a positive match.'

'And if we don't?'

Wiik looked over at her, then went back to the road. 'We will,' he said. Though he didn't sound so sure.

Gunnarson's lawyer was, as expected, a pit bull.

Jamie and Wiik had waited on him until just after eight, at which point he swept into the building in a swirl of Italian wool and leather, striding purposefully through the HQ like a lion does its territory.

He must have been in his fifties – maybe around Gunnarson's age, with a full head of hair that Jamie suspected was both cosmetically planted and dyed – and a jaw chiselled enough to use on a lathe. His shoulders pumped back and forth as he moved, his briefcase swinging at his side.

The lawyer, a man by the name of Lassen, entered Interview Room 1 without a word, and went around to Mikael Gunnarson's side of the table, sitting next to him and pulling his case onto the surface.

He opened it without looking at either Jamie or Wiik, and pulled out some papers, closing the lid after a moment.

Lassen then shuffled them around and placed them in front of Wiik, taking a pen from his jacket and placing it on top.

'Sign this,' he said, smiling like a wax figurine and clasping his hands together in front of him.

Wiik looked down at it. 'And what is *this?*'

'Release papers – to say you're not charging my client with anything, have no intention of charging him with anything, and are therefore releasing him immediately. He was the victim of a crime, not the perpetrator, and you have no reason to hold him for questioning. As such, I would strongly recommend he be released immediately. Especially considering his personal circumstances and the horrific loss that he just—'

Wiik held his hand up to silence the man. 'Shut up,' he said with a sigh. 'You're right, we're not charging Mr Gunnarson with anything.'

'Then you should—'

Wiik held his hand up again, closing his eyes this time. The vein bulged in his temple, but he was keeping his temper. So far, at least. 'If we let your client go, the person who made an attempt on his life could try again.'

'My client has suffered a great personal loss,' Lassen said.

Gunnarson stared blankly at the table in front of him, face and neck still splattered with his wife's blood. His clothing had been taken from him for analysis, and he was in a set of grey sweatpants and a grey sweater. But he didn't look especially grief-stricken. He didn't look especially anything. Just vacant. He must have been somewhere around sixty – but he looked good for it. Healthy. Barring his stubbled chin, bagged eyes and dishevelled hair.

Jamie watched him carefully as Wiik and Lassen squared off.

'I understand,' Wiik said. 'And believe us, we don't want to be here longer than is absolutely necessary.'

'Then let him go.' Lassen scoffed and shook his head, sitting back in the chair. 'I don't see any reason that any questions couldn't be answered at my client's leisure in a place of his choosing, at a time more befitting.'

Wiik's hand quivered on the table, threatening to make a fist. 'Whether your client is directly involved in an ongoing case or not, my colleague, Detective Johansson, was on the way to speak to him last night, when she intercepted the person trying to murder him. And as his attorney, I would hope that you have his wellbeing at heart. We understand and *appreciate* the situation your client is in, and if you'd like to get him out of here, then I advise *you* to advise *him* to answer our questions quickly, and truthfully. And then he may go.'

Jamie was impressed by Wiik's temperament. She didn't think he was capable of exercising that kind of restraint. Mostly because Lassen seemed like the biggest jackass she'd ever met. Solicitors like him were the bane of detectives' lives. But Wiik was smart, he knew his rights, and so long as he held firm and didn't torture Gunnarson, they could still hold on to him for a while.

'Unless, of course,' Wiik said, sitting back himself now, 'he has a reason not to cooperate?'

Lassen looked at Gunnarson, who shook his head just a little, but didn't look up.

The lawyer drummed his fingers on top of his briefcase. 'Fine. Go ahead.'

Wiik exhaled with relief.

Guys like Lassen could do this all day. Back-and-forths like that were like breathing for them. And they'd been butting heads so long all sense had been knocked clean out of them. They just had an on switch, and a goal: to get their client off, no matter what. And, of course, an extortionate hourly rate to go with that indefatigability.

Jamie measured Lassen across the table and wondered why Gunnarson had called him in? Why had he called for an attorney at all? Let alone one that would do everything in his power to excise him from police custody.

Wiik didn't waste any more time. 'Mr Gunnarson, do you know of any reason someone would make an attempt on your life?'

Lassen tsked. 'If that's the best you've got, then just sign the papers now.'

Wiik ignored him and focused on the man with his wife's blood on his face. 'I'm sure that a prominent businessman like you has made some enemies over the years,' Wiik said. 'Green energy steps on the toes of a lot of powerful people who are desperate to hold on to their business interests.'

Gunnarson looked up and met his eye.

'But I don't think that this was anything to do with your business. This was to do with Tilde.'

'Tilde?' Gunnarson's voice was weak, his eyes wide and sad. 'She's been dead twenty-five years.'

'I know,' Wiik said, stepping lightly. He knew he couldn't reveal too much of the active case. 'But another girl has been murdered. And we're looking at possible connections between this case and Tilde's.'

'The Angel Maker.' Gunnarson's words echoed around the sound-deadened room, and Jamie shifted uncomfortably in her chair, her mind going back to the clearing. Her first night in Sweden. The girl, on her knees, the boughs driven through her back.

'He was caught,' Gunnarson said, more firmly now. 'Put in prison.'

Wiik nodded. 'He was. But more information has come to light now. Other deaths have been linked to that case.'

'Other deaths?'

Lassen sighed loudly. 'Is there a question coming?'

Wiik held Gunnarson's attention. 'It appears that as well as the girls that were killed, that parents were also targeted.'

Gunnarson stayed quiet.

Jamie tried to read his face, but all she found was confusion.

'Did you or Åsa ever experience anything that might have led you to believe that your lives were in danger? Then, or after?'

Gunnarson stared at Wiik and then shook his head slowly. 'No, not until…' He trailed off, jaw quivering, and wiped his eye with his thumb.

Wiik nodded. 'Last night. Okay.' He took a breath, changed tack. 'We're just trying to connect the dots right now, looking for more leads. What can you tell us about Tilde?'

'Tilde?' The name of his daughter got caught in Gunnarson's throat. 'She was a sweet girl. Kind, beautiful.'

'You and your wife never had another child?'

'We hadn't planned Tilde – but Åsa, she was…' He found it difficult to say her name, too. He'd lost his daughter, and now his wife. Jamie was surprised he was keeping it together at all. 'She was thirty-six when we found out she was pregnant.'

Wiik and Jamie both just listened.

'We had always worked so much – we didn't have time for children. But then, suddenly, we were having one. We went to see a doctor – and they told us that waiting any longer would only decrease the chances of having a healthy child. That the older Åsa got…'

Wiik nodded, encouraging him to go on.

'But work was difficult. We always had nannies, au pairs, to look after her. She didn't have many friends, you know?' Gunnarson looked up over Wiik's head. 'So we were,' he started again, his voice catching, 'we were recommended this group – a church group.'

Jamie felt her pulse quicken.

'It was a Sunday-school type thing. Not heavily religious, but apparently there were other girls there around Tilde's age. Lots of them. They met a few times a week. We thought it would be good for her, you know? To meet new people...' He sobbed then, breaking down a little.

Lassen glared at Wiik but kept his mouth shut. He knew that curtailing things here would only prolong the time spent in this room.

Jamie watched Gunnarson, not able to imagine what he was feeling. The guilt he must have felt. He and his wife didn't have time for Tilde, so they'd sent her to a church group to make friends. And it just so happened to be the church group run by Hans and Eva Sjöberg. The one that would ultimately get her raped, kidnapped, murdered.

Jamie swallowed the lump in her own throat and sat up straighter. 'Who recommended the church group to you?'

Gunnarson was a little thrown by the question, but looked over at Jamie anyway. 'Uh,' he said between sobs. 'I don't know – the nanny, I think? She was from the city. She attended the church.'

Wiik already had a notepad at the ready and glanced at Jamie, nodding her to go on.

'Do you remember her name?' Jamie asked.

Gunnarson shook his head. 'No, I don't. There were lots – we were with an agency. They would arrange them.'

Lots? The word set something off in Jamie's head. 'Why were there *lots* of nannies?'

'I don't know – Åsa dealt with it. Some weren't suitable – others were just here on exchange programmes or doing it for a little money while studying. We had nannies from the time she was born until…'

Jamie nodded. 'The nanny that recommended the church group – was she with you long?'

Gunnarson shook his head. 'No, not long. A few months, that was all.' He gave a little sideways glance at Lassen.

Jamie and Wiik both picked up on it, exchanging a glance themselves, that momentary look enough to set them on edge.

Jamie swallowed. 'Why was she only with you for such a short time.'

Gunnarson looked at Lassen again now and the pit bull gave a slight nod of approval that he could go on.

Jamie didn't know whether he had any idea what Gunnarson was about to say, but he sat a little straighter, ready to interject if need be.

Gunnarson began kneading his hands. 'Tilde, uh – she didn't like her – I think.' He added the last bit quickly, then coughed a little, looked down at the table.

Jamie didn't want to stray too far from the original line of questioning, but her back was firmly up. 'Didn't like her? Why not?'

He shook his head, and then looked at Lassen, whose eyes had now narrowed as he watched his client. This was a fine line to tread for him.

'Mr Gunnarson?' Jamie asked, pressing.

He set his jaw and then exhaled shakily. 'I don't know – she just didn't. I don't remember why. And I don't see why this is relevant anyway—'

'It's not,' Lassen said, cutting off his own client. 'It has nothing to do with anything and I'd appreciate it if you'd stay on-topic rather than trying to dredge up decades old, irrelevant information that you couldn't reasonably expect my client to have any memory of.'

'Okay.' Jamie nodded. This wasn't going anywhere. But the reaction alone from Gunnarson and his lawyer told her that they needed to look into it. And that was something. They could get the agency's name, look up the dates leading up to Tilde's death, track the nanny down. Question her, too. 'Do you remember her name, at least?' Jamie asked, giving it one last try.

Gunnarson shook his head, refusing to meet Jamie's eyes, and then looked at Lassen hopefully.

'This won't take much longer,' Jamie said, feeling the air change a little. 'The last nanny' – Lassen opened his mouth but Jamie held her hand up to signal that she wasn't going to keep asking the same questions – 'was she a regular at the church?'

Lassen didn't look at him, but touched Gunnarson's arm in a way he had probably done a hundred times before.

Gunnarson seemed to relax a little, a signal definitely given. 'I don't know,' Gunnarson said, more definitely now. 'It was twenty-five years ago.'

Wiik seemed to sense the sudden wall that had gone up too, and repositioned himself on his chair, letting Jamie carry on with the questions, watching Gunnarson like a hawk.

'Did Tilde know any of the other victims, do you know? Were they friends, or…?'

'I'm sorry, I don't know.'

Jamie was growing uneasy. 'Do you know how many girls were in that church group?'

'I don't.'

'Did you ever attend the church yourself?'

'No.'

'Are you religious?'

'No.'

Lassen stepped in now. 'This interview is going nowhere and these questions are pointless. I hardly think Mr Gunnarson or his wife were targeted because of their religious views.'

Jamie ignored him. 'Mr Gunnarson – it's difficult to imagine that you just placed your child in the care of this nanny and allowed her to take your daughter to a church group that you'd never been to and didn't know anything about.' She was pushing, just a little, just to see.

Gunnarson's sadness boiled into anger. 'You don't think I feel guilty enough about it already?'

'Would you say,' Jamie said, very carefully, 'that you neglected Tilde, or just ignored her?'

Lassen slapped his briefcase now and pushed back from the table, buttoning up his blazer. 'This interview is over,' he said coldly. 'Mikael, we're leaving. Any further questions that you have, you can direct to me, and Mr Gunnarson will reply at his earliest convenience. You have no charges to bring, no reason to keep my client in custody, and he's been more than accommodating. But we will not sit here and allow his parenting skills to be slandered without cause the night after his wife has been murdered – and by the sounds of it, because of historical police negligence.' He cast a scornful eye at Jamie and then Wiik, and then frogmarched Gunnarson out of the room.

Wiik didn't say a word, and didn't move. The door closed behind Gunnarson and his attack dog, and then Wiik let out a long sigh, tapping his pen on his blank notepad.

'Sorry,' Jamie said. 'I shouldn't have pushed so hard.'

Wiik reflected for a moment. 'No, you were right to. I sensed something was off too. And now we know.'

'What do we know?'

Wiik stopped tapping and looked at her. 'That Mikael Gunnarson knows more than he's saying about his daughter's death.'

33

WIIK WAS STANDING BEHIND JAMIE, his arms folded, staring down at the screen in front of her. His screen, in fact. On his desk.

'You know,' he said, pressing his lips into a line so his cheeks puffed a little. 'Hallberg is really good at this stuff.'

Jamie didn't look around and instead kept scrolling down the page she was reading. 'I like doing my own research,' she said, scanning a column of text. It was difficult to focus with Wiik breathing quite literally down her neck.

She was looking up Mikael Gunnarson to see exactly what he was doing at the time of his daughter's death, but all she could find so far was that his company was in the midst of negotiating a major investment from an early-adopting green-energy corporation. Åsa, similarly, was dealing with a huge case that had spread her entire firm thin. But otherwise, nothing seemed of note, though Jamie didn't exactly know what she was looking for. She did know, however, that Mikael Gunnarson knew something he wasn't saying. And that whatever it was, it must have been incriminating, otherwise he wouldn't have refused to say anything without his solicitor present.

Jamie sighed and leaned back in the chair, reaching for the statement he'd given last night at the crime scene again.

'You won't find anything there you didn't the first ten times you read that,' Wiik said, sighing.

She exhaled through her nose and lifted the page. 'You could help, rather than just standing and reading over my shoulder.' The truth was that they were at a wall. And neither wanted to admit it. As soon as Gunnarson had left the room, they'd worked on a series of requests for information that they knew he wouldn't have given during the questioning. Name of the agency used for the nannies, name of the nanny herself. A list of potential enemies or people who may have had it out for him and Åsa. While Jamie and Wiik were almost positive that the shooting and Tilde's death were related, they couldn't rule out that it was just pure coincidence. Though neither of them believed it.

And with Eriksson still in the wind, they were no closer to solving this thing.

Jamie checked her watch. It was almost midday now. The news would be circulating the girl's photo again. But if they hadn't had a hit yet, it was becoming more and more unlikely by the hour that they would.

'Coffee?' Wiik asked from behind her, probably noticing she'd been staring blankly at the same page of Gunnarson's report for the last few minutes. It said they were having dinner, awaiting the arrival of the detectives from Stockholm, and then he saw a flash from across the valley, out of the fog. Then he felt the hot spray of blood on his face and fell off his chair in shock, screaming, scrambling for cover as the shooter put more bullets into the house.

But Jamie hadn't heard any screaming – and she'd been close enough to the house to have been in range.

And while Mikael Gunnarson's chair was pushed back

from the table, it didn't look like anyone had toppled off it.

Though none of that meant anything. Maybe he'd not screamed loudly – rather squealed. Maybe he'd fallen sideways off the chair. Maybe he'd not screamed at all and had dived for cover the moment his wife's chest had been blown all over his face.

Whatever happened, Jamie had a feeling that there was more to him than met the eye. The question was, though, how much they'd get out of him with Lassen on defence.

Wiik laid a hand on her shoulder and she looked around.

'Coffee?' he asked again, raising an eyebrow.

'Sure,' Jamie said, dropping the statement onto his desk and rubbing her eyes.

Wiik disappeared towards the coffee machine and Jamie watched him go. Though the case was getting worse, the leads drying up and the suspects disappearing, Wiik seemed in reasonable spirits.

Jamie thought about what Falk had said – that Wiik was the temperamental type, that losing his partner had really shaken him. But he seemed to be more himself now. Or what Jamie thought 'himself' might be. She just hoped he wasn't getting any ideas about her hanging around.

She dragged her eyes from him and sighed, jolting in shock as she realised Hallberg was standing at the corner of the desk, clutching a piece of paper.

'Jesus,' Jamie said, shaking it off. 'You scared the shit out of me.'

'Sorry,' Hallberg said, breathless. She looked like she'd been running. 'Where's Wiik?'

'Getting coffee, what's wrong?' Jamie asked, reading the haste in her voice.

'Nothing's wrong,' Hallberg said, thrusting the piece of paper at her. 'We just got a call – positive ID on our victim.'

Jamie grabbed it and stared down at the photograph of their victim on the pathologist's slab. Under it was a photograph of a young girl. She was maybe a year or so younger in that photo and was standing next to a woman at what looked like a birthday party. They had their arms around one another. The woman was grinning. The girl wasn't. She looked uncomfortable and was wearing a pin with *13* on it, Jamie doubted of her own choosing.

Wiik appeared just then, holding a single cup of coffee. He handed it to Jamie and took the paper out of her hands at the same time. He must have spotted Hallberg from the machines and hightailed it over.

She stared down into the brown liquid. Looks like he didn't have time to get both.

Jamie took a long, scalding gulp, and then pushed to her feet, crowding Wiik to read the paper.

'Emmy Berg,' Jamie said, reading the name. 'Thirteen years old.'

'The call was made by…' Wiik said, scanning the words. 'Anna Hansen, is that right?' He glanced up at Hallberg.

She nodded.

'Who is Hansen to Emmy Berg?' he probed.

'Foster mother,' Hallberg said quickly. 'Emmy Berg was orphaned, has been placed at several homes – Anna Hansen said she had a habit of running away. From previous homes, and theirs, too. Her and her husband Jan have been fostering her for a little over ten months – Anna said she thought the girl was happy. She wanted to report her missing, but Jan insisted that she would come back when she was ready, or they'd get a call from the police that she'd been picked up. She seemed upset by the whole thing.'

Wiik shook his head in disgust. 'Who would leave a thirteen-year-old girl to the mercy of the city?'

Hallberg looked like she was about to hazard a guess before she decided against it and kept quiet.

Jamie nodded to her that it was the right call and she looked away bashfully.

'Right,' Wiik said suddenly, smacking the paper with the knuckles of his other hand. 'We have a positive ID. Finally.' He looked at Hallberg, as if deciding, and then landed on Jamie. 'You ready? I want to speak to them in person as soon as possible. Just in case our shooter gets any more bold ideas.'

Jamie bit her lip and glanced at Hallberg. 'You should come with us—'

'No,' Wiik said, looking at her. 'Hallberg can stay – carry on your research into Mikael Gunnarson. You're terrible at it anyway.'

Jamie was knocked off balance by the bluntness of the insult. 'My research is—'

But Wiik wasn't listening, or he didn't care. Or both. He was already striding back towards the corridor, leaving both Jamie and Hallberg standing in silence.

After a second Jamie exhaled and looked at the girl. 'He does that a lot, huh?'

'Insults you, cuts you off, and then walks away?' Hallberg raised an eyebrow. 'More than you'd think.'

'Great,' Jamie said, reaching for her jacket, and her coffee too. 'Good work on getting the ID,' she said. 'You're going to make a great detective.' She smiled at the girl, took another sip from her coffee, and then went after Wiik, suddenly full of energy.

She didn't know if they made the coffee stronger in Sweden, or if it finally felt like a break in the case, but either way, she was moving fast and had no intention of slowing down.

34

WIIK WAS DRIVING QUICKLY.

Whether he thought they were racing another shooter to the punch, or whether he was just angry and not paying attention to the speedometer, Jamie didn't know. But either way, he was doing nearly twice the speed limit. And on slick roads, too.

His phone buzzed in his pocket and he wrestled it out, glancing down at the screen. 'Shit,' he muttered, looking back up and weaving around a car pulling left into a side street. They laid on their horn as the car straightened out and slipped away, deeper into the city.

'What is it?' Jamie asked, reading the look of frustration on Wiik's face.

'Forensic reports have just come back on Eriksson's, Eva Sjöberg's and your place.'

Her place? Wiik meant her father's house. But yes, she guessed it was hers now. It just felt strange to hear it come out of someone's mouth.

She didn't have much time to process it as Wiik went on. 'Eriksson's was clean – if he was doing anything sick with

Emmy Berg before he murdered her, then he wasn't doing it there.'

Jamie made a disapproving *hmm* sound at Wiik's conjecture, but didn't slow him down.

'No prints, no DNA, nothing. And his computer is gone, too.' He sighed hard, brake-checked as a car in front flew out of the distance towards them, and then started weaving back and forth in the lane, looking for space to overtake.

Jamie hadn't ever seen him drive like this. He'd not been a slow driver before, but it was always measured. Now, it was bordering on erratic. He'd been in a good mood that morning – brought her coffee. But now… It was as though getting the ID on Emmy Berg had done something to him. Had stoked his fire. The cool, detached man she'd first met had now been replaced by a father with a grudge, his hands in fists around the wheel.

Was it a daughter he had? He'd said he had a kid, but Jamie couldn't remember if he'd said a boy or girl. Divorced, though, he'd said, right? She'd barely been listening. And though she'd been living in his pocket for the last four days, she didn't know a damn thing about him. But if he was half as difficult to get on with in a marriage as he was in work, she wasn't all that surprised.

She glanced across at the man, noted that his usually impeccably clean jaw was now covered in one-day stubble.

Then again, she doubted she looked runway ready either. She'd not washed her hair since she'd arrived and her long sleeve was wrinkled from the sink-wash it had suffered the night before. That, combined with the total sixteen hours of sleep she'd had over the last four days, probably made her look like she'd just crawled out of the gutter.

She could smell the faintest whiff of sweat in the air and had assumed it was coming from Wiik. But looking at him now – unshaven but washed, in a perfectly pressed shirt – she came to the conclusion that it was either coming from her hair or her own top.

Jamie cleared her throat and focused on the task at hand. 'So Eriksson's running,' she said. 'No news there. What about Sjöberg's house?'

Wiik looked at his phone again. 'Tracks in the snow indicate a single person gained access through an unlocked bedroom window, then exited the same way. The tracks were doubled-back on to remove any trace of tread marks and to make sizing impossible. Sound familiar?'

Jamie looked ahead, thankful that Wiik was coming up on a wall of cars and a red light. He pressed the brake and they slowed. She noticed then that her hand was around the safety handle on the door. 'Yeah, it does.' Jamie thought back to the crime scene. The killer had backtracked on his footprints for the same reason. And she guessed it was the same at her father's house, too. 'What about DNA, fibres, particulates—'

'Nothing. They scraped the whole place, found lots of skin and hair they've positively matched to Eva Sjöberg – but nothing else. Killer probably wore gloves, a hat...'

'Like every person in this city in January,' Jamie remarked, shaking her head. 'Shit. And uh,' she said, finding it hard to say. 'What about *my* house?'

Wiik's eyes were on the road now, but even from briefly skimming what Jamie had assumed was a summarising email from Hallberg, he'd committed all the details to memory. 'No signs of forced entry, tracks doubled-back on. There was no moisture in the house, either, no snowy prints on the floor – so the CSTs assume that it happened sometime the day before. Pinpointing time is difficult. Which makes looking for nearby CCTV practically impossible. Or at least more time consuming than we can afford.'

Jamie set her jaw. Damn. If she had reported it when she first got there the night before, would there have been prints? Other evidence that had degraded through the night? Evidence that she'd walked out the front door on the bottom of her own shoes and destroyed? Jamie swallowed and tried to move the conversation on as quickly as she could.

'Did they say if anything was missing?' She'd already removed certain items – ones she didn't want bagged and tagged and stuck in an evidence locker for years.

'Nothing apparent – but it will take a while to catalogue everything. And I'm sure they'll ask you some questions, too, just to confirm.'

Jamie nodded, glad Wiik hadn't mentioned anything that suggested they knew she'd arrived home a full twelve hours before she'd called the CSTs in. 'So, timeline,' she started, raising her hands. 'We visit Eriksson, the second we walk out the front door, he's out the back, in the... church bus? He races over to Eva Sjöberg's house, gets in through the window, takes the letter he sent to Hans to stop us from using it in evidence – maybe lifts Hans's hunting rifle if he has one, then slips back out.'

Wiik sort of scoffed. 'For all we know, he rang the front doorbell and asked Eva Sjöberg for them right to her face. The woman will be completely useless as a witness when this goes to trial. We'd get as much sense painting a face on Hans's urn and asking that questions instead.'

Jamie wasn't sure if that was supposed to be humorous or not. She thought Wiik was even less funny than she was. And that was saying something. Someone had once asked her to tell a joke, but the only one she knew – and still knew – involved the words 'knock, knock' and an owl. And she'd somehow managed to screw that up the one time she'd told it, too. Jamie pressed on anyway. 'So he leaves Eva Sjöberg's house with the letter, then goes to my father's house? Picks the lock to get in, looks around – maybe takes a notebook, or a page from one?'

'And then follows you out to Rättvik,' Wiik added. 'Leaves you a note to try and scare you off the investigation.'

'And when I don't get the message, and then show up at the Gunnarsons' place…'

'He's got the rifle in hand, and a chance to kill two birds with one gun. Literally.'

Jamie pursed her lips, thinking. 'But why break in at all? He couldn't think that we wouldn't connect the dots. That we would go see him, he'd make a comment on my notebook, and then, when a threatening note shows up under my windscreen wiper, that we wouldn't immediately leap to him?'

'Maybe that's what he wanted. If he didn't think we'd home in on him, why would he run? Taking a page from your father's notebook was as much of a message to back off as the message itself.'

Jamie nodded. That was her first thought at the scene, too. 'No doubt he was looking for this, as well.' She pulled out the red notebook she had in her pocket. It wasn't the Angel Maker notebook – that was still back at her hotel. But Wiik didn't and wouldn't know the difference. 'He was probably looking for all evidence from the original case, anything he could remove to lessen potential evidence against him. Except he didn't find it.'

'So he changes the plan, snatches a page from one of your father's notebooks, and writes you a little letter to try and get you to back off.' Wiik narrowed his eyes.

Jamie watched as he fitted the puzzle pieces together in his head.

'And then follows you out to Rättvik, note in hand.' Wiik glanced over at her. 'But how would he pick up your trail?'

Jamie thought on that. 'He knew about Annika Liljedahl,' she said, recalling their conversation. 'He told me about her – he knew I'd go there. He put me on to her. He could have withheld that information, played dumb. I'd never have known the difference.'

'What does he gain from getting Annika Liljedahl wrapped up in all this?'

Jamie bit her lip. 'Annika's story about Hans Sjöberg was the reason my father believed he was guilty.' Jamie scoffed a little, shaking her head. 'And it was the reason that his guilt was called into question in my mind... The story doesn't implicate Sjöberg in the Angel Maker case – it just calls Sjöberg's character into question.'

'And Eriksson knows that,' Wiik said. 'So he sends you out there to throw the original conviction into question... You come away believing Sjöberg was wrongly convicted... And it all leads back to Eriksson.'

'Shit,' Jamie said, understanding then. 'He's playing with us. It's all just a big game to him, and he's got us out here chasing our tails.'

Wiik sort of grunted his approval of the theory and his growing disdain for Eriksson.

There was still one thing she couldn't figure out. 'But what does he get from killing the parents? From putting a bullet between Åsa Gunnarson's shoulders and trying to blow Mikael Gunnarson's head off?'

Wiik drew a slow breath. That one escaped him, too. 'I don't know. The court transcripts don't tell much of a story – Sjöberg pleaded innocent, to begin with, but didn't contest the signed confession. The transcript shows no mention of him announcing that the confession was coerced as Eva Sjöberg said.' He looked over at her to gauge her reaction to that, Jamie thought.

She tried not to show any. She only had one person saying that her father had brutalised Hans Sjöberg to get that confession, and a distinct lack of corroboration to argue against it. No confirmation wasn't the same as opposition.

'The evidence was overwhelming, and by the time they'd presented what they had on the third victim, Hans Sjöberg offered to change his plea – and then plead guilty to all seven murders.'

'Jesus,' Jamie said. Wiik had been busy in Jamie's absence. Between the trip to Rättvik and then the run out to the Gunnarsons', it looked like he'd done his homework. 'So he pleads guilty to the seven murders to cover up the killings of the parents? But that doesn't make sense if it was Eriksson all along.'

'The evidence was overwhelming. Maybe a guilty plea got him a shorter sentence?' Wiik offered.

'If you were innocent, would you plead guilty to the rape and murder of seven teenage girls for a shorter sentence?'

'I don't know,' Wiik said, sighing now. 'But either way, we can't rule him out. There was solid evidence on top of the confession… which means there's a good chance he was the Angel Maker.' He looked at Jamie now, his features grave. 'Or at least one of them.'

'What do you mean?' Jamie eyed him now.

Wiik moved his head back and forth. 'Seven girls and their parents? Twelve total victims in the space of a year – nearly thirteen if you include Leif Lundgren? That's prolific.'

'You think Sjöberg and Eriksson were in on it together?' Jamie hadn't considered that.

'Who knows? Both were religious men – both believed in whatever fucked-up version of God and faith drives men to rape and murder children. Sjöberg had the medical knowledge and training from the army, Eriksson knew his way around a hatchet. Maybe one did the girls and one did the parents. Maybe they took turns with the girls—'

Jamie cut him off. She'd heard enough. 'So they get together, cook this scheme up over a bottle of whisky, a couple of buddies, and then they just, what, start murdering?'

'I've had wilder theories that have panned out.'

Jamie exhaled hard, her head spinning suddenly. 'And then when Sjöberg gets picked up, he takes the fall for Eriksson. They part ways, keep the radio silence for appearances, Eriksson goes into the church to cover his tracks.'

Wiik nodded. 'They think they'll get together when Sjöberg gets out, maybe do another one for old times' sake.'

'But then Sjöberg gets sick. Reaches out to his old friend, tells him he's not getting better...'

'Eriksson goes to visit him, they have a nice off-the-record chat. Just like they used to, plan another kill. Plan how to get away with it – what he'd need to do. Nyström, the case files...'

'And when Sjöberg dies...' Wiik said, rolling his head left and right, looking for an opening for another overtake.

'Eriksson chooses a girl and gets to work. Pays tribute to his friend and the good old days...'

'And throws doubts on the original investigation, too – potentially exonerating his friend. Muddying the waters for us. Splitting our focus.'

'Or at least giving Eva Sjöberg some peace.' Jamie bit her lip. 'Sounds like he did care about her.'

'It's all a lie,' Wiik said coldly. 'He's a piece of shit and he's playing a game. That addled old woman is just one more part of it. He's a twisted child-killer, a rapist, and he thinks he's a lot smarter than he really is. Just like they all do. And with Nyström in the bag, the case files missing, he thinks he's gotten away with it all.'

'Except he doesn't bank on me showing up,' Jamie said, feeling Wiik's anger start to rub off on her.

'Right. And when you come asking about Sjöberg, Annika Liljedahl, it sets alarm bells ringing. He knows we're getting close, so he bolts – tries to clean up his mess. He goes after the letter to Hans, he tracks down the Gunnarsons' to sweep up his mess. He goes out to Rättvik, banking on you being there, tries to scare you off the case.'

'Why not just try and kill me then, too?' Jamie asked. She had to play devil's advocate. It was the job.

'Kidnapping an old, semi-retired detective is one thing. Especially because he needed Nyström. But he's older, too. Remember how he winced when he leaned against the desk in his bedroom?' Wiik glanced at her for confirmation. Damn, he really didn't miss a thing.

'I did. You don't think that was bullshit too?'

'Who knows. But either way – you're a few decades his junior, and you've only got to take one look at you to know that you wouldn't go quietly.'

Jamie restrained a little smile.

'Maybe he sized you up, thought he was going to be biting off more than he could chew if he came after you face to face.'

'But with a rifle from across the valley…' Jamie sighed. 'Damn,' she said tiredly.

'"Damn" what?' Wiik asked, indicating at the last second and swinging down another street.

Jamie jostled in her seat but didn't think twice about the standard of driving anymore. 'Damn – it all fits.'

'It does.'

'So you think Eriksson is our guy?' Jamie asked, watching the buildings go by. They'd changed now from central-city offices and apartment blocks to suburban townhouses.

'I do,' Wiik said. 'Whether Sjöberg was in on it too, or Eriksson hung him out to dry, I can't say. But I know one thing – innocent men don't run.' Wiik decelerated sharply. 'The main question now, is how he chose Emmy Berg, and more pertinently, whether he's going to stop at one.'

The brakes squealed as they came to a stop and Jamie lurched forward and then slumped back in the chair, looking up at the pretty townhouses on her left. Tall, narrow, three-storeyed. Picturesque.

'Come on,' Wiik said, stepping out. 'Let's go and question Jan and Anna Hansen.' He closed the door and buttoned up his coat against the cold. 'And with any luck,' he said, looking across the top of the car at Jamie, 'we're not already too late.'

35

JAN HANSEN WAS an accounts manager for a software development company in the city. And he made a lot of money doing it. His wife, Anna Hansen, retired from work at forty-three years old to foster children full time.

They had been married for over twenty-five years, and had one child of their own. Anna fell pregnant at just seventeen, and they got married as soon as it was legal. Now that their own son had flown the nest, Anna had wanted to fill that hole.

They were currently fostering two children. A boy, William Martinsson. And their victim, Emmy Berg.

By all accounts they were good, wholesome, generous people. Neither had criminal records, or anything to suggest that they were anything else. Except for the fact that both Wiik and Jamie unanimously agreed that Jan Hansen was one of the least caring and rudest people that they'd ever met.

'It's not our fault,' he said flatly, arms folded, sitting back into the corner of the sofa in his living room.

The house was sizeable – three floors, four bedrooms. His wife and his was on the first floor – along with the one that

Jan had converted into a home office – and the children's on the second.

Jamie could see that Jan's general demeanour was like nails on a chalkboard to Wiik. His temple vein was back again. So she took the lead. 'No one is saying it's your fault, Mr Hansen,' Jamie offered diplomatically.

Anna Hansen spoke up then. 'Emmy was such a sweet girl—'

But then Jan Hansen cut her off for what must have been the fifth time in as many minutes. 'She was a rambunctious, uncontrollable teenager. She was a runaway. And she was a thief,' he said bitterly.

His wife's lip quivered. 'For God's sake, Jan!' she said, throwing her hands down but keeping her eyes on the floor. She didn't dare shout *at* him. 'She was just a girl! An innocent girl. She'd been bounced from house to house, from family to family – she was scared, and she didn't think anyone could ever love her.'

Jan sneered. 'She didn't know how good she had it.'

'No, she didn't!' Anna nearly yelled this time. 'But we were getting there with her. She would have understood. If you'd have just been a little…'

Jan leaned forward on the sofa now. 'A little what?' he spat. 'Nicer?' He laughed now, his words dripping with bile. 'She had a warm bed, food in her stomach, and a roof over her head. And what did she give us? Nothing but sullen grunts, angry silences and grief.' He looked at Jamie and Wiik now. 'Either of you ever fostered?'

They both shook their heads.

'Well *don't*. More trouble than it's worth. And now the agency is going to try and say it was *our* fault. You know how many times that girl ran away?'

They shook their heads again.

'Six times. Six times in ten months.' He shook his head and sneered again. 'She'd wait for an opportunity, and then *bang.*' He clapped loudly and threw his right hand into the air. 'Out the door with whatever she could stuff in her pockets.'

Jamie set her jaw. 'You don't seem to like fostering, Mr Hansen,' she said slowly, glancing at the ceiling.

'Until this one,' Jan said, laughing again, 'It's been a dream. But Emmy?' He tutted now.

Anna was silent. Submissively so. Jamie expected that it was Anna's wish to foster the children, and that Jan just went along with it. Though Jamie couldn't understand why. Anna obviously wasn't the dominant one here.

Wiik asked a question now. 'What kind of things did she take?'

'What *didn't* she steal?' Jan said.

Jamie noted the use of the word 'steal' versus Wiik's 'take'. Whether it meant anything, Jamie didn't know. But it felt harsher to hear. More blame-laying, that much was certain. Jan was playing himself off as the victim. Or trying to. He didn't look like one, though. He actually didn't look like much except for a gigantic dickhead. She watched him with his voice on mute as he counted off the things Emmy had taken on his hands – very animatedly, she realised, without any sound. She caught the words 'ornaments', 'silverware', 'an iPad', before she got rid of his voice altogether. Jamie was glad he was easy to tune out, and instead focused on the 'loving' husband and wife in front of her.

Anna was slight, with a short brown pixie cut. She had a pointed chin and a small nose, sunken eyes and prominent cheekbones. She was wearing a high-collared dress that stretched down to her shins, a brown cardigan and house slippers.

Jan, on the other hand, was big – a little overweight, maybe hovering around six feet or so. He had a thick neck and a narrow head so that it looked like someone had painted a face on a finger. She remembered what Wiik had said about Sjöberg's urn and tried not to smirk to herself. Jan Hansen's ears stuck out of his tapering, bald head, and supported thin and what she was sure he was told by the optician were 'trendy' glasses. They hugged his face and covered his beady eyes. She watched as the roll of skin wobbled under his weak chin, her eyes moving down to his open short-sleeved white shirt, the hairy exposed forearms, and then she slowly turned the volume up, just as he was getting to the end of what seemed to be an exhaustive list.

'—which is why we started hiding the electronics,' he said, finishing with a flourish of his arms.

Jamie refocused on Anna now. 'Anna,' she said, waiting for the woman to look up. 'Can you tell us what Emmy was like?'

'The girl was—' Jan began before Wiik laid daggers into him.

'Inspector Johansson was talking to your wife,' he said coolly, staring the guy out.

Jan, like all bullies, shrank at the first sign of someone standing up to them.

'Anna,' Jamie said again.

'I thought… I thought she was happy,' Anna Hansen said quietly. 'She was sweet.'

Jan scoffed behind her, and then sat back again, pouting, crossing his hairy arms over his belly.

Anna went on after a few seconds – once she realised Jan wouldn't speak again. He knew better with Wiik still staring at him. 'She was… she was scared, I think.'

'Scared of what?' Jamie asked, trying not to lean in too expectantly.

'Scared of being loved.'

Jamie's jaw tightened. Not the answer she wanted, but it was one that tugged on the heartstrings. Hard. Anna was distraught by it. Jamie could see that. 'How many children have you fostered?' she asked, changing the way she was going to approach this.

'Emmy was our... fourth? Fifth.' She corrected herself. 'We usually try to take one teenager, and one younger. Often it's difficult to place teenagers – not many families want them. And they can often be more difficult than the younger children.'

Jan looked like he wanted to weigh in, but Wiik wasn't looking like he wanted to be tested, so instead he kept quiet and resigned himself to sulking.

'I can imagine,' Jamie said. 'The other child you have now – has he been with you long?'

'William?' Anna asked. 'Yes – about two years now. Maybe a little longer.'

'And how old is William?'

'He's eight,' Anna said.

'Good.' Jamie offered her a warm smile. The woman seemed genuinely nice. What she was doing with a guy like Jan, was anybody's guess. Though Hallberg had said she didn't have a job, and the house wasn't cheap. Jan must have earned a lot on his own to afford it. She expected that he reminded Anna of that often. 'And before William?'

'Elias – he was with us for seven years. From the time he was eleven to when he was eighteen.'

'He was lucky to have you,' Jamie said.

Jan couldn't help himself this time. 'And the boy knew it, too.'

Wiik growled, then stood up. 'Mr Hansen – could you show me to Emmy's room, please? We'd like to take a look at it.'

He looked at Wiik, then at Jamie. 'Why? The girl was never there. Always out, doing who knows what with who knows who.'

Wiik straightened his jacket. 'All part of the investigation,' he said, forcing a smile. 'Would you mind?'

Jan Hansen looked at his wife now – staring at the back of her head as though afraid to leave her alone with Jamie.

'Now, Mr Hansen.'

The man reddened visibly, then heaved himself off the sofa. 'Fine,' he said. 'Top floor. After you.'

He trailed after Wiik, glancing back a dozen times before he disappeared up the stairs.

Jamie breathed a little easier, but Anna looked more apprehensive than before.

'Are you alright, Mrs Hansen?' Jamie asked.

'Yes,' she replied quickly. 'It's just…'

'What?'

'Jan didn't want me to call you,' she all but whispered.

'Why not?' Jamie asked quickly, aware that Jan was probably doing all he could to hurry Wiik along and get back down here.

'I don't know – he said that no one would care that she was gone. That it would be easier for everyone if we just left things as they were.'

Jamie measured the woman, aware she had to tread a fine line here. 'Mr Hansen said Emmy had run away before – six times.'

'That's right.'

'Did she always come back?'

'Yes – eventually. She knew where we kept the spare key

for the side gate, and the back door. She'd usually slip in during the night. I'd find her in bed in the morning.'

'And how did she seem when she came back?'

'What do you mean?'

'Children who run away don't usually try to come back – not unless something has happened to them, or—'

'Oh, no, I don't think it was anything like that,' Anna said dismissively. 'I think she just realised it was safer here than out there, you know? For a girl of her age. She wouldn't tell me where she went or why she left… But I trusted her to talk to me when she was ready. She just never… got the…' Anna Hansen broke down into tears then and began to sob quietly.

Jamie steeled herself. She had to maintain distance. She cleared her throat, looked down, gathered her thoughts, and then spoke again. 'Fostering children can be difficult. You can take solace in the fact that you provided a solid, dependable, safe environment for her. But girls like Emmy – if they've been in the system for a while – it can be hard for them to build trust.'

Anna nodded, not stopping.

'Did Emmy have a phone by any chance? Did you contact her while she was away from the house at all?'

Anna shook her head. 'No, I gave her a phone,' she choked out. 'But Jan said she sold it…'

Jamie cursed inwardly but kept going, conscious of time. 'Do you know where she might have gone? Did she have any friends or contacts in the city?'

Again, Anna shook her head. 'No – William is… he has friends, you know? But Emmy – she struggled to meet people. She was nervous. Quiet. She liked to be alone.'

'I know the feeling. Life can be tough at that age,' Jamie said honestly. Her childhood had been better than some, but worse than others. But compared to girls like Emmy, it had been a breeze.

Anna nodded her confirmation. 'After the phone – Jan said we couldn't give her anything like a laptop, or a TV, so Emmy read mostly when she was here.'

Jamie swallowed. 'Mr Hansen said she went out a lot – do you know where? Was it in the day, at night?'

'At night, mostly – she would go out before Jan came home, come back after he'd gone to bed. He would always lock up – said it would teach her to tell the time. But I'd always leave a key out.'

'She was lucky to have you,' Jamie said, trying to keep her voice straight. 'Did she ever say where she went?'

Anna shook her head again, stifling the sobs. 'No. She didn't talk to me much.'

Jamie gritted her teeth now. They were going around in circles. No phone, no laptop. Nothing. No friends. No contacts. She coughed into her fist to shift the lump in her throat and asked the question she needed to. 'Was Emmy religious? Do you think she might have been going to a church, or—'

'A church?' Anna looked up now, her expression quizzical. 'No, I don't think... she was— she liked science, and I never heard her talk about it – Jan and I aren't religious. And I didn't read anything about it in her file – and they always include things like that. Any requirements or beliefs – allergies, religions, things they like and dislike. What you can do to make their stays easier, you know?'

Jamie nodded, taking it in. Then how the hell did she connect to Eriksson? 'Thank you,' Jamie said. 'I'm sorry this has happened.'

Anna quietened then and looked down at her hands. 'I just wanted to help, you know?'

'I know,' Jamie said, thinking about her own youth – those formative years. Where she remembered everything that passed between her mother and father so vividly. The arguments, the tears, the screaming. 'But sometimes, children don't want to be helped. No matter how much they need it.'

'It's not about helping them – it's just about loving them.'

Jamie let that hang in the air for a few seconds, listening to the footsteps ringing down from above. 'Is William here now?' Jamie asked after a moment.

'Yes, he's in his room,' Anna said.

'How was his relationship with Emmy?' Emmy wasn't talking to Anna and certainly not to Jan, but kids often spoke to each other. Though William was only eight, so Jamie wasn't holding out much hope. Still, she had to try. All they knew so far was that Emmy would be out of the house for long periods of time, would steal and sell what she could to get by and that she was abducted while she was out of the house. It was clear she was trying to scrape money together – probably for a train or a bus ticket. For something. A fresh start, maybe – to get away? Jamie didn't know. But she'd only come back when she ran out of money or realised she wasn't going to make it. Except for the last time. She was going *somewhere*. She was meeting *someone*.

The Angel Maker's MO wasn't to just abduct girls off the street. They were chosen. They were groomed or coerced. They went willingly into the cars. There were so signs that any of the victims had been harmed physically other than the sexual assaults, which meant that either they knew their attackers or at least felt safe enough to go with them willingly. The reports – old and new – had shown the same thing. That the girls were assaulted, and then afterwards – but not immediately – they were suffocated, and then quickly mounted and displayed in succession. A picture was forming:

either Sjöberg or Eriksson had groomed the girls in that church group, abused them, and then when they'd got bored, they'd killed them. Or it was a joint effort from the start, or one got off on the rape and the other on the murder. But either way, there was a connection here between Emmy Berg and Per Eriksson. All they had to do was find it.

Somehow, that sick fuck had managed to get his claws into this girl, and now she was dead.

Anna spoke then. 'Their relationship was good, I think. William liked her – he liked having an older sister.'

'We'll need to speak to William, if that's alright?'

Anna looked apprehensive. 'Is that really necessary?'

'I'm afraid so – he may not realise it, but he may know something important.' She smiled at Anna. 'Don't worry, we can do it here if you'd prefer. Not now, but we'll come at a time that suits you and William, and there'll be a children's welfare officer with us.'

'A welfare officer? We treat William like one of our own—'

'No, it's nothing like that,' Jamie said, shaking her head. 'It's just to ensure that William isn't becoming distressed by the questions, and that we're not pressing too hard. It's just standard procedure. Nothing to worry about.'

Anna nodded slowly. 'I can't imagine that he'll know anything – he's only eight. Emmy wouldn't have told him anything.' Anna looked into space now. 'William did all the talking – he was always asking her to sit with him, to watch him play his games.' Anna smiled weakly.

'What games?' Jamie asked warmly, just trying to get a better picture of the situation here.

'I don't know – something on his iPad – where you build things with blocks, you know the one?'

'Minecraft?' Jamie asked.

'I think that's it, yes,' Anna confirmed. 'He's always playing on it.'

'It's a popular game,' Jamie said.

'He was always so keen to show Emmy what he'd built, and she'd help him out, too – when he couldn't do something. It's over my head, of course. Jan understands it more than I do. He says they shouldn't play on it, and that Emmy's as likely to steal William's tablet as she did her own.'

Jamie wasn't listening, though. Something had twigged in her head. 'You said that Emmy would help William out with his games?'

'Yes – Jan didn't want her to. But I thought it was a good way for them to bond.'

Jamie leaned forward now. 'You said Emmy sold her tablet, didn't you? Her phone too?'

'That's what Jan said.' Anna looked at her, a confused expression on her face.

'How did he know?' Something wasn't sitting right with her.

Anna sort of stuck her bottom lip out and shook her head. 'I don't understand what you're asking.'

Jamie drew a slow breath. 'It's okay – don't worry. I wonder if you can do something for me, though?'

'What is it?' Anna was apprehensive, kneading her hands.

'Would you give us permission to search your home? And conduct a cursory examination of any computers, tablets, phones that we find.' Jamie said it casually, as though it was just a simple request. She tried not to let on that everything might hinge on it.

'Our computers and phones?' Anna asked. 'Why?'

'We just need to check whether Emmy might have reached out to anyone. It's all just standard procedure –

nothing to worry about, I'm sure. But it could help us find out who took her. You want that, don't you?'

Anna looked at the empty stairs, at the place Jan had been before Wiik had led him away.

'Anna?' Jamie said, her voice a little sterner.

The woman looked around at her.

'You want to help us find Emmy's killer, don't you?'

She swallowed and then nodded, her head barely moving. 'I do,' she all but whispered.

'Good,' Jamie said, feeling the tension drain from her shoulders. 'That makes everything a lot easier.' She smiled at the woman. 'You're doing the right thing.'

She said nothing, but her quivering lip told Jamie she thought Jan would be angry.

In Jamie's eyes, though, that was all the more reason to find out what he was hiding.

36

JAN HANSEN'S voice carried from inside the house down the street to where Jamie was standing. He was yelling at the officers walking up his steps and in through his door, protesting and telling them to get out. But they had written consent to be there – courtesy of his wife – and whether he was a controlling piece of shit or not, her name was on the deed too, and that was all they needed.

Jamie tore her head away as the last of the officers filed in to do their sweep and looked at Wiik. He was watching her.

'You did good,' he said.

'Do you think we'll find anything?'

He raised his shoulders into a shrug and then let them fall. 'I don't know. But Hansen never moved from my shoulder, and every time I opened a drawer, he'd say, "There's nothing in there."'

'Like he knew?'

'Like he'd already emptied the room out.' Wiik scowled up at the pretty townhouse.

'The question is whether he was smart enough to get rid

of whatever was left altogether, or if he just thought hiding it was enough.'

Wiik smirked a little. 'I'm more curious as to why he removed or hid anything to begin with. And if he did – how he knew Emmy wasn't coming back.'

Jamie clicked her teeth together, listening to Jan Hansen's diatribe at the presence of the officers in his house carry on the cold wind. She shivered and pulled her peacoat tighter around her body. 'Any word yet from Hallberg on the Gunnarson thing?'

Wiik cracked his neck, reached up and flattened his hair against his head, and then replaced his hands in his pockets. 'Hallberg has followed up with Gunnarson's lawyer, but hasn't got anything back. Gunnarson's too grief-stricken to answer our questions, supposedly. She also managed to make a list of agencies in the city that supplied nannies and au pairs between '95 and '96. Though most of them aren't operating anymore. She's going to reach out to the owners today and see if any of them had Mikael and Åsa Gunnarson listed as clients. Then we'll see if we can track down the nanny in question and get her talking.' He sighed. 'But that's a lot of ifs.'

'Shit,' Jamie said. 'In the meantime, we should probably put a watch on Leif Lundgren, just in case the killer wants to take another swing at him.'

'Already done.' Wiik said, looking at her and smiling a little.

'I'm guessing by your face he didn't take to the idea.'

'No. But his options were being left to the wolves or being followed by a police car. He chose the lesser of two evils.' This seemed to amuse Wiik. Jamie recalled that he'd said Leif Lundgren was a bit of an asshole.

'Leif Lundgren and Jan Hansen,' Jamie muttered after a few seconds.

'What was that?'

'It's just weird, right? Both Hanna Lundgren and Emmy Berg weren't Lundgren's and Hansen's biological children. Hanna Lundgren was adopted, Emmy Berg was being fostered. Have Hallberg go back and check the relationships of the deceased parents with the original victims.'

'What are you thinking?'

Jamie shook her head. 'Not sure. Just a thought. But I'd bet they're not biological relatives. At least not all of them. Step-parents, foster parents…'

'Okay, I'll get her on it.' Wiik nodded, seeming to trust her instincts more now. He pulled his phone out and started tapping away.

Jamie turned to look back at the sea of police cars up ahead, wondering what the neighbours would think. She'd task a uniform with getting statements from them too. See if they knew anything about Emmy Berg.

It was now getting late in the afternoon and the sky had dimmed to a dull and lifeless grey. The streetlights would be coming on any minute now.

They had an interview set up for the following morning with William Martinsson – the boy that Anna and Jan were fostering. She was bringing him to HQ at nine, and they'd conduct the interview there. When Jan had come downstairs and found out that officers were on their way in force to toss the house, he'd all but blown his top. There was no way that they were going to do an interview at the home with Jan anywhere near it. If Emmy was avoiding him like the plague, there was a good chance the boy wasn't too fond of the man either. And they needed him talking. And if that meant him being as far away from Jan Hansen as possible, then they were happy to oblige.

Jamie heard Wiik's phone buzz in his hand and turned back to him. 'That was quick, even for Hallberg,' Jamie said, trying to lighten the mood. But Wiik's expression told her that nothing would have done the job. 'What's wrong?' she asked.

He swore under his breath and lowered the phone, looking over at her. 'Tomas Lindvall has just been found.'

'That's good, isn't it?' Jamie asked, knowing it wasn't.

'No, it's not. He's dead.'

'Dead?' Jamie was surprised. 'How?'

'He threw himself off a bridge.' Wiik looked angry about it.

Jamie wasn't missing something here. 'Jesus,' she said. 'When?'

'About an hour ago,' Wiik replied, the anger draining out of him. He hung his head now. 'I just got an email from *Avdelningen för Särskilda Utredningar.* They want to interview me. Immediately.'

Special Investigations Division. The SPA's equivalent to the Professional Standards departments back in the UK.

'They're investigating my conduct when it came to Lindvall's apprehension and interrogation.' Wiik ran his hand over his head again, blowing out a hard breath. 'Apparently, he made a phone call to his estranged sister while he was on the bridge – telling her that he was sorry for what he did and that he'd been made to realise the man he really was. That the world would be better off without him. She tried to talk him down but he wouldn't listen. And she's also saying that the last words he said before he jumped were "the detective was right."'

Jamie swallowed, watching Wiik closely. This was the last thing the investigation needed.

'I, uh,' Wiik said, rubbing the back of his head and looking around quickly. 'I've got to go and deal with this.'

She reached out and put her hand on his shoulder, squeezing hard. 'It'll be okay.'

He looked at her briefly but said nothing.

'You did nothing wrong – Lindvall was unstable, off his medication, on drugs. He wasn't in his right mind. A psychotic break,' Jamie tried to reassure him.

'Yeah,' Wiik said, shrugging her hand off. 'And that's because I pushed him into it.' He exhaled hard again and started walking. 'You okay to find your own way?' He turned, back-pedalling, but not stopping.

'Sure,' Jamie said. 'Good luck.'

He gave her a weak smile and then showed her his back, making up ground on his car quickly. A second later he was in it and peeling away from the cluster of marked cars assembled outside the Hansens' house.

The tyres scraped, spun on the damp asphalt, and then gripped, slingshotting the car into the distance, leaving Jamie alone in the street, with nothing but the biting wind and darkening sky for company.

37

JAMIE CAUGHT a ride back to HQ and then headed down to the underground car park to collect her car.

There was no sign of Wiik's Volvo, and she'd not heard from him in the last hour.

Afternoon had descended and the darkness was heavy now. She thought about calling him but decided against it. He was no doubt in the midst of a very serious talk with Falk, and maybe even the SID. Jamie had been worried that Wiik had pushed too hard with Lindvall, and her hunch had proved right. She just wished she'd stepped in sooner.

The Special Investigations Division, if they were anything like the Professional Standards Department, wouldn't give two shits about an ongoing investigation, and would be up Wiik's ass so far he'd be tasting them before the day was out. By the way he'd scurried off, she suspected they were already.

Jamie would leave him to it. Not only was he not her partner, this wasn't even her police. Or her country. She hovered next to her car, thinking about it. During Lindvall's arrest, she'd tripped him, and then put him down for the count, too. Would this blow back on her? No, she'd done nothing but defend herself. He'd come at her. She was safe. She hoped.

Jamie got in the car and cranked the engine, setting the heating to max. She'd been standing around far too much today and she was cold to her bones.

The question now was what the hell was she supposed to do with her afternoon? The investigation was stalled. Gunnarson had his walls up. Leif Lundgren was under surveillance. Hallberg was in the process of contacting the parents of the original victims for statements. Per Eriksson was still in the wind. And while Jan Hansen was a giant dick-head, that wasn't a prosecutable offence. The techs would have to go over the electronics recovered from the Hansens' house and let her and Wiik know the results. Hopefully, it would be before William was brought in the next morning. She expected Jan Hansen to have lawyered up by then. But Anna had signed the form and agreed to bring William in. Jan Hansen had no reason to block that unless he had something to hide.

She was reserving judgement until the techs were inside his computer, but even thinking about the bastard made her skin crawl.

The only other thing she could think of was Robert Nyström. The one missing piece of this puzzle, the one crime that everyone seemed to have ignored.

The first crime in this tangled web.

Someone had abducted a former police officer, and no one seemed to care.

She thought about the man then as she waited for her windscreen to defog.

He'd been a good friend to her father. And a friend to her,

too. The number of times she'd heard a car pull up outside and watched as Robert Nyström had carried her father in through the door, blind drunk, barely conscious, and laid him on the sofa.

The number of times that he'd got her father out of a bad situation, had vouched for his sobriety when he was drunk on the job, had lied to Jamie's mother about where he was. Had brought her hot chocolate when her father had abandoned her at his desk to go and get drunk or high in the middle of the day.

He'd always ruffle her hair, and say, 'Hey, you want to play with my gun?' and then snatch it away at the last second. 'Maybe when you're older,' he'd add, and then ruffle her hair again.

She always hated him doing it. But he was a good guy.

Jamie would feel sad for him that he worked late so much – that he'd stay after hours at his desk when all the other officers had gone home. She realised much later that he did it for her sake. That he stayed to keep an eye on her when her father disappeared. Wordlessly, thanklessly. Just because he was a good man. Jesus, he was the best. And now he'd been taken.

Jamie brushed her hair off her forehead, feeling a tight knot in the pit of her stomach.

Hell, he was probably dead in a ditch somewhere. Buried in a shallow grave.

But she could find him.

And she had nothing else to do.

Jamie let the handbrake down and slotted the car into gear, pulling out of the car park and creeping into the frozen city of Stockholm.

Her city.

Through the frozen streets.
Her streets.
Towards a frozen house.
Her house.

38

JAMIE STEPPED into the dark interior, the smell of dust still hanging thickly in the air.

The whole place felt like it had been violated. The CSTs had been through everything. Plastic sheeting stretched through the rooms, forming gangplanks they'd walked on. Print dust was sprinkled on the surfaces, and little white paper stickers littered the house – markers for items to check for prints, photograph and catalogue.

The house may have been hers, but it had never felt further from it.

'Alright, Robert,' Jamie muttered, pushing the door closed behind her. 'Where are you?'

Jamie pulled her phone from her pocket and flicked on her torch. She'd dropped a message to Hallberg on the way over to forward any information they had on Nyström that might have helped. But it looked like he was living a frugal life. His apartment was mortgage free, his car was paid for, and he got by on his pension as well as a little consulting work with the SPA every now and then.

The CSTs had gone over his apartment but found nothing

of use. No particulates, no fibres, no prints, no DNA. Though that didn't surprise Jamie, considering the circumstances of the other abductions. Eriksson was skilled, he was smart and he was *very* experienced. And perhaps worst of all was that he was completely unassuming – friendly faced. A damn priest, for God's sake. The perfect disguise. On top of that, there was no CCTV inside Nyström's building either. There were two exits, a number of directions they could have gone in, and no specific time on the abduction itself. Neighbours reported hearing nothing out of the ordinary, and no one saw a damn thing, either. It was as though Nyström vanished into thin air.

All they had was the grainy photograph from the toll-booth, but that didn't put a time on anything except when that car passed through. Which could have been an hour or a day after Nyström was taken. Probably the latter, because it hadn't been clocked coming the other way, and there were at least four other routes that could have been taken out of the city that were free of tolls. The photo told them that the driver wanted to be clocked there. Which told them that it was an obvious misdirect. Or an un-obvious non-misdirect. Or a double, triple or quadruple bluff.

Basically, it meant shit. Just one more thing to make sure they didn't know which way was up in this investigation.

And with the Angel Maker case now breaking on national news, the assassination of Åsa Gunnarson smeared across every front page in the country, Emmy Berg's photo in every tabloid, Leif Lundgren under police protection, every CST in the city being bounced from crime scene to crime like pinballs, the primary suspect on the run with every patrol car from here to Svalbard on the lookout, and now the SID breathing down the neck of the primary investigator, the case was stretching the SPA thinner than it ever had been.

Per Eriksson was running rings around them, and Jamie couldn't help but feel like he had them chasing their tails on purpose. Every clue seemed to lead them deeper into this maze, and every stone they turned over only pushed everyone further in different directions.

It had been a tiring, difficult, dangerous four days, and Jamie didn't think things were about to ease just yet.

And lost in the maelstrom of it all was Robert Nyström. A man who dedicated his life to catching bastards like Per Eriksson. A man who'd worked alongside her father to put Sjöberg behind bars. A man that everyone seemed to have forgotten about.

Jamie paused at the open door to her father's office, took a breath, and went in.

Inside, it was pitch black. There were no windows in the office – her father had made sure of that. He wanted the place completely inaccessible. The door was heavy and equipped with a bolt lock too. Just in case.

Jamie swung her phone around, its pale light casting a ghostly glow, and then she paused, noticing a small battery-powered LED floodlight that had been affixed to the top of the door. It was hanging on the back. No doubt the CSTs had put it up there while they were working and missed it when they were leaving. Jamie wasn't complaining though. She pushed the door to and reached up, flicking it on and blinding herself at the same time.

It cast a harsh, shadowless glare on everything and she swore, ducking out of the light and jamming the heels of her hands into her eye sockets. 'Son of a bitch,' she muttered, seeing stars and turning back to the room.

Everything was illuminated now.

She sighed, not knowing what she was looking for. Or where to start. Her childhood was fuzzy to her – just repetitive snapshots of her arguing parents, of sitting at her father's desk at work, of her father asleep on the sofa, of her mother slamming the front door and storming out, of hovering at the top of the stairs as they moved through the house in a twister of profanity and tears. Jamie shook the memories out of her head, and moved forward.

With every book she read, every surface she ran her hand over and every drawer she opened, her childhood split in two and revealed itself to her. The shell was cracking a little more with every minute she spent on Swedish soil, and soon, it would all be exposed.

She wondered whether inside she would find memories Robert Nyström and the Angel Maker case. Or whether she would simply discover more reasons that she'd repressed the first decade of her life.

Jamie scanned the room before approaching her father's desk. It didn't look like the CSTs had taken anything during the search, and everything that had been touched and moved had been put back.

Still, it felt violated.

Jamie sat at her father's desk, the ancient chair squeaking horribly as she rolled back on it, trying to picture Robert Nyström. But she didn't have to think hard. She stared at the wall behind the desk, under the shelves, at the photographs pinned up there, and let her eyes rest on the picture of two men in angling gear holding a fish up between them. It was a river pike about three feet long. A *gädda*. On the right was her father – six-two, burly, blonde with a big face, wide teeth that always reminded Jamie of a carthorse's, and pale blue eyes. On the left was Robert Nyström. He was an inch taller than her father, but half as wide. He had narrow shoulders and a narrow head. His chin was strong, his hair cut short. It was nearly white in this photo – even though he must have only been about forty. Jamie never remembered it being any other way. But that's probably because she was more focused on his eyebrows. He had prominent cheekbones that, when coupled with his large, dark bushy brows – which a horned owl would be proud of – made his eyes look sunken. He was smiling in the picture, his grin cutting into his cheeks. As was her father.

Jamie reached out and took the photo off the wall, listening as the pin dropped somewhere behind the desk.

She studied it more closely.

Her father and Nyström took a lot of trips like that. Fishing, hunting. Every winter, they'd travel north to icefish near a little village called… Jamie rocked back in the chair, trying to remember the name. But for the life of her, she couldn't. It began with 'V', she thought.

She sighed, rocked back, and then turned the picture over, laughing at herself. On the back, the words *Vemdalen, 1992* were written. Jamie would have been nine.

She went back to the other photos and scanned across them, feeling her throat ache at the sight of herself and her father. In one she was just a baby, in another, she was a little girl – maybe five or six – in another she was a teenager. Her mother was distinctly absent from each.

Jamie paused on the last one, looking at it. Her and her father were standing on a rise above a lake. She was probably thirteen – God, that must have been during the Angel Maker case.

Jamie narrowed her eyes, trying to recall it.

She was standing there, holding her father's Remington Model 700, grinning. Her dad couldn't have looked happier. She always hated hunting. Never liked the idea of killing anything for sport. Her father didn't, either. Anything they shot, they ate. Her father would gut the thing right there in the woods with his knife – a beautiful stag-horn-handled hunting knife that he carried in a sheath on the back of his belt. To work, when hunting. It never left his person.

Where it was now, Jamie didn't know. She'd not found it when she'd gone through the office the first time. Her mother probably had it with her father's effects. She'd picked them up at the coroner's office when she'd ID'd his body before the funeral. Jamie never saw what was in that bag. Her mother had kept it from her and then said she'd thrown it away. 'Nothing you'd want to keep,' she said.

Jamie realised now her mother had probably lied about that, too.

She exhaled hard, staring down at her father.

Deer was his favourite. They'd stalk one for days, sometimes. One well-placed kill shot, only when it was guaranteed. 'Through the heart,' he'd say, pointing to his chest. 'Or through the head.' And then he'd hold his hand up to his temple like a gun.

She laughed sardonically at that image – at the cruel irony of it as she sat ten feet from the blood-stained wall – and then felt her eyes burn with tears. She wiped them away and went back to the photo, remembering that weekend. Teasing it from the tumult of her childhood.

He had one arm around her, the other across his body, on her shoulder. She looked at the image more closely and noticed her father's ring. It had always irked her mother that he'd worn it, as he'd always refused to wear a wedding ring.

It was a family thing – his father's before him. Big, brass, with a crest on it. He'd often joked that it was a good reminder for the people on the wrong end of it not to step out of line again.

She'd always thought that was great. Hilarious. Brave. Exciting.

Now, she saw it for what it was.

But it was a part of her father, for better or worse.

Mostly worse.

The picture lingered in her fingers and she realised then that the photo didn't only contain her and her father. There was a third there, Nyström. The man behind the camera.

She scanned it for anything else she might recognise and saw the land falling away behind her and her father, a lake in the background, the weak, cloud-blocked light playing off the surface. It looked to be in a rolling valley beset with larch trees, a narrow strip of water stretching into the distance.

A small cabin stood at the near side of the lake, smoke curling from its chimney. Jamie could just make out the tiny outline of her father's car in the gravel stretch before it.

Jamie furrowed her brow, trying to recall the cabin. And then it burst into life in her mind. It was an old hunting cabin – damp and raw. Sap oozed from the walls, the inner surfaces rough with uncut bark. The seams were sealed with gum, the pitched roof awash with cobwebs. Jamie could remember lying on the top bunk of one of the bunks in there, staring up at them, watching as the spiders scuttled around in the lamp-light on their silver webs, fascinated but not scared.

The cabin had no electricity, no running water. Her father and Nyström would fill plastic jugs from the lake and boil it every morning over the fire in the stone hearth.

No one owned the cabin. It was built long ago by those passing through and maintained by those who stayed there. She could picture her father and Nyström sawing wood to repair the leaky roof one summer while she skipped stones on the lake.

Something in Jamie's head twigged then, and she reached into her pocket, pulling out her father's notebook.

She flipped through a few pages, still holding the photograph, and stopped at the entry she wanted, re-reading the note written to her. The words said, '*There are things I want you to have. That they would take. Things that only you can find. I know you will. One day.*'

Jamie went back to the photograph now and stared down at that tiny cabin. They were there once – it was cold. Jamie remembered that. Just her and her father. Snow had been beating against the windows. Maybe it was a Christmas one year, Jamie didn't know. The fire was small and they were huddled around it. Her father had leaned the thin mattresses from the bunk beds up against the window and door to stop the wind getting in.

They'd made soup and drunk hot chocolate for the best part of two days, just talking. About her father's life, about what Jamie wanted to do when she grew up. About all the things she wanted to be. He'd told her to make a list – write a letter to her future self. Telling her all the things she wanted to do. She remembered some of them – she wanted to be a figure skater – no, a hockey player. Her *mother* had wanted her to do figure skating, not hockey. She'd wanted to be a zookeeper – or a park ranger – in Africa. Someone who protected elephants and rhinos from poachers.

Jamie bit her lip, dredging the riverbed of her mind.

She wanted to be a detective, like her dad, of course.

And she wanted to be an Olympian – yes, that was it. Biathlon. Skiing and shooting. Her father had loved the biathlon. She'd trained so hard in those last few years she'd been here. After moving to England, her mother had refused to let her continue.

Jamie felt anger well in her, sadness, and then regret.

When she'd left her father behind, she felt like she'd left herself behind, too.

Jamie let out a rattling breath and summoned the strength

to return to that cabin – to her shaking, frozen, eleven-year-old fingers scribbling on that grubby paper.

What had she done with it?

Her father had written a letter, too, but wouldn't let her read it. Because she wouldn't let him read hers.

She laughed now at that. Christ, they could have both frozen to death in there. The lake had frozen solid in hours, the temperature plunging as the storm rolled in – one of the most fierce the country had ever faced. At the time, it didn't even enter her mind. There, with her dad, nothing could have hurt her.

She closed her eyes, reliving those moments.

After they'd finished, he'd taken the notes and folded them up, placing them inside a piece of hide, all rolled up. And then he'd bound it in leather string, had her put her finger on the knot as he'd tied the bow. And then he'd pried up one of the floorboards with his stag-horn knife and put the parcel underneath it. He'd said, 'We'll come back here in twenty years, and find these letters. And we'll see who you grew up to be. Who knows, maybe we'll even bring your daughter here.'

Jamie had made a loud, long *ewwwwuegh* sound to express her disgust at the idea of having kids of her own. The noise she'd make now at the thought wouldn't be too far away.

She lowered the picture slowly. 'There are things I want you to have. That they would take. Things that only you can find. I know you will. One day,' she said out loud to herself. She turned on the chair to look at the near-black stain on the wall and held back tears. 'What things, Dad? What things?'

39

JAMIE ROSE FROM THE CHAIR, exhausted.

The photo just had a date on the back. It said, *December 1995*, but it made no mention of where the cabin was.

Jamie had to find it, though. Her father's note to her had said that he'd left things for her.

And if they'd be anywhere, they'd be there.

She just knew it.

He wouldn't risk leaving anything at the house in case her mother found it. But her mother would never be caught dead on a camping trip.

She found herself nodding, bathed in the blinding light of the flood lamp.

It was making her eyes ache.

Jamie checked her watch – it was nearly six in the evening now and once again her stomach was empty. She sighed, rubbed her eyes, and then set about thinking of dinner. Sweden had nearly one hundred thousand lakes, and visiting them one by one until she found the cabin wasn't the solution.

But she couldn't seem to come up with a better one just then, but nor did she need to.

The cabin could wait.

Eriksson was still out there, and the case was far from over. Every minute that passed was a minute closer to the next body. The next victim. The next girl.

And with still no new leads on Nyström she was no closer to finding him either.

As for her father's parcel — it had waited twenty years. It could wait a few more weeks.

For now, she'd get back to the hotel, get some food in her stomach. Grab a hot bath and a good night's sleep. Or at least as good as she could hope for. Closing her eyes just meant being alone with the things that lived in her head. The things she'd done.

She had to admit, as much as she hated to, that working a case again was giving her focus. Purpose. Though while it blocked out those thoughts while she was awake, nothing much could be done for the times that she was asleep.

Jamie placed the photos – of her father and Robert Nyström, and of her and her father – into the notebook, along with a few others above the desk she didn't want to leave behind, and made for the door.

She switched off the lamp above her head, a deep throbbing pain developing behind her eyes, and opened the door to her father's office.

Jamie's skin hackled, gooseflesh coming out on the back of her neck, a shiver erupting through her body. And not just from the near-zero temperature in the house.

She held her breath between her teeth, staring out into her darkened dining room. The table was just a black slab in front of her, the sideboard with the glass windows, glass shelves, and decanters a ghostly outline, the faintest rays of light playing on the edges of the bottles.

But it was the window Jamie was transfixed on. Nestled between the archway into the kitchen and the unit, it was about two feet across by three high and shuttered. Jamie could just make out the pale lines of the shutter slats. They caught the orange light from the street lamps at the kerb and cut through the dust.

She could only just see through them from this angle – a millimetre or two between each slat. Barely anything. Basically nothing. And yet her brain was telling her not to move a fucking muscle.

It was blackness on blackness, the tiniest hint of yellow. Shadow in the absence of light. Emptiness to the eye. But something was screaming at her. Something that made her blood run colder, her muscles all strain tight and fill with blood, her heart kick up a few gears, her heels grind into the floor for traction, and her fists curl at her sides.

Jamie narrowed her eyes, forcing herself to breathe, not daring to look away.

And then the darkness moved.

A ripple beyond the shutters in the veil of night. The flap of a hood or the flutter of hair. It didn't matter which. But they were running.

And now so was Jamie.

She plunged forward on instinct, and then cut left into the kitchen, shoving one of the chairs out of the way as she slid across the tiled floor and made for the hallway.

The sound of footsteps sloshing in snow echoed through the shuttered windows, reaching Jamie from the right-hand kitchen window, then the front window, then through the front door as she hit the porch.

Jamie tore the door open and pressed herself to the inside

wall in case the figure was armed, watching as the shadow lurched towards the fence at the end of the front garden, spraying snow everywhere as he slung his feet in wide strides.

The whole picket fence, rotten with age, swayed violently as he pitched over it and into the street, stumbling before he managed to find his balance.

Jamie hauled herself forward, running down the icy path, the treads of her boots fighting for grip as she made for the street.

She slid onto the kerb, squinting into the darkness – no sign of the figure.

Shit.

Jamie turned and circled into the roadway around one of the neighbour's cars and caught a glimpse of a coat flashing between two bumpers twenty metres ahead.

She filled her lungs and took off, bolting straight down the street to make up some ground.

The figure was headed for the city. It was maybe a kilometre or so before the houses and gardens gave way to apartment blocks and offices, but the guy was moving fast.

Jamie skidded on the slick ground and shoved herself through the gap between the two cars, back up onto the opposite pavement.

She glanced left and right, looking for any sign of him. The same person that had been lingering in the alleyway across from the hotel? Maybe the same person who'd shot at her at the Gunnarsons'. Per Eriksson, the fifty-something priest with the bad back? The way they were moving, she didn't think so. But she'd been wrong before.

Jamie stopped, tweaked her ears for any sounds or signs of movement. Cars were trundling past now, coming home from work. Windows were lit up, casting glare onto front gardens. Voices carried – the sounds of TVs and families sitting down to dinner.

Shit, she was going to lose him.

Something clanged and her head snapped around, seeing the glint of metal moving in the streetlights as a side gate swung closed and bounced on the jamb two houses up.

Jamie was running again.

She hurdled a low fence into someone's garden, trusting her footing more on the snow than she did on the frozen pavement.

Her knees came high, her heels nearly clipping her hamstrings as she tore through the slush, blinding herself with a thick cloud of breath-mist after every heaving exhale.

She was fit – more so than most – but running in these temperatures was hard. The air slashed at her lungs, felt like it was tearing into her throat. Her chest tightened and threatened to clamp shut.

Jamie fought it off, leaping the dividing fence, her hip just clearing the chain-link as she vaulted over it.

It sang behind her, wobbling madly as she adjusted her course and closed ground on the gate.

Her feet came free of the snow and she was through it. The gate hit the wall and swung shut behind her and then she was at the side of a house and charging forward, fists pumping through the frigid air.

Something banged and then echoed up ahead, and Jamie came around the corner and into another back garden, watching as the figure scrambled to its feet and took off again, an overturned plastic see-saw shaped like a triceratops lying up-ended on the grass, the broken snow on the ground telling Jamie the man fleeing had fallen face first over the thing.

She wasted no time in closing the gap, and ran the guy

down just as a security light flared to life overhead, filling the entire garden.

The figure slid, looked for an exit, and then made for the back-fence.

He ducked between the swings on a children's swing set and then leapt onto the panelled fence at the back, toes scrambling as he tried to haul himself over it.

Jamie was too close, though, and too fast.

She circled the set and took three big steps, kicking into the air.

Her fists hit the back of the figure's jacket, just at the shoulders, and the sudden extra weight tore the fence from his grasp.

Jamie and the man toppled backwards, hitting the ground and sprawling onto their backs.

The figure reacted quickly, glancing over, his face obscured by a mask pulled up to the eyes, a black beanie hat pulled low to his brow, and lifted his right arm.

His fist sailed into the air above Jamie and he swung it down like a mallet, right at her face.

She threw her arms up, taking the blow against her forearms, and then rolled away as the figure tried to get to his feet again, skidding and sliding in the snow, his hands and heels gouging divots in the earth beneath, sending mud everywhere.

But Jamie was quicker, already on her feet.

She came forward now again and tackled the man to the ground, her shoulder hitting him in the middle of his back, forcing him onto his belly.

His legs flailed, arms swimming for freedom, but it was no good. Jamie had her right knee firmly in the small of his spine, her hands going for his. She snatched the man's right hand out of the darkness and folded it up behind his back,

leaning him left at the same time so his other arm could do
nothing but bend awkwardly against the earth.

He cried out in pain, but the yell was muffled as Jamie
shoved her free hand against the back of his head and pressed
his face into the snow, sweat dripping from her brow as
she did.

She was panting hard, fighting to stay on top of him, but a
quick twist of the captured wrist settled him down and told
him there was no getting away.

A voice rose from the snow. 'Don't kill me!' it yelled,
followed up with a mewling whimper.

But it wasn't the voice of a man.

Jamie released the wrist a little and unfolded it, standing
just enough that she could flip the woman underneath her
over.

Before she could try anything, Jamie pulled her arm down
to her side and pinned it under her knee again, straddling the
woman's midriff.

'I can't— I can't breathe,' she choked out breathlessly,
throwing her free hand to her face and dragging the ski mask
down to her chin.

She had her eyes closed, her chest rising and falling under
her heavy parka. Her skin was pale, rosed in the freezing air,
her dark curly hair sticking out from under the brim of her
hat. She panted wildly, coughing and spluttering. But Jamie
didn't release any pressure. She just caught her own breath
and kept her fists curled in a loose attack position above the
woman's head.

'Who are you?' Jamie demanded, feeling the cold of the
ice soak through the knees of her jeans.

They both drowned in a sea of steam. It peeled from their
exposed skin, streamed from their noses and mouths.

'I— I—' the woman began, stammering.

Jamie leaned into the woman's wrist, crushing it under her knee.

She squealed in pain. 'Get off!'

'Who are you?' Jamie asked again.

'My name is... my name is Rachel, Rachel Engerman!' she practically screamed it now, her straight, white teeth gritted in pain.

'And who are you, Rachel Engerman? And more importantly,' Jamie said in a low, hard voice, twisting her knee a little more, 'why are you following me?'

Tears formed under Rachel's eyes now, and she sobbed with pain, her free hand flapping around wildly at her side, at a loss for anything else to do.

It seemed to have no intention of harming Jamie now.

'It's about Hanna,' she said, devolving into sobs. 'I killed Hanna Lundgren.'

40

JAMIE RELEASED the woman and stood up, backing off a step or two, processing what the hell she'd just heard. 'What did you say?'

Rachel Engerman – a woman roughly the same age as Jamie – maybe a year or two older – curled onto her side, her back soaked with snow, and cradled her right wrist, the hand locked into a claw shape. She clutched at it with her left, crying into her fingers.

Jamie looked around at the house they were behind, could see a man and a woman standing at the patio doors, a pair of little girls clutching at their legs. 'It's okay,' Jamie said, fishing her police lanyard from her pocket. She held it up. 'I'm with the Stockholm Polis,' she called commandingly, glancing down at the woman on the ground, who seemingly had no intention of running anywhere now. 'Nothing to worry about,' she called again, smiling. 'Sorry about your, uh… garden,' she finished, glancing down at the mess they'd made.

She stepped back towards Engerman and reached down, taking the girl by the arm and dragging her to her feet. 'Come on,' she said. 'It's not broken.'

Jamie kept a vice-like grip on the woman's arm, and half pulled, half pushed her back through the garden towards the side gate, holding her badge up to the family in the window as she passed. 'Everything's fine,' she called again. 'Sorry to disturb you.'

They peered around the corner as best they could to watch Jamie and the stranger go, but the second they were out of sight, shielded by the side of the house, Jamie stopped and threw Engerman against the wood panelling. 'Start talking,' she said, pointing into her face. 'Now.'

The woman looked frightened, and shook her head innocently, unable to muster words.

'Why have you been following me?' Jamie demanded.

She held her hands up beside her shoulders now. 'I haven't,' she said quickly.

'Bullshit! I saw you across the road from my hotel.' Jamie thought then. 'Were you in my house?'

'What? No!' the woman said.

Jamie's fist curled suddenly and plunged into the panelling next to her head. 'Don't fucking lie to me!'

'I wasn't!' She began to well up again.

Jamie exhaled and pulled her hand back. Her knuckles were throbbing. She was soaked, freezing, shivering and exhausted. 'Were you at my house a few days ago?' she asked, more calmly now.

The woman nodded slowly, not daring to move.

'But you didn't go inside?'

She shook her head.

'Why were you there?'

'I was looking for you.'

'Me? Why?' Jamie narrowed her eyes.

'I... I needed to talk to you.'

'About what? Hanna Lundgren?'

She nodded, her teeth beginning to chatter.

'Then why did you run?'

'I wasn't sure if it was you.'

'Who else would it be?'

Engerman lifted her shoulders a little, offering a weak shrug. 'I don't know.'

She looked scared. Which told Jamie she might have had an idea. But this wasn't the place to have this conversation.

'You know I'm not police, right? At least not Swedish police.'

Rachel Engerman nodded. 'I guessed.'

'So why didn't you try to contact my partner, or—?'

'I wasn't looking for *you*.'

'Who were you looking for?'

'Jörgen Johansson. The detective from the old case. I looked it up online when I read the news – about the Angel Maker – that he was back, I wanted to reach out, to... to make things right.'

'Jörgen Johansson was my father,' Jamie said. 'He's dead.'

'Oh,' Rachel said, looking at the ground. 'I didn't know – I'm sorry.'

'I'm helping with this case, though,' Jamie added quickly. If Rachel Engerman had something worth saying to say to her father, then she was damn well going to hear it herself. Jamie studied her for a second and then sighed. 'You going to try and run again?'

She shook her head.

'Then put your hands down and come on.' Jamie slapped them out of the air and beckoned the woman after her. 'It's freezing out here.'

. . .

Jamie pulled the car into a nearby coffee shop and led the way into the overly bright interior.

The two women entered – soaked and bedraggled – and headed for a booth in the corner. It was quiet in there now. The only other patrons were a man in the far corner tapping away on a laptop and a young couple leaning over a little table at each other, laughing and whispering about who knew what. Something innocent and fun, no doubt. Jamie grimaced and tore her eyes from them, looking back at Rachel Engerman.

They stared at each other in silence, sizing each other up, and then a waitress appeared.

'Can I get you anything?' she asked, looking at both of them in turn, dying to ask, but too afraid to.

'Black tea,' Jamie said, not looking away from Engerman.

'The same,' she replied, unable to resist looking at the waitress and smiling. 'Thanks.'

Jamie bit her lip. She was polite, well-spoken. She seemed nice, by all accounts. Not the murderous type at all. But those words had stuck with her. *I killed Hanna Lundgren.* Jamie didn't think she'd raped her, suffocated her, and then rammed birch branches through her back. But you couldn't ignore a statement like that.

'Start talking,' Jamie said, the second the waitress was out of earshot.

Rachel Engerman swallowed and then cleared her throat. 'Hanna Lundgren was my friend,' she said slowly, choosing her words. 'I thought I was helping her.'

Jamie's fingers had gone numb now and the backs of her legs were stinging with the cold. 'Talk faster.'

'We were childhood friends – neighbours. She was two years younger than me, but we grew up together.'

'You said you killed her,' Jamie said plainly. 'So either

explain what the hell you meant, or I'm going to put you over this table and cuff your hands behind your back.'

Rachel Engerman looked at the table and let out a long breath, as though summoning the strength to say what she needed to. 'Hanna Lundgren was raped.'

The waitress approached the table and put down the two teas. She waited to see if anything else was going to be said, but Jamie and Rachel just stared at each other in silence until she left.

Jamie waited until she was sure she wouldn't be overheard, and then leaned in, clasping the mug with her cold hands. 'All of the Angel Maker's victims were raped,' she said. 'It was part of his—'

'No,' Rachel said, shaking her head. 'It was Leif Lundgren.' She basically spat his name, and the look of disgust on her face told Jamie exactly what she thought of the man.

'Hanna Lundgren's father?' This was coming as news to her, but she tried not to let on her surprise.

'Leif wasn't her real father. Hanna was adopted.'

Jamie knew that already. But it didn't make it any better.

'Hanna was a pretty girl – and when she hit thirteen, she started to... develop.'

Jamie watched Rachel closely.

'Her parents – Helena and Leif – they couldn't have children of their own. And by all accounts, they were good parents, you know?'

Jamie reserved judgement, but offered Rachel a soft look as the woman stared at her. Trying to hurry her would do no good. She just had to listen.

'But then, as Hanna got older, Leif started to change. He became... strange. Quiet, angry. I think... I think he knew it was wrong. He hated himself for it. But he couldn't stop. It didn't start out like *that* at first. But Hanna said it got worse over time, and then one night...' She looked out of the window, her eyes filling, and then she took a sip from her tea. 'She didn't want to tell me, at first, but she said Leif was starting to get scared. He'd threatened her.'

'Threatened her?' Jamie's voice was low, and she was almost over the table now, trying to catch every word. Rachel was practically whispering.

She nodded. 'Yeah, said that if she told anyone that he'd... he'd kill her.'

Jesus, Jamie felt like saying. But she kept quiet, nodding Engerman on.

'She needed help,' she said, voice cracking.

'And you gave it to her?' Jamie asked tentatively.

Rachel Engerman nodded. 'Yeah – I told her about the church.'

Jamie's back stiffened, her heart picking up a little in her chest.

'My family went there – and I went to this group that they ran. It was like a kids-group type thing – but for all ages. We did some Bible study, that kind of stuff, but mostly... mostly it was just somewhere to go, you know? Where you could talk to people. Where you could feel safe.' Rachel's lip began to quiver.

Jamie needed to keep her on track. 'And you took Hanna there. Introduced her to Hans and Eva Sjöberg?'

Rachel met her eye now and nodded. 'Yeah, I did. Eva was so sweet. So caring. And Hans, too – he was so nice. Really caring people. And I thought, you know, that if Hanna wanted to tell them, that they could, you know, *protect* her. From Leif.' She was barely holding it together. 'We all knew that Hans was in the army. So I thought that... that...'

She trailed off. Her shoulders jerked, then she began to sob.

Jamie sat there, clenching her teeth.

The waitress appeared at the side of the table. 'Is every-thing alright?' the young girl asked. She must have been eighteen, no more. Jamie fired her a look that said a thousand words, and the girl receded from the table as quickly as she'd arrived.

Jamie reached out and took one of Rachel's hands. 'It's okay,' she said. 'You didn't know.' She left that for a second, and then spoke again, keen to hurry Rachel along. 'What happened then?'

'Hanna came... a few... times,' she said between little sobs. 'And then, suddenly, she didn't. I went to her... house... and, uh... she wasn't there.' She swallowed and looked at Jamie. 'Leif told me to go home – he looked scared. I thought... I thought that he'd killed her.'

My father thought that, too, Jamie wanted to say. Again, she just watched, waited, and listened.

'But then, when they arrested Hans Sjöberg... I-I knew those other girls. All of them. We were all friends. And one by one... I thought, I mean... I thought that they were leaving? Just not coming anymore. The Bible stuff could get a little heavy sometimes. Some people thought it wasn't cool – others just sort of dropped in and out. It was mostly for kids with nowhere else to go. But it was popular – a lot of kids went there.' She took a second and collected her thoughts. 'I never thought Hans could have...'

Jamie processed it all, trying to work out what it meant. What it meant for the original case. What it meant for *this* case. Whether her father had this information. Whether it would have changed anything. 'Did you tell anyone about Hanna back then?' Jamie asked, her voice subdued suddenly.

Rachel shook her head. 'No – I thought if I did, that Leif would have killed me, too.'

'Why didn't you tell anyone you thought Leif killed Hanna?'

'I did,' Rachel said, picking her head up.

'Who?'

'Hans Sjöberg.'

Jamie set her teeth. 'After Hanna disappeared?'

Rachel nodded.

'What did he say?'

'He said… He said not to worry. That— that men like that always got what was coming to them in the end.' She scoffed a little and shook her head. 'Heaven-and-hell bullshit, you know? That's all it was. Forgiveness. Turn the other cheek. All of that crap.' Rachel looked at her now, but Jamie's brain was still on the last thing she'd said. *Men like that always got what was coming to them…*

Just then, Jamie's phone started vibrating in her pocket. She pulled it out, seeing Hallberg's number flash up on-screen. 'Excuse me a second,' she said to Rachel, sliding out of the booth and answering it. 'Hello?'

'Jamie,' Hallberg said quickly. 'Is Wiik with you?'

'No, he's not.'

'You know where he is?' She sounded stressed.

'No, I don't. Why? What's going on?'

'We just had an email from Tech – it looked like one of the tablets recovered from the Hansens' house wasn't password locked. The son's tablet.'

'William?'

'Yeah – they just pulled the history from it now, and—'

'And they found evidence that Emmy Berg was being sexually abused by Jan Hansen.' The words came out of her mouth before she could stop them.

'Yeah,' Hallberg said, surprised. 'How did you know?'

'I didn't.' Jamie let out a long, shaky breath, and turned to look at the woman sitting in the booth. The woman who had just changed the entire case.

You don't understand.

Jamie gritted her teeth.

She was beginning to.

41

'EMMY WAS ACCESSING a support forum for victims of sexual abuse from her brother's tablet,' Hallberg said. 'And from the looks of things, this may have been how the killer targeted her.'

Jamie stirred her tea slowly, listening as Hallberg confirmed her hunches, the phone pressed to her ear. She stared across at the empty seat opposite. Rachel Engerman was gone, as were the sickly sweet couple and the man with his laptop. Just Jamie and the two girls behind the counter remained. They were talking to each other and glancing over, probably trying to assess whether Jamie was some bedraggled homeless woman who'd wandered in off the street, or if she just looked like it.

'If Hansen knew,' Jamie said, 'then it explains why he took her phone and computer off her.'

'Or even if he was just afraid she might tell someone,' Hallberg added.

'Right. Do we have details of the other children they've fostered?'

'I've sent an email over to the agency, but they're closed for the night. We won't get a response until the morning.'

Jamie picked up her tea and sipped, embracing the bitterness of the liquid. 'What did they find on the forum?'

'It looks like Emmy was posting under the username EBStockholm06. The techs have trawled the site and found a few messages posted by her. She initiated two threads – one entitled – "Help" and the other entitled "Need to talk". The first said that she thought an older man in her life was trying to initiate some sort of physical relationship, but she wasn't sure. It goes on to list the things this man is doing – touching her arm, stroking her back, things like that.'

Jamie's stomach churned a little, anger rising in her. 'Does it mention any names?'

'No,' Hallberg said, sounding as disappointed as Jamie felt with that answer. 'But from the responses she gave to people commenting and replying, it's pretty clear that it's Jan Hansen.'

'Clear enough to use in court?'

Hallberg cleared her throat. 'That's not for me to— uh, I don't know, is what I mean.'

No, in other words, Jamie thought.

Hallberg went on. 'That was back in September – which puts it about six months after they began fostering her. Sounds like Jan's advances had been going on for a while, but there's no exact date.'

'And the other thread?'

'"Need to talk",' Hallberg said. 'That was posted about two and a half weeks ago.'

Jamie sat up a little straighter. 'So about a week before Emmy was killed?'

'Eight days, yeah.'

'What did it say?'

'It's sparse on details, but it intimates to the fact that she was raped.'

'Jesus,' Jamie said, knowing she had to get all the information she could. 'And the responses?'

'All supportive, kind. People offering the numbers of local helplines to call, offering to speak to the authorities for her. Some even offering places that Emmy could go if she needed to get away.'

Jamie perked up at that. 'Places she could go?'

'Yeah, it looks like two of the commenters were from Stockholm – and both said that they'd be happy to protect Emmy if she wanted to leave the house.'

'We have their names?'

'Usernames, yes. Real names… That could take a little while. The forum is running on a fairly new system, and considering the nature of what's discussed there, anonymity is a big priority for them. Security isn't lax, the techs said. They'll need to contact the host to gain access. Trying to break in will take a long time, and we'd need a warrant to even attempt it, so—'

'What did Emmy say back? Did she agree to go to any of them?' Jamie didn't have time for a discussion over the finer points of data protection law. She needed information.

'This is the weird thing,' Hallberg said. 'Emmy didn't seem to want to take them up on the offer. She said thank you, but she'd figure something else out.'

'Something else? Like what?' Jamie furrowed her brow.

'I don't know, but there are thirty-seven replies to her post, all offering different things. When Tech gets hold of the forum hosts, we can look at getting into Emmy's account and seeing the activity associated with it, and from there, hopefully, we'll know more. Maybe someone messaged her, or deleted their reply, or… or… I don't know.' Hallberg sighed.

Jamie processed. 'This is good,' she said.

'Good?'

'We're getting closer. There was always that question –
why Emmy Berg? With Sjöberg, he was choosing girls from
the church. From what Engerman just told me, they were
confiding in him. That's how he was choosing them.'

'He was choosing abuse victims?'

Jamie nodded to herself. 'Yeah.'

'And then he was raping them?'

'No,' Jamie said slowly. 'I don't think so.' She took a
moment, rearranging the information in her head. 'I think
that's what my father always had wrong. He thought that
Sjöberg was raping them, then suffocating and mounting
them. That it was all some sort of weird crime-apology-
redemption act. That he was making them into angels to
restore their purity after he took it from them. And I think
once he spoke to Annika Liljedahl and found out that Hans
Sjöberg had slept with her when she was fourteen, he put
those two pieces together, found that they fit, and that was it.'
Jamie drew a breath, finding the next part hard to say. 'He
confronted Sjöberg about it then, and when he wouldn't
confess – because he wasn't abusing those girls, at least not
in that way – my father tried to beat it out of him.'

Hallberg was silent.

'But he had it wrong,' Jamie said. 'The Angel Maker
wasn't raping his victims. He thought he was saving them.'
Jamie let out a long, shaking breath. 'Whether it was Sjöberg
on his own, or Sjöberg and Eriksson, or just Eriksson, I don't
know. But the forensics supports it, right? In all cases, the
examinations showed proof of sexual assault, but in all cases,
it wasn't immediately before death. It was assumed that
Sjöberg was abusing them over a period of time, and then
once he was finished with whatever twisted intention he had,

he would suffocate them, and then he'd take them into the woods, and he'd make them into angels.

'But he wasn't doing that. He had their trust. He would take them for a drive somewhere,' Jamie said, imagining it. 'Telling them he was taking them somewhere safe. It would be at night. They would be tired.' She remembered her own childhood, the long drives in the back seat of the car. The hypnotic strobing of the streetlights. 'They would fall asleep there, thinking that it was over. And then he'd stop somewhere and pipe the exhaust fumes into the car while they slept. He'd go down into the woods at the side of the road and get things ready. Cut the boughs, find the right spot. While the girls slowly suffocated, not even waking up.' Jamie took another sip, her hand quivering, and then put the cup down, watching the black surface of the liquid shimmer. 'They'd go quietly, painlessly, without even knowing. Their last thoughts would be happy – that they were being saved. And then…' Jamie tried to clear her throat to shift the lump there. It wouldn't move. 'Then, when they were gone, he would carry them into the woods, and he'd make them into angels. He'd make them the angels they were – give them back what had been taken from them.'

Jamie heard Hallberg swallow on the other end of the line and then sniff twice. She coughed away from the receiver and then spoke, her voice cracking. 'That's, uh… that makes… um…'

'But that wasn't it,' Jamie went on, the words coming on their own. 'That was only half of it. He would need to save the girls. But then he'd also need to make the people who hurt them pay for what they did. He promised them that. He promised Hanna Lundgren that. She didn't know it at the time, but Sjöberg knew. And I think…' she said, hesitating for a moment. 'I think he felt it was necessary. A necessary evil. A duty. He didn't enjoy it – the killing. The kills are remorseful in the case of the girls. He thought he was doing right by them. And then, in killing the parents... it was... detached. He ran one of them off the road, another was supposed suicide. Maybe he convinced them to do it? Maybe he confronted them, and got them to do it themselves or face justice? Gave them an out. The others... disappearances? We don't know how he did it, but I don't think he relished it.'

'What about Lundgren?' Hallberg asked, her voice quiet. 'He was garrotted. That's not detached?'

Jamie shook her head and let out a long breath. 'I don't know, Hallberg,' she said. 'I don't know is the only answer I have. It was twenty-five years ago, and the man is dead. He denied it all in court, then plead guilty. But he never made a statement, never explained himself. You'd think, if in his mind it was honourable, that he'd want to say it, right? That he'd want to shout that from the rooftops?'

'Unless it wasn't him.'

Jamie pinched the bridge of her nose. 'Yeah. There's that.'

'If he didn't do it, then he wouldn't be able to explain why. He could have confided that in Eriksson at the end, and all the while Eriksson could have been the actual killer.'

Jamie touched her cup and felt it cold against her skin. 'We could sit here all night theorising,' Jamie said, 'but none of it will matter if we don't catch the guy who's killing *now.* Whether Sjöberg had righteous intentions then – fucked up as they were – and whether it was him alone or Eriksson too – at the end of the day, it was vigilantism, and it was murder. Whatever way you spin it. And now, whether Eriksson's picked up this noble fucking crusade again, or he's just doing it because he loves killing, I can't say. But what I do know is this – seven girls were murdered. And then five parents were

killed. Now, Åsa Gunnarson is dead too. As is Emmy Berg. And the pattern shows that Jan Hansen is next on the list. And whether he deserves it or not, our job is to stop people killing each other. If Jan Hansen is guilty, then he'll face justice. *Real* justice. That's how it has to be. Or what the hell are we even doing?'

'Right,' Hallberg said, regaining her voice slightly.

'But the killer is smart, and he knows what he's doing. If he thinks Jan Hansen is going to be a difficult target, then I don't expect him to try anyway. He's patient. As patient as a saint.' An image of Per Eriksson in his dog collar popped into her mind. 'Waiting more than two decades to go after Mikael and Åsa Gunnarson proves that. If he needs to wait to move on Hansen, he will. But that doesn't mean he'll stop killing. I bet he's already searching for the next girl.' Jamie pushed away the cup of cold tea and stood up, staring through the window at the city she'd once called home. 'That is,' she said, heading for the door, 'if he hasn't found her already.'

42

JAMIE,

There are fleeting moments of clarity now. But they are filled with regret. I find it easy to take another drink then, if only to drown them.

I am scared. Of who I am. Of who I have become. I look in the mirror and don't recognise the person staring back.

My only solace is that I will not have to be him that much longer.

I will not have to be *at all.*

43

Jamie walked into Polis HQ just after eight the next morning.

Falk had sent her a text asking her to come in, and as she strode between the empty desks on her floor, Hallberg rose from behind a computer screen.

'Jamie,' she said, looking a little surprised.

'Hallberg,' Jamie replied, slowing. 'You get a text from Falk too?'

The woman looked back at her quizzically. 'No, I didn't.'

'Then what are you doing here?'

'I always come in by eight,' she said brightly, finding a smile, even in the midst of all this.

Jamie resisted the urge to scoff. That'll wear off soon enough, she felt like saying. 'Got to get a head start on that paperwork, eh?' she said instead, struggling to find any enthusiasm herself.

'Right,' Hallberg said, laughing. Jamie detected some nervousness there, and she knew why. She saw a lot of herself in Hallberg. Eager to please, boundless energy and absolutely nothing else in her life except for work. She woke up in the morning thinking about work, and went home at night missing it. It was early to bed because there was nothing else to do, up early because you'd been in bed since nine, and then in work at eight because sitting around your flat in your clothes for another hour seemed like the worst kind of torture available.

Jamie didn't know whether to tell her what was in store, or let her work it out for herself. The saddest thing of all was that she was looking at Jamie like the girl aspired to be her. Like she thought Jamie had it all together. That a string of cracked cases under your belt and the battle scars to prove it were worth all the shit that came with it.

It wasn't. But when you were this far in, there was nowhere else to go. A normal life, a normal job… They were the only things that seemed even less appealing than stopping. All this was just another kind of addiction. Some liked the bottle, others pills. Some people liked sex. But for Jamie, and for this poor girl in front of her, it was the job. The only thing that kept them going was the thought of nailing one more piece of shit to the goddamn wall.

That fix.

Fleeting as it was.

Jamie cleared her throat and glanced at Falk's office. She was sitting behind her desk, staring at Jamie.

She took the cue, gave Hallberg a nod, and then headed for the glass office.

Jamie was halfway through the door went Falk held her hand up. 'No, go get Hallberg,' she said flatly.

'She said she didn't have a text,' Jamie answered automatically, caught a little off guard.

'That's because I knew she'd be here,' Falk replied, raising an eyebrow.

Jamie folded her lips into an apologetic smile and nodded.

All it took was a glance over her shoulder at Hallberg, and the girl was already on her feet and heading over.

Jamie went inside and Hallberg hung at the door, looking expectant.

Falk nodded to the chairs in front of her desk and they both sat down.

She looked at Jamie, then Hallberg, then leaned on her elbows and interlinked her hands on the nape of her neck, hanging her head. She took a long breath and then sat up straight, letting her hands fall to the desk and clasp together. 'There's no point skirting around this. Wiik is being investigated by the SID for misconduct. Which means the case is on hold until I say otherwise, alright? I've told Wiik to take a few days off, to prepare himself. I don't want him working while SID are sniffing around. That will only make things worse.'

Jamie stayed silent. She'd been in the office of a senior officer enough times to know when it was time to talk and when it was time to listen. Hallberg obviously hadn't.

'An investigation?' she asked incredulously. 'For what?'

Die-hard loyalty for a man who treated her like a doormat. Jamie had to respect that. But that's what a love of the job did. Hallberg was in that frame of mind where she thought it was a rite of passage. That she had to earn Wiik's respect. The ironic thing was that when she stopped trying so hard, she would.

Falk took a second and then responded, hoping Hallberg would apologise for asking and retract the question. She didn't.

'Following the death of Tomas Lindvall, the Special Investigations Division are looking into whether there's a solid link between his treatment while in police custody and his suicide.'

Hallberg shook her head. 'Lindvall was high. Judging by the drugs recovered from his flat, he was mixing, too. They will have done a blood panel when they admitted him at the hospital,' she said confidently. 'That will show what he'd taken – and whether he was mixing it with, or had stopped taking, his antipsychotic prescription. We can't be held accountable if—'

'We are not being held accountable,' Falk said evenly, holding her hand up to silence Hallberg. '*Wiik* is. Lindvall was clearly not of sound mind, and knowing his history before he went into that interview room, he should have exercised restraint. The investigation will be into whether he used excessive force or caused Lindvall's psychotic break. Luckily, Johansson here,' Falk said, glancing at Jamie, 'seemed to quell him before he did anything *really* stupid. So I'm hopeful that, as you rightly pointed out, the SID see that Lindvall has a long history of both violence and self-abuse, that he was mixing his medication with illegal drugs, and that it was negligence on behalf of the hospital that led to his death. Lindvall was not being restrained, despite being admitted while in custody. It seems that they put him in for a battery of tests while unconscious and didn't restrain him afterwards.'

'So it's their fault,' Hallberg said, nodding assertively.

Falk sat back and opened her hands. 'That's not for us to decide. A string of events like this will have everyone pointing fingers. We apprehended Lindvall with less than circumstantial evidence—'

Jamie cut in now, unable to resist. 'He did run from us.'

'And from Wiik's report, you shoved him to the ground and then kicked him in the stomach,' Falk retorted.

Hallberg looked shocked.

'Well, not while he was *on* the ground,' Jamie said in her

defence. 'And he did try to punch me in the face. What would you have preferred me to do? Get hit?'

'I would have preferred that you'd apprehended him without the use of unnecessary force.' Falk wasn't budging.

'I thought it was necessary.' Jamie wasn't either.

'Great. That means so much coming from the British detective who's working under my authority as a civilian consultant, who is also currently on administrative leave for shooting a suspect.' Falk's cold gaze bored a hole right through Jamie's chest.

She quietened, realising then that she'd overstepped. She was surprised that Falk didn't have her on a plane already. In fact, why didn't she?

Falk exhaled slowly. 'Look – there's going to be a lot of accusations. Lindvall's family are looking for someone to point the finger at. And as far as they're concerned, both the SPA and the health service have deep pockets. We're on the defensive here, and the hospital will be trying to push them towards us.'

Jamie found she was shaking her head. 'They can't seriously be trying to lay the blame for Lindvall's death on us?'

'Who do you think tipped off the SID?'

Jamie was speechless.

'Look,' Falk said, softening. 'I wanted to bring you two in early so you were aware of the situation. Wiik is meeting with Legal this morning to go over some things. But our hands are tied. SID have governance now. All we can do is see what they say.'

That hung in the air for the moment, and then Hallberg spoke again. 'So we just abandon the case?' she asked in a tone that suggested Falk either didn't care or didn't know what was going on.

'The case is on hold, for now.' Falk reiterated it carefully, but sternly enough that Jamie wouldn't have asked again.

Once again, Hallberg exhibited what she thought was tenacity, but Falk was no doubt reading it as borderline insubordination. 'But you know that we *just* got evidence to suggest that Emmy Berg was abused by Jan Hansen. *And* William Martinsson is being brought in this morning for questioning. *And* Jamie was approached by a potential witness in the original case last night, who's attesting to Leif Lundgren abusing Hanna Lundgren. We can't just let these guys—'

Instead of raising her hand again, Falk simply leaned back and spun around on her chair so that she was facing out of the side of her office instead.

Hallberg stopped speaking and then looked at Jamie for an explanation. Jamie offered her a shake of the head that quite clearly said, *Shut up.* Whether Falk was a career pencil-pusher or not, she was smart, and Jamie had no doubt that she'd already thought about all of these things. The bags under her eyes that the make-up she was wearing was doing its best to hide told Jamie that Falk had had a late night, or an early start, or both, and had no doubt agonised over the plan moving forward.

Hallberg exhaled, unable to contain herself. 'These men are *targets.* Jamie said that the witness, Rachel Engerman, said that Hans Sjöberg said' – she was chopping one hand into the other with each item of information she was reciting – 'that men like that get what's coming to them in the end. We can't prove abuse with any of the other victims yet, but if there's a pattern here, then we could be looking at a potential vigilante-style case.' She was showing no signs of letting up, but Falk didn't seem all that interested. 'We need to put more protection on Lundgren and Hansen – bring them in for questioning. Get them talking. Show the killer that we're ahead of him. If we don't then—'

Falk spoke from her position facing away. 'Then perhaps the killer won't know that we know.'

That seemed to throw Hallberg, but Jamie was right there with Falk. 'You're using them as bait,' Jamie said as everything came into focus.

'I had a call from a solicitor representing Jan Hansen about thirty minutes ago. William won't be brought in for questioning. And any questions we have for Jan Hansen will be dealt with through his legal counsel. Much in the same way that any questions we have for Mikael Gunnarson are. And as for Leif Lundgren... This investigation is spreading everyone thin. But we'll keep a car close by.'

'That's...' Hallberg began. 'You're... *hoping* that the killer comes after them?'

Falk turned back in her chair now. 'And condemning these men to death?' She was stony-faced. 'Of course not. That would be unethical.'

Jamie watched Falk carefully and put her hand on Hallberg's knee, squeezing hard enough that she finally got the message.

Falk laid it to bed once and for all. 'We have an unmarked car parked outside both Hansen and Lundgren's house. They've been there since you told me about the evidence on William Martinsson's tablet and about Rachel Engerman's testimony. As for Mikael Gunnarson, he's spending his time in his penthouse flat in the city, but is well connected enough to look after himself. I don't think that the killer will make an attempt on his life again so soon. As for Hansen and Lundgren – if the killer sticks to his pattern, then we'll be there to intercept.'

Hallberg didn't know what to make of this. Jamie could

see it in her face. She was right that not telling them that their lives were potentially in danger wasn't completely ethical. But Falk was right in saying that the killer was more use to them not knowing the extent of their knowledge.

And anyway, even if Lundgren could be brought in on the two-decade-old withheld testimony of a friend – who was a child herself at the time – and questioned, they had no evidence to take it anywhere unless he confessed. Which Jamie didn't think he was about to. And as for Jan Hansen, all they had was some circumstantial evidence pulled from a child's tablet. Something that any solicitor worth their salt would get thrown out of court in a heartbeat.

They had nothing solid to bring any charges with, and dragging them in here would only serve to upset the investigation.

No, as hard as it was, right now, all they could do was nothing. They had all the devices from Hansen's house. The techs would scrub through them and catalogue everything they found. But it would take a while to beat their security measures into submission and extract what was hidden inside. An innocent man would provide the passwords to expedite the process. But Jan Hansen wasn't an innocent man. And the longer it took, the longer he had to come up with some bullshit to cover his ass.

It was a waiting game now.

But that was almost worse.

Jamie had worked enough cases like this to know one thing for certain.

Wait long enough, and people die.

44

'WHAT DO WE DO NOW?' Hallberg asked, rocking back on her chair.

Jamie was leaning against her desk. It still wasn't close to nine o'clock yet, and the office remained empty.

Falk had told Jamie and Hallberg that they could take the day. That she'd inform them if anything developed. But Jamie didn't feel like walking in circles at the hotel. She had plenty to do.

She pushed off the desk and cracked her neck, shaking out her legs. They were a little sore from the exertion the night before. 'Do whatever you want,' Jamie said. 'Take a day off.' She raised a hand over her shoulder and bid Hallberg a quick goodbye, heading for Wiik's desk.

She was sure that Falk would set her up with a temporary log-in if she asked, but there was no need. She knew Wiik's password now. Lucas110708. His son's name followed by his birthday in reverse. She'd been told once by a digital technician at the Met that any passwords containing the names and dates related to loved ones were utterly hackable. Which she'd then proved by hacking Jamie's log-in details. And then her partner's, too, for good measure.

Jamie had taken that to heart.

But Wiik hadn't got the memo, obviously.

She'd seen him type it in over his shoulder the day before.

Jamie arrived at his desk, pushing away the *Min pappa är en superhjälte* mug, which now had a furry, grey blob swimming on top of the coffee left in the bottom.

She sat and logged in quickly, pulling the photograph of her and her father from her jacket pocket. She stood it up under the screen and inspected it again in the full light of day, racking her brains for any memory of where it was. Searching for the slightest hint in the landscape that offered any identifying data.

She found none.

Jamie let out a long breath and closed her eyes. This might be harder than she thought.

But she needed to find it. To find what her father had left her.

Jamie opened her eyes and jolted in her seat.

Hallberg was hovering at the corner of the desk like a child. 'What are you doing?' she asked.

'I'm, uh,' Jamie started, sitting forward and looking at the blank search engine on her screen. 'I'm looking for a lake.'

'A lake?' Hallberg wasn't following. 'Why?'

Jamie glanced at the photograph, deciding how much she wanted to explain. 'My father and I left something at a hunting cabin years ago. I want to see if it's still there.'

'What kind of something?'

'Just personal stuff,' she said, brushing it off, hoping Hallberg would get the hint.

The woman nodded back at her, but didn't make an

attempt to leave. She just hovered, pushing some pens around a stationery caddy next to Wiik's desk.

'Do you need any help?' she asked after a few seconds.

'You don't have anything else to do?' Jamie raised an eyebrow.

'Wiik offloaded all of our other cases when we took the Angel Maker.'

'Paperwork?'

'Done.'

'Forensic reports?'

'All catalogued, filed, earmarked.'

'The questions for Gunnarson?'

'Sent to his solicitor. I followed up with another email a few minutes ago.'

'Parents of the original victims?'

'I have requisition forms in with the Vehicle Licensing Agency for updated addresses and contact details. It could take a while.'

'The agency they used for the nanny?'

'There were five possibles operating in Stockholm at the time of Tilde Gunnarson's death. I've reached out to the two that are still running for their records, and I pulled the names and addresses of the owners of the other three from the national business registry, and followed up with the VLA for up-to-date contact details on them, too. Fingers crossed they get everything over at the same time. I'm hoping we can track the nanny down from there, but if the owners haven't kept records for that long... And as there's no proof of any criminal activity, we won't get a search-and-seizure warrant for the Gunnarsons' personal files. If Mikael doesn't have the records or isn't prepared to hand them over, then we're at a dead end with this one.'

Jamie didn't like the turn of phrase, but she accepted the

possibility. She was continually impressed by Hallberg's ability to just get work done. She was efficient and focused, and Wiik was lucky to have her. 'So you have nothing else to do?' Maybe she could use her.

Hallberg smiled and shrugged. 'Do you need help?'

'Sure,' Jamie said, grabbing the photo from the desk and handing it to her.

'This is you?' Hallberg said, inspecting it. 'And your dad.'

'That's right.'

'And you need to find out where this lake is?'

'If I can.'

'That's the hunting cabin?'

'It is.'

'And this car – what is it?' Hallberg glanced up at Jamie.

'I don't know. A Volvo – early nineties model.' She inflected it like a question. She never took any notice of what the car was. She was just a kid.

Hallberg nodded, as though that was enough. 'And you have no idea where it is?'

'My dad used to go fishing to a lake near Vemdalen, but I don't think it's this one.'

'There are a lot of lakes around there.'

'Yep,' Jamie said, sighing. 'That's kind of the problem.'

Hallberg nodded. 'Leave it with me. Do you mind if I borrow this for a minute? I can just make a copy and bring it back if—'

'No,' Jamie said quickly, not sure why that bothered her so much. 'Don't make a copy. Just… just look after it, okay?'

Hallberg held it against her chest. 'Of course,' she said. 'I'll let you know if I find anything.' She smiled widely at Jamie, as though relieved to have something to do. Like an itch had been scratched. Like an addiction had been fed, if only for a little while.

Jamie watched her go for a second and then turned back to her own screen. To the empty search bar there. 'Okay,' she said to herself. 'Let's go.'

Thirty minutes later, Jamie was on page seventeen of Google Images, the words 'lakes in Sweden' in the search bar. She was trawling endlessly through photos of them, looking for anything that looked anywhere close to hers.

So far, she'd made a note of two. One on page three, and another on page eleven. Neither was it, she thought. But she didn't really know what else to do. Maybe Wiik was right and she had become terrible at research. She supposed she was a little out of practice.

Hallberg was walking towards her then, grinning, a piece of paper in her hands, the photograph held against, pinned it under her thumb.

She slowed at Jamie's desk, looking proud of herself, and laid it down.

Jamie took the photo off the top and put it back in her coat without a word and then lifted the paper in front of her. On it were a list of eight lakes, separated into columns. It had their names, their coordinates, their sizes, volumes, and whether or not they fell within national parks.

She knew Hallberg was good, but she was gobsmacked. 'What... How did you find these?'

'Oh,' Hallberg said, thrown by the question. She probably never got asked, or thanked, by Wiik. She just produced. 'I just looked up the dimensions of that model of Volvo, and then used a 3D-modelling software to calculate the approximate size of the cabin. Using that, I determined the height of the surrounding valley, and then calculated its width, then cross-referenced that with topographical survey maps for similar prominence and size. Then I checked which of those valleys held bodies of water. I can't see any tributaries feeding this, so I discounted all those that were fed into by rivers. Then I checked which of those lakes fell within the areas where hunting was allowed during the nineties, and then finally I pulled up satellite imaging, and checked the remaining lakes against the shape of this one to get rid of the outliers.' She reeled it off casually, and then sighed. 'I'm sorry I couldn't narrow it down any further. But over the last twenty years, the size and shape of the lake could have shrunk or grown, so I didn't want to cross out any potential matches.'

'No, this is amazing,' Jamie said, still amazed by the list in front of her. There was an ache in the back of her throat now, her eyes burning a little.

'At first, I tried to grab the measurements of the lake in order to calculate its relative volume – but that can be unreliable because we don't know what the depth is, as well as variables like seasonal fluctuation and things like weather, glacial melt if it's near to a—'

'Hallberg,' Jamie said, cutting her off. 'You did great. Thank you.'

The woman blushed violently. 'With some more time, I could—'

Jamie didn't want to hear any more. She felt like they were already burning daylight. 'How fast can you calculate a route through all eight?'

'What do you mean?'

'Driving from here – which is closest? Can I get to them all in a day?'

'You want to go there?' Hallberg seemed surprised. 'Oh, er, yeah. Just give me a minute.' She pulled her phone out and started tapping in the names of the lakes. Jamie waited, while she did. Hallberg had no intention of leaving her desk, it seemed.

'Okay, this one is closest,' she said, turning her phone around. 'There's two more within about half an hour of it. And then there are a few further north. The last three are too far to drive in a day.'

'We can take them off the list then.' Jamie nodded assertively. 'My father used to drive – and it was never more than a day. A couple of hours. Maybe four or five at the most, I think. I don't know, but it wasn't an overnight journey. We'd get there in the afternoon.'

This seemed to spur Hallberg on. She checked her watch, dashing back to her desk and grabbing her jacket. In seconds she was back at Jamie's desk. 'If we leave now, we should be able to reach the first by about eleven.'

Jamie raised her eyebrows. 'You want to come with me?'

'Of course,' Hallberg said. 'Why wouldn't I?'

'I don't know.' Jamie didn't really have an answer. But if someone asked her to drive aimlessly around the Swedish countryside all day, looking for a lost lake which may or may not have a hunting cabin next to it, which may or may not contain a package left there two decades prior, she would probably have politely declined.

'Come on,' Hallberg said, heading for the door, striding powerfully.

Jamie laughed a little, watching her go. She was another Wiik in the making with a walk like that. And had no doubt modelled herself on him.

Jamie stood and threw her jacket around her shoulders.

There were worse detectives to be inspired by, she supposed.

But then again, she really didn't know if the world could endure another Anders Wiik.

At the very least, she couldn't.

45

THE CLOUDS WERE thick and oozing, the light beginning to fade. It was two in the afternoon now.

Jamie had elected to drive this time. She remembered the track leading up to the cabin had been rough and rutted, no more than an old horse-track churned back to the stone by semi-regular use. Hallberg's Mercedes was riding on low-profile tyres and had expensive alloys. The ride wasn't altogether made for comfort and it sat low to the ground. Jamie's rental on the other hand was on skinny wheels with lots of sidewall, steel alloys and soft suspension that soaked up bumps. It wasn't a four-by-four by any stretch, but this time of year, all rentals came with snow chains, and its plucky little hybrid-petrol engine would have no problem hauling Jamie and Hallberg around.

They'd already visited the four lakes at the top of Hallberg's list, excluding the ones over a day's drive away. Number five was just around the next bend.

Jamie slowed and pulled off the main road at Hallberg's direction, into a stony lay-by, and then she eased down a narrow track lined with snow. This far north, the ground was completely covered with it. But the lay-by looked well driven over, and two deep tyre marks had been carved into the snow, the stone clearly visible beneath. They looked nearly black in the closing gloom, vivid against the virgin snow.

Hallberg and Jamie jostled like they were on a riverboat, neither speaking.

They were both tired and cold.

Several times they'd driven up tracks like this, got stuck in the snow, and had to get out to put the snow chains on. The trouble was that even after they'd managed to dig the car out and attach them, when they got to the end of the track, they realised they were in the wrong place and had to go back. Then, upon reaching the road, they had to take the chains off again, as the roads themselves were clear.

As such, neither could feel their hands, and they were both ready to call it a day.

The radio was droning static now, the valley sides around them blocking out any signal.

Jamie switched the lights to full beam, and they cut through the crisp air, setting the snow alight.

They ventured further from the road towards a break in the valley wall. The track began to climb now, heading for a crest that would take them down into the otherwise inaccessible bowl that held the lake.

Hallberg had given her the name, but it didn't sound familiar. The road in didn't feel familiar either. And this track was as alien as all the rest.

She'd never taken much notice of the trips up as a girl, but she thought she'd have recognised something.

Jamie sighed, focusing her eyes. They'd been on the move for six hours, and both were running low on energy. This was the last one. Neither said it, but both knew.

The car's tyres fought for grip as Jamie eased it up the

slope, listening to them slip and then bite on the rocks and ice. The car would shudder and rev as the wheels began to slide and then lurch forwards as they found purchase again.

Up and up they moved at a snail's pace, the sky darkening ahead, the road no more than a black paint stroke behind them.

The city was hours away, as was any sort of rescue. If Jamie lost it here and the car slid sideways into what she had to assume was a snow-filled ditch, they'd be stranded.

But she didn't say that to Hallberg. She just kept her eyes on the tracks ahead, and hoped to hell they wouldn't have to get out and do the chains again. The temperature had plunged now to minus nine, and the windows were fogging at their flanks as they both breathed heavily, the tension rising by the second.

The engine whined as the car hauled itself over the last ridge, and then they were on flat ground, the sky lightening in front of them. The sun was directly at eye level now, fighting against the cloud cover as it sank towards the horizon.

Then the nose was dropping again, and they were trundling down into the shaded valley. The lake stretched out ahead, in the shape of a dead fish. Larch stretched around the walls of the bowl, shadowed and jagged. Snow had piled up next to the road, the valley sides sheltering it from the wind. It rose up next to the car as Jamie wrestled to keep the wheels straight, feathering the brakes to stop them from locking.

They squealed in protest.

The car snaked lower into the valley, a thin mist beginning to settle around them as the sun faded.

In the distance, Jamie could see a little cabin, nestled among the edge of the trees. The tracks cut right up to it, the muddy mess of tyre marks telling her the place wasn't empty.

She could make out the shape of two vehicles, but from this distance, it was difficult to put any sort of guess on them.

She needed to focus on the track, anyway. The terrain was more than treacherous. She just hoped they could get back out when this turned out to be the wrong lake too.

She still wasn't having any familiar pangs.

All the lakes on Hallberg's list could have been it.

But she was afraid that none would be.

Jamie exhaled and loosened her grip on the wheel, her fingers aching.

Hallberg was leaning forward, squinting into the distance as they descended, the fog thickening with every metre.

They reached the bottom and the car flattened out, the bumper scrubbing on the snow. A rock scraped the undercarriage and Jamie squirmed in the seat, feeling the wheels sink in the mud.

She shifted up a gear to keep the revs down and gave it a little throttle, squeezing the clutch to limit the power output.

The car twisted left and right, and then picked up speed, bouncing over the uneven surface.

Jamie sighed with relief, her eyes fixed on the ground ahead.

She stole a glance up at Hallberg, who was practically pressed against the windscreen. 'Is that…' she started. 'Is that the…'

Jamie followed her line of sight, doing her best to pick out the thing she was looking at. Ahead, about a hundred metres out, the headlights were reflecting on the side of what looked like… 'The church minibus,' Jamie said, her voice strained suddenly. She eased off the gas instinctively, all the tiredness gone from her mind.

'Eriksson,' Hallberg said, her voice barely a whisper. 'What the hell is he doing all the way out—'

But she didn't get to finish that thought. A flash burst out of the darkness ahead, somewhere in the general vicinity of the cabin. A small, white plume.

Jamie's brain barely registered it before the bullet punctured the windscreen, tore through the cabin and blew the back window out.

The glass shattered behind them and rained down onto the parcel shelf. In front, a spider's web of cracks rippled out in all directions, blinding them.

Hallberg ducked forward, shielding her head.

Jamie swore in shock, the bullet missing her face by inches, and ripped the wheel to the side, stamping on the brake.

The front wheels locked up, and the car began to slide, spinning the passenger side towards the shooter.

Jamie didn't have time to think before another bullet hit the back passenger window and buried itself in the opposite side's door pillar. The noise of it hitting the metal frame of the car made the whole thing vibrate like a bell.

The wheels dug into the soft mud in the centre of the track, the front diving into the gulley on the left, sending snow up over the bonnet.

The whole thing threatened to tip over for a moment, and then came to rest on its wheels.

Hallberg was swearing in a continuous stream. They were pinned down, in the open. And the shooter had clear line of sight.

Jamie's brain reverted to a primal mode and she threw the driver's door open and dived out into the snow.

She landed heavily on her front and rolled around, getting to her knees, ignoring the stinging of the ice on her fingers. She scrambled herself back against the car, panting hard, her breath rising in front of her like smoke.

Hallberg was still inside, her head between her knees, swearing.

Another shot rang out, a bullet glancing off the top of the car, sending sparks into the blackening sky.

The noise echoed as the bullet ricocheted into the distance, a deathly cry in the otherwise silent wilderness.

Jamie gritted her teeth and rolled into the open doorway, keeping low as she reached across and unfastened Hallberg's belt, grabbing for her hand.

The girl snatched it away, cupping the back of her head, but Jamie took it again and pulled hard.

Hallberg looked at her, wild-eyed.

'Come on,' Jamie said, dragging her across the centre console. 'You've got to get out of the car!'

Hallberg nodded quickly, slithering over the handbrake on her belly and kicking herself down into the snow next to Jamie.

Once she was clear, Jamie pushed the driver's door closed and took stock of the situation. 'Are you hurt? Did you get hit?' she asked, roughly running her hands over Hallberg.

'No – no, I don't think so,' she squeezed out. She looked like she was about to throw up. She obviously hadn't been shot at before.

Jamie would have liked to have said you get used to it, but you didn't. Her heart was hammering so hard in her chest she thought it was about to burst.

'What do we do?' Hallberg asked, frantic.

Jamie forced air into her lungs and got her heels under her. She started lifting herself up, turning her head to peek through the back window.

'What are you doing?' Hallberg hissed, as though the shooter might hear her.

Jamie edged higher, trying to get a good look at what was ahead.

The ground was flat from here to the cabin. The church van – complete with decals of a crucifix and the words *Jesus Räddar* – Jesus Saves – was pulled off to the left, its nose facing the frozen lake. Beyond that, the cabin stood, no more than a dark square. There was no light burning inside, no smoke rising from the chimney. Nothing to suggest life.

Jamie narrowed her eyes, trying to pick out anything else in the monochrome landscape.

Another flash rippled from just above the cabin, at the treeline, and Jamie dropped back down, wincing as the window above her exploded, showering her with glass. 'Fuck,' she said, protecting her skull, spitting flecks of saliva through gritted teeth.

'What do we do?' Hallberg asked again.

'I don't know,' Jamie said, feeling the vibrations in the metal as Eriksson put another bullet into the side of the car, just for good measure. Running perpendicular to a shooter, moving from cover to cover was one thing. But from this angle, straight on – with this much open space – there was nowhere to run. And no chance of getting out of there alive.

Eriksson was no prize marksman, but it was a hundred metres up a snowy slope before they had any chance of safety. To the right was deep snow rising into a steep valley wall. And to the left was the lake. Five hundred metres of slick ice and zero cover.

She growled at the lack of options and laid her head back against the frozen metal.

'What do we do?' Hallberg asked again, sinking her fingers into Jamie's arm.

'I don't know!' she practically yelled back, making the woman shrink away from her.

Hallberg's eyes began to fill. She was terrified.

So was Jamie.

But she had to think. There had to be a way out of here. Could she get in the car? Swing around, drive out? No, not a chance. The track was narrow and the car was already half off it. They'd have to get the chains on to have any chance of moving it at all and there was no way in hell they could get to the open side without taking a bullet.

They weren't going on foot, and they weren't going by car.

Could they call for help? How long would they take to arrive? Jamie didn't know.

Too long.

She forced herself to breathe. To think.

The shooter had gone quiet. Conserving ammunition, choosing his shots.

Shots.

That was it.

'Hallberg,' Jamie said, turning to her. 'Your pistol.'

Hallberg's eyes lit up a little. She pulled it from the holster on her ribs and held it aloft like it was the answer to their problems.

'Can you shoot?' Jamie asked.

'Shoot? At what? I don't even know where he is!'

'It doesn't matter,' Jamie said, her brain beginning to work again now. The fear was there, but with a loose plan forming in her mind. 'I just need you to draw his fire.'

'Draw his fire? I'm not going out there!' she protested.

Jamie turned to her now, taking her by the shoulders. 'I don't need you to. I just need you to keep him occupied long enough.'

'Long enough for what?'

Jamie met her eye, a strange coolness seizing her. 'Long enough for me to shoot back.'

Hallberg looked confused. Jamie wasn't surprised.

'Look,' she said, scuttling to the back of the car. 'He's set up somewhere at the treeline, just above the cabin. I don't expect you to hit him – it's probably impossible from this distance with a pistol.'

'I'm a good shot,' Hallberg said, trying on something like confidence. It slipped off her like a silk veil.

'Good. Then it'll make him duck.'

'I don't understand what we're—'

'When I give the signal, I want you to pop up and fire—' Jamie cut herself off, looking at the pistol in Hallberg's hand. 'What is that, a P226?'

'Yeah,' Hallberg said, seemingly thrown by Jamie's intimate knowledge of guns.

'Thirteen-round magazine?'

'Yeah,' she said again.

'Good. Then fire six shots – count them off – every few seconds – evenly spaced. I need fifteen – no, twenty seconds.'

'For what?' Hallberg asked, shaking her head.

'Ready?'

'No!'

Jamie was at the back of the car now, and she wasn't waiting. 'Now, Hallberg! Go!'

Keeping close to the bumper, Jamie edged into the open.

Hallberg had no choice. Either follow the plan or watch Jamie get blown apart. She rattled out a long, shaky breath, and then moved, rising up over the bonnet, squeezing off the first round prematurely, sending it wheeling into the sky. The next was closer to the target. The third was pretty close.

Jamie just had to trust Hallberg, focus on what she was doing.

She traced across the metal of the boot and found the latch for the door. She popped it, keeping as tight to the back of the car as she could. Inside there was an old blanket. She grabbed it and pulled it towards her, the contents heavy.

Jamie listened as Hallberg put round number four into the darkness, and threw back the top flap, exposing her father's Remington Model 700 hunting rifle. She stared down at it for a second before taking hold of the barrel, along with the small box of ammunition she'd taken from his office too, and scrambled back into cover.

She'd not wanted the CSTs to see it. Any firearm found in a search needed to be queried – and without knowing where the documents for the rifle were, Jamie didn't want to risk it being seized. What she intended to do with the thing, she hadn't been sure. She couldn't take it back with her. But she didn't want it taken into police custody.

And she was glad she'd removed it now.

Because it was about to save her life.

Hallberg sank next to her, breathing hard, clutching the shaking pistol in both hands. She had her eyes closed and Jamie thought she could see her heart hammering through her coat.

As the first round slipped into the magazine of the rifle, Hallberg's eyes opened, then widened in shock. 'Jesus!' she said, recoiling from it. 'Where the hell did you get that?'

'It was in the boot,' Jamie said calmly, pushing more rounds into the magazine. Each clicked into place. Five. Six. Full.

Jamie exhaled hard and snapped the magazine back into the body, dragging back the bolt. It ground a little on the metal. It had been twenty-five years without use. But her father had always maintained it perfectly. She had no doubt it would shoot.

She looked back at Hallberg. 'Ready? Same drill.'

'Wait – what are you going to—'

'On my mark, okay?'

'Jamie, wait—'

'Now.' Jamie moved before she lost her nerve, spinning to a knee and moving beyond the protection of the car. She pulled the rifle to her shoulder and held it tight, closing her left eye and sighting through the scope with her right. There was no wind in the bowl, and at a hundred metres, she hoped she wouldn't have to account for bullet drop. But that was all assuming she could even see who she was shooting at.

Jamie blinked hard and scanned the landscape, forcing her eyes to focus in the dwindling light.

The sound of Hallberg's shots echoed around the valley, the reports bouncing off the sheet ice of the lake and reverberating into the sky.

The scope was grubby, the dust on the lens stinging her eye. She could feel it tickling her eyelashes.

Jamie squinted down it, her heartbeat making the whole thing shake in her hands.

She counted off Hallberg's trigger pulls, trying to pick out any sort of shape from the darkened trees.

One, two, three.

Jamie gritted her teeth and held her breath, jamming herself against the back corner of the car for stability.

Shit. Come on, where are you?

Four. Five.

Jamie growled, going back over the same patch of darkness for the third time. He was there. Somewhere, she knew it. She just couldn't see him.

Six.

One shot left in Hallberg's magazine.

And she didn't have another.

A white rose burst from the trees ahead. An instantaneous flash of muzzle fire that disappeared as suddenly as it had appeared.

Jamie homed in on it.

Metal on metal sang behind her as Eriksson's bullet hit the bonnet of the rental car.

Hallberg screamed.

Then she hit the ground, hard.

Was she hit?

Jamie couldn't think about it now.

The last remnants of air left her lungs, the crosshairs falling just to the right of the flash.

She squeezed the trigger.

The rifle kicked back into her shoulder, her ears ringing, not even registering the report.

Jamie was blind for a moment, then refocused her eyes.

She couldn't see anything.

Did she hit him?

Jamie lowered the rifle and ducked back behind the car. Her fingers were stinging from the cold, her knees frozen and wet from the snow.

She turned quickly to Hallberg, who was lying on her back, clutching her face.

'Jesus,' Jamie said, dropping the rifle in the snow and sliding towards her. She scrabbled through the slush, spraying mud and snow everywhere, and reached out. 'Are you okay?' She pulled Hallberg's hands from her face, seeing the stark crimson of blood on her pale skin.

Jamie's heart seized in her throat as she looked down at Hallberg's face. She had it screwed up, tears streaming from the corners of her eyes.

Across her right cheek and ear, Jamie could see cuts – little marks sliced into the skin running towards her hairline.

Eriksson's shot must have hit the bonnet of the car just in front of her. The shot had missed, but it had sent shrapnel flying. Paint chips, pieces of metal, shards of bullet. Jamie didn't know, but Hallberg's face was a mess. The shards had missed her eye – just – but Jamie counted maybe a dozen individual cuts – some deeper than others.

Blood had begun seeping into her hair now.

She was whimpering, tugging against Jamie's hands to hold her face again.

'Hey,' Jamie said softly. 'I need you to look at me, okay? Hallberg?'

The girl's eyes fluttered and then forced themselves open.

She squinted into the bludgeoned sky and then focused on Jamie.

Both eyes open.

She couldn't see any damage.

That was a relief.

She'd be okay.

Jamie sighed a little and pulled Hallberg to a seated position, brushing snow from her shoulders. 'You're okay,' she said, nodding. 'You did good. Hold on.' Jamie swivelled backwards and pulled the car door open, reaching into the tiny back seat where she'd thrown a beanie hat and a scarf the day before. She grabbed them both, folding the scarf up and handing it to Hallberg. She guided it towards her face and pressed. Hallberg hissed and winced.

But Jamie wasn't paying attention to her anymore. Her ears were pricked for any sound beyond the shelter of the car.

Hallberg would be fine, if not in pain for now. Jamie's main concern was the shooter. Had she hit him? If she hadn't, they were all out of options.

Jamie returned to the car now, scooping the Remington out of the snow, and shook it clean. She took the beanie then and slipped it over the nose of the rifle, holding it upright so it balanced on top like the hat it was.

She stuck close to the front wheel and slowly lifted it up, motioning Hallberg to stay down with her other hand.

The top of the hat poked over the car and hovered there.

Jamie watched it, counting.

She got to ten seconds.

Nothing.

Twenty.

Nothing.

She tried to relax.

How long would she wait? How long would the shooter wait? Had he seen it? Would he take the bait? He hadn't blown a hole through it yet, or even tried to take another shot.

Maybe Jamie had scared him off.

She lifted her head slightly until it hovered next to the wing mirror. She glanced over at Hallberg, who was staring up at her through her uncovered eye, and then nodded in reassurance.

Jamie exhaled hard and then peeked over the sill of the door, squinting into the distance.

Nothing moved.

The cabin stood silent.

Jamie swallowed and got a little higher into a crouched position now. 'Wait here,' she said to Hallberg, moving towards the back of the car.

'Where are you going?' she asked. 'Jamie?'

But she was already gone.

If there was one thing she had in her favour, it was that she was fast. Jamie Johansson could run. She was built for it.

Rifle in hand, she got to her feet and took off, moving as fast as the conditions allowed.

She kept to the edge of the track, hammering through the

fresh snow, her chest heaving and aching beneath her jacket. She told herself that if there was any hint of gunfire, a flash of a muzzle, she'd throw herself into the undergrowth. Just hurl herself into the thick ferns and snow at the side of the road. It was all she could do.

But as she ran, eyes fixed on the trees, none came.

The cabin came up quickly and Jamie suppressed a wave of memories. The smell of the larch sap, the fish hanging on a rack outside. The black coals of a burnt-out fire. They were all familiar things that were lodged deep in her mind.

Jamie blinked hard, her brain not fully grasping the situation.

She passed the church van on her left, filthy and quiet.

The vehicle next to it, too. She recognised it. It was—

She ducked instinctively, a noise coming from up ahead.

Jamie was frozen for a moment, the rifle rising to her shoulder again.

She pricked her ears, heart thundering.

Groaning.

She could hear groaning.

Low and pained.

Jamie was in the open now. She had to move.

She turned and went the other way, circling the cabin. She didn't know whether it was a trick, a trap – or what kind of other weapons Eriksson might have. Had she winged him? He was alive. She knew that much.

The snow deepened and snatched at Jamie's thighs as she waded behind the cabin and up the slope towards the trees.

She was breathing hard, her fingers numb, her head and neck slick with sweat.

Night was falling quickly and it was all but dark in the shadow of the trees.

The groaning was back, and louder now.

She was getting closer.

Jamie moved past the cabin completely and out onto a path in the snow – a worn track leading from the door to the woods.

She glanced back at the dark cabin, listening for any sound – any hint of a second presence.

She found none, and pushed on, following the pained cries, coming up from what she hoped was the blind spot.

She followed the path, pace quickening, and picked out the shape of a body in the dwindling light.

There, at the line where the ferns met the trees, she could see a section of snow that had been tramped flat. A rug had been laid on it – animal skins by the look of it – and some brush had been laid around the edges to form a makeshift hide. Larch branches, twigs, ferns, all dusted with snow.

She could see a rifle, the barrel poked through it, the stock laid on top of a rolled-up blanket. She looked at it for just a second – thought it was maybe a Sauer 202 – she wasn't sure. But it was a bolt-action deer rifle, by the looks of it. Long scoped. Maybe a tactical model or modified to take the world-ending rounds it had been dishing out. But whatever it was, it packed a hell of a punch.

Her eyes moved quickly from the rifle that had nearly killed her twice now to the man who'd been firing it.

He was lying on his right side, clutching at his ribs with his right hand, his left reaching for the gun that was out of reach. Jamie could see blood oozing through his fingers – it looked like she'd hit him in the side.

He was wearing a quilted black body warmer, what looked like a jacket under it, tatty, old jeans, and a full-face balaclava. He was groaning, his lips puckered, pink and flecked with blood in the opening of the mask.

His eyes were slits, screwed up in pain.

His legs kicked sporadically, raking dirt and snow around.

She couldn't see the exit wound – didn't know at what angle she'd hit him, if the bullet was still in there.

But as she stepped closer to kick the rifle further out of reach, her boot squelched in a pool of blood. It was soaked into the rug and still leaking through the shooter's fingers.

'Jesus,' Jamie said, looking at her feet. She lifted her head towards the car in the distance and lowered her rifle. Hallberg was still over there. Hiding.

Jamie's brain began to work. This amount of blood, the way the bullet had struck him... She swallowed. He didn't have long left.

But who was to say that he wasn't already dead when she got there?

Jamie watched him on the ground, coughing now, spraying blood onto the pristine white snow.

His eyes opened, a milky green and sunken, and he stared up at her. 'J... Jamie?' he said, barely a whisper.

Jamie looked down at the man on the ground and her blood ran cold.

She clamped her jaw tight to stop it from shaking and knelt down in the pool of blood, suddenly very far removed from herself. She reached out for the ski mask, her fist closing about the crown of the man's head, his name forming on her lips before she even pulled it off.

'Robert Nyström,' she said, dragging it from his face.

The withered man she'd known as a girl looked back up at her – the same white hair, the same thin face, the same bushy eyebrows.

Confusion came over his face, a droplet of blood running from the corner of his mouth. His head shook. He could barely hold it up. 'I... I didn't mean to—'

'Shh,' Jamie commanded, regaining herself and moving forward. 'Don't talk.'

She batted his hand from his flank, pulling off her jacket and stuffing it against his body.

He made a pained whine as Jamie held it against the entry wound, hard, fishing her phone from her pocket.

Robert Nyström stared up at her in silence as she dialled the emergency line.

It rang once, then connected.

Jamie spoke fast, keeping her eyes on the man who'd been as close to her father as a brother, who had helped catch the man who killed those girls. Who'd been there for her a hundred times – and wondered how long it would take for an airlift to arrive.

Jamie watched Nyström's blood soak into the coat clamped beneath her fingers and realised that, however long it took, it was probably going to be too long.

Nyström was dying right in front of her.

And though her brain was trying every combination of the information it had, she just couldn't make sense of it.

But she knew one thing for certain, as painful as it was to accept.

Robert Nyström was the Angel Maker.

She just didn't know why.

46

WHEN THE DISTANT chug of rotors first broke the air, Jamie wasn't sure if it had been minutes or hours.

She was shivering with the cold, her skin prickling, fingers completely numb. The snow and blood had soaked through her jeans and travelled to her hips. She couldn't feel anything below the waist.

Her hands had turned completely red with Nyström's blood, which had now begun to crystallise around her fingers.

Her coat was sodden.

The man had slipped into unconsciousness at some point, and Jamie wasn't far off, either. Hallberg had arrived at some indeterminable time, and had knelt next to Jamie, putting an arm around her. It had done nothing.

She'd then gone to the cabin and come back with a blanket of some kind. She'd put it around Jamie's shoulders, but she couldn't feel any cold or warmth now. Her brain wasn't working like it should have been.

Then there was whipping snow. It hit her skin like needles. Bright lights. A deafening roar. Men in red jumpsuits.

They came up quickly, pried Jamie from the man on the ground and sat her back in the snow.

A man was in her face then – he had a huge, white domed head and alien eyes the size of saucers.

A helmet, Jamie realised after a few seconds.

His mouth was moving, but Jamie couldn't hear his words.

She nodded absently and he was replaced by Hallberg, who had her by the shoulders. She was yelling, but it was as though someone had turned the sound off to Jamie's world.

The two dome-headed creatures in red loaded Nyström onto a stretcher and then lifted him, walking quickly down towards the source of the light and noise.

Jamie looked at it, knowing she'd seen one before. But she couldn't remember what they were called.

The rotors beat the frigid air like drums. She felt it in her bones.

Her eyes drifted then, away from the strange machine to the little cabin.

A blonde girl appeared in the doorway for a moment, her hair long and plaited, luminescent in the glare of the floodlights.

Her eyes shone out like little opals. Glowing.

A shape loomed behind her, large and imposing.

Jamie held her breath, afraid for a moment, and then it stepped into the light.

His eyes. The same as the girl's. His face, kind.

He put big hands on her shoulders and then nodded to Jamie.

She swallowed hard and tried to get up.

Hallberg tried to hold her down, but Jamie pushed her away.

She got to her feet and loped down towards the pair.

They seemed to fade as she neared, her vision closing down to a tunnel.

The doorway lurched towards her and her hands raised automatically.

She bounced off the frame, feeling something sharp dig into her palm.

And then she was inside.

The interior was dark, the smell of smoke thick in the air. She coughed, feeling the last dregs of warmth coming from the coals in the hearth against her cheek as she passed.

The flames had long since died.

Jamie turned on feet not her own, looking for the man and the girl.

She couldn't see anything.

Then, a glimmer – in the darkness. Like cats' eyes.

And gone again.

She moved in that direction, shoving a chair from her path.

It banged against a table and toppled over.

Jamie stumbled forward, towards the corner of the cabin, and sank to her knees, using her hands like shovels.

She pushed an old stool out of the way. A metal bucket fell from on top of it and bounced behind her.

She could barely see, the only light that which was streaming through the door from the machine outside.

Jamie traced the rough floorboards with her fingers, feeling for the join, and then dug her nails into one of the seams.

She was breathing hard – painfully, now.

Her eyes were burning, her throat tight.

Jamie thought her nails were going to snap off.

She cried out, she thought, but she wasn't sure.

Dust choked her.

And then the board began to move.

It levered upwards, frozen in place by the years, and then came free.

Jamie tossed it aside and plunged her hands into the dark void beneath. She couldn't feel anything, her fingers still numb, soaked with the blood of a man she'd known her whole life.

A voice behind her then, calling a name. *Jamie.* Her name. That was her name.

She looked around, saw the woman from outside again. Hallberg. Yes, that was it. She had her hands on Jamie's shoulder. She was grabbing her arm. Pulling at her.

Jamie tried to fight her off.

No. Not yet.

But she wouldn't let go. She was dragging her, yelling something.

Jamie could just hear a distant throbbing. A high-pitched whistle. She wasn't sure what was outside and what was in her head.

She was moving then, being pulled to her feet.

Her hands clamped down on whatever was in the hole. She couldn't make out the finer details under her fingertips.

Something soft.

She pulled it tight to her chest and held on as she was guided towards the door.

Outside, the swirl of snow blasted them both.

Jamie shuddered violently, still clutching the package in her hands.

The man in the red jumpsuit with the domed helmet was beckoning to them frantically, yelling something.

Jamie slipped and slid through the snow, and then the beckoning man took her by the arm.

One on each side, they dragged her towards the machine with the bright lights and pushed her up into the doorway.

Someone put a hand on the back of her head, making her duck, and then sat her on a seat.

A belt fastened around her waist and her stomach lurched.

The ground fell away beneath her, the cabin becoming very small, very fast.

The lake, shining a dim silver, twisted around and then moved into the distance.

It shrank and shrank through the window of the machine, and then Jamie finally looked down.

Between her feet was the head of the man with the bushy eyebrows.

His eyes were closed and there was an oxygen mask on his face.

His stomach was wrapped in white bandages and the two men with the helmets were kneeling either side of him, affixing a tube to his arm, putting little sticky pads on his exposed, hairy chest.

Jamie sat there, staring down, wondering what had happened to him, watching absently as the two men did their strange work.

All the while clutching the parcel in her arms, only knowing that whatever happened, she couldn't let it go.

47

It was nearly midnight by the time they cleared Jamie to leave the hospital.

She had been treated for stage-two hypothermia, and although she couldn't remember much of it – like trying to recall a dream your mind is trying to forget – she knew what had happened.

She had shot Robert Nyström.

The doctor handed her a clipboard and asked her to sign. She obliged, her mood foul, her stomach churning from all the hot, sugary tea they'd forced down her, and scribbled her name. The doctor had receded quickly then, telling her to come back immediately if the nausea and disorientation hadn't passed by the morning.

He left the little space, pulling the curtain to the side and leaving it that way. As Jamie looked up, she noticed Wiik standing there in the gap. He had his arms folded.

His usual pressed white shirt and sweater combo was gone. He looked altogether more casual, but not by a large margin. He was wearing jeans, a dark blue chequered button-down, and though his hair was as pristinely groomed as it always was, his face was sporting two days' worth of stubble. He'd not shaved today either.

His expression was blank, his eyes fixed on her. She couldn't tell if he was judging her or not. And if he was, what for.

Jamie broke his stare and looked down, sitting at the edge of the bed. Her boots were on the floor next to her, caked in blood. She'd cleaned her hands and arms off and slipped out the sodden long sleeve she was wearing, leaving just the T-shirt she had on underneath. They'd given her a pair of scrubs to wear for bottoms, which felt itchy against her bare legs.

Her jeans and her top, both soaked with blood, were in a plastic bag next to her boots, along with the package she'd recovered from the cabin.

She'd thought about opening it a thousand times, but wanted privacy to do so. Privacy that a hospital ward didn't afford.

'How are you feeling?' Wiik asked, not moving forward. Or moving at all. He just hovered at the edge of her curtained cubicle, arms folded across his chest, sleeves rolled to the elbows.

Jamie tilted her head one way and then the other. 'I've been better,' she said, not lying. 'How's Nyström?'

Wiik ran his tongue along his teeth, as though displeased with the answer before he gave it. 'He's in a coma,' he said, seeming weary. 'Lost a lot of blood. Stage-three hypothermia. Plus, the bullet punctured his small intestine before lodging in his pelvis. He's been out of surgery for a while, but the doctors say it will be touch-and- go for a few days. They're not sure if he'll regain consciousness, and if he does, whether he'll have any brain damage. He probably won't walk right again, at the very least.'

Jamie grimaced, but she was glad he didn't say it.

And then he did.

'You really did a number on him.'

Jamie swallowed and looked up. 'And what the hell was I supposed to do?' she spat.

Wiik sighed, letting the tension drain from between them. 'Falk is furious.'

'I didn't do it on purpose.'

'Shoot Nyström?'

'Find him. Or find anyone, for that matter.'

'Then what the hell were you doing all the way out there?'

'I was…' Jamie trailed off. There was no point trying to hide it now. 'I was looking for something my father left me. Or hid for me. Or… I don't know.'

'In a hunting cabin in the middle of nowhere?' Wiik wasn't buying it.

'Yeah. We used to go there when I was younger.'

'And you had no idea Nyström would be there?'

'I thought he was dead,' Jamie said. 'If anything, I thought we were chasing a corpse.' She rubbed her temple, the bright halogens overhead giving her a headache. 'Any sign of Eriksson, yet? The church bus was—'

'Nothing,' Wiik said flatly. 'CSTs are combing the whole area, but so far there's no sign of him. Looks like Nyström was out there on his own.'

'Jesus,' Jamie muttered. She still couldn't wrap her head around it. 'How the hell does a man like Nyström – a goddamn detective – *the* goddamn detective who put the Angel Maker behind bars – turn out to be his successor?' She looked up at Wiik, genuinely asking.

'Maybe Sjöberg was innocent,' Wiik offered. 'And it was Nyström all along.'

'No,' Jamie said, dismissing it. 'I know Robert Nyström.

He wouldn't have. And anyway – he was my father's partner. There's no way that he could have been doing it without my father knowing. Not a chance.'

'Well, maybe your father was—'

'Don't.' Jamie raised her index finger to shut him down, her voice dripping acid.

Wiik held his hands up to show he meant no threat. 'All I'm saying, ' he went on, 'is that we may have caught Nyström off guard, but this case is far from sewn up. There are still a lot of pieces missing. Whether we got the guy or not. When he – *if* he – wakes up,' Wiik said, letting his hands drop now and taking a step forward. 'We'll question him and get our answers. For now, take it easy. The CSTs will search the scene – they'll go over Nyström's car and the bus, they'll pull the cabin apart, and we'll have some more answers. For now, you need to rest.'

Jamie let out a long breath, feeling her shoulders heavy, her eyes swollen and itchy from exhaustion. 'Have you spoken to Hallberg?' Jamie asked, easing off the bed and reaching down for her boots.

Wiik came forward a little, as though to help, and then stopped, backing off.

Jamie padded across the tiled floor towards the radiator next to the bed. Her socks were drying there. Had dried, she hoped.

'Yes,' Wiik said.

'How's she doing?'

'She'll live. Damage is superficial. Though she did have some interesting things to say about the whole ordeal.'

Jamie grabbed her socks, eying Wiik carefully. He was staring back at her.

'Oh yeah?' Jamie asked, going back to the bed. 'Like what?'

Wiik sort of shrugged. 'She was thankful to have you,' he offered, about as close to a compliment as things got with Wiik. 'You saved her by the sounds of things.'

Jamie recalled the shooting. 'Something like that.'

'Even if you did ask her to stick her head above the parapet to do it.'

Jamie stopped, one sock half-on, and glanced up.

'And shot our prime suspect in the process,' he added.

She pulled the sock on hard and set her jaw. 'Did you need something, or did you just come in here to torture me?'

Wiik watched her struggle with her socks and boots, her body stiff and sore from the day. Hell, from the week. He said nothing in response. 'Hallberg filled me in on Hansen and Lundgren – on Rachel Engerman – on Emmy Berg and the forum. On your vigilante *theory.*'

Jamie detected a hint of scorn in that last word. 'You don't agree?'

'It's a leap.'

'My father always said that a leap and a lead were only one letter apart.' She tried to inject just a hint of humour into it but failed miserably. It just sounded tired and bitter, even to her ears.

Wiik folded his arms again, stepping back a little. 'Well, whatever Nyström's intentions, we've got him. He's lying in a hospital bed, in cuffs, with an officer outside the door. Whether he wakes up or not, he's not going anywhere. And the city can sleep a little easier.' He lingered still, looking down at Jamie, though she didn't know what it was that he was after.

Jamie pushed her feet into her boots now and stood, wobbling a little.

'What will you do now?' Wiik asked then, hurriedly even.

'Go back to the hotel, sleep.' Jamie shook her head. 'Shower. Eat. Hope to hell this headache eases.'

'And then?'

Jamie laughed a little. 'Honestly, I hadn't thought that far ahead. Breakfast, probably.'

'No, I meant…' Wiik shifted his weight. 'Will you be going home?'

She met his eye. 'With no electricity or heating? I doubt it.'

'I meant to the UK.'

'Oh.' Jamie was surprised by the question. Even more so by the uncertain look on Wiik's face. 'I… I don't know. I was just sort of going day by day here. When the case is over…'

'But the case *is* over,' Wiik pressed, biting his lip. 'You got him.'

Jamie thought there was a sourness there – as though Wiik was annoyed he'd missed the action again. Or upset that Jamie had been in danger and he hadn't been at her side. Or maybe it was just at the thought of her leaving now that the case was done.

She picked up the plastic bag containing her belongings and pressed her lips into a line. 'It's late.'

'It is,' Wiik said, not moving, and not letting it go.

'I don't know what I'm doing yet. I haven't spoken to Falk, but I think she's going to be keen to send me packing.'

'I can speak to Falk.'

'Wiik, it's not about that… It's… It's…' She had to look away. He was staring at her like an old dog being left at the side of the road.

Jamie gathered herself, tightening her grip on the plastic bag. She picked her head up, ready to give her answer to the question that neither of them had said, but that was hanging between them.

But she didn't get to.

Behind Wiik, Jamie could see people running in the corridor.

She leaned around him, watching as a doctor streaked past, followed by a nurse hurriedly pushing a trauma cart.

They were yelling.

Jamie and Wiik were frozen in place, watching, both of their hackles rising at the same time, both holding their breath.

And then a uniformed police officer dashed past, shouting for people to move out of the way.

Wiik and Jamie didn't need any other incentive.

They were both already running.

48

THE WARNING ALARM from the heart monitor blared angrily.

Jamie and Wiik trailed the doctor and the nurse with the trauma cart, following the noise. Jamie hoped that they weren't headed to Robert Nyström's room, but knew that they were.

The officer just in front of them was hurrying back to the post he'd seemingly deserted, but it was already too late.

He was a tall man, slim, with a shock of dark hair. He got to the doorway first and filled it, hands pressed on the frames. 'Shit,' he said, freezing in his tracks.

Wiik got there a second later and damn near shoved him off his feet. 'Move!' he commanded, shouldering into the room behind the nurse.

Another nurse was already at Nyström's side, the doctor over him now, shining a light in his eyes, looking at the heart monitor.

It screamed at them.

The nurse with the trauma cart moved frantically, stripping gauze from packets as the doctor barked orders.

Jamie moved past Wiik now to see, and stumbled at the sight, gasping despite herself.

The doctor had his hands on Robert Nyström's throat.

Jamie did a double take, her own memories invading what she was seeing now.

Blood was pouring through his fingers.

Nyström was perfectly still, but everyone else was moving in a vortex around him.

Jamie and Wiik watched motionless. Speechless.

The monitor continued to cry, its numbers dropping rapidly.

The nurse with the wadding came forward and plunged it against Nyström's throat.

The doctor stood back, throwing his hands to his sides to get rid of the blood.

It splattered all up the wall, and then he was back at Nyström's neck, commanding the nurse to put up blood bags. To get coagulants. To start compressions. To prep the paddles.

But for all the shouting, for all the movement, for all the franticness and all the effort – it was too late.

Jamie watched as the numbers on the screen behind the doctor fluctuated, burned red for a moment, and then hit zero.

The erratic line flattened and the tone became constant and dull.

Robert Nyström was dead.

49

JAMIE COULD HEAR Wiik tearing the uniformed officer who'd left his post a new asshole outside the door. One that he'd be able to store bowling balls in, judging by the volume and sharpness of Wiik's tirade.

She was still in the room. Staring down at Robert Nyström's lifeless corpse.

He was lying there, soaked with his own blood. He looked pale. A ghost of himself.

His gown was crimson, the sheets were crimson. And the floor was black.

The puddle of blood spread beneath the bed like a hole that dropped away to nothing.

All of his blood had emptied out of him, and there was nothing they could do about it.

But it hadn't been from the gunshot wound – this was something else.

When the doctor and nurses had called it, pronouncing Robert Nyström dead at 12.02 a.m., they'd left the room. There was nothing more to be done except get cleaned up and look after the patients they *could* save. Brutal, but it was the job.

But this wasn't a hospital room anymore anyway. This was now a crime scene.

Because in the time that the officer left his post at the door, someone had come into Robert Nyström's room and had run a blade across his throat.

Jamie was looking down at him now – at his open gullet. The skin was peeled back, gruesome and raw. Under it, Nyström's flesh shone red. Then was his oesophagus, hacked in two. His tendons, slashed. The muscles, sliced.

Someone had stood over him, put a blade against his neck, and pulled. Hard.

There was no mistaking it.

Someone wanted Nyström dead, and they were not leaving it to chance.

Wiik came back into the room, pressing his hair to his head. He was exhaling, his cheeks puffed out. 'What a fucking mess,' he said, stopping next to Jamie.

She hung her head.

'CSTs are on the way. As are uniformed officers – we'll lock down the hospital, round up the staff, get the CCTV footage. We'll find out who did this.'

Jamie didn't feel like talking. She just didn't have it in her.

Instead, she stepped back and walked around Wiik, heading for the door.

'Where are you going?' he called, following her into the corridor.

Jamie didn't bother turning back. 'It's been a long day, Wiik. I'm going to bed.'

50

Dear Jamie,

You are so small, and yet bigger than I ever imagined you could be. When I held you in my arms on the day that you were born, I thought that I would break you. I couldn't conceive that something so little, so fragile, could have come from me.

And now, I look at you, and I see the strong, stubborn, smart girl that you have become. And to think that you have grown from that tiny thing into what I see now – it fills me with pride, and with hope.

You are so many things. But most of all, you are fearless. We sit here now, huddled around a fire that I don't know will last until morning, with snow piling up outside the doors and windows, the lake frozen solid, the car completely trapped – and yet, you are unphased. Whether you will remember this night in years to come, I don't know. But let this letter serve as a reminder to you. That I am not sure now whether we will last here. Why have we come at all? My selfishness. Your mother is your mother. And I'm sure you know that we have our differences. But my regret is only that you are trapped between us. And I have brought you here because I did not wish to be alone. Because when I am, I become a different man. A worse man.

With you, though, I want to be better.

If I ever lost you, I don't know what I would do.

When it is you and I, forgetting work is easy. Forgetting everything is easy. I am never happier than when we are driving away from the city. When we are leaving that life behind.

And every time it is time to leave here, time to go back, I think what would happen if we just stayed. If we just left it all.

The only thing that stops me from saying it out loud – because you, Jamie, you spirited, rambunctious little devil would want to. Would want to live out here like an animal. And hunt and fish and sleep under the stars and gather fire-wood and explore the world you still believe to be wild and untamed. One free from humans and their goddamn fucking evil – the only thing that stops me is knowing I would be taking you from your mother.

For all her faults, she loves you, Jamie.

As do I.

Remember that always.

You are sitting here now, at my side, with a pencil in hand, drowned in the light of this little fire, in this stinking, damp, frozen cabin in the middle of nowhere, in the middle of a storm that might well kill us, writing a letter to your future self. Telling your future self what you always wanted to be when you grew up.

You have made me write this letter, too. And have made me promise not to show it to you – if I promise not to look at yours. These are secret letters. And while I thought that I would sit here, and pretend to write something, I found that there are many things I want to write. Things I want to say to you that I can't bring myself to.

Jamie – you are everything to me. And if I have one wish in this terrible world, it is that you grow up to be happy.

I don't know how to be. And it is because of what I have made of my life.

The decisions I have made. The things that I have done. The people I have hurt.

There are good people, and there are bad people. And then there are people like me, who place themselves between. Who try to convince themselves they are one, when really they are the other.

Do not grow up to be like me, Jamie. Don't grow up to be unhappy.

I was selfish enough, stupid enough, to delude myself into thinking I could have both. Could be both. Could do what I do and have a normal life as well.

You can't.

You can't split yourself.

There is only so much that we can give, and I gave too much to this job. I let it consume me. Like the flames are consuming the little fuel we have left, the flames of this world have consumed any goodness that was within me.

If there is one thing, Jamie, that I will do my best to ensure – as long as there is breath in my body and love in my heart – it is that you do not grow up to be like me.

I fear you do not know the real me.

I have done my best to keep it hidden from you.

If you did, you would think differently of me.

You would be afraid of me, ashamed. I have no doubt.

And one day, you might. And you might feel those things.

Which is why I treasure these moments together.

Because I know, no matter what I do, they may be fleeting.

I love you, Jamie.

And I always will.

No matter what happens.

Dad

51

JAMIE LAY on the bed in her hotel room, reading and re-reading the letter. It was nearly 3 a.m.

It had been in the parcel hidden beneath the floorboards at the cabin. Along with her father's stag-horn-handled hunting knife, his family ring, his badge, the deed to their house, and a photograph of her father holding Jamie as a newborn baby at the hospital. He was grinning.

Jamie sniffed back fresh tears, wiped the ones already at the corners of her eyes roughly from her cheeks, and then rolled over onto her side.

She stared down at the collection of items on the bed in front of her, and pulled her knees up so that they were cradled, protected. She laid the letter down and picked up the gold ring, pushing it onto her thumb – the only finger it remotely fit, and rolled it slowly around.

Jamie closed her eyes then, and let out a long, slow breath. This time, she didn't wipe away the tears. She just let them fall.

And slowly, but surely, let sleep come for her.

52

It was just after seven when Jamie's phone began buzzing on the nightstand.

She roused slowly, pulling her head up from the pillow, and reached across the bed for it, sweeping the letter, photograph and knife all onto the floor.

'Shit,' Jamie muttered, coming around instantly. She rolled over to the edge, grabbing her phone and answering while she bent to collect the things from between her feet. 'Yeah?'

It was Hallberg's voice. 'Hey – how fast can you get ready?'

'Uh,' Jamie said, collecting the items in her hand and laying them on the bed. 'I don't know. Ten minutes or something. Why?'

'Prelim on the cabin has come back – and Tech heard back from the forum. Falk wants everyone on the same page today before we wrap up.'

'Wrap up?' Jamie detected an uncertainty in Hallberg's voice. Not a nervousness as such, more disappointment than anything.

Hallberg didn't respond to the question. 'I'll pick you up.'

Then, the line went dead, and Jamie was left sitting on the bed, wondering what the hell was going on.

After the day she'd had yesterday, the last thing Jamie wanted to do was hang around on the kerb. And yet, here she was.

Hallberg arrived in her Mercedes hatchback about five minutes later than agreed. And while usually that sort of thing wouldn't bother Jamie in the slightest, she was functioning on very little sleep, and the last week had been hell.

The car braked hard and stopped in front of Jamie. She wasted no time getting in. 'What's going on?'

Hallberg pulled away, not looking around. Her face was flecked with little cuts. One, just on her cheek, was held together by a butterfly stitch. She seemed tense. 'Falk is on the warpath.'

Jamie scoffed a little. 'I'm not surprised.'

'The case is being taken off us. The Chancellor of Justice has ordered the National Operations Department to step in and take over the manhunt for Eriksson.'

Jamie raised an eyebrow. 'The NOD?'

Hallberg nodded. 'We're doing a handover to the *Nationella Insatsstyrkan* this afternoon.'

The National Task Force, or the *Nationella Insatsstyrkan,* were a counterterrorism and high-risk intervention unit that were brought in to manage the worst cases. Hostage situations. Terror threats. Mass shootings. Serial killers… The bodies were stacking up, and Jamie suspected that Falk would be glad to get rid of the case now. Her best detective was under review from the SID for misconduct, a former detective and current consultant of the Stockholm Polis was seemingly complicit in and responsible for several murders, and a uniformed officer under her command had left his post and allowed that former detective to have his throat cut open by a fugitive in the middle of a public hospital. And that wasn't even mentioning the visiting London Met detective who had put a bullet into their prime suspect. Jamie swallowed hard.

'Why did the officer leave his post outside Nyström's room?' Jamie asked.

'Bathroom, apparently.'

Jamie could hear the scorn in her voice. 'Jesus,' she muttered a little disbelievingly. 'Seriously?'

'He said it was late – there was no one around. No one knew Nyström was there. And the bathroom was only down the hall.'

Jamie was shaking her head. 'I don't know what's worse. That he left his post to go and take a piss, or that he missed Eriksson standing twenty feet away.'

Hallberg looked around at her. 'What?'

'Well, think about it. If we're operating under the assumption that this is a two-person job – that Eriksson and Sjöberg did this together twenty-five years ago, and now Eriksson had recruited Nyström to take Sjöberg's place – he'd have plenty of reason to try and make sure that Nyström didn't wake up, right?'

'Right.'

'And he didn't slip into that room coincidentally when the officer went to the bathroom, did he?'

'Unlikely.'

'So he must have waited – in sight of Nyström's room – until he had opportunity. And then…'

Hallberg's frown turned to a scowl. 'How could he miss him?'

Jamie shook her head. 'I don't know,' she said, sighing. 'But I suspect he'll be paying for it for a while.'

. . .

Jamie, Wiik and Hallberg were all in Falk's office, the rest of the floor deserted. Wiik was in jeans and a pair of brown walking boots, a faded T-shirt and a thick charcoal parka jacket. He'd not shaved again and his hair was decidedly untidy.

He seemed to be taking the hiatus from the case seriously. How was his review going? She'd never asked.

'Johansson,' Falk said.

Jamie looked up from Wiik's boots. 'Yes.'

'You with us?' Falk looked even more tired than before, the circles under her eyes darker, her mouth now a puckered, sour circle.

Jamie nodded.

Falk put her fingers on her brow and scanned the documents in front of her. 'The NTF will be here by mid-morning, and they want a full rundown of the case so far, as well as all of our forensics reports, case notes and anything else we have that will help them track Eriksson down. He's slipped through our fingers twice now.' She held up two fingers to illustrate.

Three times, Jamie thought about saying, if you counted the original case. But she didn't.

'The prelim has come back from the hunting cabin. They found the original case files – or what was left of them. CSTs have done their best to pull fragments from the hearth, but they were all but incinerated.' She looked down at the reports again. 'They also recovered a disposable mobile phone, several sets of clothing and two hunting rifles from the scene – a Sauer 202 and a Remington Model 700.' Her eyes went to Jamie now. 'I presume the second one is yours?'

Jamie nodded reservedly.

'And am I right to presume that it is the weapon you used to shoot the suspect?'

Jamie nodded again, breaking eye contact.

Falk kept her eyes on her. 'And am I right to presume that it belonged to your father?'

Another nod.

'But that you don't have any of the paperwork to show that?'

Jamie stopped nodding now, but Falk kept going.

'Or any paperwork showing that *you* now own it?'

Jamie met her eye, but kept her expression blank.

'And seeing as it wasn't in the chattels catalogue that the technicians carried out when they swept your house, I won't even ask *when* you took possession of it, *where* you've been storing it, and *why* you were carrying around live ammunition.'

Jamie cleared her throat. When Falk said it like that, it did sound bad. She'd not really thought about anything other than making sure the CSTs didn't take it. An unlicenced firearm like that needed to be seized. Jamie had no intention of using it, and she'd only taken the ammunition because if the CSTs had found it, they'd ask what weapon it was for. The fact that it had saved hers – and Hallberg's – life seemed almost inconsequential.

Falk smiled at her now – a thin veneer laid over the bitter disappointment. 'Let's just hope that the NTF don't scrutinise it too hard. Otherwise we're all in trouble. Okay?'

Jamie tensed her jaw and looked down. She could see Wiik eyeing her out of the corner of his eye.

Falk turned the page emphatically and shook her head, refocusing her eyes. 'The cabin was rife with both Nyström's and Eriksson's DNA. And along with the van from the church, that places Eriksson as our top priority. For the next few hours, anyway. He's on the loose, he's dangerous, and he's not letting up anytime soon. We know from the original pattern that he'll be lining up Jan Hansen. And I have no doubt that Mikael Gunnarson will be on his radar, too. Have we had anything back from Gunnarson's solicitor or the childcare agencies?' She looked at Hallberg now.

'I still haven't been able to track down the nanny that the Gunnarsons used. The companies operating back then are mostly out of business now, and the ones I have been able to get a response from don't have a Mikael or Åsa Gunnarson listed as clients. It's not looking good.'

Wiik jumped in. 'But I think it's fair to assume that if Eriksson wanted them dead, it was because of what they did to Tilde. Gunnarson said that Tilde didn't like the nanny before he clammed up. That it was the reason they got rid of her... So whether she was the one abusing Tilde or it was the parents...' He trailed off, exhaled and cradled the back of his head. 'I don't know. But Eriksson wanted them dead – and I think that says a lot.'

Falk looked at Wiik. 'The NTF will follow up with Gunnarson. And I'll be curious to see what his solicitor does then. They carry a lot more weight than we do and don't like taking no for an answer. Still, we should make sure to tie up as many loose ends as we can this morning. I don't want the NTF to have anything to come at us for. Hallberg?'

She nearly jumped out of the chair. 'I'll keep going. I have another few names to track down, will follow up with the Vehicle Licensing Agency for updated contact details, and I'll reach out to Gunnarson's solicitor again.'

'Good. Wiik,' Falk said. 'Make sure that email states very clearly that the NTF will be taking over the case, and that if he wants to continue to deal with the very amicable and friendly Stockholm Polis, then he needs to do so quickly.'

Wiik sighed and then dipped his chin, showing his reluctant agreement.

Falk went on, intent on covering every base. 'Forensics are transporting the vehicles back from the scene this morning – including your rental car.' Falk glanced up at Jamie before going back to the report. It seemed like Falk had had enough of chewing her out, and Jamie couldn't say she wasn't thankful. 'It looks like Nyström was using his car to suffocate the girls. Techs found traces of adhesive residue on the ceiling – their best guess is that he taped a film or screen up to separate the front from the back seats. They'll conduct a thorough investigation of the car when it's in the workshop – and are already trying to match hair found in the back seat to Emmy Berg. We should have the results in the next hour or so to confirm.' She closed the file on the cabin and pulled another one in front of her. 'Our cyber techs were able to get in contact with the hosts of the forum that Emmy Berg used and recovered a set of private messages that tie Nyström to the abduction.' She coughed into her fist and then picked up the file to start reading. 'Message sent from username WeCanHelp: "Hi sweetheart, I read your message and I wanted to tell you that you're not alone. I know things seem bleak, but don't worry, we can help."' Falk looked up at each of them.

All three were hanging on her every word.

'It goes on,' Falk said. '"We've helped lots of girls like you. My friend and I have been doing this for a long time. Men like the man who hurt you are everywhere, and it may seem like there's no way out, but there is. The first thing we need to do is get you somewhere safe. My friend is a policeman. He can pick you up wherever you want, and he can take you somewhere safe. Then, we can deal with the man that hurt you. We can make him sorry for what he's done. And we can make sure that he never hurts anyone else ever again."'

Falk laid the papers down. 'They sent a phone number at the bottom of the message. Emmy didn't respond via the forum messaging service, but we suspect that she called the number listed.'

Wiik spoke now. 'Does it match the phone recovered from the cabin?'

Falk shook her head. 'No, it doesn't. But Nyström's phone only shows one number saved.'

'And it's the same one from the message,' Jamie said, putting it together as Falk said it.

'Right.'

Wiik leaned forward now, his elbows resting on his knees. 'So we track the phone? Eriksson must be this WeCanHelp person. He goes on the forums, he finds the girls, he approaches them. Then he uses Nyström's position to make them feel safe.' Wiik clapped suddenly, making them jump. 'And that's how he gets them.'

Hallberg nodded. 'It explains why he targeted Nyström to help him.'

'It does,' Falk said. 'But it doesn't explain why Nyström actually did. And to answer your question, no, we can't track the phone. It was last pinged by a data tower outside the city three days ago. Since then, it's been off. And if Eriksson is half as smart as we're giving him credit for, he'll have destroyed it and will be using another disposable phone by now.'

'What about the forum?' Wiik sounded desperate now. 'Has he messaged anyone else? Replied to any other posts?'

Falk shook her head slowly. 'No, that account was disabled and then deleted less than twenty minutes after the message was sent. Tech have tracked down the IP address used to register it and send the message, but it traced back to a popular internet cafe in the city.'

'CCTV?' Wiik asked hopefully.

'That's what makes it popular,' Falk said tiredly. 'There is none. They also offer free use of VPNs. Tech spent forty minutes trying to figure out why the account seemed to have been registered from Turkmenistan before it clicked. The place is owned by an outspoken leftist who is very much in favour of online privacy and freedom, data protection, etcetera, etcetera.' She cycled her hand through the air in front of her. 'Makes the place very popular with white-hat hackers and the like.'

'Son of a bitch,' Wiik muttered.

Jamie took it all in. Eriksson really was smart. And he had it all worked out. He needed someone to do the heavy lifting for him – to take the girls, to kill them, to display them. To go after the parents. Someone with skill. Sjöberg was perfect – military background, smart. Nyström would be a good substitute. He was trained to use weapons, trained in the use of tactics and strategy. He was police, which gave Eriksson something to lull the girls into a sense of security with. And crucially, he'd killed before, Jamie would bet. If she looked up Nyström's service record, she knew she'd find that he'd shot someone in the line of duty. And the first one was always the hardest.

She could attest to that herself.

Jamie grimaced. 'What's the connection between Nyström and Eriksson? How did he find him after all these years? He would have known him from the original case, but to reach out after two decades?'

Falk addressed Jamie directly, already ahead of her. 'We're looking into Nyström now. I have Tech and Forensics combing through his life, looking for anything Eriksson could use. Debts, medical troubles, anything like that.'

Jamie pursed her lips. 'Eriksson wouldn't need that.'

'What do you mean?'

'He's a master manipulator. A chameleon. He emulates, he mirrors. And he's good at it. One of the best I've ever met. And trust me – I've met them before. But he didn't set anything off for me. Not a single alarm bell. He was charming, easy-going, funny.'

'I didn't like him,' Wiik interjected.

Falk ignored it, focusing on Jamie.

She went on. 'He wouldn't try to blackmail or bribe Nyström into this. The Angel Maker has always been a planner and a manipulator. He got Hans Sjöberg to do his killing for him, and then to go to prison for him too. Hans Sjöberg could have rolled on Eriksson in a heartbeat for a reduced sentence. Gone home to his wife instead of dying behind bars. But he didn't. And that's loyalty you can't buy, and you can't threaten to get. That's earned – whether the victim realises it's insincere or not. No, Eriksson didn't leverage Nyström into it. He chose him, he studied him, and then he closed in on him. Was Nyström lonely?'

'I'm sorry?' Falk seemed thrown by the question.

'Was he lonely?'

'I don't... I don't know.'

'Family? Wife?'

'Widower, no children.'

'Brothers, sisters?'

'Only child,' Falk confirmed.

'And he was retired.'

'Semi-retired.'

'Stayed on to consult, right? Because he had nothing else in his life but his job. What about friends?'

Falk didn't have an answer.

'I know his best friend died nineteen years ago,' Jamie said.

Falk's eye twitched a little.

'He was alone, he was vulnerable, and he was an easy mark,' Jamie finished. 'You dig into Nyström and you'll find that. And that's the link. An innocuous friendship that built up to one important question: how would you like to make a difference in this world again? That's how he got him.'

Falk watched Jamie, something like a smile creeping onto her face. She looked down before it took hold and then began speaking again. 'Well, whether we can surmise the reasoning behind Nyström's involvement or not, our top priority is finding Eriksson. I've already got Tech scrubbing through CCTV at the hospital for any sign of him, but it looks like the camera in the hallway facing Nyström's door was covered before the attack. CSTs found a latex glove stretched over the lens.' She shook her head in disbelief. 'Looks like the moment the guard left his post, Eriksson blinded the camera, and then killed Nyström.' She sighed. 'Tech are combing the other cameras for any sign of Eriksson, but so far, there's nothing. The man is a damn ghost.'

'We'll get him,' Wiik said with something like confidence in his voice.

'Right – well, it looks like we won't have to. Or at least we won't get the chance to. Hallberg, can you make sure this is all in the handover report for the NTF? I want everything summarised, itemised and laid out neatly. Wiik, make sure your paperwork is all up to scratch and that you're available to field any questions. Forensics and Tech are bringing everything up in boxes this morning, too so that NTF have it all in both physical and digital. The place is going to be a zoo today.' She looked out at the empty office floor almost wistfully, and then back at Wiik. 'I want this to go smoothly, and I want it to work to the benefit of the relationship between the SPA and the NOD. As far as they're concerned, they're stepping in to save our asses, and I don't want them to think for a second we're not seeing it the same way. Got it?' She reiterated to Wiik specifically.

Jamie glanced over and saw his temple vein bulging slightly, teeth clenched. He was sitting forward in the chair, fists curled between his knees.

'Got it,' he said quietly.

No detective liked having their cases taken from them – especially when they were this close to being solved. The NTF would step in, they'd find Eriksson, and they'd take all the credit for bagging the Angel Maker. Something that the Stockholm Polis had failed to do. Twice.

And whether it was on Wiik or not, it still left a sour taste in the mouth.

'Okay then,' Falk said. 'You all have your jobs. Go.'

Jamie noticed that Falk wasn't meeting her eye now. 'What about me?' she asked before anyone could get out of their seats.

'You?' Falk seemed almost amused by the question. 'You've done your part. And in about' – she checked the clock on her phone screen, her thin wrists absent of a watch – 'two hours, this won't be our case anymore. As such, Jamie – as thankful as we were for your help – I think it's time that you went home.'

53

WIIK STRODE out of Falk's office, straight across the room, and disappeared without looking back. He was clearly unhappy with those parting words.

Jamie didn't know how she felt.

She watched him round a corner, wondering if it was the last time she'd ever see Anders Wiik. And how she felt about that, too.

'It'll be a shame,' Hallberg said, grabbing Jamie's attention. 'To see you go, I mean.'

'Yeah,' Jamie answered. 'But you've got things under control.' She smiled at the girl. 'Wiik will come around, don't worry. Just don't try so hard. You're doing great.'

She blushed a little. 'Thank you,' she said, nodding. 'That means a lot coming from you.'

Jamie laughed at that a little. *From me?*

'You're a great detective,' Hallberg said. 'I hope that I—'

Jamie turned and put a hand on her shoulder. 'Hallberg – don't turn out like me. Like Wiik. There's more out there than killers and these four walls. I realised that too late.'

Hallberg swallowed, nodding then.

Jamie didn't know what else to say. She didn't think there was anything to say.

'Are you leaving straight away?' Hallberg asked after a second.

'I don't know,' Jamie answered truthfully. 'I've still got one or two things to do at the house, I'll need to sort things out with the car rental company, too. Hope that their insurance covers bullet holes. Then I'll need to check out of the hotel, book a flight.' She sighed. 'I'll be here for a little while.'

She looked up at the corner Wiik had rounded. For all his teenage moodiness and annoying quirks, Jamie thought she might miss the man. Or at least working with him. And even if he was petty enough to walk away without a goodbye, she wasn't.

But beyond that, there was something else. Something niggling at her that she couldn't put her finger on. Some loose end that wouldn't be tied up with paperwork. That wasn't in the forensic reports.

'Okay,' Hallberg said, seemingly cheered up by the news. 'I'll see you before you go.' She reached out and touched the back of Jamie's arm before melting away, leaving Jamie alone in the middle of the deserted office floor.

She stood there for a moment, rolling it all over in her head, and then wondered if it was even her problem anymore. Falk had said, fairly unequivocally, that it wasn't.

And yet, Jamie wasn't the sort of person to let something like this go.

Especially when she was pretty sure that whatever she was missing, everyone else was, too.

· · ·

Jamie was sitting in the corner of the office at a desk that had been used to store the boxes and files that the NTF didn't want to look at. She was leaning back, her feet propped up on a two-high stack of them, rolling her father's ring around her thumb.

The entire floor was abuzz with bodies. There were no less than twenty NTF guys in emblazoned jackets sorting files, carting boxes back and forth, cataloguing everything and formulating their own reports and assumptions about the case.

Hallberg appeared and waved her hand in front of Jamie's face to grab her vacant stare.

Jamie's eyes focused and she looked up at her. 'Hey,' she said.

Hallberg was holding a piece of paper between her hands. 'Here.' Hallberg held it out quickly.

Jamie took it and turned it over, reading the text.

'It's a statement that says you told me about your father's rifle and I confiscated it before we travelled out to the cabin,' Hallberg said before Jamie had a chance to read it.

Jamie glanced up at her, surprised.

'You found it in your house, reported it to the closest officer – me – and then I took responsibility for it. I was going to log it officially when we got back.' She smiled at Jamie. 'That's why it was in the car.'

Jamie furrowed her brow. 'Hallberg... this is... you don't have to do this. You could get in a lot of trouble.'

She shrugged. 'You saved my life. If that rifle hadn't been in the car...' She trailed off. 'It's my way of saying thanks, okay?'

'What about the CSTs? They went through everything in the house. This statement basically claims they missed the rifle.' Jamie couldn't keep the doubt out of her voice.

Hallberg curled a smile. 'So, they missed it. After all, who better to hide a weapon from the police than one of the finest detectives the city's ever known?'

Jamie couldn't help but return it. 'You're right there. My father would have hated anyone touching his things.'

'And if anything comes back – I'll stand by that.'

Jamie held the paper up. 'This means a lot. Thanks, Hallberg.'

'Of course.' She lingered then. 'Did you get everything sorted with the rental company? Manage to find a flight?'

Jamie nodded slowly, going back to her vacant stare. 'Yep.'

'So you'll be leaving then?'

She nodded slowly again. 'I suppose so.'

'Seen Wiik?'

'No. He's avoiding me.'

'That's not surprising.'

'No,' Jamie said, laughing a little. 'I suppose not.' She looked up at Hallberg again then. 'Can you do something for me?'

'Sure. What is it?'

'Do you still have access to the files?'

'For the case?' Hallberg raised an eyebrow. 'Yeah, why?'

'I'm sure it's nothing. Just want to confirm something for my own peace of mind. Could you get a few things for me?'

'Name it.'

'The court transcript for Hans Sjöberg's file, a copy of the note stuck under my windscreen wiper, and I'm going to need access to Robert Nyström's apartment.'

'Nyström's apartment?' Hallberg seemed unsure about the last one. 'Why?'

'Just a feeling.'

'A feeling?'

Jamie nodded.

'Okay,' Hallberg said after a few seconds. 'But it's still technically a crime scene. You can't go out there on your own.'

'Then you'd better get your jacket.'

They slipped out without Falk seeing. And despite the last two trips they'd taken together ending with gunfire and death, Hallberg didn't seem too tense to be sitting next to Jamie.

'So,' she asked curiously, tapping her fingers on the steering wheel. 'What are we looking for at Nyström's?'

Jamie was reading the transcript from Sjöberg's trial. 'Papers, notes, anything like that.' She kept her eyes fixed on the words in front of her, a pen in her other hand, flipping back and forth between her fingers. 'A diary would be good. But a shopping list will do in a pinch.'

'I don't understand,' Hallberg said. 'What are we doing?'

'It's probably nothing,' Jamie said. 'It's just my brain is telling me we're missing something. And if I leave now, it'll just bother me the whole way home.'

Hallberg looked over.

Jamie was trying to keep her expression light, but the feeling of unease in the back of her brain had become a chained-up dog, gnawing at its own leg. And it wasn't going away.

They arrived a few minutes later and climbed the stairs to Nyström's modest apartment on the third floor.

Police tape was still stretched across the door. Hallberg carefully unfastened it from one side. She pulled on a pair of latex gloves and handed Jamie a set. Then she unlocked the door and they stepped inside.

The interior was musty, and about what Jamie expected to find.

Nyström was always a studious man, and his apartment felt apt. It was clean, neat and sparsely decorated, if a little dated. A small sofa was pushed against the right-hand wall, and a single wing-back chair with a brown velveteen covering faced a TV. Sitting between them was a folding dinner table.

Jamie looked at it for a moment and then moved on, taking a slow circle around the room.

On the wall, a few pictures were hanging. Nyström and his late wife. Nyström and his late wife. Nyström and his late wife. Nyström and Jamie's father. Another fishing trip.

'When did Nyström's wife die?' Jamie called out to Hallberg, who'd already gone on the hunt for the notes and shopping lists.

'Uh – six, seven years, I think?' Hallberg called back from the bedroom.

Jamie kept going, taking that in. It was still outrageous to think that he was capable of doing something like this. He'd practically raised her at times. And he'd definitely looked after her more than his fair share in her father's stead. And not once had she ever found him anything other than caring, gentlemanly and, above all else, fatherly.

She stopped as she got to the end of the photo gallery, and then stepped away from the wall, heading for the kitchen instead.

Jamie pulled open the fridge and was hit by the smell of soured milk. She grimaced and closed it again, just as Hallberg reappeared behind her. 'Will this work?' she asked, holding up a little notepad with a hole in the top of it.

Jamie took it from her and flipped through the pages, seeing lots of notes jotted down on the pages. Little reminders to do or buy things. She looked over Hallberg's shoulder at a house phone on the wall next to the bedroom. There was a corkboard next to it, a nail hanging there. As the notepad had been moments before.

'Yeah, this will work,' Jamie said.

Hallberg stared at her for a moment, and then it twigged. 'The note from under your windscreen,' she said. 'You want to compare the handwriting.'

Jamie looked up at her. 'I don't suppose Forensics are going to be pushed to make a positive match now that Nyström is dead, are they?'

Hallberg rolled her lips into a line. 'You think they'll be a match?'

Jamie thought for a moment. 'I don't know,' she said, meeting Hallberg's eye. 'I just don't know.'

It was getting dark by the time they got back to HQ.

Jamie and Hallberg stepped out of the stairwell, expecting things to be winding down, the NTF mostly cleared out, and for the situation to be a lot calmer.

But it was exactly the opposite.

Things were frantic. Phones were ringing. People were moving in a maelstrom. And in the middle of it all, Falk and Wiik were standing in front of a guy from the NTF, listening diligently.

Falk and Wiik caught sight of them at the same time. Falk beckoned them over.

The guy from NTF turned to look. He was about five foot eight, with sandy-coloured hair, dark blue eyes and a beard that was a retro combination of stubble and moustache.

Falk did the introductions. 'This is Polisöverintendent Dahlvig.' Police Superintendent. 'He has been given command of this operation.'

He nodded curtly, glancing from Hallberg to Jamie, and keeping his eyes there. 'You are the one who shot Nyström?' he asked, his voice bordering accusative.

Jamie met his eye, then nodded.

'And as I understand it, you're not a part of Swedish Polis, yes?'

'No.'

'You are from the London Metropolitan Police?'

'Yes.'

'Then why are you here?'

Surprisingly, it was Wiik that jumped to her defence. 'She is here at my behest,' he said boldly. 'I asked that she assist on the case as she has unique insight and knowledge on the—'

He cast Wiik a cold glance. 'I wasn't asking you.'

Falk tried to play the diplomat, smiling broadly. 'Please, Polisöverintendent – Detective Inspector Johansson's involvement in the case thus far has been in an advisory role. The incident involving Robert Nyström was unfortunate and purely coincidental, I might add, but I assure you that she was only acting in both self-defence and the defence of one of our own detectives, Polisassistent Julia Hallberg.' Falk gestured to Hallberg then. 'But now that the NTF are involved, Inspector Johansson's services are no longer required. And she'll be on a plane back to the UK by the end of the day. Isn't that right?' She looked at Jamie now.

If Jamie said no, she felt like she was going to regret it.

'That's right,' Jamie confirmed.

This seemed to annoy Wiik, but stood between Falk and Dahlvig, he knew his place. And speaking out now would only hurt his position further.

'If she's not,' Dahlvig said, his voice like ice. 'I'm holding you personally responsible, Falk. There's no room for tourists in the SPA, and especially not for ones who *shoot* my suspects.' He glared at Jamie then, making sure everyone there knew exactly where he sat in the pecking order. 'Now – Hallberg, is it?'

She looked up at Dahlvig.

'Falk here tells me you're good at paperwork. That right?'

She lifted her chin to show her enthusiasm. Feigned as it was.

'Good. Then I'll be correct in assuming that you've already produced a list of Eriksson's contacts, family members, friends – anyone who might help him in a situation like this.'

'Yes,' she squeezed out. Jamie thought it was the first time she'd ever seen Hallberg look angry.

'Good. Then you're with me.' He nodded decisively. 'And you,' he said, turning to Wiik. 'You've met Eriksson, yes?'

'Yes,' he replied stiffly.

'Then you're coming, too. Falk has briefed me on the mess you made with… Lindvall, was it?' He glanced at Falk for confirmation and she nodded reluctantly. 'But none of that matters right now. So consider your holiday officially over. We're going to hit every address on Hallberg's list – full incursion, dogs, tactical.' He sliced through the air with his hand. 'You and Hallberg will need to be there to provide intelligence and a positive ID on Eriksson if we see him. This is now a shoot-to-kill operation. Got it?'

Hallberg and Wiik both agreed, though getting a chain jerked tight around their necks didn't appear to sit well with either of them.

'Good,' Dahlvig said. 'Afterwards SID can do whatever they want with you.' He turned to Jamie now and stepped a little closer. 'And you,' he said, meeting her eye. 'Don't let me see you again. You've done enough to fuck up this investigation already, and you'll do no more. Understand?'

'Perfectly,' Jamie said, standing firm.

Dahlvig snapped his fingers over his shoulder at Hallberg and Wiik, and then stormed past Jamie, brushing her with his elbow and knocking her off balance like a schoolyard bully.

Jamie had to smirk at that – that she could pirouette on her left foot in half a second and sling a roundhouse into the side of his head before he could even react.

But she didn't. She just let Dahlvig go, his no doubt undersized penis swinging.

Hallberg gave Jamie one last, solemn nod. 'It was a pleasure working with you,' she said, voice a little shaky, and then lowered her head and followed Dahlvig.

Falk offered a hand to Jamie, and she took it. 'Thank you, Jamie,' she said, smiling. 'Your father would be proud of the woman you've become. I have no doubt of that.' She let go, and then turned away, heading to her office.

Jamie looked after her, voice caught in her throat.

Wiik cleared his own then and stepped towards her. He seemed less perturbed by the authority being impressed upon him. 'What will you do now?' he asked.

'You heard Dahlvig – I couldn't stay if I wanted to.'

'Do you?' He still had hope in his eyes.

'That's not my decision.'

'But if it was?'

Jamie turned her head and stared at Dahlvig, barking commands to his men. They were gearing up to leave. To go and hunt Eriksson into oblivion like the animal they thought him to be. 'Do you think it's him?' Jamie asked after a moment.

'Who?'

'Eriksson.'

'Do I think *what's* him?' Wiik leaned in a little, trying to catch Jamie's eye.

She couldn't give it to him. 'Do you think that Per Eriksson is the Angel Maker?'

Wiik looked troubled then. 'It can't be anyone else. Eriksson was an original suspect. He had means, opportunity. He knew the girls. He had access to the dresses they were placed in. He knew Sjöberg. They were best friends. He was contacted by Sjöberg before his death, they exchanged letters. He knew that Sjöberg was dying – to coincide the crime with his death. He would have known Nyström, too, from the original investigation. And what better way to screw with us than to manipulate the very detective who worked the case into committing the crime he'd convicted a man for years before?' Wiik ran his hand over his head now, smoothing down his hair.

Jamie noticed then that he had shaved at some point since their meeting that morning. And had fixed his hair, too.

Wiik began putting his fingers in his other palm one by one as he counted the mounting evidence. 'Eriksson knew we were looking for the letters to match the handwriting, which is why he was ahead of us at Eva Sjöberg's and stole it before we got there. And then he ran, too. Got the hell out of town right before the net closed. In my experience, innocent men don't run.'

Jamie inhaled slowly, filling her lungs, thinking of Tomas Lindvall. But Wiik wasn't done yet.

'He's been ahead of us at every turn – always just out of reach. Staying that way. It was pure chance that we stumbled upon the hunting cabin – if you hadn't have been looking for it, then we never would have found it. Nyström was the only person in the world who would have known about it other than you and your father. And with him dead nearly twenty years, and you living in another country, they were safe. And we know they were both there – because we have Eriksson's bus, his clothes and his DNA all over the cabin. He staged Nyström's kidnapping to throw us off balance, used him to get the case files, take the girls and to find them somewhere safe to hide. He did all of those things. But then we caught him off guard. And as much as I hate to admit it, Dahlvig is right. Now that Eriksson's pushed, he's going to be thinking on his feet – something he's not used to. He's a planner. He left nothing to chance. Killing Nyström? That was reactive. He was adapting to a quickly changing situation, and he took a big risk going to the hospital. They're still searching CCTV for him, and they'll find him. No one is invisible. No one can stay hidden forever. He'll be running now – looking for a way out. We're on to him, Jamie,' Wiik said, trying to catch her eye again. 'And he won't get away. They'll run him down, smoke him out if they have to. And when he's in the open, they'll put him down. There's nowhere left for him to go now. His face is everywhere, and there's not a uniformed officer in the entire country that isn't looking for him.'

Jamie listened to Wiik, processing and filing every scrap of evidence, every line of reasoning. Weighing them, measuring them, fitting them together into that complete puzzle.

And she couldn't argue. They all fit.

Perfectly.

Jamie hung her head and sighed.

'You don't think it's him?' Wiik asked, folding his arms now and sinking his teeth into his bottom lip.

Jamie looked at him now for the first time. 'You said it yourself, Wiik – really, there's no one else it *could* be. Right?'

54

JAMIE ROLLED to a stop outside the house and stared up at it.

There's no one else it could be.

Those were the last words she'd said to Wiik before he'd walked away towards Dahlvig. He strode purposefully as always, but this time, he slowed, stopped for a moment, and looked back.

Jamie shook him out of her head, zipped up her jacket and opened the car door, stepping into the frozen evening.

Overhead, the clouds had broken, revealing a sky as black as ink, studded with stars. The moon shone down, casting a pale light on the snow at the sides of the road, which seemed to glow blue.

The temperature was well below zero, the air still, clear and as cold as Jamie had ever known. It clawed at her cheeks as she walked, the street silent, the houses dark.

It was growing late now, and those who had braved the weather earlier in the day had receded to the safety of their homes.

She closed the door of the car Falk had let her borrow to

drive to the airport – after she'd made just this one quick stop, she'd promised – and looked around.

The street was deserted.

Jamie sighed, pushing her hands into her pockets. She wasn't really here, was she? She didn't really think...

And yet, the dog in the back of her head, gnawing on its leg, was down to the bone. The wound was raw and angry, bleeding all over the floor.

It needed to be addressed, and it needed to be addressed now.

Jamie started forward, crossing the road, and walked up the front steps to the door.

There were no lights on inside.

She lifted her hand and knocked, hard.

Nothing stirred.

Jamie knocked again, her skin breaking into gooseflesh under her collar.

She clenched her fists and stepped back, looking around.

Her breath was tight in her chest. She told herself it was just because of the cold. But her heartbeat, fast and light in her throat, told her it wasn't.

Jamie looked around for any signs of life, spotting something at the sides of the path. Tracks in the snow, heading towards the gate.

She ventured back down onto the frozen paving slabs and followed it back onto the street, looking left and then right.

Her eyes settled on a building up ahead and she began walking.

The road ended and Jamie slowed to a halt, seeing the tracks pick up again in the snow, cutting their way into the darkness.

Her muscles tightened, her eyes searching the darkness for any hint of what lay ahead.

She could see none.

But it was too late to turn back now.

She pressed on, treading carefully not to disrupt the tracks, tracing them further and further.

Behind, the lights from the street grew dimmer and dimmer.

Jamie's skin prickled, sweat beading around her jaw, her eyes darting left and right, breath held between her teeth.

And then she stopped, a shape swimming out of the gloom.

She blinked to make sure she was seeing what she thought she was, and then edged closer.

The tracks in front of her ended.

Two lines carved deeply through the untrodden snow, leading to an abandoned wheelchair.

Jamie stepped around it slowly, eyes fixed on the ground.

In front of it, leading towards the old, burnt-down church, were footprints.

She let out a rattling breath and pushed forward, leaving the discarded wheelchair where it was – beyond the reach of the streetlights and prying eyes.

The church loomed ahead, the red-brick front steps leading up to the old porch. It had remained intact – and the once white doors were standing firm against the years. They had been chained to stop anyone entering, but now that chain lay in a coil on the ground like a sleeping snake.

Jamie looked down at it, and then back up at the doors, the word *murderer* spray-painted across them.

She reached out and laid her hands on the cold wood, pushing.

They swung into the ruined interior, creaking mournfully as they did.

The snow-dusted boards groaned as Jamie entered, stepping slowly.

Around her, the support pillars rose out of the foundation like the ribs of a great beached whale, ending in charred, pointed tips. Blackened wood panelling clung between them – the last remnants of flesh on this gruesome skeleton.

This truly was the belly of the beast.

To either side of the aisle, old pews were sitting haphazardly, destroyed, rotten, and cast aside.

At the far end, Jamie could see a crucifix affixed to the central support strut that had once held the steeple aloft.

It was nearly eight feet tall and looked down upon all the sinners.

But they had long gone from this place.

All except one, that is.

Jamie mustered her voice. 'Eva Sjöberg,' she called out, the words echoing around her.

The woman was on her knees before the cross, hands clasped in prayer.

She lifted her head slowly, placed her long, bony fingers on the snow-covered wood either side of her, and pushed to her feet.

Eva Sjöberg uncurled until she was standing straight and then turned to face Jamie. Her once vacant expression was now razor-sharp, shadowed in black gouges by the moonlight. Her glasses had gone, the long, brittle grey hair pulled into a loose ponytail now hanging dead straight at her back.

She was a little shorter than Jamie, and slight. In her wheelchair, she'd looked withered, like a dying flower. But now, she looked like a poised viper.

'You found me,' she said, her voice barely a whisper, but carrying in the space between them. 'I wondered how long it would take you.'

The elderly, frail, fading woman Jamie had met was now gone, and in her place stood the true Eva Sjöberg. A woman who never missed a thing. Who planned everything, down to the most minute detail. Who had evaded capture twenty-five years before, orchestrated the abduction and murder of eight girls, the killings of six parents and the manipulation of two men into committing some of the most brutal, evil crimes Jamie had ever witnessed.

Jamie dragged air into her lungs, pulling her shoulders back, finding her voice. 'Is Per Eriksson dead?' she asked.

Eva Sjöberg said nothing, but the corners of her mouth cut up into her cheeks until she was grinning, her yellowed teeth like fangs in the darkness.

'It was you,' Jamie said then. 'It was always you.'

Eva Sjöberg stepped forward.

'Don't move,' Jamie commanded, her fists coming out of her pockets.

'I'm curious,' Eva Sjöberg said, lifting her chin to listen to the air. 'Did you come alone?'

Jamie's eyes narrowed, going to the woman's hands. They were hanging loosely at her sides, her shoulders low, knees soft. She wouldn't be fooled by the woman's age. She wouldn't be fooled by anything anymore.

'How did you find me?'

'You weren't as careful as you thought,' Jamie said, sliding her heels backwards in the snow, taking up ground, keeping Eva Sjöberg at a distance.

'No?' She stepped forward again.

'No,' Jamie said. 'You had everyone else fooled. Eriksson was a good patsy. But not good enough.'

'What gave it away?' Eva seemed amused by the conversation. As though almost excited by the idea of being caught.

'Little things,' Jamie answered, stealing a glance behind

her. She was closing on the threshold now. She had to watch her footing. 'Eriksson was the perfect suspect. Too perfect. The evidence was overwhelming. The letter Hans sent him – the letter he sent back. The kidnapping of Nyström. The kill coinciding with Hans's death. It was all laid out so carefully. It made Eriksson the perfect villain, the pieces of the puzzle just difficult enough to fit together to really sell it. But I've met men like Eriksson was *supposed* to be. And he wasn't it. He really was just a nice guy, wasn't he?'

Eva Sjöberg sneered. 'Nice? He was *weak*. He was supposed to be Hans's friend. And he turned his back on him. He deserved it. Just like all the others.'

'Deserved it?' Jamie parroted. 'Those poor girls – did they deserve it?'

Eva held her chin high now, her thin lips quivering with sudden rage. 'We *saved* them,' she spat. 'What was done to them – what they suffered through – no child deserves that. I *know*. They would carry it with them for the rest of their lives. That pain. They would never escape it. *Never*. It would haunt them forever. We did the only humane thing. We saved them. Released them from that life of suffering. We made them—'

'Angels,' Jamie said, swallowing. She read the expression on Eva Sjöberg's face. The anger there, the turmoil. She wasn't a cold, calculating psychopath. She was just a broken woman, her view on the world twisted and skewed by her own experiences. You could ask her a million times, and a million times you'd get the same answer. That she thought she was doing the right thing. That there was no cruelty in her actions. Just kindness.

'We gave their innocence back to them.' Eva looked up over Jamie's head and then met her eye again, squeezing her wrinkled mouth into a bitter pucker. 'And then we made the men and women responsible for it pay. More than you or your kind ever could.'

Jamie thought of Jan Hansen, of Leif Lundgren. Of what they did. And she hated that Eva Sjöberg was right. They'd never truly suffer enough under the protection of the law for what they did. 'Is that how you got Nyström?' Jamie asked. 'The old "greater good" speech? The lesser of two evils? Or maybe you just told him he could be the man he always wanted to be.'

'Men are easy,' Eva said coldly. 'They just want someone to whisper in their ear. To tell them everything is going to be alright. To have someone hold them, and stroke their hair, and reassure them that they're good, strong, righteous men.' She twisted her mouth into another evil smile now. 'That's what your father wanted, too. I could see it in him from the moment I met him.'

'Shut up,' Jamie said, her voice taking on its own hardness now.

Eva Sjöberg ignored her. 'He was the one I really wanted. Big, strong – not afraid of a little... *violence*.'

'Shut up.' Jamie's voice grew now.

'I watched him – I watched him tear himself apart over the case. He was weak, quick to anger. Driven by his emotions, plagued by his own darkness. He would have been...' She trailed off for a moment, then locked eyes with Jamie, hers flashing in the moonlight. 'He would have been perfect. But then he went and killed himself. Before I could get to him. Before I could give him meaning again.'

Jamie's fists were clenched so hard her nails were cutting into her palms, the skin on her knuckles threatening to split under the strain.

'Nyström resisted at first,' Eva said, rolling her head left and right, flexing her fingers at her sides. 'But it didn't take long. They made it easy. The Polis was all he had – and they were turning their backs on him, too. Casting him aside. All he wanted was to matter. To do something again. To save just one…' Eva Sjöberg stepped forward again. 'More.' Another step. 'Life.'

Jamie was at the doorway now, holding firm.

Eva Sjöberg was closing in.

'Now then,' she said, lowering her head. Her hand moved at her side and a blade appeared in it. She turned it slowly so it caught the moonlight, glinting. Single-edged, sharp, small. Easy to conceal, the blade hooked. Perfect for slashing tyres. And throats. 'What are we going to do with you…'

Jamie's heel hit the threshold and she lifted it over, stepping back over the chain and onto the porch.

Eva Sjöberg advanced slowly. Her footsteps light and sure.

Jamie was on the bricks now and moving towards the steps.

'You can't run,' Eva said, bringing the knife in front of her. 'Your father wouldn't have run.' She grinned down at Jamie, stepping over the threshold. 'Your father would have stayed and faced me.'

Jamie was down the steps now, heels crunching in the fresh snow. She locked eyes with the woman in front of her and let the tiniest hint of a smirk creep across her lips. 'My father also wouldn't have come alone.'

Eva Sjöberg froze, a faint click to her right stopping her in her tracks.

Anders Wiik stepped from the shadow of the wall, the muzzle of his pistol hovering about six inches from her temple.

His fingers flexed on the grip, his hand steady in the frozen air. 'Drop the knife,' he ordered.

Eva Sjöberg began to grin again. 'You're smarter than I gave you credit for,' she said, still fixed on Jamie.

Jamie let her smirk broaden now, the tension finally draining from her shoulders. 'And you, Eva Sjöberg,' she said, turning away to face the city she had once called home. 'Weren't.'

55

THE STREET outside Eva Sjöberg's modest one-storey house was a flood of blue flashing lights.

There were three uniformed police cars, two canine units, Wiik's Volvo and a whole fleet of officers.

Eva Sjöberg sat like a statue in the back seat of one of the marked cars, staring blankly at the metal cage in front of her.

You'll have to get used to it, Jamie thought. *You'll be looking through bars for a long time.*

Wiik was standing with his arms folded, staring at her, bottom lip turned out in disdain.

'Hey,' Jamie said, coming up beside him.

He looked at Jamie briefly, then went back to his scowling.

She was about to start talking when Hallberg appeared from the jungle of blues.

'So it turns out,' Hallberg said, shaking her head, 'that Eva Sjöberg was in a car crash in 1993 that damaged her pelvis and spine. Hospital records show that she needed to have surgery which would have prevented her from being able to have children, as she said – *but* the spinal injury was minor. She needed the wheelchair for eight to twelve weeks, from the notes, but made a full recovery. The follow-up consultation stated as much. Since then, it was all just a cover.' Hallberg lowered her head. 'If we'd have just thought to check…'

Wiik eyed her.

Jamie could tell he wanted to say something encouraging, but couldn't bring himself to.

So she did instead. 'You couldn't have known. No one could have. There was no reason we should have confirmed that.' Jamie made a point of smiling at her. 'What matters is that we got her.'

'But how did you know?' Hallberg asked, looking up at Jamie in awe.

Jamie squirmed under her gaze. It felt uncomfortable, and she certainly wasn't deserving of any enamour. She was just doing her job. And a lot of the time, playing devil's advocate was part of it. 'There was too much evidence,' she said quickly. 'It *had* to be Eriksson. Everything we knew said that. The DNA, the circumstance, the means, the opportunity. Everything.'

Hallberg didn't look to be following the train of thought.

'But what if it wasn't?' Jamie shrugged. 'There are no certainties in this game. And if it wasn't Eriksson – who else could it have been?'

'And you thought of Eva Sjöberg?'

'Not at first.' Jamie was tired of this explanation before it began. 'But outside of what we *thought* we knew, he didn't make sense as the killer. How does a six-foot-plus priest hide in plain sight of a hospital room and uniformed officer for hours without garnering a second glance? How does he evade CCTV, slip in and out unseen? How does he reach the ceiling to put a latex glove over a camera?'

'He doesn't. But an old woman in a wheelchair…'

'Can move freely around a hospital without turning a head.' Jamie nodded.

'And she could get up on her chair and reach the ceiling no problem,' Hallberg said, huffing in realisation.

'Exactly. Eriksson wasn't visible on the CCTV because he wasn't on it. But go back through it now and I bet you'll see Eva Sjöberg rolling through the corridors, as cool as a cucumber.'

Hallberg tutted, then looked at the woman in the car, mustering as much disgust as her friendly face could manage. 'And the court transcript? Nyström's apartment?'

'Just pulling the thread. The transcript said that Sjöberg pleaded innocent to begin with – but then did a U-turn and pled guilty with no explanation. At first I thought he was doing it to protect Eriksson – they were best friends, after all. But Eriksson said that he turned his back on Sjöberg. They didn't speak for twenty-five years. And during all that time, it seemed odd to me that Sjöberg would continue to protect him. It all hinged on who was telling the truth – Eva Sjöberg or Eriksson. And if Eriksson wasn't lying.'

'It meant Eva Sjöberg was.'

'Hans went to prison for her. Took all the blame. And he protected her until his last breath.'

'And Nyström's place?'

'He had pictures of his wife everywhere – years after her death. He was lonely – we had that much right. But he missed his wife more than he missed my father. Eva Sjöberg was more likely to have been able to twist him up than Per Eriksson.' Jamie watched the woman who'd been running circles around them for two decades through the window of the police car. 'Once I compared the handwriting at Nyström's apartment to the note under my windshield wiper, I saw they

were a match. I knew the killer wouldn't be sloppy enough to
leave a clue like that – but Nyström did it because it was *me*.
He knew me. Didn't want to kill me. But it created a trail. A
trail that Eva Sjöberg then had to mop up. If we'd got the
Eriksson letter from her house, we'd have been able to elimi-
nate Eriksson as the person who left it. And she needed to
maintain that illusion – keep us chasing a ghost. And that's all
it was. It was her, pulling the strings all along. She wanted us
to believe that Eriksson had fled. That he'd stolen his letter
back to protect himself. But he wouldn't need to. If Eva was
as infirm as he said, he could have walked right in the front
door. Why risk breaking in in broad daylight? And why leave
her alive, a potential witness? No, if it was Eriksson, he
would have taken Eva along with the letter. Tied up all the
loose ends.' Jamie turned away from her now and looked
back at Hallberg. 'The double-tracked footprints to obscure
the size, the misdirection, the loyalty Hans Sjöberg showed at
trial, the link to Nyström through the original investigation…
Each piece on its own would be ignorable. But all together…'

'It had to be her.'

'If it wasn't Eriksson, there was no one else.'

Hallberg took it all in, her eyes still shining like a child's.

Jamie cleared her throat and folded her arms, then looked
at Wiik and saw he had his folded too. She unfolded hers
quickly. 'Eva always planned to frame Eriksson. And getting
rid of him was a part of that. She lured him to her house
under the guise of taking him up on his offer of picking her
up to attend church. When he got there, she killed him, took
the letter and Hans's belongings, drove his bus out to the
cabin and dumped them there. Then her and Nyström got rid
of the body, and he drove her back. He's out there somewhere
– buried in the earth or under the ice in that lake.' Jamie
grimaced at the thought. 'Killing Nyström was the icing on

the cake. The public act of brutality that would send the whole of the SPA into a blind rage. The NTF took the bait, came in with numbers, ready to run Eriksson down. And they would have tried. All the time, looking at the wrong person. It was a perfect plan. She thought of everything.'

'Everything except what would happen if you showed up,' Hallberg said, grinning at Jamie now.

'Yeah,' Jamie said, shrugging. She didn't take praise well. 'If you say so.'

'So your father was right, all along then. About Hans Sjöberg.'

Jamie nodded. 'Yeah, he was. He just only had half the picture.'

Hallberg put her hand on Jamie's shoulder and squeezed. It felt awkward and strange. 'It was a good thing you were here to finish what he started.'

Jamie felt her throat tighten. 'Yeah, I guess it was.' Her eyes drifted to Wiik, who was still standing, looking at the unassuming woman in the back of a police car responsible for it all.

Hallberg read the cool silence between them and excused herself tactfully. 'I've got to follow up with some of the officers,' she said, hooking a thumb over her shoulder, and then left the two of them alone.

After a few seconds of silence, Wiik spoke, but didn't look around. 'With some luck, her testimony will help us go after Lundgren and Hansen.'

'Guess there will be a silver lining, then.'

'And maybe she can shed some light on what Mikael Gunnarson did to Tilde.'

Jamie swallowed, not sure she even wanted to know.

Wiik said nothing for a while, eyes still fixed on Eva Sjöberg. 'How did you know I'd come?' he asked.

Jamie stood a little closer, pushing her hands into her pockets. She nudged him with her shoulder. 'And miss the party for the third time?'

He turned his head and looked at her, narrowing his eyes a little.

'You looked back,' Jamie said.

'When?'

'At HQ. After I asked you if you thought it was Eriksson.'

'And you drove out here alone, hoping that I'd get cold feet with Dahlvig and come running after you, based on a *look*?'

Jamie laughed a little. 'A look can say a lot, Wiik.'

He shook his head a little.

'I knew that my question would bug you. And I knew you wouldn't be able to let it go. That you'd check with Falk. And that when she told you where I was going, it would click and you'd come running.'

'I wouldn't say *running*.'

'I'm happy you did. For a second I thought I'd have to face her on my own.'

'You could have taken her,' Wiik said, shifting his weight from foot to foot.

'Yeah, maybe.' She looked at him now and he at her. 'But I'm glad I didn't have to.'

That sat between them for a second, and then he spoke again.

'What time are you leaving?' he asked, the blue lights playing on his expressionless face.

Jamie stared into the distance for a while, letting him suffer. 'You know,' she said slowly. 'I never actually booked my flight.'

He twitched a little, trying not to seem eager. 'No?'

'Or checked out of my hotel.'

He cleared his throat. 'Why not?'

Jamie tried to keep the smile from her face. 'I don't really have anywhere to go back to. The Met isn't missing me, and all my stuff is in storage in a locker in London. The place I was staying in Scotland was...' She just sort of trailed off. 'It was nice. But I'm in no hurry to go back. That's a part of my life I think I'm ready to leave behind. And anyway, I feel like I have some things to sort out here. There'll be outstanding bills on the house that will need clearing before anything can happen to it. And it needs some work before it can be lived in.'

'You're thinking about living there?' Wiik tried his best to keep the excitement from his voice.

'Living in it, selling it. I'm not sure. There are a lot of memories there for me. Some good. A lot bad.' She shrugged. 'But either way, I'm not going to let it rot.'

'What about work?' This time, he didn't try to suppress it.

'I hadn't given it much thought,' Jamie said, meeting his eye finally. Answering his question, finally. 'I don't suppose you know of any detectives looking for a new partner, do you?'

Wiik looked down, smiling to himself, and then looked at Jamie. 'Oh, I don't know,' he said coyly, reaching up and flattening his hair against his head. 'I'm sure I could think of someone.'

EPILOGUE

JAMIE SAT BACK on her heels, her knees aching, and wiped the sweat from her brow.

It was early March and the snow was melting in the city. A string of warm days had spurred Jamie on to begin the clear-out she'd been dreading. Eva Sjöberg had been in custody for nearly six weeks and was awaiting trial.

Now, it was out of their hands.

Jamie's phone vibrated in her pocket and she pulled it out, dragging fistfuls of mail from the space next to the TV with her free hand at the same time.

'Hallä,' Jamie said, not even checking the number. So few people called her it could only have been Wiik or Hallberg – or Falk. But that last one was a rarity and she wasn't assigned to any cases just yet. Not until her paperwork came through fully and her loan to the Stockholm Polis officially started.

'Johansson.' It was Wiik. 'How's it going?'

Jamie sighed, jiggling the black bag to get the mass of envelopes and old papers to settle. She stared around her living room, a sea of dust swirling through it. 'We're getting there. What's up? The idea of a day off is to have a break from your partner. You know that, right?'

He sucked on his teeth and it made a squeaking noise in Jamie's ear. Wiik wasn't much of a laugher. Neither was she, really. But this was about as close as it got to *light patter* between them. 'Just received Sjöberg's written statement and confession.'

'Oh right,' Jamie said, sitting up and focusing a little more. 'Don't tell me she's going for a deal?'

'No – she's pleading guilty,' Wiik said with something like relief in his voice. 'Not to all the murders – she didn't want to steal credit from Hans, of course.'

'Of course.'

'But enough to put her away for the rest of her life.'

'Good,' Jamie said, letting herself smile a little. 'You call just to tell me that?'

'No – thought you'd want to know that she details her experiences with both Leif Lundgren and Jan Hansen, too, as well as recounting the conversations with Hanna Lundgren and Emmy Berg. She's prepared to testify to their guilt. Supposedly her and Hans had a process, did their due diligence to make sure they weren't going after anyone wrongfully.'

Jamie scoffed a little. 'Gotta love a serial killer with a moral code.'

Wiik harrumphed. 'With the original forensics reports placing Lundgren's DNA under Hanna's nails, along with both her confession to Rachel Engerman, who is also prepared to testify in court, we'll be able to get a conviction.'

'If we're lucky,' Jamie said, swallowing. Sadly, she knew how these things went a lot of the time.

'And with both Hansen's wife's testimony, along with

what we pulled from the tablet, and William's confirmation that it was only him and Emmy using it...'

'I hope you're right,' Jamie said.

'We'll get them,' Wiik answered affirmatively. 'Eventually.'

Jamie stayed quiet, waiting for more.

Wiik cleared his throat then. 'Sjöberg also gave us an explanation on the Gunnarsons and why they were both in the crosshairs.'

Jamie didn't know if he was speaking metaphorically, but she guessed not considering the nature of Åsa Gunarsson's death. She said nothing.

'The nanny they hired was abusing Tilde. She told Mikael and Åsa, and apparently they fired the nanny – and get this,' he said, huffing incredulously, 'Eva said that they actually *paid her off.*'

'What?' Jamie said, feeling her brow crumple in shock. 'They paid her off for what?'

'To keep quiet, supposedly,' Wiik said angrily. 'When Tilde told them, they confronted her. But Mikael was in the midst of a big negotiation for investment in his firm, and Åsa was working a huge case. They didn't want to risk any police involvement or scandal so they paid her some money to go away, and then told Tilde she'd been arrested.'

'Jesus,' Jamie muttered. 'Paying the woman who did that to your...' She swallowed the bile rising in her throat. 'How does Eva Sjöberg know all this?'

'Apparently her and Hans hunted the woman down, and then tortured her to—'

'Actually,' Jamie said, shaking her head. 'I don't even want to know.' She'd not liked Mikael Gunarsson from the get-go, but this was something else. The kind of people who'd be capable of doing that. She couldn't imagine.

'Sjöberg said that Hans went after her, though – she doesn't know where the body is. And with her testimony coming second-hand, Gunarsson's lawyer will call it hearsay and have it thrown out of court in a second.' He drew a slow breath in and let it out. 'I don't think we'll be able to get anything to stick on this one.'

Jamie clenched her teeth, wondering if the guilt of having to live with what he'd done, as well as the loss of his child and wife would be enough punishment for the man. The words came to her lips then without her thinking about them. 'Men like that always get what's coming to them in the end,' she said quietly.

'What was that?' Wiik asked, not quite catching it.

'Nothing,' Jamie said, shaking her head. 'Just something I heard somewhere.' She coughed up some dust lodged in her throat. 'What about the bodies of the other missing parents? Eriksson?'

'Sjöberg gave us some leads – but it was more than two decades ago now, so we're not sure how many we'll be able to turn up. As for Eriksson – he's out there somewhere in that valley. She knows that much. But doesn't know what Nyström did with him. She says that...' His voice drifted off in her ear as she turned her head towards a knock at the door.

'Let me call you back,' she said, and he fell quiet.

'Hejdå,' he said then, and hung up. Bye.

Jamie stood and brushed herself off, going for the door. She hoped this wasn't Hallberg 'spontaneously' showing up to help. The girl had been hanging on her shoulder in the office, asking to go for a coffee at least twice a week, and had even asked Jamie if she could join her on her morning runs. She was sweet, and she wanted to learn to be a better detective — but Jamie was by no means the sort of person she thought anyone should model themselves on. And she was

still trying to work out how best to tell her to go away
without shattering her feelings too badly.

She pulled the door open widely, forcing a smile. It
slipped off and she did a double take, surprised to see a man
she very much didn't expect to see standing on her step.

'Doctor Claesson,' Jamie said, blinking at him. 'What are
you doing here?'

He twisted the woollen flat cap he was holding in his
hands and looked at her nervously. 'Inspector Johansson,' he
said, smiling briefly. 'I was wondering if I might come in?'

Jamie stepped back automatically and proffered him the
hallway, her mind working to give reason to his visit. 'Sorry
about the mess,' she said then, closing the door behind him.
'No one's lived here since…'

He nodded, giving her another quick smile, and then
turned to face her, glancing in at the living room and kitchen.
He seemingly had no intention of venturing deeper.

'What can I, uh,' Jamie started, folding her arms, 'do for
you, doctor?'

He swallowed. 'I wanted to speak to you about your
father.'

Jamie felt her body stiffen a little, reading the conflict on
the small man's face. His bald head was beaded with tiny
droplets of sweat and the skin in his neck pulsed with his
quickened heart.

'I'm guessing that Wiik told you about the… *incident*
between your father and I?'

Jamie nodded, not able to find her voice.

'Yes, it was quite the talk of the station from what I heard,
but… but I think you deserve to hear the truth of what
happened.'

Jamie braced herself, not sure if she wanted to. Had it

been worse than she knew? Had her father been even more brutish than anyone realised?

'He was working a case when it happened,' Claesson started, wanting to get it out before he lost his nerve by the looks of things. 'A strange case – I don't know if you remembered that I mentioned I was just a junior pathologist at the time?'

Jamie nodded briefly, leaning in slightly.

'The case he was working – I didn't know anything about it. But I was under strict instructions not to file the autopsy reports and tests we had in the archives.'

'Is that odd?' Jamie queried, knowing it was.

'Yes, very,' he said, meeting her eye suddenly. 'And what's even more odd is that the case appeared to be far above the pay grade of a junior pathologist. The head pathologist at the time, a man by the name of Svensson, was intentionally kept out of the loop by the SPA. The bodies were delivered by night, the examinations conducted in a closed lab. I was sworn to secrecy, and told to hand the reports directly to your father.'

Jamie's jaw was clamped firmly shut now. She stared at Claesson, willing him to go on.

'The incident occurred after the third body was delivered. Each victim was killed distinctly, but there were common elements at work. Each of the three victims' – he lifted his hands now and made three box shapes in front of him – 'had faint ligature marks on their wrists consistent with being suspended upright, each had damage to their eardrums, and each was presented as though they had killed themselves.'

Jamie's heart picked up and she sank her teeth into her bottom lip to stop them from trembling.

Claesson kept going. 'The first had cut their wrists, the

second threw themselves from a building, the third was drowned…'

Jamie didn't know if she liked where this was going.

In fact, she *really* didn't like where this was going.

'The third victim, who had supposedly drowned — I called your father to tell him what I had found. Traces of propofol in his system.'

'Propofol?' Jamie asked, her voice catching. 'Isn't that an anaesthetic?'

Claesson nodded. 'Yes – but more than just an anaesthetic, it has curious barbiturate effects, too. It lowers inhibitions, makes the person pliable, and essentially, it is amnesia-inducing. In studies performed with the drug, subjects under the influence are unable to recall anything that occurred—'

'Okay, okay,' Jamie said, cutting him off. 'I get it. So what happened with my father?'

Claesson gathered himself. 'I could see he was getting worse. The case, whatever it was, was taking a toll on him. We weren't *friends*… not quite, but we had worked together for several years, and we were casual, you know?'

She wished he'd get on with it.

'That night that I called him, to tell him about the propofol – just trace amounts – I thought the killer had perhaps kept the victim alive for a few days to let the drug disperse in the body before…' He saw the look on Jamie's face and curtailed his own story. 'I called him in, and he arrived. Drunk.'

Jamie swallowed. She wasn't surprised. But she was still upset to hear it.

'He could barely stand. But he came anyway. I was being kept there late – doing this after hours – not allowed to tell anyone. Thanklessly. Without extra pay. Told by the SPA that if I didn't comply, and keep my mouth shut, that I'd be shipped off to the forensics lab in Luleå. So when he arrived – drunk, cheeks smeared with lipstick,' he said, and then pointed to his face, 'nose white with…' He stopped again, shook his head, and then looked at Jamie once more. 'Anyway, I was angry. Here I was being confined to my lab while he was out there, partying, having a grand old time.'

Jamie's head was whirling.

'I spoke… harshly,' Claesson said. 'I can't remember the conversation specifically – it's all rather a blur. But I remember what I said before he picked me up by the collar and ran me through a counter full of glassware.'

'Which was?' Jamie's voice was barely a whisper.

'That behaving like this, it was no wonder your mother and you left him.'

Jamie closed her eyes, just hearing the words a knife to the heart.

What her father did wasn't right, but she couldn't help but understand why that would hit home.

'He left me there, then,' Claesson said. 'Bloodied, alone. I wasn't found for hours – unconscious by then. The cleaner who discovered me called for an ambulance. The surgeries. The recovery time. There was no way it could be kept quiet. And I was still angry – but I knew what I said was wrong. Below the belt. And… and…' He stumbled over his words. 'And I thought I could help him, then.'

'By filing a charge against him?' Jamie tried to keep her voice free of scorn.

Claesson nodded. 'Yes. I thought that he was going off the rails, that maybe it would scare him straight – get him to realise what he'd done. Make an effort to get help.'

'It got him suspended.' Jamie thought she'd failed to keep the scorn away that time.

Judging by Claesson's expression, she did. He went back

to twisting his hat between his hands. 'I know that. But I fear it did more than that.' He paused, collecting his thoughts. 'When I left the hospital, I returned to the lab to see what had happened in my absence, and found it empty.'

'What do you mean *empty?*'

'The bodies – gone. The test results – gone. The files, the reports, everything – gone. It was as though the case never existed.'

'But why would they… I mean, *who* would…?'

Claesson shook his head. 'I didn't know, but who could I tell? Or ask? My superiors had no knowledge of it. I had been sworn to secrecy by your father, and I didn't know who to contact at the SPA. I feared I had already done something I shouldn't have by filing that charge. I didn't think at the time – but I had to detail what we were doing at the lab late at night, and why we were there…'

God, she wished he'd stop trailing off and just hurry up.

'And then, two nights later, he came to see me. At home.'

'My father?'

Claesson nodded. 'Yes, it was late – I don't remember what time – but he knocked on the door to my flat.'

'Okay.'

'When I opened it and saw him, I was frightened, as you can imagine. I suspected that he'd heard about the charge, and come to finish me off.'

Jamie swallowed, seeing the fear return to his face for a moment.

'But that wasn't it at all. He looked tired. Exhausted. But he was sober. And sorry.'

'Sorry?'

'Yes. He said that he was sorry about what had happened, that he hadn't meant to, but that what I'd said… He'd just lost it. He said he couldn't tell me what he was working on, but it was a big case. He thought I should know. It was all hush-hush. Under wraps. Need-to-know. Just a handful of people were in the loop, and he couldn't tell me anything else.' Claesson cast his mind back. 'In those previous weeks when he had come to see me, he'd been dressed differently to normal. Not his usual day-to-day, you know?'

Jamie nodded, but she didn't.

'And that night at the lab – he was in a suit.'

'A suit?' Her father hated suits. The only time she'd seen him wear one was in photos of her parents' wedding.

'I surmised then that it must have been an undercover operation, or…' He trailed off for the umpteenth time, his face screwing up. He looked ready to cry.

Jamie saw it then. 'And by filing that charge…' She closed her own eyes, the words hurting to even say. 'You might have blown the whole thing up.'

'I had no idea.'

'No, of course not,' she said, her voice quietening. 'You couldn't have known.'

'But he said,' Claesson went on, more determined now. 'That it was almost over. That he was closing in on the people responsible, and after it was done, he was getting himself together.'

Jamie picked her head up and looked at him now. 'That he was going to stop drinking, and he was going to fix up the house, and get on top of things, and… and… and he was going to get you back.'

Jamie held her breath, measuring the man for any hint of falsehood. 'What?'

Claesson nodded. 'That's what he said – that once it was finished, he was going to get you back. Even if he had to go to England himself to do it.'

Jamie's throat clamped shut, her eyes burning. 'Why would he tell you that?'

'I think… to show that he was serious. He wouldn't have joked about something like that. You know that he carried a photo of you and him in his wallet. Everywhere he went.'

'When, uh,' she said, her voice trembling, 'when was this?'

'About a week before…'

'He…'

Claesson nodded and Jamie hung her head, looking around. 'He must have slipped,' she said, the words coming to her naturally. 'I'm not surprised—'

'No,' Claesson said then, forcefully almost. 'He didn't.'

Jamie looked at him cautiously.

'He was serious. And I believed him. I could see that he had changed in those final few months. Whatever that case was… it pushed him. Too hard. And he knew it. But he was going to come back from it. I've never seen a man so determined.'

'But he didn't.'

Claesson ploughed on, ignoring the comment. 'The next morning, I withdrew the charge against him. It took a few days to process, but once it had, I tried to find him, to tell him. But I couldn't.'

'You couldn't?'

He shook his head. 'No. I couldn't. I came here, but he wasn't home. His car wasn't in the driveway. He wasn't picking up his phone. No one from work had seen him. His partner, Nyström – he hadn't heard from him. I even checked with the bars local to the station – the places I knew he went. His partner got a little worried then, tried to find him, too. But… there was no trace.'

Jamie didn't have words now.

'And these bodies,' Claesson said, looking at the ground. 'From the case – the three men killed – they weren't just nobodies. They were important people. One of them was a judge, another was a high-profile solicitor. The third was a politician. Whoever killed them was good. They were smart. They were clean.'

Jamie watched the man in front of her more closely than she'd watched anyone in her life. Listened more intently than she'd ever listened before. Felt more sick than she'd ever felt.

'He was going to get his life together. He was. And then he disappeared. And a week later, I read in the paper that…'

Jamie held her breath.

'I don't know what happened to him,' Claesson said slowly, readying himself to say something he had been holding in for two decades. He looked up, met her eyes, and then uttered the words that would shatter her world. 'He didn't kill himself, Jamie. Your father was murdered.'

AUTHOR'S NOTE

Angel Maker. It feels *different.* If you've come to this novel first – and it is the first you've read of my work, and of Jamie, then I sincerely hope you enjoyed it.

It was not the first Jamie Johansson novel, however – it's actually the fourth. But for me, it feels like the first. The original three are London-set crime thrillers that allowed me to cut my teeth in this genre, and get to know the woman who has haunted these pages. Those three books let me discover who she was and what she could do, and when it came time to put pen to paper for Angel Maker, I felt good about what was to come.

For me, writing is a mode of reflection and revision. I write, I release, I read every review, every comment, and I take it in. Then I re-read, refine, revise, and allow the work to mutate and grow organically, guided by both my own experience and that of the reader. I had always hoped to write a methodical whodunnit police-procedural that was high-concept, taut, and expertly written. But I have quickly come to realise that the last thing on that list was a stumbling point. I began writing in science fiction and dystopia – and through that education, my strengths have revealed themselves to be in the action elements of the work. The fight scenes, the chases, the confrontations – they are where I feel most at home. And so I write in this ebb and flow – an inhale-exhale – fashion that allows the reader to breathe and take stock of the story before being plunged into the next action sequence.

Though I have known and consulted those in the police, and forensics, and psychology, I am not any of those things myself. And so I have let go of that desire to create a deep and realistic procedural novel, and instead lean into my strengths and my more human-focused desires. To create a cast of deep characters driven by their emotions and experiences. And to create a novel that unfurls itself like a rose (excuse the poeticism here but unfurling like an onion doesn't have quite the same ring to it) to reveal layer upon layer of characterisation. This novel is not a police procedural, it is a thriller novel. A crime thriller, I suppose, as it revolves around that single *crime*. The fulcrum of the novel is the killing. And the characters move around it like a vortex, closing in until that final convergence, wherein the crime is finally laid bare.

This, in my mind, is how this novel began, transpired, and then ended. It was guided by its genre, but developed organically. And it is truly my hope that you feel this stepping away from the rigour of the procedure involved in policing, and instead placing two humans at the centre of a harrowing mess, and allowing them to write their own story free from convention, has resulted in something that is, at the end of the day, enjoyable to read.

The list of to-dos stretches on when you're writing a novel. Every sentence and clue and thread needs to coexist with all the others, needs to build towards the finale, and then needs to be tied up. There are many within this novel – bread crumbs, false starts, red herrings, suspects, outliers, misdirects, and finally, a twist that I did my very best to obscure until the final seconds. Did I do that? Did you see it coming? Honestly, I'd love to know. If you did, then when did you think it? This is what I am most curious about.

I could write forever here, and often feel the need to ramble. As it's a way to decompress after a solid two and a half months of sitting at my desk and churning out words. My writing is borderline fanatical. But I am in love with the idea of it. Not in love with my own writing, but with the concept of writing something that people will enjoy. That aspiration to create something with impact and weight, that people will carry forward. That is what drives me. It is what keeps me up at night and what wakes me in the morning. It is what makes me want to drag myself back to the keyboard after finishing one novel and immediately begin the next.

So this is probably a good place to leave you. Because the next story is calling. And it's not something I can ignore.

If you did enjoy this novel, you'll be glad to know that the next one is Jamie Johansson's next adventure. She has become a character close to my heart, and I can't wait to torture her a little more. But honestly, I wouldn't if I didn't know she could take it.

She's strong, and she's about to embark on a journey that I hope will span decades. If you'd like to know what comes next for Jamie, read on. The next book will be out later this year. Until then, stay safe.

All the best,
Morgan Greene

———

If you enjoyed Angel Maker, please consider leaving me a review on Amazon in order to help new readers discover the novel.

Read on to discover more about Rising Tide, the next novel in the DI Jamie Johansson Series.

RISING TIDE

Book 2 in the DI Jamie Johansson Series

It is ten below in the Norwegian Sea, and the Bolstad B Drilling Platform stands dark among the jagged waves. The wind whips across the surface of the ocean at sixty miles per hour. Land is 342 miles away. There are no boats. There is no escape. And a body has just been discovered hanged from the edge of the platform.

A six-month shift is due to end in five days, and a dozen weary, strained drilling engineers are about to go home. A helicopter will arrive to take them back to the mainland. But there is a killer among them, and people are scared.

If they are transported home, they will all be arrested upon arrival, interrogated. It will be an international scandal. And the Swedish-owned Bolstad Oil Company cannot afford it. Their drilling rights are drying up, their stakeholders selling their shares. This could end them. But worst of all — a killer could walk free.

Is someone using the Bolstad Company's problems as a

smokescreen to cover their tracks? Or is something much bigger going on?

Detective Inspector Jamie Johansson is on loan to the Stockholm Polis, and she and her new partner, the pragmatic and stern Anders Wiik, are pulled into the investigation when one of the stockholders calls in a favour with their boss. They need this solved quickly and quietly before the workers are brought home. If the helicopter is cancelled, it will raise flags and people will start asking questions.

Bolstad won't risk it. Which means the clock is ticking.

Jamie and Wiik are flown out to the middle of the Norwegian Sea with one job – find the killer in five days.

But the platform is only so big, there are only so many places to hide, and the killer doesn't like being cornered. They have a home-field advantage. They know the platform inside and out. And they have no intention of going quietly.

Jamie and Wiik are on their own. They've got no support, no help from the mainland, and there's a storm rolling in.

As the rain begins to pelt the platform, drowning out the sound of the screams, the crew begin to go missing. One. By one. By one.

It's only a matter of time before Jamie and Wiik are next on the list.

This is a cat and mouse game with the ultimate stakes, and no hope of rescue. Tensions are reaching boiling point, and as more secrets are revealed among the crew, Jamie and Wiik begin to realise that finding the killer may not be their top priority. Five days is a long time to try to survive when there's nowhere to run.

The badge means nothing when you're this far from home.

Out here there is no police.

There is no law.

There's just oil and blood.

And lots of it.

———

Rising Tide is the brutal and taut next instalment of the DI Jamie Johansson series. A claustrophobic mystery with no shortage of suspects and murder, this case will test Jamie and Wiik's investigative skills, as well as their will to survive. Will they crack the case before the killer comes for them, or will they buckle under the pressure? Jamie has faced evil before, but never with her back up against the wall. Pre-order Rising Tide now to get your hands on a copy as soon as it releases.

Order your copy of Rising Tide today. Available on Kindle, Kindle Unlimited, and Paperback.

FOLLOW ME ON FACEBOOK FOR THE CHANCE TO WIN SIGNED COPIES

Follow me on Facebook to stay up to date with all the latest news and giveaways I run.

I regularly give away signed copies, the opportunity to name characters in my books, become an advanced reader, and lots of other great prizes.

Check out my page by heading to and like or follow to never miss a your chance:

facebook.com/morgangreeneauthor

ACKNOWLEDGMENTS

Writing an acknowledgements page is something I wasn't sure I'd ever have to do. I used to read them in books and always find myself thinking – how could so many people be a part of a single book? That was probably because I always wrote things on my own. I did my own research, my own editing, my own revisions. And then I put them out there. And so there was a part of me that thought I'd never get here.

And yet here I am. The first outings for Jamie Johansson were penned within a closed environment. And I believe that really shows within the reception and the reviews – not all of them wholly positive. And understandably so. I'd do a lot different if I had it all to do again.

So when it came time to begin work on Angel Maker, I sought the help that I needed. And the assistance, both big and small, that I received, has been instrumental in making this book feel more authentic and rich — feel more real, and hopefully, feel like a more complete and satisfying work to read.

So, here we go then.

Firstly, I would like to thank my editor, Rebecca. Self-publishing as an indie skips a lot of vital steps in the editing and refinement process, so having a trusted voice of reason and editorial advice is indispensable. The edit of Angel Maker has been the most intense of all my books, and has come with a steep learning curve for me. But I believe the manuscript is all the better for it. And that is down to you, Rebecca. And for that, you have my eternal thanks, as well as loyalty. So if you were hoping to scare me off with all those corrections and suggestions, tough luck. You're stuck with me now, and you've only yourself to blame.

Next, I would like to thank my friends and colleagues in Sweden who advised tirelessly on the grammar and translations included, as well as the feeling of the setting, the descriptions included, and everything else that helped to place this story in and around the wonderful city of Stockholm. Julia Karlsson, Jennifer Hallberg, Shannon Oehlschlager, Anna Abrahamsson, and Linnea Grunnesjö. This book would have been a lot worse without you. And for that I thank you.

I would to thank those first faithful readers and reviewers who deigned to take a chance on Bare Skin. *You picked it out of a pile of free-to-read novels, and gave it your time and energy. And then, you were kind enough to give it your support. Your words, your enthusiasm, and your feedback fuelled me to continue writing during what has been a difficult year — both globally, and personally. Honestly, without you, I probably would have just given up. Abbie James, Kathi Defranc, Kelly Hansen, Samantha Wells, Rosie Bray — your words mean more than you can know to a writer trying to make it.*

I would like to give my thanks to those who's undying enthusiasm of this genre has allowed them to find a little more space in their hearts and minds for a new author. To discover readers offering such a warm welcome and reception was something I never expected, and something for which I will always be grateful. So thank you, Donna Morfett, Joe Singleton, and Samantha Brownley. I hope that you will continue to let me eat up your time with my words and presence. Meeting you will no doubt become something I will look back on fondly in years to come.

Finally, I would like to say thank you to those closest to me, who have supported me unwaveringly through not only this latest phase of writing, but who have always been there while I chased this dream. Julie, for always being the first to read, and for unfailingly pointing out stumbling in my grammar. I'm sure my work would be a flaming mess without you. And to Sophie, my partner, who has watched me try and try again at this whole writing thing, and who has never once been anything other than stalwart. There comes a time for pragmatism, and a time for blindly pushing on even when there is no light at the end of the tunnel, and I cannot thank you enough for encouraging me to do the latter, rather than applying the former. I am where I am because of you, and I'll never forget that.

ALSO BY MORGAN GREENE

The DS Johansson Prequel Trilogy:
Bare Skin (Book 1)
Fresh Meat (Book 2)
Idle Hands (Book 3)

The DS Johansson Prequel Trilogy Boxset

————

The DI Jamie Johansson Series
Angel Maker (Book 1)
Rising Tide (Book 2)
Old Blood (Book 3)

Printed in Great Britain
by Amazon